MW01181589

THE COLOR LINE

LIZZETTE GRAYSON CARTER

Genesis Press, Inc.

Indigo Love Stories

An imprint of Genesis Press, Inc.
Publishing Company

Genesis Press, Inc.
P.O. Box 101
Columbus, MS 39703

ISBN-13: 978-1-58571-263-2
ISBN-10: 1-58571-263-9
Manufactured in the United States of America

First Edition 2005
Second Edition 2007

Visit us at www.genesis-press.com or call at 1-888-Indigo-1

DEDICATION

To my family members and loved ones who've passed:
Grandma Brown, Aunt Lillian, Tyrone (Man), Gregory,
Grandma, Aunt Betsy, Steve, Cathy, Miss Chris, Herbie,
Uncle John, Shirley, Aunt Ida, Daddy George & Aunt Ruby;
you are truly missed.

ACKNOWLEDGMENTS

First and foremost, I must thank my Lord and Savior Jesus Christ. You've blessed me so much, Lord and I'm truly humbled. To my husband Michael for making me laugh and looking beyond the physical and seeing the inside. Love and kisses to my daughter Brienna you are my blessing and a joy. I'm proud to have such a God fearing, good-natured child. Thank you to my inspiration and solid rock Marie Brown Golden and Daddy George is truly missed. To my mom, Emaline Creamer, you raised me through trials and tribulations, and you're always in my corner. To my dad, James Grayson thank you for given me a shoulder to lean on and allowing me to still be daddy's little girl. My step-dad, Gregory Creamer thank you for constantly being there and loving my mom. To Herbert and Doris Carter (Mama and Daddy) thank you for loving me from the start and being amazingly devoted second parents. To Charlie and Gail Banks for being there for my family when we needed you most. Thank you to my brothers and sister: Bryant, Rodney, Gregory and Georgette for bringing harmony in my life. To my aunts and uncles: Martha Ann Paden, Faye Shackelford, Julia Leonard, Jane Hayward, Lucille Blakey, Shirley Golden-Carter, Virginia Golden, George Carter, Roger Golden and David Grayson thank you for your never-ending guidance and comfort. To the Carters, Goldens, Graysons, and other thank you for love, laughter, tears and memories. To Reverend & Mrs. Eric D. Robinson and the Ebenezer Baptist Church Family, Nikki Turner, and Sha-Shana Crichton thanks for keeping my best interest in mind. Thank you to the Genesis Press Family for helping make my dream become a reality and a special thanks to my editors Sidney Rickman and Angelique Justin. For your love and support Tawanda Ferguson, Lettice Mayfield, and Lisa Shields Robinson, Christy Henderson and the Henderson family, Vanessa Boyd Knight, Esther Ware, Kitty Riley, Sheila Rucker, Becky Norwood, Darlene Patterson, The Overnite Transportation and Times-Dispatch Newspaper family, to Mathews County residents and Mathews County Public School's teachers, faculty, staff and students.

CHAPTER 1

Thank God, it's Friday!

I stepped off the elevator of my warehouse apartment building in Manhattan. It was a cool evening in New York—the first week in September. I was glad to be home. My arms were full of groceries and I was tired.

It had been a very exciting day at the office. We had given a going away party for my boss who was leaving our company to join another. I'd been an employee for five years and I was glad he was leaving. He wasn't the easiest person to work for. Now, at seven in the evening, all I wanted to do was put my feet up and relax and enjoy some peace of mind.

When I unlocked the door to my apartment, I noticed a stack of mail on my threshold. I knew my next door neighbor Robert had put it there. He's an attractive guy, but quiet and distant. Ever since I moved in, he's always been nice enough to put my mail at my door, but never once has he asked me out.

I was grateful that he'd brought my mail up, but figured it wasn't anything important, probably just junk mail or bills. That's why I hadn't looked in the mailbox. I needed no reminders of my liabilities.

With one free hand I picked up the mail and went into the kitchen to put the groceries on the counter. I looked at the mail for a few seconds without opening any. Oh yeah, it was junk mail. Not caring that I would eventually have to come back and look through it later, I slid the pile into the garbage. Frankly, I was too tired to be bothered. Unpacking the groceries, I noticed a small, white card on the counter, which I must have overlooked. When I picked it up, I immediately recognized the handwriting.

Just a reminder about our date. I'll see you at eight tonight.

Love,

S.T.

S.T. was Steven Turner. We'd been seeing each other for approximately three months. We'd met on the job. I'm one of the top administrative assistants in a large investment firm and he's one of many financial analysts working there, hoping to become a partner.

Before Steven, I had made a point of avoiding relationships with any male co-workers, but when he asked me out, I didn't hesitate. He was attractive and I was twenty-seven and not getting any younger. I hadn't had a date in months and needed quality time with a man. Why not go out and have some fun? So I went out with him. That was my first mistake. My second mistake was letting him practically move in with me.

Every day Steve wanted sex. Now, I like sex. As a matter of fact I love it; but sex is not good if there is only one satisfied partner. I often wondered if he realized that I was even there. One time while we were in the act, I decided not to move a muscle, moan or anything—just to see whether he would notice. Well, he didn't. He just continued doing his thing.

Another thing that bothers me about Steve is that we have absolutely nothing in common. He rarely likes to eat out, because he's leery of eating restaurant food. Whenever we do eat out, there's only one restaurant that he takes me to. He hates going to malls because he says they're too crowded. And as long as we've been together, he's never taken me to the movies. "Why go to the movies when you can wait for the movie to come out on video tape," he'd say. Steve is cheap and insensitive and I've had it with him. When he finds the time to think about me, then maybe I'll find the time to think about him. Nevertheless, I was committed to this date.

My watch showed seven-thirty. I had a half-hour to get dressed. Damn! I didn't want to see him and didn't want to go out with him. Out of the blue, I heard a knock at the door. *It had better not be him.* When I opened the door I saw my sister Reneé with three duffel bags on her shoulders.

I took in everything and said, "What's going on, Reneé?" I knew what was going to come out before she opened her mouth and said the words that I didn't want to hear.

"Mom and I had a fight and she kicked me out," she answered. Brushing past me, she put her bags on the floor in the living room and sat down on the sofa.

I closed the door and walked over to her. "Okay, spill it," I commanded.

"You know my boyfriend Danny, right?" she asked.

I nodded my head. I remembered Mama mentioning him. I hadn't met Danny, but I knew that he was the only guy Reneé had been seeing for the past year and Mama wasn't too happy about it.

Reneé continued. "Well, Danny and I've been getting really serious and we decided that I should get on the pill—just as a precaution. So I asked Mama if she would take me to a gynecologist."

My jaw dropped.

"She started screaming about how she would not have her seventeen-year-old daughter having sex and said that she didn't want me to see him anymore. I tried to reason with her. I told her it wasn't fair for her to stop me from seeing him. Then she said she could tell me to do whatever the hell she wanted, as long as I was under her roof. So I packed up and here I am," she explained easily.

This was great, just great. I sighed and looked at my sister. She was looking at me expectantly. Damn!

"Okay, you can stay here," I mumbled reluctantly. Her eyes lit up instantly. "This is only for tonight, though. You can sleep upstairs in the spare bedroom. Now before you get comfortable, I want you to call Mama and tell her that you're here."

"C'mon, Lacie!" Reneé exclaimed. "I can't do that. You know how irrational Mama is. She's gotten even worse since Daddy passed away."

Daddy was Martin. He was Reneé's father and my stepfather. He'd been gone for about a month now and since the funeral, Mama'd been giving Reneé a hard time. It was evident that Mama was having difficulty dealing with his death.

"Lacie, she wouldn't even listen to me," Reneé continued. Her eyes widened. "Why don't you call her?

She won't yell at you. Please, Lacie. You know I can't talk to Mama when she's like this," she pleaded.

She had a point. If Reneé called Mama, she'd be over here in minutes, screaming her lungs out for Reneé to come home. If I called Mama, the chances were better for Reneé to stay.

Reneé followed me into the kitchen. I put my index finger to my lips, signaling her to be quiet while I dialed Mama's number. She picked up on the first ring.

"Hello?"

"Uh, hi, Mama. I'm calling to let you know that Reneé is over here. She wants to sleep over here tonight."

"Uh, huh. I figured as much," Mama mumbled. "I'm on my way to pick her up."

Oh, boy. Here we go. "Mama, why don't you come by tomorrow?"

"No! I want her back here tonight!"

"What's the hurry?" I asked gently. "Listen, why don't you just tell me what's going on?"

"Lacie, I don't need this right now. I'll be over in…" Mama began.

"Wait a minute, Mama," I interjected softly. "We need to talk this out and I don't think it's a good idea if you come over tonight. You know that as soon as you come over here, you two will start arguing and shouting and I don't need that. Why don't we let things settle down for the night?" I looked at Reneé and shrugged my shoulders.

"I don't think so, Lacie. Reneé is getting too grown. She thinks she can get away with a lot of things and I'm not having it," Mama voiced.

"That may be true, but come over here tomorrow and we'll talk about it then, okay?"

There was a long pause. "All right. But you tell her to be ready to come home."

It was time to get off the phone before she changed her mind. "Okay, Mama. We'll see you tomorrow and we'll talk then," I said hastily.

I heard Mama mumble, "There isn't anything to talk about," as she hung up the phone.

I was so glad that was over. I hate being in uncomfortable situations. I glanced at Reneé. She had a huge grin on her face.

"Don't you dare smile at me, Reneé. You know very well what kind of position you put me in," I scolded.

"Oh, please, Lacie. You did great! All you have to do now is convince Mama to let me stay with you permanently." She got off the bar stool and went into the living room and sat on the sofa.

I know she didn't say what I thought she'd said. I followed her and stood in front of her with my hands on my hips, then caught myself and put my hands down. I'd suddenly recalled how Mama would always stand over me with her hands on her hips whenever I did something wrong, and how I hated to have to listen to her talk first and then beat my behind. I don't know which I hated most—my mother's mouth or her beatings.

"Reneé, what are you talking about?"

She looked at me dolefully. "I don't want to go back home. I want to stay here with you."

"What?" I heard an alarm go off in my head. No, it was the telephone. I ran to the kitchen to pick it up before the answering machine came on.

"Hello?"

"Hey, girl!"

It was Dawn Robinson. She was my best friend and just like another sister to me. We'd known each other since we were kids.

"Hey, girl, what's up?" I responded wearily.

She caught on instantly. "Girl, you sound awful. What's wrong?"

"Reneé is here. She had an argument with Mama and she wants to stay with me permanently," I answered.

"What!"

"Yeah, that's exactly what I said."

"What are you going to do?"

"I don't know. I haven't decided if I'm going to let her stay or not," I said loudly as Reneé crept up the stairs. "She is going to stay tonight, though."

"What happened?" Dawn asked.

"Girl, I can't get into that right now. Steven will be over here in fifteen minutes and I'm not even ready."

"I thought you were going to quit him?"

"Well, I was. I mean, I am. I just haven't done it yet." I sighed. "I really don't want to be with him tonight."

"So don't. Tell him you already made plans with me. Then we can go to the club."

"I don't know. He's already on his way," I started to say.

"I don't even want to hear it. I'm on my way over. See you in about ten minutes."

"Where are you?" I asked. Dawn lived in Brooklyn, so I knew it wouldn't take her ten minutes to get to my place.

"I'm here in the city, calling from my cell phone."

"So you went ahead and got it, huh?"

"Yeah. Ronnie thought it would be a good idea if I had one so he could call me whenever he wanted," she explained.

"Dawn, you already have a pager."

"I know, but let's not get into that right now. I'll be over there shortly," she said and hung up.

She never wanted to get into it. She knew I didn't care for Ronnie. Why would I? He was no good. He had tried to make a move on me when I first met him, but I didn't dare tell Dawn that. They'd been together for only a month and already he'd bought her a one-carat diamond ring, a new wardrobe, and they were living together. I just didn't trust him.

The clock showed seven forty-five. I ran upstairs to my room to get dressed.

In ten minutes I was ready. I hate being in a rush for anything, much less a man. After glancing at my watch and seeing that I had five or so minutes before Steve's arrival, I decided to get something to drink. Seeing Dawn's behind blocking the refrigerator door when I walked into the kitchen was no surprise, considering she had a key to my apartment.

Dawn stayed hungry and stayed thin. I took one look at her skinny frame and got angry. How anyone could eat so much was beyond me. She was five-feet-ten with long legs, a chocolate complexion and a very pretty face. Dawn worked for the same firm that I did, but on another floor. She was a struggling actress and model and vowed that her job at the firm was temporary.

Knowing that she hadn't heard me come downstairs, I snuck up behind her. "Just what do you think you are doing?" I yelled.

She whirled around with a fried chicken leg in her mouth. "Dammit, Lacie, you scared me! Why do you always sneak up on people?"

I laughed and reached into the cabinet for a glass. "Why do you always have to come over to my house and eat up all my food?" I teased. "I thought you were on a diet anyway. Although you don't need to be."

"I am on a diet," she declared. "I'm eating this only because it looked so good."

Although my back was turned, I could feel her eyes on me and turned around. "What?"

"Are you ready for your big date?" she teased.

If she weren't my friend, I would have punched her in the mouth. "Look, it will take some time to get rid of him, but I will, eventually. I just haven't had the nerve yet," I explained.

"Uh, huh," she murmured, still chewing on the now meatless chicken bone. "I'm sorry, Lacie, but I just don't understand why you ever gave him the time of day."

"I don't know either. I guess I was lonely and needed some sex," I shrugged. "I mean, he's a nice looking guy, but we just don't click and he doesn't give me the attention that I need."

"Then let's do something about it. Let's go out to the club."

"I told you. I can't. Steve and I already made plans. He should be here any minute now."

"Then we'll break them. You need a man and I need to shake it up. So we're going."

"All right, then you tell Steve."

"I will," she returned indignantly.

There was a knock at the door. I didn't even have my drink yet. When I went into the living room, Dawn followed and sat on the sofa. I looked through the peephole of the door and opened it.

"Hey, baby," Steve said casually as he came in and strolled right past me, without giving me a kiss or a hug. That's exactly why I was dumping his behind. I should have slammed the door in his face. "Hey, Dawn. What are you doing here?"

"Lacie and I have a dinner date with my mother and I came to pick her up," she explained innocently.

Steve turned toward me. "Lacie, I thought we were going out tonight?"

Dawn didn't give me a chance to answer. "I'm sorry, Steve, but Lacie forgot about it as well. She didn't remember until I came over."

"Can't it wait?" he asked.

"No, my mother and Lacie get along really well. She's looking forward to seeing Lacie and she'll be quite upset if she doesn't come. You know how these things are, don't you, Steve?"

"I guess we can do it another night. I'll hang out with Ronnie, then."

"Uh, Ronnie's out of town. He won't be back until next Saturday," Dawn lied.

Steve looked from me to Dawn. I thought he was going to object again, but he didn't. Looking me straight in the eye, he said, "I guess I should go then. I'll see you later, Lacie." He walked swiftly to the door and slammed it behind him.

I turned toward Dawn and caught her smile.

"You see, that wasn't so hard," she said triumphantly.

"He knew it was a lie, Dawn. You saw his expression."

She stood up and grabbed her coat and purse. "Well, Lacie, I got rid of him like you wanted to. Now let's go out and have some fun."

"I'll meet you downstairs. I'm going to check on Reneé," I said, already heading for the stairs.

"Okay, but don't take too long," Dawn said as she walked out the door.

Reneé was watching television. "Hey," I said. "Dawn and I are leaving. There's plenty of food in the refrigerator and the number to the club is on the table."

"How long will you be out?"

"Not too long, I hope. Call me if you need me," I said and closed the door.

I left the apartment thinking how much I wanted to stay home.

The club was small and hot. Dawn chose a table right in front of the dance floor so she'd be able to see the men. I wanted to sit in the back so I could just sit and watch, but I went along with what she wanted. Shortly after we ordered drinks, one guy came over and asked her to dance and she jumped at the chance. I drank my strawberry daiquiri and watched them, shaking my head. The guy was cute, but he couldn't dance a lick.

While I continued drinking my daiquiri and looking around, I sensed someone standing alongside me. I looked up and blinked. This man was gorgeous! He appeared to be about six feet tall, maybe an inch or so taller, with the most beautiful brown complexion I'd ever seen. His muscles were everywhere.

"Would you like to dance?" he asked, offering his hand.

Was he serious? "Sure." I took his hand

As he led me to the dance floor, "Between the Sheets" by the Isley Brothers came on. *Damn!* I'd gotten into many compromising positions because of that song.

We started to dance and boy, did it feel good! He had one arm around my waist and held my hand against his chest with the other. He held me so tightly I could hardly breathe.

He whispered in my ear, "My name is Joe."

"I'm Lacie," I replied.

"Lacie. That's an unusual name, but it's pretty."

"Thank you." He could have hated my name for all I cared. He smelled so good that I just closed my eyes and enjoyed the feel of his arms around me. The last thing I wanted was for our dance to end.

Once I opened my eyes, I noticed Dawn signaling me with wide eyes. Evidently she had been trying to get my attention for the past few minutes. I figured her eyes were wide because she saw how attractive Joe was, but when I looked where she was pointing, I saw Steve! He was standing on the side of the dance floor with his hands buried in his pockets. Oh, man!

Joe, feeling me tense up, looked in Steve's direction. "Boyfriend?" he asked.

"Kind of," I answered reluctantly.

"Do you want to stop?"

No, I definitely did not want anything to stop. I said, "Let's wait until the song ends; then I'll go over there."

We continued to dance and I avoided looking at Steve. After the song ended, we let go of each other slowly.

Joe cleared his throat. "I guess you'd better go over there before he comes over here. Don't be so hard on him, now. I can understand why he looks so mad. You're a beautiful woman and of course he would be upset if he saw you dancing with another man. I would."

I smiled wearily. "Thank you. It was nice meeting you, Joe."

He smiled in return and his teeth were beautiful. "It was my pleasure as well. I hope to see you again. Take care," he said before he walked away.

I walked toward Steve, my anger building as I did so. I turned back around to get a last look at Joe, but he was gone. I walked that mile to Steve, and the first thing he said was, "I thought you were going to Dawn's mom's?"

"Change of plans," I replied nonchalantly.

He looked at me as if I were a child he'd just caught stealing a cookie from a cookie jar. "I knew this was where you would be. C'mon, we're going home."

"Wait. Let me tell Dawn I'm leaving," I said, already heading for the dance floor.

He came up behind me and grabbed my arm roughly. "No. I'm ready to go now," he uttered through clenched teeth.

Oh, no he didn't! Seeing the expression on my face, he immediately released my arm from his vice grip. *Calm down, Lacie. Play it cool.* "Wait here, Steve," I commanded and walked off.

Dawn met me halfway. "Girl, what's going on with Steve and who was that fine looking man dancing with you?"

"Steve's taking me home and I'll explain everything to you later."

"Are you sure you don't want me to take you?"

I knew she was having fun and was only asking because she felt it was the right thing to say. I glanced at the guy she'd been dancing with and decided she should stay.

"No, I'll be okay. Just give me a call later. No, better yet, I'll call you."

"All right. If you say so," Dawn mumbled uncertainly, although I knew she was glad I didn't take her offer.

"I'll see you later on, okay?"

"Sure. Don't forget to call me."

"I won't."

I met back with Steve and we left the club.

I didn't say anything to Steve on the way home. I merely sat in his car and seethed. When we arrived at my apartment, I went upstairs to change while he made himself comfortable on the couch. I checked in on Reneé and saw that she was asleep. Next, I changed my clothes and got ready to deal with Steve.

He had his feet propped up on my oak coffee table when I went downstairs. I slapped them off, sat in front of him and spoke calmly. "Steve, what you did tonight was inexcusable. You really pissed me off. I have had it with you. Enough said, I want you to pack your stuff and get out." I stood up and headed into the kitchen for a drink.

Behind me, I heard him say, "Wait, Lacie. Can't we talk about this? Don't you think you owe me an explanation?"

I stopped dead in my tracks. *No, Lacie. Don't respond.* Then I continued en route to the kitchen.

"Lacie, I'm talking to you!" Steve yelled, following me.

Once in the kitchen, I grabbed a soda from the refrigerator, took one huge swallow and said, "Steve, I don't owe you a damn thing. I mean, I can't believe that you're even asking me for an explanation after the stunt you pulled tonight. I am not some child who will jump to attention and do whatever you tell her to do. You embarrassed the hell out of me making a scene like that! Who do you think you are?"

He looked shocked at my outburst. "I'm your boyfriend, Lacie. That means something, doesn't it? How do you think it made me feel to see you in another man's arms? What's even worse is that you lied to me."

"I didn't lie to you. That was Dawn."

"You know what I mean. You went along with what she said and you don't seem sorry about it, either."

"No, I'm not," I said defiantly. "All of a sudden you see me dancing with another guy and now you want to act like my boyfriend? Steve, give me a break. You haven't been acting like one since we've been together, so don't try it now."

"What are you saying? You don't want me anymore?"

I sighed. "Steve, we've known for a long time that this was over. We're not right for each other. You can't give me what I want in a relationship."

His expression turned bitter. "If that's what you want, fine. I'll call you when I'm ready to pick up my things. I'm getting out of here."

When he closed the door behind him, I immediately felt as if a huge weight had been lifted from my shoulders. Steve wasn't right for me and I think deep down he knew it. Dawn was right. I had to be upfront with him. Too much of my time had been wasted with men that were not giving me what I wanted. It was time to get myself together, and ultimately that was what I would do. But right now, I had to figure out what to do about tomorrow.

So much for a night of rest.

Knock. Knock.

"Lacie, wake up, Mama's here." I heard Reneé's voice on the other side of my bedroom door.

I turned over and looked at the clock. It showed eleven in the morning, but I turned back over.

"Lacie, wake up!" Reneé yelled.

"All right, all right. I'm on my way down," I mumbled into my pillow.

I heard the door open and close. Reneé was standing over me with her hands on her hips.

I raised my head and gave her a stupefied look. "Wait a minute. Did I tell you to come in?" I asked. "I said I was on my way down."

"Sorry, Lacie, but I couldn't hear you." She pointed to my pillow.

I looked at the pillow. "Oh." I pulled the cover off and sat up. "Well, what's up?" I asked with a yawn.

"Do you remember that you're supposed to talk to Mama for me?" Reneé asked.

"Umm, now how could I forget? She's right down-stairs," I grumbled cynically and walked tiredly to the adjoining bathroom with her on my heels.

Reneé stood in the doorway of the bathroom with her arms folded and watched me squeeze toothpaste on my toothbrush. "When are you going to tell Mama that I'm going to live with you?" she asked after I started brushing my teeth.

I almost gagged on the toothbrush. "Excuse me?" I asked, looking at her with a mouthful of toothpaste.

"You know…we agreed that I could stay here," she said innocently. "So when are you going to tell her?"

I rinsed my mouth out. "Reneé, I didn't agree to anything except you staying for one night."

"I can't stay with her, Lacie. I'll have no life. Mama will lock me up and throw away the key. Please, Lacie. I promise I won't get in your way," she pleaded.

I rolled my eyes. She could be so dramatic. "Don't do this, Reneé. I'm not ready for this. I like living alone." After I washed my face, I walked to the closet to pick out something to wear. Reneé followed. "I mean, how am I supposed to take care of a seventeen-year-old? I'm not ready for that kind of responsibility. *I'm* not even through growing up yet."

"I'm not a kid. I'm a senior in high school and I don't need a baby-sitter. I can take care of myself," she insisted.

"That's what I'm afraid of," I retorted.

Reneé stamped her foot.

I whirled around and looked at her. "Now you see. That's exactly why I don't want your spoiled behind to stay here. If you're not a kid, then stop acting like one."

"I'll tell Mama you're on your way down," Reneé mumbled and closed the door behind her.

I finished dressing and looked in the mirror. I'd seen better days. I knew I'd get a lecture from Mama. I always did. But I went downstairs.

Reneé had tears running down her face and she and Mama appeared to be in an intense conversation. I took one glance at Mama and knew she was not happy.

Mama's full name was Josephine Brown Taylor. An extremely beautiful, slender woman standing five-feet-six, inches tall, at forty-three, she didn't look a day over thirty. All of my life, people have told us that we look alike— despite our difference in complexion and hairstyles. Her complexion was a deep mahogany color and I was a couple of shades lighter. She always wears her hair short and I've always kept mine long.

"Hi, Mama." I kissed her on the cheek.

"Hi, Lacie. I was wondering when you were going to come down," she said. "You look awful."

I ignored her remark and started walking toward the kitchen. "Yeah, well…I'm sorry. I had a long day yesterday and a long week. Do you want some coffee?"

"No, Lacie. We're getting ready to leave. Get your things, Reneé," Mama commanded.

I stopped. "You just got here. Don't you think we should talk?" I suggested, signaling for Reneé not to get up.

"Not really," Mama said dryly.

I guessed I had to start the conversation off. I took a deep breath. "Mama, Reneé feels as if she can't talk to you and she's not happy."

"I know how she feels, Lacie," Mama said. "However, Reneé is getting too hot and I'm having a time trying to control her hormones."

"Mama, that's not true," Reneé said. "All I wanted was to go to the doctor for…"

"I know why you wanted to go. You don't have to repeat it!" Mama snapped. "You don't want to listen and obey me—especially when it comes to Danny. I don't want you to see him anymore and that's that."

"I told you this would happen, Lacie!" Reneé exclaimed.

"Mama, she's seventeen years old. Most young adults her age are dating," I said in Reneé's defense.

"I said I don't want her to see him and I mean it!" Mama yelled.

"That's it. I've had it." Reneé jumped up.

"Reneé, sit down," Mama said sternly.

"No!" Reneé yelled.

"What!" Mama's eyes widened.

"I don't…" Reneé began, but didn't finish because Mama walked over to her and slapped her face so hard it echoed.

Reneé touched her face in disbelief. I couldn't believe it either. Sure, Mama had hit us before, especially when I was growing up, but never over something so small. I had to get them apart before things got worse.

"Reneé go upstairs. I want to talk to Mama alone for a few minutes," I said softly.

Reneé ran upstairs crying and closed the door.

"Mama, what's wrong with you? Why did you do that?" I asked, once Reneé was out of earshot.

Mama sat down heavily on the sofa. "I don't know. I don't know."

"What do you mean, you don't know, Mama? Have you any idea what you did?"

"Yes, I know. This is becoming too much for me." She brushed a hand through her hair, a gesture I inherited from her. As if making a decision, she stood up with a drained expression. "Lacie, would you mind taking care of Reneé for a while? I need some time by myself. Ever since Martin died…"

Oh no, not again. I shook my head. "Mama, I can't do this. I'm too busy for a child."

"She's not a child. It'll only be for a little while. Reneé's old enough to take care of herself. She won't need a babysitter or anything."

"So I've heard," I mumbled and shook my head. I couldn't believe this. First Reneé and now Mama. I sighed. "How long is a while?"

"I don't know, really. I may need a few weeks or a month. I need some time to get myself together, Lacie," she uttered weakly.

All of a sudden I started to feel guilty. Mama was still mourning Martin's death and I wasn't being considerate.

"All right," I agreed reluctantly. "But let's focus on a few weeks." Her weary smile thanked me. "Where are you going? What are you going to do?"

"I don't know...start getting rid of Martin's clothes, I guess. I may go back home to North Carolina. I haven't decided." She looked sad. I didn't know what to say. She breathed deeply then said, "Well, I'm going to leave. I'll send Reneé's stuff over here sometime this week. Tell her that I didn't mean..."

"Sure, Mama. No problem. You just do what you have to do."

She smiled thinly. "Thanks, Lacie. I really appreciate this."

$$ \mathcal{C} $$

I went upstairs to Reneé's room after Mama left.

"Are you okay?" I asked gently.

"Yeah, I'm fine. Did Mama leave?" she asked.

I nodded. "She just left." I decided to break the tension. "You know what? You and Mama must have ESP or something, because she just asked me if you could stay with me for a while."

"What did you say?"

"I agreed, just as long as you had your shots first."

Reneé smiled and then we both laughed. I walked over to her bed and sat next to her.

"Hey, everything is going to be fine. Mama just has some things that she needs to work out for herself. Then, once she's better, I can kick you out and I'll have the place to myself again," I joked. "Listen, I'm kind of new at this stuff, but we'll try to make the best of this situation. I'll spend as much time with you as I can. How does that sound?"

"Sounds good," she replied, and gave me a hug.

"I'm hungry. Let's go out to eat so we can get your mind off all this."

"Where to?"

"Anywhere you want. Just not any place too expensive. I'm not used to having a dependent yet."

"How about Chinese? There's a nice little place here in the Village that I know of. Danny's taken me there a few times and it's not that expensive."

"Chinese, it is then," I said.

CHAPTER 2

At eight fifty-five Monday morning, I entered my high rise office building. I was running late and in a hurry. The trains had been unusually slow and my alarm hadn't gone off on time. What was my new boss going to think?

Reneé and I had spent a lot of time together over the remainder of the weekend. Lunch at the Chinese restaurant, followed by a movie, and then church on Sunday kept us in good spirits. We seemed to relish each other's company and I was glad. We didn't talk much about Mama, but I knew she was in both our thoughts.

"Hold it, please!" I yelled as I ran for the elevator, tripping in the process and spilling my purse and briefcase on the floor.

"Hey, are you all right?" I heard a deep male voice say as he helped me up with a gentle hand. We were the only two in the elevator. Usually, I don't speak to people in the elevator that I don't know, but I wasn't thinking.

"Yes, I'm fine. Thanks for holding it for..." I stopped when I looked up and saw a pair of amazing blue eyes and coal black hair. "...me." I couldn't believe what I was seeing.

When he pulled me up, I was an inch from his face and could smell his cologne. He was saying something, but I couldn't hear him.

"What?" I asked, watching him look me over for any visible injuries.

"Which floor are you getting off?" he asked.

"Oh...ah...push the twentieth, please." I eased out of his reach and bent down to pick up all of the papers that had been in my briefcase and were now scattered all over the elevator floor.

Out of the corner of my eye, I watched him push the button and bend down to help me. "You don't have to help. I can get all of this myself," I said, avoiding his eyes.

"It's no problem," he said. "You could've really hurt yourself. Why were you running?"

"I'm a little late," I explained as we finished gathering up all my things. "I have a new boss and I don't want him to be upset."

"What company do you work for?"

"Ryan and Company. I'm an administrative assistant."

"That name sounds familiar."

"Yeah, well...it's a pretty big firm." The door opened on my floor and I said, "See you around and thanks for your help. I really appreciated it."

"You're welcome. Glad I could be of assistance."

I got off the elevator and hurried down the hall. Putting my stuff on my desk and rushing to my new boss's office to introduce myself and apologize for being late, I was surprised to see no one there. The office was empty except for a desk, two chairs and a few boxes. That was a relief. I went to the kitchen to make some coffee and saw Carrie Weaver walk in.

Carrie was in her mid-thirties, married and has three children. We sat not too far from each other and although I've known her since my first day at the firm, we just recently became very good friends when she was transferred into my department. We were the only top black administrative assistants in the department. Carrie often knew everything before everybody else and she always had gossip to tell me in the morning.

"Hey, Lacie. Did you hear about the new exec—your new boss?"

I shook my head. "No. What did you hear?"

"Girl, I hear he's handsome, rich, young and single," she said emphatically. "I can't wait to see what he looks like. Child, let me get back to my desk. You're coming to the meeting, right?"

"I guess so."

"It's in five minutes."

"What? I thought it was after lunch?"

She rolled her eyes upward. "They decided they wanted everyone to meet the new asset to the company early. That's why it was changed."

"Oh."

"Come by my desk when you're ready."

"Okay," I said as she walked off.

It was already crowded when Carrie and I walked into the huge conference room, so we decided to sit in the back. Everyone there looked familiar; there was no sign of a new face. Once everyone was seated and had gotten quiet, Mr. Ryan, the CEO of the company, walked to the stand. He said something about introducing a major asset to the company and how proud he was to have someone join his team of leaders. I paid little attention to him because I only wanted to find out who my new boss was.

My daydream ended when I felt Carrie elbow me in the ribs and point to the front where Mr. Ryan was shaking my new boss's hand. It was the guy from the elevator! I got hot! He'd known who I was the whole time and hadn't said a thing. I could feel my cheeks burning with embarrassment.

Carrie was talking rapidly, but I barely heard her. My attention was glued to the front at the guy from the elevator making his speech. Once he finished, Mr. Ryan adjourned the meeting.

Returning to our floor in the elevator, Carrie started getting on my nerves. She talked nonstop about how nice my new boss seemed and how lucky I was to have him. I didn't say anything. As soon as we got off the elevator, Carrie begged me to call her after I met him. She wanted to know everything, as usual. I decided I'd call her when I was ready and not anytime sooner. Right now, I was seething with anger and went into the kitchen to make another cup of coffee to calm my nerves.

I was so into making my coffee that I didn't feel him behind me.

"Would you mind making me a cup also?"

Surprised, I whirled around. His blue eyes were on me something awful. I tried to get myself together and somehow managed to speak. "Sh, sh ...sure," I stammered.

"Thanks, I'd appreciate that. I like my coffee with a little bit of milk and no sugar. Oh, and after that, I'd like to talk to you for a minute."

"Do you need me to bring a note pad?" I asked.

"Yes, please. I'm going to need a few things for my office." He looked at his watch. "See you in five minutes?"

"Sure, no problem," I uttered as I watched him walk out of the kitchen.

After the coffee was made, I went to my desk, gathered a pen and pad and stuck them under my arm. Although I felt Carrie's eyes on me, I ignored her. His cup of coffee in my hand, I knocked softly on my new boss's open door.

"Come in," he said. "You can close the door."

"Uh, here's your coffee," I said awkwardly, handing it to him.

"Thank you," he said and took a sip. "Have a seat." He motioned toward the soft leather chair in front of his desk, then put the cup down. "First off, I apologize about earlier in the elevator. I should have told you who I was, but I was afraid you'd be embarrassed if I told you. I'm sorry," he said, waiting for my response.

I shrugged. "I accept your apology, but I wouldn't have been embarrassed," I lied.

"Really?" He grinned skeptically. "You practically ran to the office when the elevator stopped."

"I didn't run. I was walking fast. I didn't want to be late, remember?" I raised my eyebrows.

"Touché," he said with a nod. "Let's start over, okay? We haven't been formally introduced. What's your name?"

"I think you know my name," I answered stubbornly.

"Listen, I'm just trying to break the ice, that's all. Now, what's your name?"

"Lacie Adams," I muttered.

"I'm sorry. I didn't hear that." He put a hand to his ear.

Damn him. He was enjoying this. "Lacie Adams," I repeated louder.

"Well, it's nice to meet you, Lacie. I'm Anthony Douglas." He reached over the desk and offered his hand. I gave him a limp handshake, but it didn't bother him. "Now that we've been formally introduced, let's get down to the real matter at hand."

I wondered where the firm had found this guy. He was unlike any boss I'd ever had and he'd sounded sincere when he apologized. I didn't trust him. Actually, I've never trusted a white man—especially the ones that I've worked for.

He explained my duties. He didn't drink much coffee, so it wouldn't be necessary to fix any for him in the morning; he'd fix it himself if he wanted it. He didn't like dictation, so that was one thing I didn't have to worry about. If he needed to travel, I'd have to make all the arrangements, and if clients came to the office to see him, I'd meet and greet them. He said that he wasn't a hard man to work for. The only thing he required was for me to be ready to travel whenever he needed me to. This, I had a problem with. Any other time it wouldn't have been a big deal, but now Reneé was living with me.

"What do you mean, Mr. Douglas?"

"I mean that I'll probably need you to go on a few trips with me because some of my business might be done out of town."

"Will this be often?" I asked.

"Probably." He saw the concern on my face. "Don't worry. I'll give you plenty of time to make arrangements."

"Oh, okay."

"Now is there anything you want to ask me?"

I was taken aback. I'd never been asked that question before. "Uh...no," I replied.

"Good," he said. "Here are a few notes that I need typed." He stood up and handed me a small stack of crinkled notebook paper with chicken scratch handwriting on it. "I know my handwriting isn't great, but it's the best I can do. Blame it on my mother. I was born left-handed but she would tie my left arm to make me use my right. So bear with me," he explained. "If you're unsure of anything, just ask."

"Okay," I said, looking at the papers he'd given me. "When would you like this completed?"

"There's no rush. If you can have them typed by tomorrow, I'd appreciate it. Oh, one more thing. I'll be busy and in meetings most of the day, so if I get any calls, just take messages, even if I'm in my office. I've got a lot to do."

"Okay, Mr. Douglas."

"Well, good," he said, looking at me with an expression that I couldn't make out. "If you need anything, all you have to do is ask. I hope this works out, Lacie."

"I hope so too," I said. I got up and walked to the door, still unsure of what to think of him.

His voice stopped me at the door. "Oh, and Lacie...you don't have to call me 'Mr. Douglas.' 'Tony' will do just fine, okay?"

I turned around and looked at him. "Okay...Tony," I said. His smile followed me out the door.

Carrie called me the instant I reached my desk. "How did it go?" she asked.

"Pretty well, actually. He's different."

"What do you mean?"

"Carrie, the man wants me to call him by his first name and he says that he'll probably need me to go on business trips with him."

"Lacie, don't you read your e-mail? They're starting to do that in every department now. It's supposed to promote positive attitudes or something like that. And you know I've already been on a few trips with my boss."

"That's right. I forgot about that," I mumbled thoughtfully.

"Lacie, what's wrong with you?" Carrie asked. "You've got a handsome boss who seems to be nice and you act as if you don't want anything to do with him."

"I don't know. He just makes me uneasy."

"You're attracted to him, aren't you?" she asked suddenly. I could picture her smiling.

"No, I'm not."

"Child, you don't have to deny it. I saw it all in your face when we were in the meeting. That's okay. He's good looking. Why didn't you tell me that you liked a little vanilla?" she teased.

I had to get off the phone. She was irritating me. "I've got work to do, Carrie. I'll talk to you later," I said and hung up as she started singing "Jungle Fever."

ℭ

True to his word, Tony stayed in meetings all day and I didn't see much of him. I refrained from taking my lunch break to avoid getting the third degree from Carrie and the rest of the ladies in the office. Instead, I started on the stack of papers Tony had given me. I'm glad I did because his handwriting was awful. His mother should have let him stay left-handed.

I was so busy typing that I didn't notice the time until the phone rang. It was Carrie.

"Hey, are you ready? It's almost five."

"No," I replied. "I've still got one more page to type and then I'll be finished. You go ahead."

"Okay, I'll see you tomorrow." She hung up.

As soon as I finished typing the last page, Tony came out of his office wearing a black trench coat and carrying a briefcase.

"You're still here, Lacie?"

"Yes. I wanted to finish all of this before I left." I handed him the stack of papers.

"Thanks," he said with surprise. "You didn't have to finish these today, you know."

"I know. But I figured I should since I gave you such a hard time earlier. Anyway, you didn't leave me with much else to do and I didn't want you to think I was slipping on the job." I smiled, stood up and walked to the kitchen to straighten up. "So how was your first day?"

"It went well, as a matter of fact, considering the way it started this morning," he replied as he came in and watched me.

I caught the tone in his voice. "Ah…yes…this morning. I guess I really didn't make much of a good impression on you. I wasn't very hospitable," I said. "Look, I apologize for the way I acted this morning. I'm not usually like that with people that I work with. I was embarrassed, is all."

He chuckled. "Really, I should have introduced myself to you as soon as you told me the name of the firm." He watched me empty and clean the coffeepot. "So, is this a truce?"

I smiled. "I guess it is. We have to work together, so we might as well make the best of it."

"Don't make it sound so awful. I'm not that bad to work for."

"Well, you may not be too hard to work for, but your handwriting is awful," I teased. "You really need to brush up on that. It took me forever to differentiate between your *I*'s and *T*'s."

He grinned. "Do you always talk to your employers like that?"

"Hey, I'm just being truthful," I defended. "One thing you need to know about me is that I'm very straightforward. I'm probably the most honest person you'll ever know."

"I'm glad you told me that," he said, moving closer. "I guess we'll get to know each other pretty well then."

What did he mean by that? I stopped what I was doing and looked at him. His eyes were fixed on me.

I cleared my throat and turned around to put the coffee can in the cabinet. "Well, it's getting late. I should get going," I said.

"I'll wait for you and walk with you to the parking deck."

"I don't drive to work. I live in the Village and it's a lot cheaper to take the subway." I walked to my desk to get my coat and briefcase with him behind me. "Thanks for the offer, though."

"Would you like a ride home?"

"No, thank you. I'll be fine. I've got one or two stops to make before I go home and I don't want to be any inconvenience to you."

"It wouldn't be."

"Maybe. But even so, I think I'll take the subway."

He nodded with a little smile. "Okay. Have a nice evening and I'll see you tomorrow then."

"Sure, I'll see you tomorrow."

I was pensive on the way home. Maybe Tony would work out. He seemed nice enough and easygoing. Maybe this would even be my chance for advancement. I'd been with the firm for a long time and had a strong interest in a particular position that I'd applied for a month earlier. There were two other women vying for it that I knew of, but because I had a degree and knew the business inside and out, I wasn't worried.

I stopped at the corner store on my way home to get groceries for dinner. At the entrance to my building, I ran into my neighbor, Robert, who was standing at the door with what was apparently my mail. When he saw me, he immediately grabbed the paper bag from my hand.

"Don't you think it's about time we introduced ourselves officially? How many times are you going to get my mail before I can invite you in for a cup of coffee?" I asked, putting on my best smile.

He seemed stunned, but then he smiled, stuck out his hand and introduced himself as Robert Payne.

"Well, Robert Payne. It's nice to finally meet you. I guess I don't have to introduce myself. You seem to know my name already," I bantered, indicating the mail in his hand.

We took the elevator to our floor, both eyeing each other warily. He was a handsome, slender man about six feet tall, with brown skin, and almond eyes. When we reached my apartment door, I asked him if he wanted to come in for a while, hoping he would say yes.

His voice was soft, but masculine. "No, I'd better not. I've got dance class in about thirty minutes and I don't want to be late."

Dance class? "How about another night, then? Let's make it dinner instead of coffee. I'll cook dinner and we can get to know each other."

"You don't have to…" he began.

"I insist. You've been more than kind and this'll be my way of saying thanks."

He contemplated my offer for a second and then nodded. "Okay, when would you like to have dinner?"

"How about Friday around seven?"

"Sure, that'll be fine. I don't have class that day."

"Good. It's a date then?"

"Yeah. I guess it is."

I reached for my keys and opened the door. "Great. I'll see you at seven on Friday."

He handed me the grocery bag and was about to walk away when he stopped and asked me if I wanted him to bring anything.

"You can bring something to drink," I suggested.

"Okay, I'll see you Friday then." He headed downstairs.

Walking into my apartment, I wondered if I had been too forward. He'd seemed surprised when I asked him to dinner. I called out to Reneé and walked into the kitchen.

"Hey, Lacie, what happened?" she asked, walking into the kitchen wearing her nightclothes.

I took one look at her and suddenly remembered. "Oh my God! I am so sorry. I was in such a hurry this morning because my new boss was arriving, that I forgot to give you the keys to the apartment."

"It's okay. I didn't mind staying home." Reneé smiled.

"I bet you didn't. Here." I reached into my purse and gave her an extra set.

"You don't have to give these to me now."

"Yes, I do. Knowing me, I'd forget again. And if you tell Mama about this, I'll kill you," I joked.

"So how was work today?" She came around the counter and started helping me with the groceries.

"Okay, I guess. My new boss seems nice. I think it's going to work out."

"Sounds good," Reneé said softly. "Uh...listen, Lacie...I wanted to ask you something."

"Sure. What's up?" I asked, getting ready to put a pot of water on the stove to boil for spaghetti.

"How old were you when you lost your virginity?" she asked quickly.

I almost dropped the pot of water. Where was this coming from? A second ago she was asking me about my job and now she wanted to know about sex? Why me? I didn't know what to say. I groaned inwardly. I wasn't ready for this. I continued what I was doing with my back turned.

"Well...I was seventeen..." I began carefully.

Reneé came up next to me with an intense look. "Did you love him?" she asked.

"No. I barely knew him. We never even went out on a real date," I replied.

"Did it hurt?"

I couldn't believe these questions. I blew hard. "Uh...no...fortunately it didn't. Uh...I was very nervous...and I guess, in a way, I was coerced into doing it. It's not something I really like to talk about because it wasn't all that great. I do wish that I had been stronger back then, because I always wanted my first time to be with someone that I was in love with or when I was married."

She watched me for a long time. I was afraid of what she'd ask next. Then she kissed me on my cheek. "Thanks for answering my questions and being honest," she said, and left the kitchen.

I watched her retreating figure and shook my head. What had I gotten myself into?

It turned out that Tony was better than any boss I'd ever had. We were getting along very well. As his assistant, I planned his luncheons, scheduled all of his meetings with clients, and even arranged his dry cleaning. I was his office wife. Occasionally, he and I would stay after work for a few hours, finishing up the day's work. And I found myself liking him more and more.

I learned a few things about him through casual conversation. He was single, but had just gotten out of a long engagement. He wasn't too interested in having a serious relationship just yet, but he was beginning to date again.

I was putting a memo on his desk when I noticed a picture of a woman. I figured she was his former fiancée and picked it up. She was extremely beautiful with long black hair and green eyes, and she looked familiar.

"Her name is Simone."

I whirled around. Tony was staring right into my eyes. "I'm sorry. I was just putting this memo on your desk and noticed the picture. I wasn't snooping," I said quickly.

He dismissed my explanation with a light wave. "No, it's okay. You're fine. I trust you." He looked at the photograph in my hand.

"She's pretty," I commented.

"Yes, she is, isn't she?" He gently took the picture out of my hand. "You've probably seen her," he said. "She's a top model. She's been in numerous commercials and magazines."

"What happened?" I asked directly.

He stared at the picture with a melancholy expression. "It just didn't work out."

"I'm sorry."

"Don't be. It wasn't meant to be. We're still very good friends and even though we're not together anymore, she'll always be special to me," he said. He glanced at me. "So what about you?"

"What about me?"

"Do you have anyone in your life?"

"No," I replied. "I did for a while. We met here and started seeing each other, but I broke up with him. He wasn't right for me and it was getting too stressful for me to continue dating him."

"Would you consider dating anyone on the job again?"

"No. I don't think I want to take that route again."

"Oh," he said and we went back to work.

Mama finally called me at work. "So how's Reneé? Is she doing okay?"

"Oh yeah, she's doing fine," I assured her. "I think she's enjoying living with her big sister."

"Good. When would be the best time to bring the rest of her clothes over?" she asked.

"As far as I know, she's got enough. So I don't think there's any rush."

"Okay…well…I'll probably come by sometime this weekend. Tell Reneé hello and that I'll be in touch. I just called to check on her. I'll talk to you later," she said and hung up.

She didn't even say, 'I love you or good-bye.' Mama had always been like that.

The week went by fast and I was anxious about Friday's date with Robert. He seemed interesting and I was hoping that we would get the chance to know each other better.

Reneé and I were bonding more and more each day. She appeared happy to be staying with me and from the conversations we had, I gathered that she was doing well in high school and couldn't wait to start applying for college. I was proud of her. She had a good head on her shoulders.

I told her about my date, so she agreed to keep a low profile and stay upstairs. I decided to make lasagna and tossed salad with Italian bread. Cherry cobbler would be dessert. I had a knack for cooking and Dawn was always telling me that I should start my own catering business. I was looking into it. After all, I wasn't planning on working for someone else my entire life.

Robert was punctual. He brought a bottle of wine with him and he looked handsome. I told him to sit down while I fixed our drinks.

"So Robert. We finally get to sit down and talk," I said, trying to start a conversation as I sat beside him on the sofa. "I hope I wasn't too forward with you the other day. I don't usually do this, but you've just been so nice to me that I figured I could trust you."

"No, you weren't too forward. Besides, I was thinking about asking you out as well. I mean, we're the only two people in this building, so I thought it would be a good idea if we got to know each other," he added.

I grinned. Now this, I liked. "Good. I'm glad you feel that way. Honestly, I've been thinking about this for a while also. I was waiting for the right time, is all."

"Exactly," he said. "I figured we could become good friends. I mean, I haven't had any luck with finding a boyfriend and I could use a good friend." He took a sip of his drink.

My mouth must've dropped wide open.

"Lacie, you didn't know that I was gay?"

I blinked and recovered quickly. "Uh...no...I didn't." Figuring I might as well joke about it, I added, "In fact, I'm kind of glad. Now I don't have to worry about how to get you to sleep with me on our first date."

We laughed and continued to talk and drink. Of course, I couldn't resist asking him that nagging question that was in my head.

"Robert, you are so good looking and you don't act gay. Are you sure you're gay?"

He laughed. "You know, my father asked me that same question. The only answer that I could give him was that I've known ever since I was a young boy."

"You have?"

He nodded. "Yes, I have."

"What's it like with your father now?" I asked.

"He's learning to accept—no—tolerate it. He stopped trying to fix me up with women a long time ago. And about your comment about my not acting gay—I'm just a man who is attracted to other men. It's as simple as that," he said seriously.

"I'm sorry," I said meekly.

"No, it's fine. I've been asked worse and if we're going to be good friends, then we have to be honest with each other," he assured.

I gave him a hug. "Okay. One more question and then we can eat dinner." I looked at him. "Are you having as much trouble with men as I am?"

"Probably more," he sighed.

Mama came over the next day. Reneé was out with Dawn, so I figured now would be the best time to talk to her.

"Where's Reneé?" Mama asked.

"She went out with Dawn for the day. They'll be back later this evening," I replied.

"Good. At least she's not out with Danny."

"Right. Ah, Mama...we need to talk."

"Really?" she said guardedly.

I nodded my head. "I get the feeling that the reason you two aren't getting along is because you're not communicating with Reneé about…important things," I said gently.

"Such as?"

"Sex," I replied.

"She's a child. She doesn't need to know about that yet."

"Mama, the last time you were here, you told me yourself that she wasn't a child. Now what's it going to be? You need to make up your mind, Mama. Reneé is seventeen. She's almost a grown woman. You need to talk to her about the birds and the bees, so that whenever the time comes she'll be prepared to handle it."

"I have nothing to say to her about that," Mama said stubbornly.

I was getting aggravated. "Is this what you're going to do? Are you going to hide the facts from her until it's too late—like you did with me?" I asked. "Right now, you have a second chance at raising your younger daughter to be responsible and you're going to blow it?"

Mama stood up. That was her usual response when she didn't want to talk about something. "I'm going," she said coldly. "Tell Reneé that I came by. I only came by to let her know that I'm going out of town for a while and I don't know when I'll be back."

I didn't bother to ask her where she was going. At that point I didn't care. I sadly watched her close the door behind her. She was never going to realize the importance of her actions.

℘

I didn't bother going to church Sunday. I wasn't in the mood, which is why I should've gone in the first place. But I was a little dispirited and felt like staying home. Dawn had stayed overnight. She'd had a huge argument with Ronnie and in return, he locked her out of the apartment. Because Dawn and her mom didn't get along either, I told her she could stay at my apartment for the time being. I didn't bother talking to her about Ronnie because I had told her he wasn't good for her too many times before. She never listened and I didn't want to argue with her. Instead, she took the opportunity to ask me about my date with Robert.

"Well, tell me what happened," Dawn urged excitedly.

"Nothing happened. We merely ate dinner, talked a lot and he's gay," I said quickly.

"What? You're joking! I can't believe it! He's gorgeous!"

I nodded my head in agreement. "I know. I know. I was all set to have some good sex before he decided to mention it," I remarked facetiously.

"So what's next?"

"Nothing's next. I'll just continue being single and not ever pursue anyone again."

"What about that guy that you were dancing with at the club the other night?" she pointed out. "Now, he was fine."

"Yes, he was, but unfortunately, Steve interrupted that magic moment before I could give him my number or get his." I shook my head. "No. I'm just going to chill. I'm not having much luck with men, so I'll let things happen naturally. I just hope I'll find the right one before I have to take a vow of celibacy."

CHAPTER 3

Weeks flew by and it was getting colder. A conference was being held in Washington, and Tony and I and certain other employees were selected to attend. I wasn't surprised at the amount of work and preparation we had to do before the conference started on Friday. This was a major event that usually lasted two days, and a lot of important people were going to be there. Tony was even on the list of persons scheduled to speak.

Carrie and her boss were also going, so Carrie and I arranged to share a room. Unfortunately, our flight schedules were different. Carrie and her boss weren't due to arrive until early Friday morning and Tony and I had booked for a Thursday afternoon flight.

The few days before we left were really hectic. Tony and I worked aggressively, staying sometimes until eight o'clock to work on proposals and speeches. Most of the time we'd be the only two still in the office. I felt guilty because I wasn't spending as much time at home with Reneé as I had wanted, and to make matters worse, I'd be leaving within the next few days. Fortunately, Dawn was there and would be some company for Reneé. She was still having problems with Ronnie and had for the time being refused to move back in with him, even after he'd asked her back.

During our breaks, Tony and I would converse. I felt comfortable with him and it became evident to me that he was more than just my boss. He was genuinely interested in what I had to say about the company and my goals.

"So you're saying that you don't feel like you have a future with this company?" he asked one evening while we ate pizza.

"No. I'm merely saying that I would feel better if I had my own business. I mean, I've had a lot of experience and I've trained a lot of people, but I'm still in the same position. Some of the same people that I trained are making more money and are in higher positions than I am. I've had interview after interview and I've never landed any of the positions that I applied for," I explained.

"If you were to start your own business, what would it be?"

I shrugged. "I don't know. I guess I'd go into catering since I've had so many compliments about my cooking. I'm not going to think about that now though, because I don't have the capital to do it."

"Maybe you should look into it. There are plenty of lenders out there for small businesses."

I didn't take his suggestion seriously. I figured he was just humoring me.

The time for the trip to Washington had arrived. I was packing when Reneé came into my room.

"Hey, Lacie. Do you have a minute? I need to talk to you," she said tentatively.

I looked at my watch. I had about thirty minutes before the limo arrived. I could spare the time. "Sure, baby. What's up?" I asked, continuing to pack.

"Remember when I asked you about your first time, and if you loved the guy you had sex with? I was wondering if you could take me to the gynecologist to get some birth control pills."

Shocked, I stopped packing and looked at her. *Oh, Lacie, grow up. She's seventeen. She's a walking hormone ready to explode. You knew this was coming.* I sat down slowly.

"You see? That's the same look Mama gave me," Reneé accused. "Just forget it." She started to leave.

"Reneé come back here," I said. "It's okay…really. I'm sorry. You just surprised me, that's all. Come here." I motioned for her to sit next to me.

"Before I say anything else, let me ask you two questions. Have you had sex yet?" She shook her head, but her eyes told me she had gone far enough. Damn! Why did sex have to be so good? "Are you sure about this?" I asked.

"Yes." She nodded. "I know this is at the last minute, Lacie, but you've been so busy lately that I haven't had any time to talk to you," she explained.

"Yeah. I'm sorry about that, honey, and unfortunately, I can't promise it'll get any better. I've got a new boss, you know and I've gotta keep him happy." I smiled reassuringly.

"I know," she said, still waiting for my answer.

"Did you ask Dawn about this?"

"No. But I almost did, though."

"Okay. That's good. You did right," I said abruptly. Lord knows what Dawn would have told her. "Okay, look. I know this is what you want and how important it is to you. As you know, I've got to go out of town today, so I'm going to need you to promise me something."

She looked at me suspiciously.

"I'll only be gone for a few days. So can we do this when I come back? I assure you that we'll go as soon as I get back. Will you promise me that you won't do anything until then?" I asked. My heart was racing as I waited for her to answer. At that particular moment, I understood the hell that parents go through.

Then she smiled. It was an answer to my silent prayer. "Sure, I think I can wait."

I hugged her tightly. "Thank you, child." I sighed with relief and we both laughed.

We were in Washington within a couple of hours. I was looking out the window of the limo, thinking about what Reneé and I had talked about.

"Lacie? Did you hear what I said?" Tony touched my arm.

I turned my head away from the window slowly. "No. I'm sorry, Tony. My mind was somewhere else."

"That's obvious. You've had that same look on your face ever since we left the airport. What's wrong?"

This man did not need to know my troubles. I quickly changed the subject. "Uh, what were you saying, again?"

He shook his head and grinned. "Smart. Very smart. I was telling you that there's a big dinner tomorrow and everyone is expected to be there. I forgot to tell you about that."

"Aren't those usually reserved for the important people?"

"Sometimes. But we little people are expected to be there this time. Aren't you glad you're my assistant?" he teased. My expression must have said it all. He chuckled. "Don't worry, Carrie didn't seem too pleased about it either."

"I'll just have to make the best of it." I sighed. "It's going to be formal, right?"

"You guessed right," he said with a nod.

"That figures," I mumbled.

Tony gave me a peculiar look but I ignored it. I had too much on my mind and I was not in a sociable mood.

Once we arrived at the hotel, Tony found out that he had a meeting. Since I didn't need to be there, I went on up to my room to unpack. Once settled in, I stood around restlessly, unsure of what to do. Carrie wasn't due to arrive until the next day and there was nothing on the tube. That being the case, I decided to go down to the bar. A lot was going on in my head and I needed to relax.

At the bar, I ordered a margarita and thought about the situation with Reneé. I had no idea how to handle this kind of thing. Yeah, I'd told her that I'd take her to the gynecologist as soon as I got home, but honestly, I had no idea if that was the right thing to do.

"Penny for your thoughts," I heard someone whisper in my ear. I jerked around. Tony was smiling that great smile at me.

"Do you always sneak up on people like that?" I asked.

"Only when I know I can get away with it," he chuckled. He ordered a drink and sat next to me. "What's going on with you? You've been this way ever since the flight. And don't tell me that it's nothing, because I'll know that you're lying," he insisted as the bartender came back with his drink.

I debated whether I should tell him. He was my boss—not my therapist. Then I realized that he wasn't going to let it go until I told him. So I did. Everything. He listened intently and nodded in understanding every now and then.

"What are you going to do?" he asked after I finished.

"I don't know. I'm her only sister and she looks up to me. She's expecting me to come through for her, and it would break her heart if I came back home and told her that she's too young to have sex. I'd sound like my mother and I know she doesn't want that. She's growing up and wants to explore new things and I guess I'm going to have to be there for her," I replied.

"Sounds as if you've already made up your mind what to do. I think you'll do a good job."

"You really think so? It doesn't sound as if I'm giving her permission to have sex, does it?"

"No," he assured me, shaking his head. "She's seventeen. Regardless of whether you give her permission, she will find a way. All teenagers do and your approval doesn't have anything to do with it. She's going to do what she wants to do—only she came to you for advice first."

I smiled and shook my head. "Do you always have an answer for everything?"

"Only when I'm asked," he said and we both laughed.

"What are you doing down here anyway? Shouldn't you be in that meeting?"

"Actually," he said, glancing down at his watch, "it ended about twenty minutes ago. I decided to come downstairs to get some fresh air and I saw you in here. You looked as if you needed some cheering up and I thought I'd give it a try."

"I did, huh?"

"Yes, you did. I don't like to see people I care about looking so glum," he replied softly.

Care about? We sat in odd silence for a moment and I stole a few glances at him, as he took a sip of his drink. He was so gorgeous. *Stop it, Lacie.*

"So," I said.

"So," he said.

I was looking at the glass in my hand, but I could feel his eyes on me. It seemed as if he wanted to say something but didn't know how to say it.

"Listen, Lacie...there's something that I've been meaning to ask you, and I don't know how to go about it," he said.

"All you have to do is ask," I said with a shrug. I was preparing myself for whatever he was going to say, when out of the corner of my eye, I saw Steve. I was taken aback. What was he doing here?

He caught me looking and headed our way. Steve's eyes were on me as he reached the bar. "Hello, Lacie. I'm surprised to see you here. Would you mind introducing me to your new friend?"

Tony, sensing hostility, didn't wait for me to answer. He offered his hand to Steve. "Hi, I'm Anthony Douglas, Lacie's boss. Everyone calls me Tony. And your name is?"

I wasn't sure if Steve was going to shake his hand, but he did. He managed to take his eyes off me and looked Tony boldly in the eye. "Steven Turner" was all he said. He turned his attention back to me. "Lacie, can I speak to you for a minute?"

I didn't want to make a scene in front of Tony. "Sure," I said. "Tony, will you excuse me? I'll be right back, okay?" I didn't wait for him to answer. This was the second time Steve had pulled this. I was going to lay him out.

"Okay Steve, you've got my attention. Now what do you want?" I said coldly as soon as we were outside.

"Are you sure you don't want to go back inside and talk? It's a little chilly out here."

"No. I'm fine. I don't plan on being out here too long. What do you want?"

He looked uncertain. "Uh...well...I was wondering if we could work something out? We had something good going on."

He led me outside for this? I tried to remain calm. "First of all, Steve, I shouldn't even be talking to you right now because of how rude you were in there just a minute ago. Secondly, there was nothing good about our relationship. It was only good in your eyes because it was all about you and nothing but you. We've been over this before. I told you I don't want to be with you anymore. Why is that so difficult for you to understand?"

Steve looked flustered and said nothing. Suddenly, with a determined look, he grabbed me and kissed me roughly on the mouth. It took me a second to realize what was happening. I wrestled myself from his arms and slapped him hard on the face. I was so furious with him for trying that. I didn't wait for him to respond after I slapped him and went back into the hotel with angry tears running down my face. I heard Steve calling after me, but I kept walking. I just wanted to go to my room.

Fuming, I didn't pay attention to what was going on around me and took no notice of the figure on the elevator that I bumped into.

"Oh, excuse me. Can you push ten, please?" I mumbled, getting in a corner.

"Lacie, what's wrong?" he asked, immediately coming to my side.

I looked up. We were the only two in the elevator. This was the second time. "Oh. Hey, Tony. I'm a little upset right now, that's all. Do you have any tissue?" I asked.

"Sure. Here you go." He reached into his pocket and handed me a handkerchief.

I blew hard without shame. It was all too common for me to get mad and start crying. I hated that. I knew he was looking for an explanation and I avoided his eyes.

"What happened?" he asked.

"Steve kissed me and I slapped him," I replied.

"Ah." He nodded. "So I take it that he's the same guy you mentioned when I caught you snooping that time?"

I didn't catch what he said at first. "Yeah, he's the one. I sure can pick them, can't I?" I sighed. Then I realized what he'd said. "I wasn't snooping!" I objected. Then I noticed that the elevator hadn't moved. "And will you please press the button to the tenth floor?"

He laughed and pushed it. "Well, I had to say something. This is becoming quite regular, me having to come to your aid and the two of us in an elevator alone."

"Hey, I'm fine. I can take care of myself," I declared indignantly.

"You sure about that?" he asked, moving closer to me.

"Yeah, I'm sure," I mumbled, wondering why the space that had been between us had now shrunk to inches. He was so close I could see the sparkle in his eyes.

"Then why are you smiling right now, when just a minute ago, you were blowing all of your nose right into my handkerchief?"

"Well, I…" I stopped when, without warning, he gently took my face in his hands. I was astounded. Why was this fine white man holding my face this way and why wasn't I doing anything about it? "What are you doing?" I gulped.

He didn't immediately answer but instead seemed to study my face. "Just this," he said at last, then smiled and slowly put his lips on mine and began to kiss me ever so tenderly. Incomprehensibly, I returned his kiss as he kissed me even deeper.

As soon as the elevator came to a halt, we stopped kissing and looked at each other in question. He released me as soon as the door opened and I walked hastily down the corridor to my room. Not looking back, I heard the elevator close.

I slept restlessly all night, and in the morning I was not a happy camper. I got up early to eat breakfast and when I came back to the room, Carrie was unpacking her clothes.

"Hey, girl, what's…?" She stopped when she saw my expression. "Girl, what's wrong? You look awful? Didn't you get any sleep?"

"No, not at all. I had a lot on my mind," I said. I sat on my bed and watched her go back and forth from the suitcase to the dresser. Then something made me come right out and tell her. I had to talk to someone and Dawn wasn't there. "Tony kissed me last night," I blurted out.

Carrie turned around from her suitcase. Her eyes were wide and she had a huge grin on her face. "I knew it! I knew it! I knew something was going on between you two," she exclaimed, pointing her finger at me.

"Carrie, there is nothing going on," I stated firmly. "He just kissed me. Nothing else happened. And what do you mean, you knew it?"

"Girl, from the moment he stepped into that office, sparks have been flying between you two," she said. "I've seen the way he looks at you, Lacie. No man looks at a woman that way without having something on his mind other than work."

"You've caught him looking at me?"

"Yep."

"Wow!" I said and blew softly. "What am I going to do, Carrie? This is too huge. I mean, what do you do when your employer kisses you?"

"I don't know. That's never happened to me."

"Carrie, I'm serious."

"You really like him, don't you?"

I didn't want to answer her question directly. I shrugged. "He's...all right...I guess."

"That's not what I asked you."

"I know. I know," I said quickly, then threw my hands up. "Okay, so I'm attracted to him," I admitted. "But I work for the man, Carrie."

She shrugged. "So?"

"*So*? What do you mean *so*?" I asked. "He's my boss. I can't date my boss. Not to mention that he's white, Carrie. I've never dated a white man before. I wouldn't know how to handle something like that. Also, I just got out of a relationship with Steve and we both know how that turned out." I shook my head.

Carrie silently contemplated what I'd said. She sat down on her bed, reached in her purse and took out her wallet. "Come here and sit next to me. I want to show you something," she instructed.

I sat next to her as she opened her wallet and showed me a picture of herself, a white man, two boys and a girl.

"That's my husband, David, and that's Sean, Patrick, and Ashley. This is my family," she said.

"Oh." I couldn't hide my surprise. I took the wallet from her and looked closely at the picture. They made a beautiful family. I was surprised that she was in an interracial marriage. "I apologize, Carrie," I said. "In the five years, I've known you, I never knew."

"That's okay, Lacie. It's not something anyone has to know. It's no one else's business, because I think of him only as the man that I love. I don't think about his color. Do you get what I'm saying?"

"How long have you been married?"

"Fifteen years. Sean is my oldest child. You see how beautiful my family is? When I look at them I don't see black or white. I see my blood and my life. Color is not something you should base love on, Lacie. Love comes from within here," she said, pointing to her heart.

I glanced at the picture again, thinking how remarkable it was that she'd maintained a relationship like that for fifteen years. I was curious and wanted to ask some questions, but I figured it was pointless. Nothing else was going to happen with Tony. I handed her the picture and stood up.

"Carrie, you have a lovely family and I'm very happy for you, but I can't do this. That's not for me. I date black men. I always have."

"Lacie, don't use color as an excuse to ignore your feelings about him. He could be the one, you know," she insisted.

"I have no feelings, Carrie. It was just a kiss, that's all."

"Sure. Whatever you say."

During the conference the next day, I avoided Tony and involved myself in meetings, which wasn't hard because I had Carrie by my side most of the time. I met many interesting people and decided to try to put what had happened with Tony behind me.

During dinner, everyone sat at designated tables. Carrie, Tony and I sat at the same table, along with others from the company. Steve was nowhere to be found, which was a relief to me. There was amicable conversation at the table as everyone ate their dinner, though neither Tony nor I said much. Every once in a while I'd catch him staring at me, but I'd quickly look away.

As it got later, a few people started to retire to their rooms. Carrie went to our room to make a phone call, leaving Tony and me alone at the table. We sat there in uneasy silence.

I couldn't stand it anymore. "Excuse me." I got up and went out to the balcony.

"Hey. Did I make you that uncomfortable?" I heard a voice say a minute later. Tony walked up beside me and waited for my answer.

"Yes, you did," I said softly, turning around to face him. "Can you explain what happened last night? Why did you kiss me?"

He hunched up his shoulders. "I don't know. You looked like you needed a friend," he answered. "At first I was only going to give you a hug, but then I looked into your eyes and suddenly, I just wanted to kiss you."

"Do you usually kiss your friends like that?"

He smiled. "Uh, no...I don't."

I took a deep breath and turned back around. "I don't know what to make of this. You caught me off guard and now I feel a little awkward. I'm unsure of how to act around you."

"I know. I'm sorry. As soon as you walked off the elevator I immediately regretted what I'd done."

I turned to him. "You did?"

He looked surprised. "Yes, I did." He peered at me. "Shouldn't I have?"

I cleared my throat. Of course he should have. "Of course you should have," I said, trying to sound stern. Then we both laughed.

"Listen, Lacie. I'm truly sorry. I put you in an awful position and I don't ever want you to feel uncomfortable around me again. I wouldn't blame you if you screamed sexual harassment."

I couldn't resist teasing him. "Well, you know, the idea did come to mind," I said. When his eyes widened, I smiled at him reassuringly. "But I immediately erased it."

"Do you still want to work for me?" he asked.

"Of course. Don't you want me to?"

"Of course."

"Then I guess the best thing to do is put this behind us and make sure that it doesn't happen again. Right?"

"Right," he agreed.

The remainder of the conference went along swiftly and without incident. I didn't run into Steve again and I was glad. Maybe this time, he'd finally gotten the hint.

On Saturday, Carrie and I did some last minute shopping before we headed for the airport to fly back to New York. I couldn't wait to get home. Although I'd enjoyed the time away, I had missed Reneé and Dawn. I decided it would be a good idea if I took them out to dinner to make up for lost time.

Our plane landed at LaGuardia Airport around seven o'clock that evening. Carrie's husband was waiting for her and she introduced us. He was handsome and also very nice, and they looked happy together. They offered me a ride home, but I declined and said I'd catch a cab. I didn't want to impose. Carrie said she'd see me on Monday and walked away with the man of her dreams. I watched them walk away and decided that one day, I was going to have what she had.

Walking out to the exit, I bumped into Tony. "Hey, what are you doing here? I thought you left on an earlier flight?"

"I did, but I got caught up in a conference call. I've been here for about an hour," he explained. "Are you just getting back?"

"Yeah. Carrie and I did some last minute shopping before we left."

"How was your flight?"

"It was okay. I was a little tired and was hoping to catch a nap, but didn't get the chance."

"I'm sorry to hear that," he said. His limo pulled up. "Would you like a ride home?"

"No, that's okay. I'll catch a cab."

"C'mon. You said you were tired. Let me give you a ride," he urged. "I need to talk to you about a few things concerning a prospective client anyway."

I raised one eyebrow. "And just think. I thought you were actually being considerate," I gibed.

"I am." He chuckled. "What do you say?"

"Okay." I smiled and nodded.

"I've been meaning to tell you how impressed I am with all the hard work you've done so far. You've helped me out a lot." he remarked, once we were on the road.

"Thank you."

"I talked to an old friend of mine on the phone yesterday and it's possible that he might be interested in doing business with the firm. I was wondering if you would help me out a little," he said, offering me a drink which I declined. "His name is Joseph Mitchell. I've known him for years. We went to college together. He has his own mortgage brokerage company and he's interested in investing."

"Why do you need my help?"

"Well, he's from Miami and he arrived in town a few weeks ago on business. He'll be staying in New York longer than he anticipated, and he's looking for a place to rent. He's coming to the office Monday and I was hoping you could help him."

"And you can't do it because you'll be in meetings all that day, right?"

"Exactly. You're my assistant, you should know." He looked at me earnestly. "This is very important," he said. "It would mean a lot if you would do this for me."

"All right, I'll do it."

"Thanks, I really appreciate this, Lacie."

"No problem," I said.

"So what are you doing tonight?"

"I don't know. I'm thinking about taking Reneé to dinner. I've ignored her long enough, so I think I'm going to spend some time with her and do sister stuff."

"I admire you," he said suddenly.

I was surprised at his comment. "Why do you say that?"

"Because it took a lot for you to take her in and have a full time job at the same time. You seem as if you'd be a good mother."

"Women do it all the time, Tony. Women raising children alone has become quite common these days. This thing with Reneé staying with me was decided on the spur of the moment, and frankly, I don't think I'm doing such a good job. I haven't spent much time with her and whenever we do get together, all we seem to talk about is her hormones."

"C'mon, it's not that bad. You're doing your best, Lacie, and that's all you can do."

"I know. It's just been kind of hard to get used to." The limo stopped in front of my building. "I'll see you Monday," I said as the driver opened the door.

"Here. Let me help you with your bags." Tony got out and grabbed them from me. "I'll walk you upstairs."

"Tony, you don't have…"

He raised his hand in objection. "You're doing me a big favor Monday, so let me do something for you."

"Okay." I shrugged.

The apartment was dark when we entered. I turned on the overhead light in the living room and yelled for Reneé and Dawn but got no answer. I figured Reneé was asleep and Dawn was probably out with Ronnie.

"Welcome to casa de Lacie," I announced with a smile. "You can put my bags over there." I pointed. "Do you want something to drink before you go?" I asked, walking to the kitchen.

"Yes, a soda will be fine. This is a nice apartment," he said, looking around. "Did you do all the decorating yourself?"

I noticed him looking at my collection of African art as I returned to the living room and handed him a Pepsi. "Thank you and yes, I did. The majority of this stuff came from art shows that I used to go to when I was in college. I've always been interested in African art—well, actually, any kind of art." I motioned for him to sit on the sofa and I sat next to him. "So you really like the apartment, huh?"

"Yes, I do. It looks as if it took a lot of time and effort to get it like this," he replied.

"Oh, please. You don't even want to know how long it took." I rolled my eyes and smiled. "But I enjoyed it. Now my real pride and joy is my kitchen. I put more effort into it than into any of my other rooms. I like to cook and I needed a relaxing environment."

"You mentioned something like that before. Would you mind cooking something for me?"

"Now?" I asked, taken aback.

He nodded. "Yes, if you don't mind."

"Do you have time?"

"Yeah. I don't have any plans right now."

"Well, what would you like?"

"Oh, anything," he said with a smile. "I just want to see if you're as good as you say you are."

"Is that a dare?"

"Not unless you take it as one," he chuckled. "Seriously though, I am a little hungry." He patted his stomach.

I laughed. "Okay, Mr. Douglas, follow me to the kitchen." I stood up. "How about a Spanish omelet?"

"Hey, you're the cook," he replied, sitting down as soon as we entered the kitchen.

"Oh no, Tony," I objected. "You are not going to just sit here and watch me cook. You can start helping by getting the ingredients out of the refrigerator."

He looked amused. "You mean you're actually going to treat your new boss this way?"

"Yes. Around here I'm the boss. The eggs are in the door and the tomatoes, onions and green peppers are in the bottom drawer," I chuckled, getting a skillet from the cabinet.

Tony put all the ingredients on the counter, leaned against the refrigerator with his arms folded and watched me. "So is cooking the only thing that relaxes you?" he asked after a moment.

I finished cutting the onions and green peppers and put them in a bowl. "No, it's not the only thing. I like to read when I get the time and on occasion I also enjoy listening to some jazz or classical music. Now if I'm by myself, then the music just puts me in a zone altogether. There's something so peaceful about those two kinds of music. You know?"

He nodded his head in agreement. "Yeah. I get that same feeling when I listen to jazz also. A little R & B isn't too bad either."

I stopped what I was doing and looked at him in surprise. "You're kidding! You like jazz and R & B?"

He laughed. "I do. Why does that shock you?"

I shrugged. "I don't know. I guess I figured you to be the Barry Manilow or Harry Connick, Jr., type," I chuckled. "I'm really surprised."

"There are a lot of things about me that will surprise you," he said softly.

I caught the tone in his voice and dropped my knife. It fell on the floor and Tony and I bent down to pick it up. Our hands touched and then our eyes met. He had an unusual look in his eyes and all I could do was gaze into them. The gaze was broken when I heard a loud thump upstairs. He heard it also and we ran up the stairs to find out what the noise was. It had come from my sister's bedroom. I opened the door, ready to scold Reneé for not answering me when I called her the first time. Instead, I found her and Danny, half naked and scrambling for their clothes.

CHAPTER 4

"What's wrong with you!" I yelled at Reneé. I was so angry with her. We were in her room and Tony and Danny had gone downstairs.

"I'm sorry, Lacie," Reneé said meekly. She sat on her bed, watching me walk back and forth across the floor.

"I don't believe this. I don't believe this," I repeated as I held my head and continued to pace. "Why couldn't you wait? I thought we agreed—no, excuse me—you promised me that you wouldn't do anything until I got back and then we would both go to the doctor to get you some birth control bills."

"Lacie, I tried," she insisted. "I really did. But things got out of control. I couldn't help myself."

"Oh, this is not good. This is definitely not good," I mumbled. I stopped pacing when I thought of something. "Did you use protection?"

"Yeah. We used a condom."

"Good. That's one thing I don't have to worry about." I looked at her and saw that she was disappointed in the way I was acting. But how could she blame me? I had basically caught the two of them in the act. "Okay. This is what we're going to do. Early Monday morning we're going to see my gynecologist. I'll just have to tell Tony that I'm going to be late for work." Her eyes lit up. "Now, listen. I want you to know that I don't condone this, but if you are going to be sexually active, then you might as well be responsible."

"Thanks, Lacie."

"Look, I know it's been kind of hard on you with me not being here and all, but I want you to understand that from now on, if you need to talk to me or if you need something, you can always come to me. Okay?"

"Okay."

"Good. Now let's go downstairs. I need to talk to you and Danny together. Do you have any questions?"

"Who's the white guy?" she asked directly.

"Oh…he's my boss, Tony. That's a long story. C'mon. Let's go downstairs."

Tony was sitting in a chair and Danny was on the sofa. I motioned for Reneé to sit next to Danny. While I was unsure of what to say, I knew I had to set some ground rules. For some reason, I didn't mind Tony being there.

"First of all, let me say to both of you that I don't ever want to catch you two in that kind of compromising position again. Since you both are now sexually active, let me remind you that it's imperative that both of you behave responsibly. Sexually transmitted diseases and teen pregnancy are major factors to consider when you become sexually active, and I don't want to worry about either of those happening to Reneé." I looked at them both sternly.

"You won't have to worry about that, Miss Adams. We're going to be very careful," Danny assured.

"Good, and call me Lacie, okay?"

There was silence in the room for a moment. Then I said, "Tony, can I talk to you in the kitchen, please? You two behave yourselves while we're gone," I said to Reneé and Danny.

"I was wondering if you could do me a favor," I whispered to him, once we were in the kitchen.

"Sure, what's up?"

"What time is Mr. Mitchell coming to the office Monday?"

"I believe he said he'd be there around noon. Why?"

"I need to take Reneé to the doctor. I was wondering if I could come in a little late. I'd probably be no later than eleven o'clock."

"No, I don't mind at all. I know the situation, so it's fine," he said. I breathed a sigh of relief. "Are you going to be okay?" he asked, touching my arm lightly.

"Oh, yeah. I just need to get that picture out of my head is all," I replied dryly. He gave me a sympathetic smile. "But I'm going to be all right."

"I'm glad to hear that. I wasn't sure what you were going to do, but I thought you handled it pretty well."

"You think so?" I asked.

"Of course, I do. I couldn't have done any better."

"Thanks." I smiled gratefully. Then I looked at the eggs and tomatoes in the bowl on the stove. "Hey, I'm sorry about the omelet. I think you would have really liked it."

"Oh, don't worry about it. I'll just get some takeout. You can fix it for me another time." He nodded his head toward the living room. "You want me to ask Danny if he needs a ride home?" he offered.

I was elated that he'd asked. "Could you? I'd really appreciate it."

"Hey, it's no problem. It's clear you and Reneé need some alone time."

"Thank you."

Once Tony and Danny left, I put my arm around Reneé and said, "You know what, kid? I think it's time we had a really good sister-to-sister talk."

She grinned. "Do you want to order Chinese?"

We were both pigging out on Chinese—shrimp egg foo young for me and moo goo gai pain for Reneé—when I started a long overdue conversation.

"So how was it for your first time? No, wait. Before I assume anything, this was your first time, right?" I asked.

"Yes, Lacie," she replied, rolling her eyes upward.

"Oh, don't even roll your eyes. I only wanted to be sure, that's all. It's not uncommon for kids your age to be sexually involved."

She pointed at me. "That's exactly what I was trying to tell Mama. I knew we would get along. Mama is just too old-fashioned."

"Now wait a minute, Reneé. I know I said that it's not uncommon, but that doesn't mean that it should become a practice." She looked confused. "Listen, what I'm trying to say is that women's bodies are a special gift to men, Reneé. What we have to offer should not be routinely given. I don't care what anybody says. And since we are special, then we should be treated as such. Get it? I know this was your first time and all, but this does not make you an expert and it definitely doesn't mean that you have to continue sleeping with him. There's an art to making love, and honestly, a lot of guys your age don't know a thing about it."

"Trust me. Danny knows what he's doing. I mean, it did hurt a little, but he was very gentle and patient. I was very comfortable and it wasn't as bad as I thought it would be. He was so romantic and even held me in his arms afterwards. There was something so right about the whole thing. I know that he really loves me," Reneé said confidently.

I stared at her enviously for a moment and then shook my head. "I've got to get some ice cream." I got up and went to the kitchen.

"Hey Lacie, you didn't finish telling me about the white guy," Reneé yelled from the living room.

I came back and sat down on the sofa with a pint of butter pecan ice cream. "There's nothing to tell." I shrugged nonchalantly. "His name's Tony and he's just my boss, that's all."

"If he's just your boss, then why was he here?" she asked.

"If you must know, Nosy, he gave me a ride from the airport and I was fixing him an omelet when we heard that loud thump you and Danny made upstairs."

"Oh." She blushed.

"Yeah. 'Oh'," I repeated.

"So, do you like him?"

"Yeah, he's nice," I replied evasively.

She looked at me pensively for a moment, then said, "I think he likes you."

"What?"

"I could see it all in his face—the way he was looking at you and everything. There's something going on and wait 'til Mama finds out that you're dating a white man."

"What is it with everyone this weekend? First, it was Carrie and now you. There's nothing going on between us. Okay?"

"Okay, okay. Why are you being so defensive? I was only teasing," Reneé exclaimed, holding up her hands.

"Well, stop. You've already brought up my blood pressure."

"What are you talking about? You're too young to have high blood pressure," she laughed.

"Yeah, well…anyway, it's getting late. Why don't you go upstairs and get some sleep? I'll clean up."

She started to get up. "I guess sleep will do me some good."

"Hey, remember what I told you, okay? This is very serious. So don't act as if we're going to an amusement park or anything like that," I reminded her.

"Yes, ma'am." She saluted.

I watched her go up the stairs and wondered how much more of this I could take. I gathered up all the trash that we had made and went to put it in the garbage. I heard the door unlock quietly. I knew it was Dawn.

"You don't have to sneak in, Dawn. I'm awake," I called out to her.

She walked into the kitchen looking guilty. "You are, huh? I was hoping you wouldn't be up. Are you mad at me?" she asked.

"No," I said wearily. "I'm too exhausted to be mad at you. Not after all the excitement."

Dawn's eyes widened, like they always do when she's scared of what she might hear. "What? What happened?"

"Sex—that's what happened. I must be really old or something, because back in the day, when we were growing up, things were very different."

"Will you tell me what happened?" she asked excitedly.

I took a deep breath and looked at her stoically. "I caught Danny and Reneé having sex."

"What!"

"Yep," I said wryly. "Bare asses and everything."

"What!" she exclaimed again. "Are you okay?"

"I really don't know. I'm still digesting it. I'm not used to seeing my teenage sister getting busy with a guy in my own house."

"Oh, I'm sorry, Lacie," Dawn said sympathetically. "So what did you do?"

"I yelled, of course. Then I calmed down and Reneé and I talked." I paused. "I'm taking her to my gynecologist to get her on the pill."

"Are you sure that's the best thing?" she asked.

I sighed. "Dawn, I have no idea. This is new for me. You know, I always promised myself that if I ever had any kids, that I would have the sex talk with them and everything. I'd be prepared. Now look what happened. It's my first incident, she's not even my kid, and I yell at her."

I must have looked pitiful, because Dawn walked over to me and gave me a hug. It was so good to have her as a friend. I could always talk to Dawn about anything.

She let go and looked me in the eye. "Lacie, listen. She's not your child and you can't be supermom for her. You're doing your best, considering the circumstances. I mean, I probably would have acted worse if I had a baby sister and found her in bed with some guy. I couldn't have done what you did. So don't feel bad."

I grabbed a tissue for my nose. "Tony said the same thing to me before he took Danny home. I don't know. I just don't want her to end up with any STDs or get pregnant like I did."

"Did you talk to her about condoms?"

"She already knows. That's what she and Danny used tonight." I blew my nose.

"Wow," she uttered. "Well, think of it like this. They were smart enough to use a condom, so that's got to mean something, right?"

"I guess."

"You know I'm right," Dawn said. "Now, who's Tony?"

"He's my new boss. I told you about him before."

She nodded. "Yeah, I remember now that I think about it. Why was he here?"

"He gave me a ride from the airport and brought my bags up for me. I was in the middle of fixing an omelet for him when we heard Reneé and Danny upstairs. That's why he was here."

"Uh, huh," Dawn mused. "So how did the conference go?"

"It went well. I mean, there was that little incident when Tony kissed me and…"

"Wait, wait, wait a minute. Hold up," she said, peering at me. "Did you just say that he kissed you?"

"Well…yeah," I said, not liking the look she was giving me.

"What do you mean, he kissed you?"

This was frustrating. "The man kissed me, Dawn—tongue and everything—in the hotel elevator," I blurted in exasperation.

"Why did he kiss you?"

I hunched up my shoulders. "Dawn, I don't know, okay? I mean, I'd just had an argument with Steve, during which I slapped him, and I was very upset. I ran into Tony in the elevator and he asked me what had happened. I told him and the next thing I knew he was kissing me."

Dawn closed her eyes tightly and held up her hand. "Okay. I'm not going to ask what the argument with Steve was about or why you slapped him. I just want to know one thing." She opened her eyes. "What are you going to do about Tony? Are you going to file a complaint against him?"

"No, I'm going to forget about it." Dawn scoffed. "Look, he apologized and said he would never do it again, and that's that. I have a good job, Dawn. I can't afford to leave right now," I maintained. "Plus, he's a really nice guy and we get along fine, so why spoil it?"

She shook her head and looked at me thoughtfully. "You're not falling for this guy, are you?"

"No, it's just that I don't want any trouble. I've got enough stress right here in my own house. I don't need it on the job as well."

"Okay. I was just wondering if you were starting to slip, that's all."

"What do you mean by that?"

"Well, he kisses you and you don't and won't do anything about it and you were fixing the man an omelet and everything…" She shrugged. "Listen. My mama always told me that if they can't use your comb, then don't bring them home. That's all I'm saying."

"Don't worry about my comb or anything else. I'm handling it."

"If you say so," she said.

That was my cue to go upstairs and go to bed. I didn't need to hear this. What she should be worried about was that trifling boyfriend of hers, Ronnie. She knew he was no good, but kept going back to his sorry behind.

The doctor visit ran smoothly. Dr. Jones was very helpful and Reneé was very happy to get her birth control pills. I was grateful when the visit was over.

I arrived at the office shortly after eleven and as soon as I reached my desk, Tony called me into his office.

I was curious about the person that I'd be guiding around town. Even though I'd told Tony that I didn't mind, I wasn't happy about it. As soon as I walked into his office, I noticed that the man in question was black, but I couldn't see his face because his back was turned as he sat facing Tony.

"Come on in, Lacie," Tony's voice welcomed as I was about to knock on his open door. "I want you to meet my friend. Joe Mitchell, this is my assistant, Lacie Adams."

Joe Mitchell rose out of his chair, turned and offered his hand. He grinned as I slowly shook his hand with my mouth wide open, because I was somewhat shaken by this weird coincidence. He was the same guy that I'd met at the club the night that I broke up with Steve. I was shocked, but he didn't seem surprised at all.

"I didn't think it was possible that you would be the same Lacie that I met a few weeks ago, but now I see you are. How are you?" he asked politely.

I smiled nervously and just stared at his beautiful teeth. "I'm doing well. How have you been?"

"I've been fine. The last time we saw each other, we really didn't get a chance to talk, considering the circumstances. Are you still with that guy?" he asked directly.

"No, I'm afraid that's ancient history. He's long gone."

"Then maybe we can start from where we left off," he flirted, holding my gaze.

"Uh, excuse me." Tony cleared his throat. "You two know each other?"

Joe Mitchell turned around and looked at Tony. "Kind of. We met at a club a few weeks ago. We were getting along quite well until her boyfriend interrupted us," he explained.

"Ex-boyfriend, Mr. Mitchell," I corrected him.

"And my name is Joe, remember?" he corrected me.

"Oh, sorry…I forgot." I blushed.

"Uh, maybe I should go with you two to look for a place," Tony suggested quickly.

"No, there's no need, Tony. Lacie and I will be fine," Joe said, turning his attention back to me. "I won't have her away from the office too long. Besides, we have a lot of catching up to do."

"So, Mr. Mitchell, where do you want to go to look for an apartment?" I asked as we sat in his limo.

"I told you to call me Joe," he reminded.

"Right…Joe."

"I don't know. I was hoping you could suggest something."

"Do you have a specific price range?"

"Not at all. Money's no object. I want a nice place with lots of room."

"All right, I'll call a realtor I know and see if he can find anything for you." I looked in my purse and realized I'd left my cell phone at home. "Do you have a phone I can use?"

"Oh yeah, sure." He reached into his sports jacket and handed me his cell phone. "Help yourself to anything in here," he said with a grin.

"As you can see, Mr. Mitchell, this is a very luxurious and spacious penthouse apartment, and if you're ready to make an offer, we can start the paperwork right now," Mr. Fisher said.

He was right. The apartment was astoundingly beautiful and huge. It had two fireplaces, one in the living room and one in the master bedroom, a whirlpool bathtub in the master bath and a huge kitchen, which made the apartment even more impressive. When Mr. Fisher told us how much it cost, I wasn't shocked. I'd known it would be expensive. I couldn't even dream of living there on the salary I was making.

"Thank you, Mr. Fisher," Joe said. "This is a nice place, but would you mind leaving us alone for a minute?"

"No, not at all. Take your time. I'll be right out in the hallway," Mr. Fisher replied.

I walked around the apartment again, admiring the marble floors and how spacious it was. I walked to the kitchen and Joe followed, watching as I looked around.

"Do you like the apartment?" he asked.

"Are you kidding? This is gorgeous! I mean, look at the view. Have you seen the view?" I asked excitedly, pointing to the window. I glanced at him. "Then again, it is a bit expensive. Are you sure you want this?"

He chuckled. "Only if you like it. I told you money is no object." He came closer to me. "How many times am I going to have to remind you of that?"

Umm, I could smell that scent again. He was so close I could easily touch him. I moved over to the stove to get cool. What would Tony think of me hitting on a potential client? That wouldn't be cute at all.

"Let me put it this way. If I had the money, I would definitely get this place."

"Then it's been decided," he said with a nod. "Let's tell Mr. Fisher the good news and then I'll take you out to eat to celebrate." He grabbed my hand.

"Wait, Joe. I can't go out with you. I've got to get back to work. Tony will kill me."

"He's not going to say anything," he assured me. "He's my friend and he wants my account."

"I know, but I don't want to take advantage of that." I gently removed moved my hand from his.

He saw that I was serious. "Okay, if you don't want to go out now, then how about dinner tonight?"

"You want to go out with me?"

"Yes, I do."

"Are you sure?"

"Yes, Lacie. I want to take you out and have a complete date without any interruptions—just the two of us."

I grinned and shrugged. "Okay."

He smiled. "All right. Now let's go tell Mr. Fisher that I'm going to take the apartment before he gets nervous."

"Right, good idea. So you really own your own mortgage brokerage company, huh?" I asked as we walked out the front door.

Joe dropped me off at the office and told me to tell Tony that he would talk to him later about business matters. He planned to use the afternoon for furniture shopping, he said, but he'd be by my house around seven-thirty to pick me up.

I was on cloud nine as I took the elevator up to the office. Someone must have heard my prayers because I was having a good day and I was going on a date with a successful black man. It was just too good to be true.

Carrie met me at my desk full of excitement. "Girl, where have you been? This whole office has been going haywire. Tony has been in a bad mood and snapping at everyone since you left with Mr. Mitchell."

"Really?" I glanced at my watch. "It's not that late. Joe told Tony he wouldn't have me out too long. I wonder what's wrong with Tony."

Carrie looked surprised. "His first name is Joe, huh?" She folded her arms. "Since when did you start calling him by his first name?"

I noticed the tone in her voice. "Since he asked me to, Carrie. We met a few weeks ago at a club and it just so happens that he's planning on doing business with the company."

"Really?"

"Yes, really," I said. "And that fine, successful black man also asked me out on a date tonight."

"Oh, so that's why you skipped in here so happily. A successful black man, huh?"

"Yes," I said. I didn't appreciate the attitude she was giving me. "What's with you, Carrie?"

Just then, Tony buzzed me. "Lacie, can you come in here for a minute?"

"Sure. I'll be right in." I hung up the phone. "Look, I'll talk to you later, okay?"

"I know you will," Carrie said and walked off.

I took my coat off, walked to Tony's office and knocked on the door.

"Come in," I heard him say.

He was standing up and looking out the window when I walked in

"Sit down, Lacie," he said in a cool tone.

I sat down and waited a couple of minutes before he said anything.

He finally turned around and sat down in his chair. "Did the apartment hunting go well?"

"Yes, it did. I called a realtor I knew and he was able to show us one immediately. You should have seen it, Tony. It was so beautiful. Joe said he was going to take it and he invited me to dinner to thank me for helping him."

"That's nice. You and Joe seem to be getting along well." He paused. "But I have to tell you that it's not a good idea to get involved with Joe on a personal level."

"Where is this coming from?" I looked at him dubiously.

He ignored my question. "I noticed the way Joe acted toward you and I'm giving you fair warning. His track record with women isn't very good."

I was beginning to get offended. "He was fine with me and I don't see how any of this is your business."

"Since you went out with him for business purposes, it is," he disputed. He sighed, then shrugged. "Hey, it's your life." He threw a large stack of papers across the desk.

"Here, I've drafted a few things that I want you to type up for me. I would like them completed today, please."

I took the stack of papers and looked at them. He had to be crazy. "Tony, there's no way that I can finish this today."

"Just do the best that you can, okay?" he said curtly. "That's all for now." He dismissed me with a little wave.

I stood there for a moment, shocked and angry at his deliberate abruptness. He was actually trying to break bad on a sister. I turned around sharply, walked out of his office and deliberately left the door open.

It was half past six when I finished. Everyone was out of the office except Tony and me.

I was packing up when he came to my desk. "Here's the work you wanted me to type," I said coldly, pointing to the stack of papers on my desk.

He took the papers and cleared his throat. "Lacie, I want to apologize about the way I acted in my office earlier. You didn't deserve that."

I started putting on my coat. "Tony, listen. When I came back it was evident that you were angry at something. For whatever reason, you took your anger out on me and in turn, you made me angry. Now, I'd appreciate you telling me what's going on. What is it? Is there something wrong with me?" I asked.

"No, it's just that..." he began, but was interrupted when my phone rang.

The look on Tony's face showed immediate annoyance at the interruption. I turned my back toward him as I picked up the receiver.

"Hello?"

"Hey, beautiful," Joe's voice rang out. "I was wondering if you were still there. Are you going to make it home in time?"

"I don't think I will. I had to finish a few things before I left, so I'm running a little late. Do you mind waiting? I should get home around seven or seven-thirty, depending on how the trains run. I'll need about an hour to get ready."

He chuckled. "Do you want me to send a car over?"

"No, that's okay." I didn't want to talk too much in front of Tony.

"How about I come by your house around eight or eight-thirty, then?"

"That's fine." I gave him the directions to my house.

"All right. I'll see you then," he said.

I hung up the phone with a small smile on my face.

"Was that Joe?" Tony asked.

"Yes, you guessed correctly," I replied.

"It wasn't much of a guess. I could tell by your smile that it was," he remarked with a disapproving look, which I ignored.

"Well, I'd love to sit here and chat with you, but I'm running behind for my date. I'll see you tomorrow." I gathered my things and started walking toward the door.

"Do you need a ride?" he asked suddenly.

I turned around. "No, I think I'll be okay."

He wasn't letting me go that easy. He walked up to me and said, "The reason I asked is because you hinted that I made you late. It'll take you longer to get home if you go by public transportation, and I know you need time to prepare for your date tonight, so why don't you let me drive you home?"

I don't know why I agreed.

We were never going to get to my apartment in time. Not only did we keep running into red lights, but Tony didn't seem to be in a hurry. Finally, I had had it.

"You're doing this deliberately, aren't you?" I asked.

He looked surprised. "What are you talking about?"

"Tony, you're driving like Miss Daisy," I fumed.

"I can't help it if we keep running into red lights," he said nonchalantly.

"All right, listen. Enough is enough. I'm fed up with this attitude that you've been giving me. What's wrong with you?"

He seemed hesitant.

"What?" I pressed.

"Lacie, I care about you, okay? I don't want you to get hurt, that's all."

"Who said I was going to get hurt?"

"All I am saying is that I've known Joe for a long time and I know what he's like."

"So maybe he's different now. I can take care of myself, you know."

"Yeah. We'll see," was all he said.

When we finally reached my apartment, I hurried out of the car without saying good-bye to Tony and ran into the building. In the process, I bumped into Robert.

"Hey, what's your hurry?"

"Don't ask," I said, trying to get past him.

He blocked my way. "Wait a minute. What's wrong?" he asked, seeing that I was upset. I didn't even have to answer him, because he guessed. "It's your boss, isn't it?"

"How did you know?"

"I saw you jump out of his car like a jack rabbit a second ago, and Dawn told me all about it."

"She did, did she?"

"Yes. We met while you were away in Washington. She invited me in for a cup of coffee the other day and we started talking."

I sighed as we stepped into the elevator. "Oh, well...c'mon then. I'll tell you all about it. I need someone to talk to and you can help me get ready for my date."

"With your boss?" he asked, raising his eyebrow.

The elevator stopped and I turned to him. "No!" I exclaimed. Then, "I'm sorry. I'm really in a hurry, that's all," I apologized quickly.

Dawn, apparently having heard us in the hallway, opened the door and stood there with her hands on her hips. "It's about time," she said.

"Don't start, Dawn. I'm in no mood." I brushed past her.

"What's wrong with her?" I heard her ask Robert.

"She's got a date, so she's in a hurry," I heard him explain.

I started toward the stairs. "Where's Reneé?"

"She's in her room asleep," Dawn replied.

At this hour? It wasn't even eight o'clock. I peeked in her room. Sure enough, she was asleep. I closed the door and felt guilty again. I should be spending more time with her. I'd have to make it up to her somehow.

"Hey, Dawn," I whispered at the top of the stairs. "Would you mind staying with Reneé tonight? I'm sorry to ask you this, but this date is spur of the moment."

"I'm going out with Ronnie, tonight." She gave me a look. "Plus, she's seventeen years old, Lacie."

"I know that, but ever since that incident with Danny..."

"Look, I can stay with her. It's no problem. I don't have anything to do anyway," Robert offered.

I could've kissed him. "Are you sure?"

"Yeah. Go and have fun on your date."

I gave him a grateful smile. He was a sweetheart. I could have smothered Dawn. What was her problem? Lately she was becoming very irritable.

"Who are you going out with anyway?" she asked coldly.

I smiled mischievously. "I'll explain later, but would you both mind helping me get ready? I'm in a rush."

They looked at each other in question, both unsure of what was going on, then climbed the stairs.

We chose a rose-colored semi-formal dress that accented my figure. Once dressed, I stood in front of the mirror with both of them standing behind me.

"What do you think?" I asked them.

"You look great," they replied in unison.

I thanked them with a smile.

"So who is he?" Dawn asked again.

I glanced at Robert, who had the same question on his face. At that moment, I heard a knock on the door downstairs. I grinned mischievously. "I think your question will be answered shortly. You two behave yourselves," I warned. I hurried down the stairs with Robert and Dawn at my heels.

I opened the door and was greeted with Joe's smile. He looked good and was immaculate from head to toe. Suddenly, I was self-conscious about what I was wearing, but his expression assured me that I looked fine.

"Hi, beautiful." He handed me a bouquet of white lilies.

"What!" I heard Dawn exclaim.

Dawn's 'what' brought me back to reality. I'd forgotten that she and Robert were watching everything. I grabbed Joe's hand and guided him into the living room to meet them.

"Joe, these are my good friends, Robert and Dawn. Robert and Dawn, this is Joe."

They looked awestruck as Joe shook their hands.

"Isn't he the same guy from the club?" Dawn asked loudly, looking confused.

I was embarrassed. Dawn could have a big mouth when she wanted to. "Yes," I replied and silenced her with a glare. She understood. I turned to Joe. "Thank you for the flowers. They're beautiful. Sit down and make yourself comfortable and I'll be ready once I put these in some water." I looked at Dawn. "Dawn, come with me," I said, walking toward the kitchen.

"I cannot believe your luck," Dawn whispered once we were in the kitchen. "How did you…? I thought you told me you didn't get his number?"

"I didn't," I answered evasively, deliberately keeping her in suspense.

"Well?"

"I met him at work. It just so happens that he's a friend of Tony's and he wants to do business with the firm." To put the icing on the cake, I added, "He owns his own brokerage company, Dawn."

"What?"

"I know. It's unbelievable, isn't it? I mean, here I was practically giving up on meeting the right man, and then he strolls back into my life."

"So is he rich, rich?"

I took a quick peek into the living room and saw Robert and Joe conversing. I wanted to make sure they didn't overhear us. "Apparently so. I went apartment hunting with him on Park Avenue today."

"What!"

"I know. I know." I shook my head, then grabbed Dawn. "Listen, I don't know how far he and I are going to go, but I must be doing something right for me to get a second chance like this. So whatever happens, please make sure that I don't mess this up, okay?"

Dawn laughed at me and gave me a hug. "Girl, you're going to do fine."

Those words were what I needed.

I was surprised to see a limo waiting when we went outside. This was my first date with him and he was already taking me out in style. I felt as if I were being given the star treatment.

Once inside the limo, Joe, being the gentleman that he was, offered me a glass of champagne. I politely declined and settled for bottled water instead.

"Are you comfortable?" he asked after a while.

"Yes, very much so. I am very curious about where we're going, though."

He smiled. "I like to keep people guessing."

"Oh, really?"

"Really," he said. He laughed and patted my hand. "Relax. It's going to be an interesting evening."

What did that mean? I glanced at him curiously and then my eyes caught sight of a helicopter. We were at the South Street Heliport. I had never been on a helicopter before.

I looked at Joe nervously as the driver opened the door. "Are you sure about this?"

He smiled reassuringly and offered his hand. "It'll be fun. C'mon. I won't let anything happen to you."

I looked down at his hand, then into his eyes, and knew everything was going to be okay. I took his hand and we walked toward the helicopter, ducking to avoid the spinning blades.

Riding in the helicopter overlooking Manhattan, I felt a new sense of appreciation for the island. New York is a beautiful city, and even more so at night. The ride was truly a breathtaking experience. Joe held my hand the entire time, which helped me relax. I was sorry when the ride was over. Feeling completely at ease with Joe, I walked to the limo with my head on his shoulder.

"Are you ready to eat?" he asked when the driver closed the door.

"Yes, I am kind of hungry," I replied.

"Good. I have a surprise for you."

In a few minutes, the limo came to a stop. We were in front of his apartment building.

"What are we doing here? I thought we were going out to dinner?"

"We are, but I forgot something upstairs. It'll only take a minute."

Once we reached his door, Joe seemed to have trouble unlocking it. He gave me the key.

"Would you mind? Maybe you can open it. I don't know what's wrong with that key. I'll talk to the manager about it tomorrow," he said.

I turned the key and it clicked with my first try. I looked at him and he shrugged.

"I don't know. I guess I didn't try hard enough."

I opened the door and was overwhelmed by what I saw. The apartment was completely lit with candles, a fire was in the fireplace and in the middle of the living room, there was an elegant table set for two with a waiter standing by. In the far right corner, two violinists and a pianist played a beautiful melody. The waiter walked over immediately and handed me a dozen pink roses.

"Good evening, Miss Adams. We're glad you could join us," he greeted, leading us to the table. "Dinner for this evening will be lobster and stuffed crab shells with potatoes and steamed vegetables." He poured white wine in our glasses. "Dinner will be served shortly," he announced as he left us and went to the kitchen.

I looked at Joe. I was grinning from ear to ear and so was he. "Thank you," I said.

"You're welcome. Do you like it?"

"Yes."

He nodded his head. "Get used to it," he said. He looked at me tenderly and touched my cheek lightly with one finger. "May I have this dance?"

As if on cue, the band started playing "Between the Sheets" by the Isley Brothers. That was the song we'd danced to when we met at the club. He took the roses from me and put them on the table. Then he offered his hand and led me to the middle of the floor and pulled me much closer than before—as if we were already lovers. This time we had no interruptions. It was just the two of us. I felt as if I were in a dream.

When the music stopped, we walked back to the table where our dinner was waiting. Two candles burned softly in the center of the table, and the musicians continued to play as we ate and talked our way through dinner. I asked him how he came to own his own brokerage company. He explained that while he was growing up, he had always wanted to have his own business. After graduating from college, he started working in a brokerage company and learned all about the business. With a few years under his belt, savings and hard work, he started his company.

"I noticed that a lot of banks were reluctant to loan black people money for homes, so I decided that I would start my own mortgage brokerage company and help my people. It was very hard at first, but in the past several years, my company has become very successful," he said. "Now, tell me about yourself."

"What do you want to know?"

"Everything."

"Let's start off with the little things," I said. "I'm not too keen on telling a guy everything about myself on a first date."

"Why is that?"

I shrugged. "I just feel that if you tell someone everything about yourself, then there's nothing left for them to learn on their own."

He shook his head. "I don't believe that."

"Excuse me?"

"I think you're afraid of letting people in."

I could have argued, but then I thought I would let him think what he wanted. Most people do anyway.

We finished eating and when the waiter came over, Joe whispered something to him. The waiter nodded, immediately went over to the band and said something. They started to leave.

"Where are they going?" I asked.

"Nowhere," was all he said. After a few minutes, he glanced at his watch, grabbed my hand and said, "Come on, let's go outside and look at the view."

We walked out to the terrace where I found the band. They began to play a beautiful, mellow song.

I turned to him. "I don't believe you."

"What?" he asked, smiling innocently.

"Do you always try to impress women like this?"

"Only those that matter," he said.

"You know, Tony warned me about you," I remarked, waiting to see what his reaction would be.

He shook his head. "That doesn't surprise me."

"It doesn't?"

"No. Tony remembers what I was like in college and that's all he seems to remember."

"So should I be worried?" I teased.

He held my gaze. "You have nothing to be worried about," he replied seriously.

I broke the gaze and looked at the skyline. "This is such an amazing sight," I commented.

"It sure is," he said. He grabbed my hand again. "Miss Adams, may I have another dance?"

I smiled. "Of course, Mr. Mitchell."

We danced slowly, as if we had all the time in the world. It was so romantic that I couldn't believe it was happening. When the band finished playing, Joe pulled me close and kissed me very slowly. The kiss deepened as we blocked the whole world from us.

"Do you want to stay the night?" he asked when we stopped to breathe.

I contemplated it, but decided against it. I shook my head. "No. I don't think that would be a good idea."

"Right." He smiled and nodded. "So, are you ready to go home?

"No. But I think I should go anyway."

He laughed.

Joe walked me to my door.

"This has been a wonderful first date and I can't thank you enough for all that you've…"

He smiled warmly. "There's no need to thank me. It was my pleasure." He kissed me softly on the lips and started to walk down the hall. "Get some rest. I'll see you at the office tomorrow."

Dawn was still up, watching television, when I walked in. I figured she'd be waiting for me. "I've got a bone to pick with you."

I sat down. "Well, pick all you want, Dawn. I've had a wonderful date and nothing can spoil it."

"Why didn't you tell me your date was with him?"

"You didn't ask," I replied. "Where's Robert?"

"I came back early, so I told him to go home," she replied. "So how did your date with Mr. Rich Man go?"

I grinned. "Dawn, let me tell you. I have never, ever, been on a date like that in my whole life. He's incredible!"

"Don't leave me hanging. Tell me how incredible he is!" she exclaimed impatiently.

"Dawn, he took me on a helicopter ride all around Manhattan, then brought me back to his place where we were serenaded by a small band and served dinner by our own personal waiter."

"I don't believe it." Dawn shook her head in astonishment.

"I can't believe it myself. This guy is so incredible and he is such a gentleman." I took a deep breath. "Girl, I don't know what to think. I mean, I meet a handsome black man at a club, we don't exchange numbers, then I find out that he's not only a good friend of my boss, but successful, and then he takes me out. What are the chances of that?" I looked at Dawn for an answer.

She shook her head. "Slim to none. But Lacie, all I know is that you need to find a way to keep him. Good men are hard to find—especially black men." She stood and went upstairs to her room.

CHAPTER 5

The next day I woke up early and fully rested and was able to talk to Reneé for a while before I went to work. Remembering what had happened the night before last, I promised her that we would go out to the movies or to dinner one weekend.

Carrie came to my desk as soon as I arrived. "So, how did your date with Mr. Mitchell go?" she asked sarcastically.

I was in such a good mood I took what she said lightly. "It went very well. We had a great time."

"Good. I'm glad you had a great time," she said and went to her desk.

I shrugged my shoulders, went to the kitchen and started the coffee. I heard Tony walk in, but I continued with what I was doing.

After a moment, he asked, "Did you have a nice time last night?"

"Yes, I did."

"Good. I'm glad you enjoyed yourself. Listen, I put some memos on your desk that I need typed today and a list of supplies that I need you to order for my office. I'll be in meetings most of the day." He started to leave, but then stopped in the doorway to say, "Oh, Joe will be here also, but I guess you already knew."

He walked out and I just shook my head. As the morning progressed, I worked on the memos while Tony went to his meetings. Occasionally, he'd come back on the floor, walk to my desk and get his messages and that would be it.

It was around eleven when Joe walked into the office. Ready for business, he was carrying his leather briefcase in hand.

He stopped at my desk. "Good morning," he greeted.

"Good morning, Mr. Mitchell," I returned with a smile.

He wagged a finger. "Now, I know you're not going to be all formal with me."

"No, I just thought…"

"No," he said softly. "I was Joe to you last night and I'm Joe to you now, okay? You don't have to treat me any differently because I'm interested in doing business with this company and we're dating."

"Oh, we're dating now?" I teased.

"Yes, we are," he replied with a grin.

Just then Tony came out his office and walked over. Ignoring me, he spoke to Joe.

"Joe, it's good to see you. I was wondering if you were going to make it here before lunch. Come on in and let's start talking business," he said, leading Joe toward his office. Closing the door, he said, "Lacie, hold my calls until I get out of the meeting with Joe and if anyone comes to see me, buzz me first," he instructed.

Forty-five minutes later Joe hastened out of Tony's office and mouthed, "I'll call you later," as he rushed past me and out the door. I wondered why he was in such a hurry. Then Tony called me into his office. I grabbed my pad and pen, walked in, closed the door and sat down and waited.

"Richard Ryan is extremely interested in landing the account for Joe's company," he stated.

"All right," I said, wondering where this conversation was going.

He continued. "I'm going to work extremely hard to get this account and I'll need some assistance. Since Joe seems to like you, I figured you would be the perfect person to help me. It's a huge account, so we're going to be doing a lot of work. In turn, this should help you move up within this company."

"What do you want me to do?" I asked.

"You'll need to attend all the meetings and luncheons with me. We need to learn everything we can about his company and what his interests are. I figure you helping will give Joe more of an incentive to work with us, and you in turn will learn more about what we do here."

I took offense at the last thing he said and replied, "Tony, I've been here for five years. I know practically everything about this firm and the business."

"Then you shouldn't have a problem." He walked toward a huge stack of books and gave them to me. "Here. I want you to go over this material—tonight if you can. It consists of legal information and technical terms you should know that'll help you get a broader view of everything. Do you have any questions?" he asked.

"Yes. You've hardly said a word to me all morning and now you want me to help you with this account. Why the sudden change in attitude?"

He shrugged. "You've mentioned before that you haven't moved any higher since you've been here, so I figured this would be the perfect opportunity for you," he said. His face was expressionless. "Do we have a deal?"

"I guess we do," I answered.

"Good," he nodded. "You're free to go home now so that you can read over all this material. I want you to be ready for the meeting tomorrow."

I took a deep breath. "Okay." I slowly got up and headed toward the door. "I'll see you tomorrow."

When I got home, Reneé hadn't arrived home from school and Dawn was still at work. I had the house to myself for a little while. I took out a pack of chicken to soak, put on some comfortable clothes and started reading the books Tony had given me. It was a lot of material.

I was really getting into the books when the phone rang. It was Joe. "Hey, beautiful," he said. I could hear that he was in his car.

"Hey. What's going on?"

"Nothing. I was just wondering if you wanted to go out tonight?"

"That sounds great, but I've got a lot of stuff to read up on and I wanted to spend a little time with my sister."

"Is it okay if I come over for a while?

"Sure. What time do you think you'll be here?"

"I'm right around the corner. I'll be there shortly."

I laughed. "Okay. Just come on up."

Minutes later, Joe was at my front door. When I opened it, he came in and kissed me on the cheek.

"Have a seat. Do you want something to drink?"

"No, I'm fine, thank you." He sat on the sofa. "So, what's this about you having a lot to read up on tonight that's keeping us from going out?" he asked.

I pointed to the stack of books and papers on the coffee table as I flopped down next to him. "Tony gave me all of this to read. Apparently, he and I are going to be working together to get your account. He wanted me to study this information so I could be ready for tomorrow," I explained.

"Oh, I see. He figures I would be a shoo-in if you were working with him, because we're going out." He grinned.

"You said it, I didn't. I'm just following the boss's orders." I shrugged. "Listen, why did you walk out of the office so fast today?"

"I had to go to the airport to pick up my lawyer and the rest of my staff. I wanted them to be on hand for the meeting tomorrow."

"Oh," I mused. "You're really serious about this venture, huh?"

"Yeah, I think I am. At first I only came here to take care of some private business, but then Tony talked to me about doing business with your company and it sparked my interest. I asked him lots of questions, and liked the answers I got back. That's when I figured I would need the rest of my immediate staff here.

"Excuse me for asking you this, but just how rich are you, exactly? Tony said that Richard Ryan really wants your account. You must be extremely wealthy for him to take such an interest in you."

He laughed. "Let's just say that I've made a lot of smart business decisions and because of that I'm financially stable."

"Whatever you say, Joe." I should've known he wasn't going to reveal how wealthy he was.

He looked at me seriously. "I'm concerned about what we talked about at the office today. Is it going to be difficult for you to work with me and date me also?"

"What do you mean?"

"I want to continue seeing you, Lacie. We had a great time last night."

I nodded. "Yes, we did. And it's not every day that I get a chance to ride in a helicopter with a successful and handsome brother on my first date with him."

He chuckled. "I know. I guess I wanted to impress you. I won't take you on any more helicopter rides. I promise."

"No, no, no. That's not what I meant. You can take me on helicopter rides anytime you want, Joe. It's just that now, it won't be much of a surprise, is all. I can read into you a little bit now. You're a very romantic person."

He searched my face. "You've had a hard time dealing with men, haven't you?"

"Let's just say that I've had my share of disappointments," I said evasively.

"Fair enough. I won't push it," he said, raising a hand. "You still haven't answered my question, though."

"You're right." I was silent for a moment, then looked at him seriously. "Joe, I have no problem dating you. You don't work for the firm, so I don't think it will be too difficult for me to handle."

"I'm glad to hear that," he murmured and started fingering my hair.

"There are two things I want to ask of you, though."

"Uh-oh," he said.

"Don't say 'uh-oh.' It's not bad."

"Okay. Then what is it?" Watching me intensely, he continued playing with my hair.

"I want us to take our time. I don't want this to become a serious thing too fast." I waited for his reaction.

He nodded. "All right. I can handle that. You're worth the wait. Now, what's the second thing?"

I took a deep breath. "I think we should keep our personal business away from the job. Someone is not taking our dating too well."

"You mean Tony?"

"Yes."

"I wouldn't worry about him, Lacie. He knows how much I like you and I don't think he wants to miss out on this opportunity."

"What do you mean by that?"

"Listen, I've known Tony for a long time. He's been a great friend to me, but I won't have him interfere with my happiness. This is between us. He knows that. We talked today and straightened everything out. You don't have anything to worry about."

"Yeah, but I still feel we should keep a level of professionalism when we're in meetings and everything," I suggested.

"I have no problem with that," he assured me. "What I do have a problem with is you not giving me a kiss."

I grinned. "You want me to kiss you, Mr. Mitchell?"

"You know I do, Miss Adams."

We were just about to kiss, but stopped when we heard someone enter the apartment. It was Reneé.

"Hi, Reneé. How was school?" I asked.

"It was okay." She shrugged her shoulders and hung her coat up.

"Reneé, I want you to meet my friend Joe. Joe, this is my sister, Reneé," I said.

Joe stood up and offered his hand. "Nice to meet you."

Reneé shook his hand. "Nice to meet you, too," she said. She turned to me. "Lacie, I'm going upstairs to do my homework. I'll probably take a nap after I'm finished. I had four tests today and I'm mentally drained. If Danny calls, just tell him I'll call him back later. Will you let me know when dinner is ready?" she asked.

"Sure, sweetie. Go upstairs," I said. "I'll call you when it's done."

"Thanks, Lacie," she said, heading upstairs. "It was nice meeting you, Joe."

"Same here," he returned, sitting back down. He turned to me. "She's pretty and she looks just like you. What's the deal with her staying with you?"

"Ahh, that's a long, long story that I really don't want to get into. Now where were we?" As I moved close to kiss him, we heard the door open again. It was Dawn and Robert. "What are you two doing here? Dawn, it's not even five o'clock yet."

"I know, but my agent called me about an audition, and after that I left work early and met Robert on the way. We just came to change. We're going to the movies and then to a club," she explained. "We didn't interrupt anything, did we?"

"Yes, but that's all right. I've got a lot of stuff to do anyway," I said. Joe and I stood up and walked to the front door while Dawn and Robert went into the kitchen. "Listen, I'm sorry about the interruptions. I had no idea everyone would be here so soon," I explained.

"Don't be. It's your house and you did tell me that you had some reading to do before I came over here. So it's fine. I'll call you later. Nope. Better yet, you call me. I don't want to interrupt you." He gave me a peck on my lips. "See you tomorrow," he said and walked out the door.

"Girl, he is just too fine! I can't believe how lucky you are," Dawn exclaimed from behind me.

I whirled around and looked at her. "Why must you always be in my business?"

"Because I'm your best friend. Besides, you're always in mine," she retorted as we joined Robert in the kitchen. "What's your problem, Lacie?"

"One, you came in here and interrupted us, and two, that little snide comment you made last night about good men being hard to find, especially black men." I said. I grabbed the bowl of raw chicken that I had left soaking and started seasoning it. "I didn't forget about that, you know."

"Lacie, I'm sorry, but that's my opinion. Why would you want to go with a rich white man when you can have a rich black man? What do you think, Robert?" she asked as she sat next to him on the barstool.

"I don't find anything wrong with the idea but I think Lacie's mature enough to make her own decisions. She knows what she wants," he said. I gave him a grateful smile.

"Oh, who asked you, Robert?" Dawn scolded. Robert and I laughed.

"Dawn, I've already explained the situation with Tony to you. There's nothing going on. As far as Joe is concerned, we're just going to take it slow. I don't want to rush into anything too fast. I mean, you know what I went through with Steve. Right now, all I want is to enjoy myself and get to know him better. So don't get too excited about this," I said to Dawn. "Now both of you come over here and help me with dinner. Robert, are you staying for dinner?"

"You didn't know?" he asked.

"Umm, hmm. I knew it. That's all you two use me for—my good cooking and getting into my business," I gibed.

We talked a lot while we fixed dinner. Dawn thought her audition had gone well and that she would hear from her agent soon about whether she got the part. She also told me that she and Ronnie had made up and she would be moving back in with him soon. I wasn't crazy about her moving back in with him, but I was looking forward to having a little privacy again. Robert had gotten a job dancing in an off Broadway play and was even seeing someone special regularly. It had been a while since I had talked to my friends and I was enjoying it.

Reneé came down to eat but said very little during dinner, then went back upstairs immediately after she ate. I went to her room after Robert and Dawn left.

"Come in," Reneé answered to my knock. She was lying on her bed.

I poked my head through the door. "Hey. Are you okay? You were really quiet at dinner and you came back up here so fast after you ate."

"I know, Lacie. I've just got a lot on my mind right now," she answered softly.

"Boy problems?"

She shrugged her shoulders. "Kind of."

"Okay. I'm not going to push the issue, but if you want to talk about it, I'm here. Don't hesitate," I encouraged. "No matter what it is."

She smiled thinly. "Okay."

"Goodnight."

"Goodnight, Lacie," I heard her say as I closed the door.

November rolled in as Tony and I started to work with Joe's immediate staff. It was clear that Joe's company was steadily growing and on its way to becoming a huge corporation. His team of lawyers and assistants really impressed me with their loyalty. With the combination of meetings and learning about his company, I began to realize how stressful the investment business could be. I was a busy woman, but I was enjoying every bit and began to feel as if I were making a difference in the firm. Apparently Mr. Ryan felt that way as well. Tony and Joe filled me in on his compliments.

Although work kept me busy, Joe and I continued to date. We saw each other nearly every day outside of the job and always had a great time together. While he was hard-nosed about his business, he had a soft side to him that no one else saw, and I liked that.

I did manage to do some things with Reneé as I'd planned. I took her to dinner one evening and then another night, I rented movies and we ate popcorn as we watched them. Bonding with Reneé reminded me of how long it had been since I'd heard anything from Mama and I wondered when she'd return.

After Dawn moved back in with Ronnie, our paths crossed occasionally at work or whenever I would go into the cafeteria to lunch with her and Carrie. We talked on the phone, but not as much as we used to. When we did, she'd always brag about her relationship with Ronnie and how good he was to her. She was even talking about marriage. This shocked me. The Dawn I remembered was not inter-ested in marriage, only her career. Since she mentioned nothing new about her audition, I figured she didn't get the part. I reminded myself that I would have to see her when-ever I got the time.

Every now and then, I'd pass Robert in the hallway of our apartment building. His show seemed to keep him quite busy. Once, I happened to see his friend. He was an attractive guy and I hoped everything was going well for Robert.

After many negotiations and a lot of hard work, Tony and I came up with a proposal that Joe and his staff liked, and we finally ended up with his account. It was Friday, a

week before Thanksgiving. Joe, his staff, and I went to celebrate at Tony's apartment, which was only fifteen or twenty
minutes from the office. We all felt like friends now. All of
us had put in many hours of work and the end result had
been worth it.

Amidst the celebration, Joe pulled me aside and said,
"Now that this deal is done, do you think it's okay to let
everyone know about us?"

I shook my head slowly at the thought. "No. I don't
think that would be a good idea. Tony's the only one that
knows right now, and I think it's better we keep it that way.
Otherwise people will begin to speculate on the real reason
why we landed your account. F-A-V-O-R-I-T-I-S-M,
they'll say."

"You are so funny," Joe chuckled. "Seriously, though. I
think you worked very hard to make this deal happen."

"I'm glad you think so, because there were times when
I was worried that it would never go through."

"It did, though. You and Tony did a remarkable job
with everything."

Tony appeared from nowhere. "Hey, did I hear my
name being mentioned?" He hung his arms around our
shoulders.

Joe laughed and shook his head. "Are you drunk, man?"

"No," Tony proclaimed, lifting his glass of champagne.
"I just feel really great. Now, why was my name
mentioned?" he asked again, looking at us for an explanation.

"I was just telling Lacie about the good job you two
did," Joe explained.

Tony shook his head. "It was more her than me. I mean, the way she caught on to everything and how she took control of the meetings was remarkable."

I smiled at Tony. "Hey, give yourself credit also. I didn't do this alone, you know."

He wouldn't hear of it. "Yeah, but if it weren't for you…"

He was interrupted when Joe's lawyer came over to inform Joe that his staff was ready to leave, but they were going to need a ride to the hotel because they were all intoxicated.

Joe moaned. "I guess I'm the designated driver tonight. Lacie, are you ready to go?" he asked me.

Tony answered for me. "Joe, you're not going to fit all of them and her into your car. I'll take her home, don't worry."

"Lacie?" Joe looked at me.

I gave him a reassuring smile. "I'll be fine. You just make sure they get home safely."

"Are you sure?" he asked again.

Tony sighed. "Will you go before they decide to drive themselves?" he commanded, indicating the obviously intoxicated group trying to put on their coats.

Joe shook Tony's hand. "Thanks, man. Take care of her for me," he said, and gave me a peck on the cheek.

We followed Joe to the door and watched him gradually ease everyone out. Closing the door, I realized that Tony was no longer behind me. I heard him in the kitchen rattling dishes. The living room was in chaos—empty

Chinese food cartons and glasses half full with champagne and wine were all over the tables.

I glanced at my watch and was surprised at how late it was, almost midnight. I'd left a message on my answering machine telling Reneé that I'd be home late, and I'd also called Robert to ask him to check on her every now and then. I figured I'd better give Reneé a call to let her know I'd be home soon.

"Tony, do you mind if I make a quick phone call? I want to check on my sister," I called out to him.

"No, go ahead. Help yourself. Use the one in my study if you want some privacy," he called back.

I went to his study and dialed my house. Reneé picked it up immediately and I told her where I was and that I anticipated being home in about an hour or so. I gave her Tony's number just in case she needed to reach me.

"Love you, Lacie," she murmured softly.

That was nice to hear. "I love you too," I returned and hung up the phone.

When I returned, Tony was in the living room throwing the empty Chinese cartons in a garbage bag.

We walked back and forth from the living room to the kitchen as I began helping.

"How's your sister?" he asked.

"She's doing okay, I think. She's been kind of distant lately and staying in her room a lot. So, I don't really know." I shrugged my shoulders.

"Boy problems?" he asked.

"I think so, but she won't say. I'm not going to pressure her, though. I figure she'll talk to me when she's ready," I said confidently as we finished putting the glasses in the dishwasher. "I mean, one thing I did have a problem with when I was growing up, was my mother's inability to communicate with me. In turn, I locked myself into my own world, so to speak. So I have an idea of what she's going through."

Tony nodded. "You think she's feeling rejected?"

"Maybe. I did." I watched him pour water into my glass.

We walked back to the living room and sat on the sofa where I continued the conversation.

"My mother and I did not have a good relationship when I was growing up. My dad left us when I was very young and that left my mother to raise me on her own. A long time ago, I did spend one summer with him. It was the best summer I ever had. Every now and then I hear from him," I said with a little smile.

"You're crazy about him, aren't you?" Tony asked.

"How did you know?"

He shrugged. "Just a feeling."

I shook my head. "You know, I have no idea why I'm so crazy about my dad. He never supported me. My mother raised me and did everything she could to help us along the way, and yet at one time I could hardly stand the sight of her," I mused.

Tony looked shocked. "Are you serious?" He watched me intensely with his elbow on the back of the sofa.

"Very," I said.

"Why did you feel that way about your own mother?"

"Because she remarried," I answered dourly. I could feel the tears welling up in my eyes. Since I didn't want to go there, I immediately switched the attention to him. "So what about you, Tony? Do you have any family problems?"

He shook his head. "No. I have a wonderful mom and dad who have been married for about thirty-five years. They live in Connecticut, in a beautiful sixty-five-year-old house on a hundred acres that I bought for them when I started making some serious money," he replied.

"No kidding?" He shook his head. "Do you have any siblings?" I asked. I was interested because this was my first time hearing about his family.

"Yes. I have twin brothers and two sisters. Thanksgiving and Christmas gatherings are a real tradition in my family. Everyone is always home for the holidays. Matter of fact, I don't think we've ever had a year when we all weren't home."

I looked at him with surprise.

"What?" he asked.

"That's wonderful. Family must be really important to you."

"It is."

"I just never figured you to be that way."

"There are a lot of things about me that would surprise you," he said.

"Umm. Now why does that sound so familiar?" I smiled.

Turning my head and looking around the living room, I noticed a beautiful, black piano sitting in the corner.

"Do you keep that as a showpiece?" I nodded toward the piano.

He followed my gaze. "No, I can play. I learned when I was very young. But I don't play much anymore."

"Why not? Something like that shouldn't go to waste. Why don't you play something for me?"

"Are you serious?"

"Yes. You had me cook for you, so it's your turn to do something for me."

"But I never did get to eat the omelet," he pointed out.

"Oh, c'mon!" I insisted.

He chuckled and grabbed my hand. "All right. I guess I can do that for you." We went to the piano and he sat down. "Do you want me to sing as well or just play?"

I sat next to him. "You sing too? Oh, this is just too much. Do both, please. I've got to hear this!"

He laughed, knowing I was teasing. "What do you want to hear?"

"I don't know…improvise. I like any kind of music— except hard rock."

He laughed again and put his hands on the keys and began to play. He started off with a piece by Beethoven and then sang Stevie Wonder's song, "You and I." I was impressed with how well he sang and played, and how he seemed to get so engrossed in the music.

"Wow. I didn't know you were so talented," I uttered softly after he finished. "Your voice is beautiful."

He shrugged. "I thought I was a bit rusty. I haven't sung or played in a while."

"No, you're very talented, Tony," I insisted.

"I surprised you again, right?" he asked, wagging his finger at me.

"Okay, okay. Maybe I have assumed too many things about you. I apologize. But I gotta tell you that I really wasn't expecting you to be that good."

"You thought the piano was just for show, right?"

I shrugged my shoulders. "You must admit that a lot of people have pianos in their houses just for decoration, not because they know how to play."

"You've got a point. But still…" he said.

"I know." I rolled my eyes upward. "I shouldn't judge."

He laughed. "Good. I see that you're learning."

I smiled. "Well, you're a very good teacher. Thanks for the little concert. I really enjoyed it."

"You're welcome. I'm glad you did."

I stared at him as he continued to fiddle with the piano keys. He was so fine. Lost in thought, I didn't realize that I was still staring, until he caught me looking and stopped playing.

"What's wrong?" he asked.

"Nothing." I turned my head quickly.

"Oh. I thought there was something on my face the way you were looking at me."

"I wasn't looking at you," I denied.

"You're lying."

I turned to look at him. "No, I'm not," I denied again, defiantly.

He grinned. "You know something?"

"What?"

"You're a very bad liar." Then he leaned close and kissed me softly.

Unconsciously I returned his kiss, but then jerked away, realizing what I was doing. I stood up with my back to him and heard him stand up as well.

"Why did you pull away?" He sounded disappointed.

I turned around and looked at him. "Tony, I'm seeing Joe. I'm involved. You know that," I said. I had to get out of there. I walked swiftly to the closet and grabbed my coat and purse. "Look, I don't like what's going on here, and I think it's time that you take me home. Now, please!" I put my coat on, went to the door and waited.

He looked disappointed as he walked over to one of the coffee tables and grabbed his keys. As he walked toward me, I looked down. For some reason I couldn't look at him. He stopped in front of me and stood there for what seemed like an hour. Still, I kept my head down, refusing to look at him. All of a sudden, he pulled my chin up and made me look right into his eyes. I almost melted.

"I'm sorry. I didn't mean to upset you," he said softly.

"It's okay," I whispered.

We stood there not speaking for a long moment with his hand cupped under my chin and our eyes locked.

When he moved to unlock the door, he was an inch from my face. He gave me a soft peck on the cheek and waited for my reaction. I didn't move. Then he kissed my forehead and looked into my eyes. I still didn't move. Slowly he began to kiss my neck with soft, gentle kisses in all the right places. I was rooted to the spot. At last, his lips moved to mine and he tasted so sweet. I muttered something as our kisses grew deeper and longer. Every inch of his tongue tasted so good that I yearned for more.

He took off my coat and I dropped my purse. Slowly he unbuttoned my blouse. Hands as smooth as butter slid inside and gently stroked my breasts. Unbuttoning his shirt, I moaned softly at the sight of his hard-muscled chest. I ran my hands across his chest slowly as we continued to kiss and touch. When he pulled my leggings down and felt between my legs, I gasped and couldn't think about anything except how good everything felt. Our hearts beating rapidly, we clung together.

Our passion mounted with every kiss and caress, and he kept whispering my name. By now I had on only my panties, and his shirt hung halfway off his shoulders. I couldn't remember how my clothes had come off.

Without warning, he lifted me off my feet, as if I weighed no more than a feather. In spite of all that we had already done, that caused an alarm to suddenly go off in my head.

"What are you doing?" I gasped breathlessly.

He said nothing, only carried me into his bedroom, kissing me along the way, then laid me gently on his bed. Finally, with a tender expression, he said, "You are so beautiful." His lips returned to dance with mine, then expertly moved down my body, planting soft sweet kisses until he reached my panties. Taking them off gingerly with his teeth, he then started licking every inch of me, while I ran my fingers through his hair.

Stopping his teasing, he reached into the night table next to the bed for a condom and expertly readied himself.

Carefully and slowly he entered me and I immediately felt an exhilarating sense of oneness. We rocked together in perfect rhythm for what seemed a lifetime. We kissed and enjoyed each other's body until we finally came to our ultimate climax and fell asleep in each other's arms.

I awoke confused by my surroundings, until I remembered that I was in Tony's apartment and in his bed. Light shining through the curtains indicated daylight. The sudden scent of cooked bacon reached me and my stomach growled.

What time was it? I looked at the clock on the night table. It showed nine-thirty. I stood up and grabbed his shirt. I needed to wash my face and brush my teeth. I always kept a toothbrush and toothpaste in my purse, but my purse was in the living room.

Quietly as I could, I walked to the living room. I could hear Tony in the kitchen. Seeing my purse, I rummaged through it and found the toothbrush and toothpaste. Suddenly I felt a kiss on my neck. I whirled around and came face to face with his smile.

"Good afternoon, sleepyhead," he greeted cheerfully. "I was just about to wake you up to let you know that breakfast is almost ready. I figured you'd want something to eat once you awoke."

I covered my mouth and said, "I...I...just came to get my toothbrush. I want to wash up a little."

"Oh…okay. There are some washcloths in the closet down the hall. Take your time." He gave me a soft peck.

I went back to the bedroom and brushed my teeth and washed my face in the adjoining bathroom. I felt better. Then I caught sight of myself in the mirror.

"Lacie, what have you done?" I whispered.

"Lacie, the food's ready," Tony called from the kitchen.

When I left the bedroom, I walked back out and was surprised to see that he had the dining room table set. Each plate held eggs, bacon, French toast and a glass of orange juice.

"You made this?" I asked.

"I did," he replied proudly. "I don't do this for everyone, you know." He pulled out a chair for me.

I looked at my plate and sat down slowly. "I don't think I can eat all of this."

"Just eat as much as you can. I think I went a little over-board with the food, so I won't be offended if you don't finish your plate." He pushed the chair in for me and walked over to the other side of the table and sat down.

"How's the food?" he asked, after a while.

"It's really good." I took a sip of my orange juice.

He smiled. "Thank you."

As we ate, we did little talking and neither of us mentioned the night before, though Tony would occasion-ally look at me as if he wanted to say something. Once we finished, I started to clear the table but his voice stopped me.

"Don't do that. I'll straighten up," he said.

Standing there, unsure of what to do, it suddenly hit me. What was I doing? I had made love with my boss. I had to get out of there. I went back to the bedroom to get dressed and was picking up my clothes from the floor when he came into the room.

"Leaving so soon?" he asked.

My heart started to race. "Uh...yeah. You probably have a lot to do, so I thought I should leave." I started to dress.

"Don't leave," he pleaded lightly. "I made plans for us to go to the movies and to dinner and everything."

I was taken aback. "You made plans?"

"Well, yes. I thought it would be nice if I took you out." He saw me shake my head. "What? You don't want to go out?"

I took a deep breath. "It's not that..."

"Then what is it?" He waited for me to answer.

I didn't know where to begin. I was speechless and could feel my eyes starting to water. "I think it will be best if I just leave."

"Why?"

I was exasperated. Gulping back tears, I threw up my hands in frustration. "Tony, think." I pointed to my head. "Think about what we did last night."

"That's all I can think about. Last night was beautiful," he said sincerely.

"No," I said abruptly, "think about how wrong it was."

He looked confused as he watched me dress. "Wait a minute. After our passionate night and breakfast, you're suddenly going to get a conscience?"

I nodded my head insistently. "Yes, that's right. Because the reality of what we did has sunk in, Tony. It was wrong."

"What was so wrong about it, Lacie? Huh? What was so wrong? We were two people attracted to each other and last night we acted on our feelings. That's all that happened," he asserted.

I shook my head sadly. "No, Tony. There's much more to this situation than you're willing to acknowledge or admit."

"Such as?"

"Tony, you're my boss!" I exclaimed. "It's not every day that I sleep with my boss and my boyfriend's friend all in the same night. Goodness! Could the problem be more obvious?"

He sighed and held up his hand. "Okay. Now that I think about it, this may be a little awkward..."

"You're damn right this is awkward!" I cried out. "I'm supposed to be seeing Joe and I sleep with you!"

"I'm not sorry that we made love last night," he proclaimed.

I shook my head. "It's very touching that you feel that way, Tony. But I don't think I can say the same thing."

He glared at me for a second, then slowly walked closer. "Are you saying that you didn't enjoy last night?"

"No, I'm not saying that."

"So you did enjoy last night?" He smirked as he moved even closer.

I caught his smirk and backed away. "Tony, let's not get off the subject."

"No, I'm not getting off the subject. As a matter of fact, I think it has a lot to do with what we're talking about." He inched even closer. "Answer my question."

I backed away again and then realized that I couldn't move any further. We were face to face, with my back against the wall and he was blocking me with both of his arms. "Are you going to answer my question?" he whispered.

I didn't have time to react as he tilted his head and brushed my lips with his. I responded, but quickly ended the kiss. This had to stop. I pushed him away gently.

He grumbled in frustration. "Oh, c'mon, Lacie."

"Tony, I can't do this," I said calmly. "This is wrong. This is all wrong."

"It didn't feel wrong when you returned my kiss a moment ago," he remarked. "What is wrong is you not acknowledging your true feelings."

I started searching the floor for my shoes. "I don't know how I feel, Tony. Okay? I'm not sure what to make of all this." I took a deep breath and looked at him. "Tony, listen. I like Joe. I really do and I can't do this to him. He's been good to me and despite all of your concerns, we seem to have really hit it off."

"Didn't we hit it off?" he argued. "Don't we get along?"

"Yes, but…" I couldn't finish and looked down.

"But…?" he urged, waiting for an answer.

I was silent.

"Oh…okay…I get it now," he said, glaring at me in disbelief. "It's because I'm white, right?"

"I didn't say that."

He shook his head. "No, you didn't have to say it. It was written all over your face."

"I just want to give this thing with Joe a try, that's all."

"Please, Lacie, save it. That's just an excuse you're using because he's black and I'm white."

"What makes you think that I don't have deep feelings for Joe?" I shot back.

"Oh, c'mon, Lacie!" he snapped, giving me an incredulous look. "Do you really want me to go there? Do you really want me to go there?"

"Listen, I care about Joe."

"Sure." He shrugged. "But not the way you care about me," he argued.

"That is so conceited of you!" I hissed.

He folded his arms. "Convince me otherwise, then. Have you slept with him yet?"

"That's none of your business!"

"Oh, so you haven't slept with him?" He gave me a satisfied grin. "Let's see. You two have been together for a month or so now, and he hasn't gotten the panties off yet." He shook his head. "You haven't slept with him. Doesn't that tell you something? Doesn't that tell you that even though you've been seeing him all this time, that maybe, just maybe, he's not who you want to be with?"

"All it's telling me is that I had a moment of weakness with you," I retorted.

"Oh, it was more than a moment of weakness, Lacie. It was far more that that."

I was seething. "This is so typical."

"What, Lacie? Is this so typical because I'm white? Is that what you were going to say?"

"I wasn't going to say that!" I refuted. "Why are you being so accusatory?"

He almost shouted his answer. "Because you're pissing me off, that's why!"

I was slightly shaken by his reaction. "Tony, look," I said calmly. "I can't help the way the world is. We're two different people with different cultures and maybe I do have a problem with the difference in our color," I reasoned. "You're the first white man that I've been with. You've got everything going for you. You're handsome, successful and rich. Why would you want to be with me? Why would you want to complicate your life by being romantically involved with a black woman? I mean, this is insane! Don't you realize how complicated this situation is?"

"I don't care!"

"Well, I do!" I groaned in frustration. "What happened between us was not a good thing, Tony. Can't you see that? Don't you have any conscience about it at all?"

"Yes, I do, but I can't help the way I feel about you, either. When we were together last night, my conscience went out the window and all I know is that I want to be with you," he said sincerely.

"I can't be with you, Tony," I said.

"You're just scared, that's all."

"Yes, I am, Tony. I am," I agreed. "You just don't understand my dilemma. I'm a female in a male-dominated world and I'm black in a white-dominated world. That's two strikes against me. I don't need a third." I found my shoes and put them on. "When people look at me, Tony, they don't see how nice or intelligent I am. They see my color. That's the first and only thing they see or ever will see."

"That's not what I see."

I didn't believe him. Now he was not being honest with himself. "Tony, c'mon. You're trying to tell me that my color was not the first thing that you noticed about me?"

"I saw a beautiful woman that I was attracted to. That's all I saw," he maintained. "Lacie, you're not the first black woman that I've been with."

"So is that supposed to make me feel more comfortable about this?"

"No, but what it should make you realize is that I don't care if you're black, blue or purple."

I pointed a finger at him. "It's so easy for you to say that now, because you have no real idea of what I'm talking about."

He appeared frustrated. "Oh yes, I do, Lacie. I know what you're talking about. I've been told, 'it's a black thing' or I'm 'not black' or I'll 'never understand what the black race has been through' and 'there's a big difference between blacks and whites.' I've heard all of this before and you know what? I'm sick of it! It's all so stupid to me. Yes, I may never truly understand, but does that mean I can't love you because of it or because I'm white? I can't help who I am, Lacie, and I refuse to hide my feelings because of a small difference in color!" he exclaimed.

It was time for me to speak. "Tony, I've spent almost my entire adult life looking for a man that was good looking, intelligent and willing to treat me the way I wanted to be treated. I believe that Joe is that person. And yes, the fact that Joe is black has something to do with it. So I'm not going to risk my chances with him because of one night of extemporaneous lust."

He glared at me coldly. "All right. I've listened to everything you've said about the difference in our color and your alleged feelings for Joe," he said. Then he walked up to me and whispered into my ear, "But after all is said and done, you just remember whose bed you slept in last night."

I glared at him really hard. "I can't believe you went there. That's okay, though, 'cause I'm out of here."

I marched toward the living room, picked up my coat and purse and slammed the door as I left.

Slamming my apartment door behind me, I dropped my things on the floor, flopped down heavily on the sofa and looked at the blank television screen. I always seem to get into complicated situations, but this time I had really done it. What was I going to do?

My thoughts were interrupted when I heard what sounded like someone vomiting in the upstairs bathroom. I ran upstairs and found Reneé crouched over the toilet seat. She looked up at me with tearful eyes.

"I think I'm pregnant," she whispered.

Just when you think you've got more than enough to deal with, something else comes along to screw things up even worse. But I couldn't let her know what I was thinking because she needed me.

I bent down next to her and held her in my arms as if she were my child. That was the only thing I could think to do.

CHAPTER 6

I rubbed Reneé's back as she continued to vomit. I knew she was glad I was there. Until she felt confident enough to know that she wouldn't need to use it for a while, we stayed in the bathroom. She told me she'd been going back and forth throwing up off and on all night.

I helped her walk to her bedroom and tucked her in. I didn't say much to her for fear it would start the tears to rolling again. Then I sat on the edge of her bed and waited for her to go to sleep.

Once she was asleep, I went to my bathroom, took a shower, then went back downstairs to gather my thoughts. I fixed a raisin bagel with cream cheese and sat quietly at the kitchen table eating and attempting to read the newspaper. When reading didn't work, I decided to try the television. There was always something that I could watch on cable.

I was deeply engrossed in *The Color Purple*, when I heard a knock at the door. It was Robert.

"Hey," he said, closing the door behind him. "Long time, no see, stranger."

"Hey," I returned wearily, walking to the kitchen with him on my heels. He sat down at the kitchen table.

"Okay. What's wrong, Lacie?"

"Nothing," I said. "Do you want a cup of coffee?"

"Yes, thank you." He smiled. "Now, I know something is wrong, so spill it," he commanded softly.

I put the coffee on to brew and sat down. I didn't want to tell him about Reneé until I knew for sure that she was pregnant.

I took a deep breath. "I slept with Tony last night."

There was a moment of silence as I waited for his reaction.

"Was it that bad?" he asked. I looked at him incredulously and he shrugged his shoulders. "I'm sorry, I couldn't help it."

"Well, to answer your question, it was the best sex I've ever had," I confessed wearily. "When I woke up, he had breakfast ready for me and everything. Then right after that, we got into an argument." I groaned and ran a hand through my hair. "Robert, I am in some serious trouble."

"Wait, wait, wait a minute. Let's slow down a bit. Tell me what happened," he said.

I sighed and told Robert everything. "...and after that I slammed the door behind me and left," I finished explaining. "I don't know what to do. I feel as if I'm in a catch-22 situation. What do you think? What should I do?"

Robert looked hesitant. "I don't think you want to hear what I have to say."

"No. I need someone's logical opinion."

"I agree with Tony."

"What!" I exclaimed, looking at him accusingly.

He wagged his finger at me. "Ah, ah, ah. Don't get an attitude with me, young lady," he scolded. "You asked for my opinion and I gave it to you. Now, I've listened to all of your arguments, and they all add up to one thing—excuses. For weeks, I've heard you talk about Tony this and Tony that and noticed how you light up whenever you talk about him. I've never heard as much about Joe as I have about Tony. You're not being honest with yourself."

"No, you don't understand. Joe is all I've ever wanted in a man. What more could I want?"

"Tony," Robert said straightforwardly.

I threw a crumpled-up napkin at him, but it missed. "Don't be ridiculous," I snapped as I got up to fix his coffee.

He rolled his eyes. "Let me put it this way. If Tony were black, you'd be his baby's mama by now," he said as I handed him his coffee.

"It has nothing to do with his color," I defended as I sat back down.

"It has everything to do with his color and you continue to make excuses and give ridiculous reasons not to be with him. There is nothing wrong with having an interracial relationship. This is the nineties, Lacie."

"Yeah, well, I'm still living in the sixties," I grumbled. "I mean, can you imagine what my mother would say? And what about Dawn, Robert? You know how she feels about that kind of thing."

"Lacie, you can't worry about what everyone else is going to think or say. I learned that a long time ago. You've got to live your own life."

"But look at all the obstacles and negativity that I'd have to face," I objected.

He shook his head. "Look at all the obstacles I face. I have to deal with prejudice everyday, not only as a black man, but as a gay man also. I hear whispers and talk behind my back but I don't pay attention to it. So don't talk to me about obstacles and negativity." He finished his coffee, put his cup in the sink and kissed me on the forehead. "I have to go. I've got rehearsal in an hour. If you want an ear, you know where to reach me."

I sat there speechless as I heard the door close. Was Robert right? I was contemplating the matter when I heard Reneé coming down the stairs. I met her at the bottom.

"How are you feeling?" I asked.

"A little better," she answered.

"Are you ready to talk?"

"Not yet. I would like something to eat, though. Would you mind fixing me something?"

I smiled. "No. Anything for my little sister." I hugged her tightly. "Go ahead and sit down and I'll whip up something as fast as I can."

I watched her as she lay down on the sofa in the living room and curled into a fetal position. She's so young, I thought. How am I going to get through this one?

As she ate, I watched her silently, then decided that it was time for us to talk.

"Reneé, are you sure you're pregnant?"

She nodded her head. "Yes. I haven't had my period in a month. When I missed the first week, I just thought I was late, but now I'm pretty certain." She sighed. "Lacie, I don't know what happened."

I reached across the table and tapped her hand lightly. "Listen, if it's any consolation, I've heard of women getting pregnant even when they have used condoms, so don't feel bad. This is probably just one of those circumstances." I took a deep breath. "I think we should get a pregnancy test just to be..."

"We already did that. Danny went with me to get one," she interrupted.

"Oh? When was this?" I asked calmly.

"A couple of days ago."

"And I'm just finding out now?" She nodded, looking guilty. "Whew!" I whispered and ran a hand through my hair.

"Lacie, I didn't know how to..."

"No, no. That's okay. This is just a lot to digest at once, that's all," I said. "Okay, so you haven't been to a doctor yet, right?"

"No," she replied.

"Then it's still not definite. We can go to the clinic today and get a blood test done, so we'll know if you really are pregnant," I suggested.

She nodded. "I'm scared, Lacie," she said.

I walked over, knelt beside her and grabbed her hand. "Don't be. There's no reason to be afraid. I'm right here for you, all right? Once we find out for sure, then we'll take it from there."

I could only pray that she wasn't.

Sitting in the exam room, I held her hand tightly as we waited for the doctor with the results. When the doctor finally came in and said that it was positive, Reneé burst into tears. All I could think to do was hold her. The doctor said that she should start her prenatal vitamins immediately, if she was planning on keeping the baby. He referred us to an obstetrician and told us to make sure to set an appointment as soon as possible.

As we rode in the cab home, Reneé cried uncontrollably. I felt her pain and continued to hold her, looking out the window. When we got home she was exhausted, and I helped her get into bed. By the time I went down into the living room, I was near tears myself. I checked my messages. There were two from Tony asking me to call him as soon as possible, and one from Joe. I really didn't feel like calling anyone.

When someone knocked at the door, I opened it to find Danny. He looked stressed out.

"Come in," I said solemnly.

We stood there silently for a second before he said anything. "I guess Reneé told you, huh?" he asked.

I nodded. "Yeah, well, I found her vomiting in the toilet, so I kind of figured it out for myself," I replied. "We just came back from seeing the doctor and he confirmed it."

He cleared his throat. "Is she here?"

"Yes. She's upstairs resting, but I'm certain that she wants to see you, so go on up. I'm sure you two have a lot to discuss."

The phone rang as Danny ran up the stairs.

"Hey, beautiful, how are you doing?" Joe's voice rang out.

Hearing his voice painfully reminded me of what I'd done with Tony. "Not so good," I replied.

"What's wrong?"

"I'm just going through some family problems right now, is all."

"Do you want me to come over?"

That was the last thing I wanted. I had too much to deal with as it was. "No, not right now. I'll call you if I need anything," I said.

He was comforting. "I understand. I'll talk to you later, then. Bye, beautiful." He hung up.

Suddenly I heard Danny running down the stairs.

"What's wrong?" I asked as he rushed toward the door, looking upset.

"Maybe you should ask your sister!" he burst out loudly as he left.

I ran up the stairs. When I opened her door, I saw Reneé sitting on the bed, staring blankly at the wall with tears running down her face.

"Reneé, what's wrong?" I asked softly. "Why did Danny run out of here so fast?"

"We got into an argument. He wants me to have this baby and I told him I don't think I want to," she explained.

I digested this information calmly and sat down beside her. "Are you sure about this?"

"I'm not sure of anything." She looked at me with sad eyes. "What should I do, Lacie?"

"Sweetie, I can't tell you what to do. This is your decision and your body," I said softly. "However, I do feel that you should really think everything over before you make any hasty decisions. You know all of your options, right?"

"Yes, I do," she replied, nodding slowly. "Mama would kill me if she knew I was pregnant. She won't let me have this baby."

"There's no doubt that it would be a difficult thing for her to swallow, but I'm sure she'd be able to handle it."

She looked alarmed. "You won't tell her, will you?"

"No, baby. I won't tell her anything. You can tell her when you decide what you're going to do. Really, though, if you're going to abort this baby, you don't have to tell her anything. If you choose to keep it or give it up for adoption, then that's okay, too. Whatever decision you make, I'll respect it, and I'll be in your corner. Somehow, I feel as if I'm to blame for all of this anyway, so if you want, I'll be there with you if you want to tell Mama."

Reneé looked at me. "Are you disappointed in me?"

I smiled at her tenderly. "No, honey. I'm not disappointed in you. I have no reason to be."

I paused and decided to tell her that I had been through this. I figured letting her know that I had been in her position would help her with her choice.

"Reneé, I'm pretty sure that you don't know this, but I was pregnant at seventeen also." Her shocked expression was no surprise. I kept on. "It was by my first boyfriend, the one I told you about. I remember the look on Mama's face when I told her I thought I might be pregnant. She was so angry with me; it was a very difficult time for us…" I was interrupted by a knock downstairs. I stood up. "Why don't we continue this later? I'll go answer the door, okay?"

"Hi," I said cautiously.

"Hi," Tony replied. He cleared his throat and shifted his feet. "Can I come in? I just want to talk to you for a minute."

Against my better judgment, I opened the door and let him in. I motioned for him to sit down on the sofa, but he shook his head. "No. This won't take long. I've got to be somewhere in about thirty minutes," he said. "How are you?"

I brushed a hand through my hair and took a deep breath. "I'm doing okay."

He looked skeptical. "You don't look it."

"I'm fine," I said firmly.

He nodded, accepting my answer. "Did you get my messages?"

"Yes, I did, but I've been dealing with some family issues, so…" I stopped. I wasn't going to explain anything to him. "What did you want to talk about?" I asked abruptly.

"When you left my house so angrily, I took some time to think about everything and what we talked about."

I wasn't budging. "And?"

"And I want to call a truce."

"This isn't one of your business deals, Tony. "

"Right. I didn't mean for it to come out like that."

"What did you mean?"

Obviously trying to remain calm he asked, "Will you give me a chance, here?"

I sat down and waited.

"Thank you," he said and blew hard. "Uh...I thought a lot about what you said and it's evident that you have very strong feelings against any kind of relationship with me. Therefore, I've decided that it would be unfair for me to pressure you in any kind of way. Obviously, this makes you uncomfortable and I don't want that. We have to work together and if we can't get along, then it's not going to work out. So I'm going to back off. From now on let's be strictly professional and do our best to be cordial towards each other."

I eyed him warily. "What does this mean?"

"I'll leave you alone. I won't try anything with you again. As for you and Joe, well I'm going to have to honor your feelings. I was being selfish and thinking only of myself," he said. "I guess the best man won, huh?"

"Tony, it's not about that at all. I want to give this thing with Joe..."

"A try—yeah. I know," he interrupted. He scoffed and shook his head. "Look, I just wanted to clear the air and let you know that you won't have to worry about me anymore. Joe's not going to hear anything about what happened last night from me. This is just between us."

"Thank you. That means a lot to me."

He looked at his watch. "I should go. I'll be late." He walked to the door and I followed.

He turned around before he left and searched my face. "I only want you to be happy, Lacie," he said and left.

I was relieved that he was gone, but yet I couldn't help thinking about what he'd said before he left. The way he'd looked at me told me that this was far from over.

After Reneé and I went to church Sunday, I felt much better. I hadn't been to church in a while and I knew that I needed to go more often more than just when things started going wrong in my life.

Later on that day, I finished telling Reneé about my pregnancy. "I never felt so confused in my life," I confided to her.

"So what did you do?"

"I ended up having an abortion. Mama was very adamant about not letting me have the baby. She didn't want it to ruin my life. So, she set up an appointment and it was done," I said sadly.

"What did your boyfriend say?"

"He didn't say much of anything. He left me right after I told him I was pregnant. That was what Mama was afraid of. She didn't want me to raise a child on my own."

"Do you regret it?" Reneé asked.

I didn't hesitate. "Yes. At times I wonder if it was the right thing to do. However, I can't imagine how things would be now, if Mama had let me keep the baby. Maybe it was the best thing for me. I don't know. But I think about occasionally."

Reneé said nothing.

"Listen, I told you this only because I want you to fully understand that this is not an easy choice for you to make.

I just want you to think this through very carefully before you decide."

I hoped I had done the right thing by telling her my story.

My heart was heavy when I went to work. Still worrying about my sister's pregnancy and what she was going to do, I tried to stay busy, hoping to keep that off my mind.

An hour before lunch, I was summoned to Richard Ryan's office. What did he want? Really nervous, I took the elevator to his floor. His secretary went into his office and returned within a few seconds. I couldn't read her expression when she told me to go in. As soon as I walked into his office, I noticed Tony sitting across from him.

"Have a seat, Lacie." Mr. Ryan indicated the chair next to Tony. "I hope you weren't alarmed when I asked to see you."

I shook my head. "No, not at all," I fibbed.

"Good," he said. "I have some wonderful news for you. As you know, this company has been trying to get Joe Mitchell's account for a long time, but for some reason, he never showed any interest in our offers. However, thanks to you and Tony, I'm happy to say that has now changed. You and Tony succeeded in landing this deal and I know that you played a significant role in it."

I couldn't take all the credit. "Well, I helped, but I don't think I deserve that much credit."

"Don't be modest. We know how hard you worked. Your input seemed to make a difference. His staff commended your drive and professionalism. They said that they really enjoyed working with you."

"That's nice to hear," I managed.

"Yes, it is," Mr. Ryan agreed with a smile. "I want to continue getting big accounts like his and I'm therefore offering you the position of director of accounts. You're perfect for this position. It calls for the same skills you and Tony used with Joe Mitchell. Tony will remain in his position and you'll work along with him, but you won't be under his supervision."

I looked from Richard to Tony. Both had smiles on their faces. I couldn't believe what I was hearing.

"This is totally unexpected," I said.

"It's obvious that you and Tony make a great team," Mr. Ryan continued. "With you two working together, I'm confident that you'll bring more major accounts to this firm and that's exactly what I want. This deal with Joe was huge and I'm very impressed with the way it was handled. So, if you are interested, I'm happy to have you on board."

All I could do was nod my head.

"We're setting you up in your very own office, and along with that you'll get a huge jump in your salary, and of course, an administrative assistant of your own, Carrie Weaver. She should be moving as we speak."

Carrie Weaver? She must have known. I wondered how this had happened. Richard stood up to shake my hand and said he was really looking forward to working with me in the future. Tony stayed in his office after I left.

Riding in the elevator, I thought about what had occurred. As soon as I stepped onto the floor, everyone congratulated me. In a daze, I realized that I'd been the last one to hear about my promotion. I walked to my desk and saw that one of my file cabinets had already been moved. Carrie came over then.

She smiled. "Congratulations, Lacie! I'm so proud of you. Girl, you made it!" she exclaimed, giving me a hug. Pulling away, she searched my face. "What's wrong?"

"I don't know. This is all happening so fast. I mean, one day I'm an administrative assistant and the next I day I get promoted to director of accounts." I shook my head and sat down. "I wasn't prepared for this."

She looked at me dubiously. "Girl, what are you complaining about? You earned it. You've put in five years here and you know everything about this business. You know more than any of the stuffed shirts around here. You deserve this."

I looked at her warily. "Carrie, do you mind working for me?"

She shook her head. "No, Lacie. You and I go way back. You're the only one around here that I really trust anyway, and I would be honored to work for you." She grabbed my arm and pulled me up. "Now, enough of this. Did you get a look at your office?" I shook my head. "Come on, then! I think it's about time you did." She led me to what was now my new office.

I stood there in awe. There was a huge oak desk in the middle of the room, equipped with a computer, phone, fax machine and other necessities. Positioned behind the desk was a beautiful, black leather chair in front of a huge glass window, which with one swivel, gave a magnificent view of the city.

Carrie smiled when she saw my expression. "I'm going to leave you alone in your new office. Go on. Get comfortable," she urged, closing the door.

At first, I just stood there taking everything in. The office was beautiful, similar to Tony's, only not as elaborate. I didn't care, though, because this was my very own office. I sat down in the leather chair and looked at the four walls surrounding me. I had finally moved up. The knock at the door made me smile. It was the first knock on my very own office door.

"Come in," I said.

Tony grinned as he came in and sat in the chair in front of my desk. "How do you like your new office?"

"It's nice, but honestly, this was totally unforeseen."

"What do you mean?"

"I'm just wondering why this happened," I hinted.

He understood and held up a hand. "Hey, I had no part in this. I didn't know anything about it until Richard called me into his office just before he called you. You earned this on your own. I didn't do anything," he protested. "You believe me, don't you?" he added.

I peered at him thoughtfully for a moment and then shrugged. "I guess I'm going to have to."

"Thank you. I just came in here to see how your office looked and how you were doing."

"I'm doing fine. I had a lot on my mind when I got in here today, but this has certainly cheered me up," I declared.

"I'm glad." He stood up and smiled. "I'm going to leave you alone to get settled in. I'm sure you'll be busy moving and everything."

"Thanks," I said as he began walking out.

He turned around suddenly. "Would you mind going to lunch with your new partner today?" he asked. "I'm buying."

I looked at him suspiciously.

He held up his hands. "Look, it's just lunch between business partners. I promise."

"Sure. I don't see why not," I decided suddenly.

"I'll be back around twelve-thirty."

I hadn't realized how much junk I'd collected over the past five years until Carrie and I started moving my things into my office.

A few people dropped by to congratulate me. Dawn was the first. She couldn't believe my luck. I didn't point out that she had only been with the company for a year compared to my five and that most of the time she had been tardy. Even though she said she was happy for me, her expression was melancholy and I noticed what looked like a bruise under her eye. In fact, her entire appearance and attitude seemed changed. I realized that I needed to talk to her and find out what was going on, but the office was not the right place to do so.

Steve came by also. I hadn't seen him since the incident in Washington. He looked very happy and said he understood why I'd broken up with him. I was glad he did. After congratulating me on my new position, he announced that he was leaving the company in a few weeks to work for another investment firm in a higher position and for more money. I congratulated him and wished him the best of luck.

It was almost time for lunch and I was putting pictures up in my office when Carrie announced a call to me from my mother.

"Go ahead and put her through," I said, sitting down.

"Lacie?" Mama asked on the other end.

"Hi, Mama. How are you?" I asked easily.

"I'm doing fine."

"That's nice to hear. It's been a while since we talked. Reneé has been asking about you. I figured that we'd hear from you before Thanksgiving rolled around."

"Well, I'm calling to let you know that I'll be back for the holidays. Are you preparing Thanksgiving dinner?"

I hadn't even thought of it. "No. Do you want to?"

"No, I'm not going to do it this year. I was hoping you would," she said abruptly.

I sighed. "Fine, I'll cook. When will you get back in town?

"Thanksgiving Eve," she replied.

"Are you arriving by plane, train or bus?"

"I'll be flying in. I'll give you a call and let you know where and when to pick me up," she said. There was a long pause. "Do you mind if I stay with you for the holidays?"

I wanted to say no, but figured a little family get-together wouldn't hurt. It wasn't as if it were anything permanent. "No, I don't mind."

"Okay, then." She paused. "Why did Carrie answer the phone?"

"I got a promotion today and Carrie is my assistant."

"Oh," she said. "Well, I'll call you about my flight plans in a few days. Talk to you later." She hung up without congratulating me or even saying good-bye.

I suddenly wondered if Mama staying with us would be a good idea after all. Reneé was going to have to make up her mind before Mama came home. I didn't want confrontation, but I knew there was probably no way of preventing it.

Tony walked in.

"Don't you know how to knock?" I barked.

He stopped in his tracks. "I'm sorry. Carrie was on her way to lunch and waved me in," he explained with a puzzled look. "We're supposed to go to lunch together, remember? Twelve-thirty? My treat?"

I immediately felt foolish. I shouldn't have snapped at him. "I'm sorry. I just got a call that disturbed me, that's all. I didn't mean to take it out on you," I explained.

He waved it off. "It's okay, I understand. If you want to postpone lunch for another day…"

"No, I'm fine. Let's go to lunch. I need something to eat," I said, grabbing my coat.

The restaurant was crowded, but we managed to get a table.

"So are you enjoying your new office?" he asked.

I nodded. "Yeah and I think I'm starting to like it more and more as I sit in that comfortable leather chair."

"I'm glad. You certainly deserve that comfortable leather chair," he said with a grin. He paused for a second. "Do you want to talk about the phone call? It's still bothering you."

I smiled faintly. "It shows, huh?" He nodded. "It was my mother."

He looked surprised. "Oh," he said. "How did it go?"

"She called to tell me that she'll be home for Thanksgiving and she wants me to cook."

"Is that why you snapped at me?"

"No, and you know that's not the reason, so stop teasing," I said. "You know exactly what my relationship with my mother is like, that we don't get along." The waitress brought our food over and we started eating. "I told her I got promoted and she didn't even congratulate me. How insensitive is that?" I said, trying not to eat too fast. I shook my head. "I am definitely not looking forward to Thanksgiving."

"You know, this thing between you and your mother has got to be resolved. You can't go through the rest of your life resenting your mother. She's the only one you have," Tony remarked, eating his shrimp scampi.

I put my fork down and looked at him hard. "Tony, please. You don't know my mother. I've been through so much with her, it's not even funny. I couldn't begin to explain it," I defended. "Besides, she's not the only reason I'm upset. I've got some other things that are bothering me."

"Such as?" he asked.

I shrugged. "I don't know if I should tell you. It's kind of a family thing."

"Hey, c'mon. You might as well. It's going to eat at you until you do."

I took a deep breath. "Remember when we caught Danny and Reneé together?"

"Yes."

"What I was afraid of happened."

"What!" he exclaimed softly. "Is Reneé pregnant?"

"Yeah." I sighed. "When I came home Saturday, she was vomiting in the bathroom and that's when she told me she thought she was pregnant." I stopped eating, appetite gone for the moment. I sat back in the chair and looked at some of the pictures on the wall.

"No wonder you looked the way you did when I came over." He frowned. "Are you all right?" I nodded. "What's she going to do? What are you going to do?"

"I'm not going to do anything. This is up to her. As for what she's going to do...I don't know. I don't think she even knows. I took her to the doctor and after he confirmed it, the poor girl cried on my shoulder during the entire cab ride home. Then before you arrived, Danny came by and they had a huge argument. He wants her to have his baby and she's not sure she wants to." My throat felt dry and I took a sip of my drink.

Tony reached over and touched my hand lightly, then quickly withdrew his hand. "I'm sorry."

"Hey, it's nothing that I can't handle. I had an idea of what I was getting into when I agreed to let her stay with me."

"If you need anything, let me know."

I nodded. "We're going to be fine." I had to get off this sad subject. "Let's stop talking about this, okay?"

We ate lunch silently for a while, both of us lost in our own thoughts.

"So, how am I doing?" he asked suddenly.

I looked up, unsure of what he meant. "How are you doing?"

He looked at me as if I should know what he was talking about. "You know," he said. "This whole platonic and strictly business thing between us."

"Oh," I said, finally getting it. I shrugged. "I think you're doing fine. I haven't felt the least amount of pressure from you. I must admit that I was a little leery of your intentions when you asked me to lunch, though."

He nodded his head. "I figured that. That's why I made sure to tell you that this was a business lunch and nothing more. I told you that you don't have to worry about me anymore and I meant every word of it. You made your choice and although I don't agree with it, I respect it. I want us to remain friends. We have to work together, so we have to get along."

I nodded. "That was exactly my point. I mean, just because we had sex the other day and it's not going to happen again, it doesn't mean we still can't be friends, right?"

He grinned. "Right. It's strictly business from now on. Is that a deal?" he extended his hand.

I reached over and grabbed it. "It's a deal," I agreed. I shook his hand and started to let go, but couldn't because he had tightened his grip.

"Oh, one more thing," he said.

"What?"

"We made love the other night. It wasn't sex. I just want to make that clear." He released my hand and resumed eating.

Twenty minutes later, we were in the elevator, heading toward our floor and I was telling Tony some of the ideas I had for future proposals. As the elevator door opened, a strange look crossed his face; then he turned ashen. I followed his eyes and saw a familiar looking woman talking to the front receptionist.

Strikingly beautiful, about five feet, eleven, with long brown hair, she was dressed in an awesome suede pantsuit. Her long fur coat was draped over her arm. I knew I'd seen her before, but couldn't recall where. I was flabbergasted when Tony left my side, rushed over to her and picked her up in a tight embrace. *What the...?* I walked over to them.

When Tony put her down, he placed his hands on her shoulders and said, "Simone! What are you doing, here? I didn't know you were in town."

So that's who she was. Simone, Tony's ex-fiancée. The model, the one that it just hadn't worked out with. Looking quite delighted, she smiled, revealing gorgeous white teeth. Unconsciously, I rolled my tongue around my teeth, then caught what I was doing and stopped to hear her answer.

"I just finished a photo shoot in Brazil and returned here to New York to wrap it up. I talked to your mother on the phone last night and she informed me that you had taken a job here and decided to drop by to see you," she explained in a soft voice that made mine sound like James Earl Jones. "So how are you?"

"I'm doing great!" Tony exclaimed as he grabbed her hand in his. "I wish you'd called me. I would have skipped lunch and picked you up."

Ouch!

Simone smiled a model's smile. "That's really nice, Tony, but I didn't call because I wanted to surprise you." Suddenly, she noticed me standing there and gave me a faint smile. "Who's this you have with you?"

Tony, still holding her hand, looked at me as if he'd forgotten I was there. I wanted to punch him in the mouth.

"Oh, I'm sorry," Tony said sheepishly as he introduced us.

Oh, how I wanted to punch him in the mouth! Simone and I shook hands.

"Uh, Lacie is my associate and partner. She and I just settled a deal with Joe Mitchell's company. She played a major role in helping us get his account," he explained.

"Joe Mitchell?" Simone asked. "I haven't seen him in a couple of years. How is he?"

"Apparently he's doing very well," Tony replied, as I slowly tuned them out. Oblivious to their surroundings they continued their conversation in the lobby.

I felt completely ignored and didn't know what to do. When I glanced at the receptionist, she gave me a sympathetic smile. What was that for?

I decided to retreat to my office. I contemplated telling Tony that I was going to my office, but changed my mind. There was a lot of whispering going on as I made my way through the department. A few people had gone up to the front to get a better look at Simone. I'd forgotten she was such a celebrity.

Carrie wasn't at her desk, so I picked up my messages, walked into my office and was sitting at my desk reading them when Carrie knocked on the open door and entered.

"Girl, did you see Simone Carr in the lobby? The whole office is buzzing about it."

"Yeah, Tony and I met her by the elevator," I replied perfunctorily.

"What's she doing here?"

"She's his ex-girlfriend."

"Really?" Carrie asked, her eyes wide.

"Yep," I said, getting up to stand by my door.

"She's even more beautiful in person," Carrie remarked behind me as we watched Tony walk Simone into his office and shut his door. She glanced at me. "Are you okay?"

"Of course, I am." I walked back to my desk. I knew what she was implying and I shrugged it off. "Why wouldn't I be?"

She walked in front of my desk. "You seem...uneasy," she said carefully.

"Why do you say that?"

"Because of the way you were looking at them."

I just shook my head. I had asked for it. There was a knock at the door.

"Come in," I managed.

Joe walked in with a frown. "What's all the commotion about out there?"

I was so glad to see a friendly face.

Carrie smiled shrewdly. "I'd better leave you two alone." She closed the door behind her.

Joe watched her leave. "Did I miss something?" he asked.

I walked over to greet him with a kiss on the cheek. "No. She was about to leave anyway. It's nice to see you. I wasn't expecting you today."

He nodded and gave me a hug. "I know. I had a few loose ends to tie up here..." He stopped and smiled faintly. "I'm lying. I just wanted to see you and to congratulate you on your promotion," he admitted.

"How did you know?" I asked.

"Oh, I spoke to Richard a while ago and he told me. I'm proud of you. You're moving up in the world," he said as his eyes roamed around the office.

"Thank you," I said. "Of course, if it weren't for you, I wouldn't be in this office right now."

He shook his head. "You have a keen mind for business and my staff really liked working with you. That's why you got the promotion," he declared. "So what's going on? There don't seem to be many people working today."

"Everyone's star struck. Simone Carr is here. She's in Tony's office right now. I've never seen so many people act like that over someone," I added.

He shrugged. "That's to be expected. I'm sure it's not every day that they get to see a major celebrity in here."

"Yeah, I guess." I wanted to talk about something else. "So how have you been?"

"I've been fine. I missed seeing you this weekend."

I returned to my desk as I was reminded again about what had happened over the weekend. "I know. It's just that a lot...well...it's a long story."

He looked concerned. "Do you want to talk about it?"

"I do, but not here. I was hoping we could go out tonight," I said. "Then maybe I could tell you what's been going on." He looked uncomfortable. I sensed he wasn't telling me something. "What's wrong, Joe?"

"I have to go out of town. As a matter of fact, I'm supposed to leave shortly," he blurted out.

I was shocked but said calmly, "This is sudden. Is that the real reason why you came here?" I asked.

He looked guilty. "That was one of the reasons, but I did want to see you."

"Where are you going?" I immediately backpedaled. "I'm sorry, I shouldn't have asked you that."

He came over to my desk, sat on the end and grabbed my hand. "It's no problem. Don't ever feel like you can't ask me anything. Okay?" I nodded. "I've got to handle some business matters, but I should be back the day after tomorrow. I was hoping to spend it with a beautiful young lady," he hinted. "Is that going to be possible?"

"That's Thanksgiving Eve. Don't you want to spend that day with your family?"

"I was, but what with going to Washington it was impossible. So, can I spend the holiday with you?"

"Are you sure? I mean, I wouldn't mind if it was just us, but my mother's coming home and I'm sure Dawn and Robert will be over. We won't have any privacy and I don't think it's a good idea for you to meet my mother just yet."

"Lacie, I'd love to meet your mother. I'm sure it won't be that bad."

"You're being very optimistic." I sighed. "Okay," I relented. "If you want to risk it, that's fine with me. I'd love to have you over. But remember, you asked for it. Mama and I don't get along well. At all," I emphasized.

"Maybe you should start trying to get along with her. She is your only mother."

He sounded just like Tony. "Joe, I try. I try very hard. It's just that we tend to have an argument every time we see or talk to each other."

"Don't feed into it," he said encouragingly. "Look, I'll be over for Thanksgiving dinner and we'll have a wonderful time."

I was doubtful. "If you say so."

He laughed and kissed my forehead. "I think it's about time for me to go." He got off the desk, pulled me up with him and held my face in his hands. "I'll be thinking about you while I'm gone," he said seriously.

Guilt came over me as he waited for my reply. "I'll be thinking about you too," I forced out. "Will you call me when you get in?"

"You know I will," he whispered. He bent his head down and kissed me lightly on the lips. For some reason, his kiss didn't feel the same.

As we walked out my office, we bumped into Tony and Simone. Tony had his arm around her and they were laughing. Simone walked over to Joe and gave him a kiss on the cheek. I didn't know if I appreciated that.

"Joe Mitchell," she announced, grinning from ear to ear. "Tony told me you were in town. It's certainly nice to see you."

"Same here. It's been a long time," Joe replied. "I came by to see Lacie."

Simone looked surprised. "Really? Are you two seeing each other?" she asked directly.

"Yes. They've been seeing each other for a while now," Tony answered before we could reply.

"That's wonderful," she said. "Now I can invite you two to the party. I was thinking about fixing you up with a date, Lacie, but now that you have one, I guess I don't need to do that, do I?"

"When is it?" Joe asked.

"Tomorrow. It's a surprise birthday party for my father. He'll be fifty years old and we're inviting a lot of his friends over. I would love for you and Lacie to be there."

Joe was apologetic. "I'm sorry, Simone, but I'm leaving for Washington today and I probably won't be back until Wednesday morning."

Simone looked a little disappointed. "Are you sure?" she asked. When Joe nodded, she turned to me. "Well, even though Joe can't make it, you'll come, Lacie, won't you?"

I wasn't thinking about it. "I doubt if I'll be able to make it, either. I'm having a few people over for Thanksgiving dinner and I want to get my house ready," I replied quickly.

"Well, if you change your mind, the time of the party and the directions are on here," she said as she reached into her purse and gave me a small beige card. She turned her attention to Joe. "Joe, it was so nice seeing you again. Lacie, it was nice meeting you. I'm sure we'll be seeing a lot of each other."

I wondered what that meant.

"She certainly is something," Joe commented as we watched them leave.

"Yes, she is."

Joe caught my look and laughed. "I was just saying…"

"Yeah, yeah, yeah," I said. "You were just saying."

He laughed again and kissed me on the forehead. "I've gotta go. I'll see you Thanksgiving."

By the time Carrie and I finished getting my office together, it was almost time to go home. Since there wasn't much else for her to do, I told Carrie to go home and finished putting more pictures on the walls. When I took a good look around my office, I was pleased with the results.

"Are you settled in yet?" Tony stood in the doorway with his briefcase and coat in hand, ready to leave.

"Yeah, just about. I'm going to need a few things to make it just right, though."

He walked in and looked around. "It looks pretty good to me. What else do you need?"

"A plant in the corner would be nice." I shrugged. "I don't know. It needs something. I guess I'll figure it out," I said. "What are you doing here? I haven't seen you since you left with Simone. I thought you were gone for the day."

"Oh, I've been here for a while. I just had to take care of some business, that's all," he said.

"Oh."

"Are you still planning on not going to the dinner party Simone's giving for her father?"

"I haven't thought any more about it. Why do you ask?"

"I think it would be a good idea if you came. There'll be a few people there that I'd like for us to get as clients. Simone's father is one of them."

"I thought it was a birthday party."

"It is, but it's a business party as well," he said. "It'll be great for the firm."

I was apprehensive. "I don't know…"

"Just think about it. I'll give you all the details tomorrow." He glanced at my desk clock. "I've got to go. See you tomorrow." He rushed out the door.

On my way home, I stopped by the Chinese restaurant. I didn't feel like cooking and since I'd gotten a promotion, I figured I was due a break. Reneé was on the sofa watching television when I opened the door.

"Hey, kid, can you give me a hand with this stuff?"

She got up instantly and helped me put the bags in the kitchen. "Chinese?" she asked.

"Yep. I was promoted today. I got my own office and more money, so I bought some takeout to celebrate," I announced cheerfully. I took off my coat and put it on the back of the kitchen chair. Then I took some paper plates and plastic utensils out of the cabinet and sat down.

"That's good, Lacie! I'm happy for you," she said as she sat down opposite me, reached in the bag and grabbed a carton of shrimp fried rice.

"Thank you." I smiled. "I see your appetite's back." I pointed to the huge portion of rice she had put on her plate.

She rolled her eyes upward. "You just don't know how awful I've been feeling," she said as she put a forkful in her mouth. "I miss eating."

"That comes with being pregnant." I stood up and grabbed two glasses and poured apple juice in them, then sat back down to eat.

"That's what I wanted to talk to you about," she said. "Lacie, I can't have this baby. I want to have an abortion."

I was about to put another forkful of shrimp egg foo young in my mouth when I heard those words and dropped my fork on the floor.

CHAPTER 7

"Are you sure?" I asked. I picked up the fork and washed it off in the sink.

"Yes," she answered. "I've thought long and hard about it and it's what I want to do."

I sat back down and stared at the floor. "I wasn't expecting you to make a decision this soon."

"I know. But I can't go through with this." Her eyes were somber. "If I have this baby, my whole life will be ruined. I want to go to college and I want to be a lawyer. I won't be able to do that with a child."

"Yes, you can. You can do anything you want to do. A baby won't stop that. It would be difficult, yes, but not impossible," I said earnestly. "What about Danny? Have you talked this over with him?"

"No. I know what he wants me to do, but I have to do what's best for me." My expression must have given me away, because without warning, she suddenly burst out in tears. "Lacie, I thought you said you'd support me in whatever I decided!"

I had said that. But had I really meant it? I shook my head and silently cursed myself. What was I doing? This child needed me and all I could do was think about what I wanted. I stood, pulled her up and embraced her with all my strength as she sobbed uncontrollably. Tears ran down my face as I felt her anguish.

"I know...I know. I did say that. I just thought you'd say something different, that's all," I whispered. "Shh...shh. It's okay. I'm here," I soothed. I stepped back and pulled her face up from my chest to make her look at me. "Listen, we're going to get through this. I won't let you down," I assured her as I embraced her again and stroked her hair. "I'll call the clinic tomorrow and try to get an appointment as soon as possible. Don't worry. I'll take care of everything."

"Thank you, Lacie," she sobbed.

As soon as I arrived at the office the next morning, I called the clinic. They'd had a last minute cancellation around one o'clock and were able to fit Reneé in. I was so glad. Although my true desire was for her to have the baby, Reneé was emotionally and physically drained. Last night, she'd thrown up all of the Chinese food she'd eaten. If having an abortion would end her sickness and if that's what she really wanted, so be it. What I wanted didn't matter. After making arrangements to leave the office early, I called Reneé and told her to be ready for the appointment.

Shortly after, Tony knocked on my door after a meeting with some board members. "Hey," he said.

Distracted, I looked up from all the papers on my desk. I had a lot of work to do before I left. "Hey," I replied.

"Have you decided if you're coming to the dinner party?"

I shook my head as I entered something on the computer. "Uh, yeah. Tony, I'm afraid I won't be able to go.

Something important came up and I've got to leave here a little early today. I'll be taking tomorrow off, as well."

"Why?"

"I've got a family problem I have to take care of and it's going to take a couple of days to work it out."

"What's wrong?" he asked.

I shook my head. "I don't want to talk about it." I stood up and walked over to the file cabinet for some documents. "Listen, I've already informed Richard that I'm leaving and he's fine with it. I've finished all the work that needed to be done, so when I return I won't be behind. I'm sorry that I didn't let you know sooner, but this came up suddenly and I can't back out of it." I walked back over to my desk and sat down.

He leaned on my desk. "You know you can talk to me. If you need help with anything…"

I smiled faintly. "Yes, Tony, I know. But I don't need your help. Besides, I'm sure you have enough to be concerned about, what with Simone and the dinner party. Everything will be fine."

"You're being quite secretive about this."

I just shrugged in answer.

He appeared uncertain as to whether to inquire further, then apparently decided against it. Straightening, he let out a deep breath. "Okay. I hope everything works out for the best," he said.

"I do, too."

Just before we left, I gave Reneé a piece of grapefruit and toast. One of the nurses had told me that she should try to eat something before she came. It was useless. She threw up as soon as she ate it. Seeing Reneé go through this, I couldn't wait for her nightmare to be over.

Once we arrived, I filled out the paper work and after that, we waited for Reneé to be called. She seemed to get increasingly nervous as we sat and waited. I was nervous as well. I didn't ask her if she had spoken to Danny again. He was the least of my concerns.

"Reneé Taylor," the nurse called out to the waiting room.

I gave Reneé an encouraging smile. She smiled weakly, rose out of her chair and walked slowly to the nurse, looking back as she did so.

"I'll be waiting right here," I assured her as the nurse closed the door behind them.

If I smoked, it would've been the perfect time for a cigarette. My mouth felt dry, so I stood up and walked over to the vending machine in the far corner. It was filled with snacks and caffeine filled sodas. I saw the Sprite button and pushed it.

I walked around the waiting room restlessly, unable to relax enough to sit down. I noticed a few girls and women I guessed to be their mothers walk in. Some of the girls couldn't have been more than fifteen. I shook my head sadly.

Before more than a few minutes passed, Reneé and the nurse came back out. I rushed over to them.

"What's wrong?"

The nurse had her arm around Reneé and she was smiling warmly. "She's decided not to have the procedure. She wants to keep the baby."

There were tears in my sister's eyes as she spoke. "I...couldn't...go...through with it," she choked out. "I went in there and realized I had to give my baby a chance."

I felt tears roll down my face as she said those words. "Are you sure?" I asked softly. "You realize that you'll be throwing up for a while, don't you?" She nodded, and smiling, I hugged her immediately and kissed her forehead. "It's going to be all right," I whispered. I glanced over at the nurse and saw she had tears in her eyes as well.

After leaving the clinic, Reneé was feeling a little better. In the interest of spending some quality time together, we went to the movies and afterward went shopping. It was almost six o'clock by the time we headed home, tired but in pretty good spirits.

I checked the answering machine as soon as we came home. Joe had called and said that he'd call again. I looked at Reneé sitting on the sofa and smiled. I was so proud of her. I took off my coat.

"Hey, do you want some tea?" I asked, then caught myself. "No, wait. You can't have caffeine. How about ginger ale?" She nodded her head, got up and followed me to the kitchen and sat on the bar stool.

"Is this what I'm going to have to go through throughout my pregnancy?" she asked.

"Huh?" I looked up from filling her glass and handed her the drink.

"You're happy I decided not to go through with the abortion, aren't you?"

I grinned. "It's that obvious, huh?"

"Yes, it is. You haven't stopped smiling since we left the clinic."

"I'm sorry," I said. "I guess my feelings about this situation have been somewhat selfish." Reneé looked confused, so I explained further. "I think I felt that if you were to keep the baby, then that would somehow make up for what I did. I still would have supported your choice, but I know in my heart that I really wanted you to keep it. And I didn't want you to go through what I did."

"What do you mean?"

I walked around the counter and sat next to her. "I went through a lot when I aborted mine. It was very hard on me emotionally and mentally." I paused as I fought back tears. "It was the most difficult thing I've ever done. I felt so guilty afterwards. All I could think of was, how could I have done such a thing?" I swallowed hard and sighed. "I realized that it was done and I couldn't go back and undo it, but it took me a long time to get past it."

I took a deep breath and grabbed her hand. "Let me tell you something, young lady." I leaned my forehead against hers. "I have never been so proud of you. You're going to be a wonderful mother to this child. I mean that sincerely. Of course, you know I'm going to be the greatest aunt this child could ever have," I asserted and we both giggled.

"Lacie, what are we going to do about Mama?" she asked suddenly.

I sat up. "I don't know. We'll worry about that when the time comes." I got off the bar stool and looked in the refrigerator. "You know what? I'm hungry. Do you want something to eat?"

"No, I'm not hungry."

"I'm going to fix me something." I grabbed the bread, sliced turkey, cheese and the mayonnaise and started making a sandwich.

"So, how's work?" Reneé asked.

I turned around, surprised at the sudden change in conversation, then continued making my sandwich.

"It's going great. I like my new office and absolutely love the fact that I'm making more money. Things couldn't be better."

Reneé nodded. "How's Tony."

"He's fine, I guess," I replied indifferently. "He's attending a dinner party for a friend of his tonight. I was supposed to be there for business reasons, but I told him I couldn't go."

"Why not?"

"What do you mean, 'why not'? I have to be here with you. What's with all the questions about Tony and the job all of a sudden?"

She looked innocent. "Nothing." Then she said, "Lacie, why don't you go. I'm fine now. I'm not going to need you here. You just got this promotion and you don't want to look bad."

"No," I objected. "I need to be here with you."

"Go!" she insisted. "I'll be fine. Robert's home and if I need anything, all I have to do is call him."

I finished making my sandwich and peered at her. "Are you trying to get me out of the house for a reason? Are you trying to bring Danny over here again?"

She rolled her eyes. "No, Lacie. You know I'm not ready to see him until I'm sure of what I'm going to say to him."

"Oh," I said. "And you're sure you want me to go?"

"Yes."

"All right, I'll go," I decided. "Call Robert and ask him if he can come over."

"Lacie, I told you…"

"Yeah, I know what you told me, but I don't want to take any chances. You haven't been feeling well and since you're kicking me out of my own house, I have no choice but to make sure you're going to be okay. I'll feel better knowing he's here. So do that for me, will you?"

"I'll call," she said reluctantly.

"Thank you. I'll wrap up this sandwich and stick it in the fridge."

"Don't do that," she said hastily. She reached and took the sandwich from me. "I'll eat it. You get dressed."

Robert was in the living room talking to Reneé when I came back downstairs. I had chosen a black dress and two inch heel pumps and put on a little more makeup than usual. Robert whistled when he saw me.

"Don't you look nice!" he appraised.

"Calm down. This is only for business. I'm trying to get some new clients," I told him as I grabbed my coat.

"With the way you look tonight, you shouldn't have any trouble," Robert teased.

"Whatever," I said, raising my palm to shush him. "I'll see you two later."

The house on Long Island that the cab pulled up to was gorgeous. A slew of cars were in the driveway and I hoped I wasn't too late. Ringing the doorbell, I was surprised to see a black doorman answer and lead me into the foyer. Unsure of where to go, I turned to ask the doorman, but he was gone.

"Lacie! It's so nice to see you!"

I turned around to see Simone coming toward me with that never-ending model smile. Her elegant silver gown made me feel very underdressed.

She gave me a little hug. "I'm so glad you made it. C'mon, everyone's in the drawing room." She put her arm through mine loosely as she led me in.

We reached the drawing room and conversation stopped. I counted about twenty white faces looking at us, each with a wineglass in hand.

"Why don't you go over to the bar, get something to drink and make yourself comfortable. I'm going to check on dinner." Simone patted my hand lightly and left.

I stood there awkwardly, while everyone returned to his or her conversation, then walked over to the bar and asked for spring water. I didn't need any alcohol.

"I didn't expect to see you here," Tony remarked as he came up behind me. "Simone was sure you'd come, though."

I turned around and looked into those blue eyes and smiled. "Well, my little emergency has been taken care of and I was told I should come so that I could make a good impression. My promotion and all, you know."

"I'm glad everything worked out and that you came." He gave me the once-over. "You look nice," he commented. "You're really trying to get clients, aren't you?"

"That's the idea, isn't it?" I asked. "Thanks for the compliment, though."

He shook his head and smiled. "C'mon, let's get to work. I want you to meet a few people." He grabbed my arm lightly, and in a proprietary manner, guided me around the room.

He introduced me to lawyers, doctors and businessmen. All of them were very nice and I started feeling more at ease with Tony by my side as I talked to them about the investment business. The last person he introduced me to was a distinguished-looking man with gray hair, green eyes and a nice tan. Simone was engaged in conversation with him as we approached and I knew immediately that he was Simone's father. Their resemblance was unmistakable.

"Lacie Adams, this is William Carr, Simone's father," Tony said.

"Happy birthday, Mr. Carr. It's a pleasure to meet you." I offered my hand and he shook it with a firm grip.

"Thank you and it's a pleasure to meet you as well, Lacie. Tony has told me nothing but nice things about you," he divulged. "You know, I'm quite interested in working with your company. You and Tony have been very highly recommended to me."

"We'll be glad to help you any way we can, Mr. Carr. I'm sure we won't disappoint you," I replied confidently.

Mr. Carr smiled and glanced at Tony. "You told me I'd like her and you were right," he said.

At that point, a black maid came in and announced that dinner was being served. So far, the only black people I'd seen were the maid and the doorman. I had to wonder. Everyone followed her to the dining room where the table was elegantly set with beautiful china and sterling silverware. In the middle of it sat a huge roast of lamb, steamed vegetables, scalloped potatoes and rolls. A wine glass was beside each plate.

Tony and Simone sat near the head of the table next to Mr. Carr, while I sat on one side. Everyone ate silently at first, but when someone made a political remark, conversation really took off. I ate quietly and listened intently as the conversation moved from politics to the stock market.

After dinner, we returned to the drawing room, where I again stood around awkwardly in the background, not knowing what to do. Even though Tony had introduced me to everyone, I still felt uncomfortable.

I observed Simone and Tony walking around the room, talking to the guests. She was acting the part of the perfect hostess, all the while clinging to him as if her life depended on it. I didn't like it.

Someone asked Tony to play the piano and everyone gathered around to watch him. I moved closer and sat on the nearest chair to get a closer look. Simone sat next to him on the piano bench. He played some tunes that were typical for that type of crowd, but still nice. He received applause after he finished and Simone gave him a tender kiss, which was also followed by applause. It made me sick to my stomach. I needed some fresh air. Out of the corner of my eye, I noticed a terrace to my right and bolted for it.

The cold air was refreshing. I had to have been out of my mind to come here. I was trying to think of a reason to leave when I heard someone behind me. It was Simone.

"Hi," I managed with a tight smile.

"Hi," she returned. "We were all wondering where you were. We're getting ready to bring the cake in to Dad." She walked over to me. "You're not enjoying yourself, are you?"

"No, no," I said, trying to sound reassuring. "I was getting a little hot and wanted some air, that's all."

"I guess it was kind of warm in there." I didn't respond. Then she said, "You know, Lacie, I understand if you're uncomfortable."

I looked at her. "What do you mean?" I asked.

"I don't know." She shrugged her bony shoulders a little. "If I were you and trying to mingle with rich people, I'd feel uncomfortable."

I raised my eyebrow. "Ah, Simone, exactly what kind of background do you think I come from?"

"It's obvious that you're not from a wealthy family." She looked at me with those wide eyes. "All I'm saying is that you have your place and I have mine. Everyone should know where they fit in and where they don't. That's all."

Bitch! Now I understood where she was coming from and immediately thought of the butler and the maid. All that Miss Nice at the office had been an act. I decided to amuse myself.

"This isn't the fifties, Simone, and the last time I checked, black people don't have a place anymore. That's what the civil rights movement was all about."

"Ah, but you do. You all do. You see, you may have freedom and civil rights, but you will never, ever, be equal."

"Wait, just a minute," I said calmly. "Who says I want to be equal? I'm my own woman. I don't have to be equal with you or anyone."

"I've noticed how you act around Tony," she said abruptly. "You're just a little too friendly with him."

"So, what's your point?" I shrugged. "We work together and we get along well. That's not a crime, is it?"

"I don't like it and I don't want you getting in my way. I know what you're about, Lacie."

"Simone, you don't know anything about me."

She cocked her head to the side. "I really don't care to know anything about you. I just want you to stay in your place—away from Tony."

"Is that why you invited me to this party?"

She coldly batted those mascara-lined eyelashes. "Yes. I got you here to hear what I had to say. I've said it and now you can leave whenever you want."

If I weren't at her house, I would have slapped her. I realized, though, that that was exactly what she wanted. That would be just the reason for me to look bad and to prove she was right. I was about to speak when Tony strolled onto the terrace.

"Hey, what are you two doing out here?" he asked.

Simone's model smile flashed on immediately. "We were just out here talking and getting a few things clear," she explained, moving over to him.

Tony was oblivious to what she meant. "Well, c'mon. Your father's ready to blow out the candles."

"Okay." As Tony started to lead her in the house, she said, "I think I'm finished out here anyway."

I took a minute to collect my thoughts, then followed them inside. It was definitely time to go. I stood around long enough to see Mr. Carr blow out his candles and cut the cake, then said a quick good-bye to him while he was alone, explaining that I wasn't feeling well, and left.

Robert was watching television in the living room when I walked in the door.

"Hey," I mumbled as I hung up my coat.

"Hey. How was the party?" He got up and followed me into the kitchen.

I rolled my eyes upward. "Please, you don't even want to know." I opened the refrigerator and grabbed a diet Pepsi. "Where's Reneé?"

"She's upstairs talking to Danny on the phone." he replied, sitting down on a stool at the counter. "How was the party?"

"How has she been? Any vomiting tonight?"

He shook his head and peered at me. "She's been fine the whole night. We even rented some movies. Now for the last time, how was the party?"

"I thought I was going to have to slap someone."

"Who?"

"Simone Carr," I replied with a grimace.

"Huh?" He looked confused.

"William Carr is Simone Carr's father. The dinner party was for him. It was his birthday," I explained.

He snapped his fingers and pointed. "Right, right. I remember Dawn mentioning her. She's that famous model and Tony's ex-fiancée. She came into your office the other day, didn't she?" he asked. "Is she that beautiful in person?"

I leaned against the counter and put my hand on my forehead. "Yes, she is that beautiful. She has the most beautiful, straightest teeth I've ever seen on anyone. She can't be any bigger than a size one, and her skin is perfect. She's so beautiful, it makes me sick," I groaned. "She was waiting in the lobby the other day when Tony and I came from our lunch break and I could've sworn she was the first woman he'd ever seen. You should've seen the way he reacted. She was all hugs and kisses with him. Blah!" Robert looked at me quizzically. "As soon as everyone noticed her, the whole office became a fan club. I couldn't believe it!"

"I know. Dawn told me it was chaotic while Simone was there," Robert said, walking around to grab a soda from the refrigerator.

"Joe came to the office shortly thereafter, and when Simone saw him, she was all hugs and kisses with him as well. She asked us, 'Are you two seeing each other?' " I tried to imitate her voice. "Then she invited us to the party."

"Sounds like someone's jealous," he murmured.

"Robert, please. Don't go there, all right? I'm not jealous. I told you, it's over with Tony," I insisted.

"I didn't say anything about Tony."

I sucked my teeth. "Anyway, I still didn't appreciate how affectionate she was with Tony and Joe," I vented.

"Okay, let me get this straight." Robert leaned against the refrigerator. "You wanted to slap her because she was all hugs and kisses with your boyfriend and the guy you are in love with, and invited you to a dinner party full of rich folk?"

"No, that's not the reason." I pointed my finger at him. "And I caught that."

He scoffed. "Lacie, c'mon! She's known them both longer than you have and she was Tony's girlfriend," he reasoned.

I looked at him blankly. "So, what's your point?"

He raised his hand. "Okay. Let's not go there." He sighed. "I'm just saying that I don't see what you're complaining about. She sounds nice."

I took a huge swallow of my soda. "Hey, that's what I thought at first, until I saw how that black butler and black maid looked at the party. Robert, the butler was Mr. Bojangles and the maid was Hattie McDaniel in *Gone with the Wind*!" I stressed emphatically.

"Lacie, you're exaggerating!"

"All right, maybe they didn't look exactly like them, but that's what I thought of when I saw them. It was such an insult and I felt as if that was deliberately arranged in order to make me feel that way."

He shook his head. "I don't believe you."

"Okay, then, check this out," I said, with a nod. "Simone sees me, gives me this little hug, invites me in and says, 'Make yourself comfortable.'" I mimicked her again. "We walk into the drawing room and all conversation stops. There was not one black person in the room, Robert! I was the only black face in that entire party, besides the doorman and the maid."

I continued telling him about the rest of the evening, including the conversation that I'd had with Simone on the terrace. Robert shook his head throughout the whole story.

"Wow...so she's a real bitch, huh?" he remarked.

I slammed my hand on the counter emphatically. "That's what I've been trying to tell you! She believes black people have a 'place,' Robert, and the doorman and the maid represented that belief. That woman is the devil incarnate! What really infuriates me is how she was so subtle about it at first, you know? Usually I can spot a person like her a mile away, but she came as a total surprise. If it weren't for the fact that it was her father's birthday and that he was interested in doing business with us, I would probably be in jail for assault by now."

The phone rang and I picked it up. "Hello?"

It was Dawn and her voice was trembling. "Hey, Lacie. Do you think you can come and get me?"

I was alarmed. "Dawn, what's wrong?"

She sniffled. "Ronnie hit me."

"I'm on my way. Have your bags packed and ready," I ordered, hanging up the phone.

Robert knew something was wrong when he saw me grab the bat from the closet. "Dawn?" he questioned.

"Yep," I said, grabbing my coat and keys.

"You need me to come with you?"

"Nope. I got this."

Yep. I was definitely going to jail tonight.

CHAPTER 8

One look at Dawn's bruised and puffy face and I almost cried. She was sure to look worse by morning. I could tell that she'd been doing a lot of crying and gave her a tight hug. She let go quickly and led me into the rest of the penthouse. It was a wreck. Clothes were strewn all over the floor and a few lamps and chairs were turned over.

"Ronnie's not here, I take it," I remarked. She shook her head slowly, as if in a daze. "When's he coming back?"

"I don't know. He took his other girlfriend home," she replied. She sat down heavily on the sofa and put her face in her lap.

"His other girlfriend?"

"Yep. I came home and they were in bed."

Ouch! I briefly remembered the sight of Reneé and Danny and shook it off. I could only imagine what was going through Dawn's mind when she saw Ronnie and that girl getting busy.

I sat down, put the bat on the floor and started rubbing her back. "Is this why it looks like World War III in here?"

She nodded a little. "I don't know what happened," she sniffled. "I saw them in bed together and I went crazy. I grabbed her hair and pulled her out of the bed and just started punching. I couldn't see straight. Then Ronnie tried to pull me away from her. When I wouldn't let her go, he punched me. Then he and I started getting into it. I've never been that angry before."

I shook my head. I had known he was no good. I continued rubbing her back and took another glance around the apartment. "Did you kick her butt?" I asked.

"Yeah. She got in a few licks, but I think I got the best of her."

"That's my girl," I commended.

Dawn lifted her head and looked at me. "You don't seem surprised about this, at all."

"I can't say that I am." I shrugged. "I've never liked him, Dawn. You know that. It didn't help when he tried to sleep with me, either," I blurted out.

Her eyes widened. "What? He tried to get you into bed?" I nodded. "Why didn't you tell me this before?"

I looked at her skeptically. "Dawn, would that have stopped you from seeing him?" She shook her head. "That's why I didn't tell you. You were so caught up in him that you wouldn't have listened to me. As a matter of fact, you didn't listen to me. It was as if his penis was gold or something."

"Okay, okay, you don't have to get graphic. You're right," she admitted dolefully. She noticed the bat and pointed to it. "What's that for?"

"I brought it for insurance. I didn't know what to expect."

"You were actually going to use it?"

"Do you even have to ask?"

"Never mind." She smiled and rolled her eyes upward, then stood up and headed for the bedroom. "C'mon, help me with the suitcases." She shook her head as I followed her. "You know, I have absolutely no idea what I'm going to do with you."

"Just love me," I said arrogantly.

On the cab ride home, I told Dawn what had happened at the dinner party. I knew Robert would fill her in as soon as he got a chance, so I decided to beat him to the punch. They were as thick as thieves when it came to my business.

"No wonder you brought a bat to my house. You couldn't kick her behind, so you decided to kick Ronnie's instead," Dawn teased.

"Hey, don't start unless you want me to use it on you," I retorted.

To my surprise, Joe and Robert were sitting on the sofa watching a game on television when we walked in. Joe rushed over and gave me a hug.

"Hey, beautiful."

"Hey," I replied, putting Dawn's suitcase on the floor to return his hug. "What are you doing here? I wasn't expecting you to be back so soon."

"Two of the meetings that I was supposed to go to were canceled at the last minute because of the holiday. So I decided to come back tonight and surprise you. Is that okay?"

I was about to speak when I realized we had an audience. Robert and Dawn stood there listening intently to our conversation. "Ah, Robert...would you mind helping Dawn with these suitcases?"

Robert took them without hesitation and they went to her room. I didn't say anything until I saw them close the door.

"I guess it's not okay with you then," Joe remarked, pointing to the bat in my hand.

I looked at the bat. "Oh," I said, slightly embarrassed. "This isn't for you." I walked to the hall closet and put the bat back and hung up my coat.

"Good," Joe said. " I was beginning to wonder."

"I thought I was going to need it tonight, that's all." I walked to the sofa and took off my heels. Joe sat next to me and I explained what had happened.

He whistled softly after I finished. "Is Dawn going to be okay? Are you okay?"

"Hey, I'm fine. I don't know how Dawn is, though."

"Why do you say that?"

I shrugged. "I don't think Dawn told me everything that's been going on. She hasn't been herself lately. She's been kind of withdrawn and I could swear I saw what looked like lines of cocaine residue on the coffee table in her apartment."

"Are you sure? Do you think he's got her hooked on drugs or something?"

"I don't know. I hope not." I sighed. "Maybe it was my imagination. I'm liable to imagine anything crazy, considering I can't stand the man." Joe chuckled softly and I looked at him. "What?" I asked.

He just smiled. "You're too much, you know that?"

"Why do you say that?"

"Just come here," he said.

When I moved closer to him, he leaned over and gave me a long, tender kiss. After a minute or so, conscious of the rest of the company in the house, I broke away slowly.

"Wow," I murmured softly.

"I'm sorry. I know it was abrupt, but I just couldn't wait to kiss you," he said.

"Don't apologize. It was nice."

"Good," he said, looking relieved. "So what's been happening? Did you miss me?" he asked.

"Oh, it's been a real adventure," I said dryly, avoiding his last question. I told him all about Reneé and the dinner party. "And to top it off, my mother will be here soon."

"Man, it doesn't sound like you missed me at all," he muttered.

"Oh, I'm sorry, Joe," I said earnestly. "Of course I missed you. I've just had a lot on my mind and tonight really didn't go well."

"I was teasing," he chuckled. "I can understand why you're kind of uptight. I don't know why you didn't call me and let me know what was going on."

"I didn't want to bother you and there was nothing you could do about it anyway. Now the only thing I have to do is figure out how to tell Mama that her teenage daughter's pregnant."

"Lacie, don't worry about it. You don't have to go through this alone. I'm here for you."

"Joe, I don't know. Are you sure you want to be in the middle of all this? I'm telling you, you don't know my mother."

"I don't think it's going to be as bad as you say it is," he said confidently. "I really want to meet your mother and get to know her. After all, she may be family someday."

"What did you say?"

He looked at me earnestly. "Lacie, we've been seeing each other for a while now. Haven't you noticed how crazy I am about you?"

"I guess," I said. "I'm just wondering how you could feel like this so soon. I mean, we haven't even been intimate yet."

"We can start right now, if that's all right with you," he murmured softly. He put his fingertips under my chin and brought my lips to his. It was a soft kiss, just like the one we'd had on our first date. We started kissing longer and I could feel his excitement.

I broke away slowly. "Uh, Joe, I don't think we should…"

"Shh," he whispered, putting a finger to my lips. "I got you."

His lips touched mine again and I sank into his kisses as his tongue tangled with mine. We didn't hear Robert, Dawn and Reneé come into the room.

"Hey, we're not interrupting you two, are we?" I heard Robert say as Joe slowly removed his lips from mine.

We looked at the three of them standing on the other side of the sofa with their hands on their hips.

"Why must you three always interrupt me?" I asked.

"Hey, this is my first time interrupting you," Reneé said. "It was Dawn and Robert last time."

Dawn looked insulted. "We just wanted to know if you two would be interested in playing a game of Monopoly, that's all. Gee, talk about touchy!"

I looked at the darkening bruises on her face and felt bad. Maybe I'd come on too strong. "Dawn, you know I don't play Monopoly anymore." I couldn't resist teasing her and added, "I don't play with you because you cheat."

"What?" she exclaimed. "I can't believe you said that."

"Hey, hey, hey," Robert broke in. "Let's leave. It's obvious that they want to be alone, so let's go," he commanded gently. "Why don't you two stay at my apartment for the night, so they can have some time to themselves. Is it okay if Reneé stays over, Lacie?"

"Sure," I said. "Just make sure you and Dawn don't keep her up too long. She needs her rest."

"I'm fine, Lacie," Reneé proclaimed.

"C'mon, you two," Robert urged as he ushered them out the door.

"Can you believe she said that I cheat?" Dawn exclaimed as they left.

I mouthed a "thank you" to Robert. He winked and gave me a thumbs up sign. Joe and I burst out laughing when the door closed behind them.

"Joe, I'm sorry," I said as I tried to stop laughing. "I guess I shouldn't have said that to her, huh?"

"Yeah, you can say that." He smiled. "But I think Dawn knows you didn't mean any harm. Does she really cheat in Monopoly, though?"

"All the time," I answered. I took a deep breath. "I'm nervous, Joe," I said suddenly.

"Why? Are you a virgin?"

I playfully punched him in the arm and he laughed. "C'mon, I'm serious, Joe. I'm really scared. I mean, we've been together for a while now, without sex or any kind of obligation and now we're about to cross that line. Things won't be the same again."

"Yes, but you see, that's a good thing. We'll be closer." He grabbed my hand. "Look Lacie, I'm not going to lie to you. I've wanted you ever since I saw you in that club and the mere fact that we found each other again, when I didn't even get your number, tells me that this is right. You are right. We are right. And if your sister, Dawn and Robert had not interrupted us, I'd be making love to you right now. You wouldn't have time to be nervous," he said. "You get what I'm saying?"

"I guess I do," I murmured.

"Good," he said, "because now I'm going to show you what I mean about not having time to be nervous."

I turned over in the bed and found him staring directly into my face. We smiled at each other.

"Good morning," he greeted.

"Good morning," I returned. "How long have you been watching me?" I asked.

"Since about eight this morning," he said, pointing to the wall clock which read ten o'clock.

"Why?" I asked.

"Why not?" he returned, then quickly moved to kiss me on the mouth.

I jerked away and covered my mouth. "No, Joe. I haven't brushed my teeth yet." I tried to get away, but he grabbed me and wouldn't let go.

"It's too late. I've already smelled your morning breath," he said as he kissed me.

"Joe, that's disgusting." I giggled.

"I don't see why. Your mouth isn't the only thing I kissed last night," he teased.

I laughed. "I don't believe you said that." I shook my head. "I just don't believe you said that. You're too much."

"Ah, but I wasn't enough for you last night," he teased again. " 'Joe, don't stop. Joe, don't stop'," he mimicked in a high-pitched voice.

"Okay, that's enough," I said, quickly getting out of the bed. "I didn't say that." He gave me a skeptical look. "Okay, so I said that—once," I admitted. "Still, you're one to talk. You enjoyed yourself also."

He got out of bed, completely naked, and came over to me. I couldn't help staring. His body was magnificent. He hugged me. "You're right. I enjoyed every minute of it. Girl, you just don't know how good you felt!"

"Joe, will you stop and be serious?" I couldn't help laughing. "What's wrong with you?"

"I don't know. I guess I'm just very happy."

Now it was my turn to tease. "Why? Because you finally got some?"

He looked at me seriously. "No, because I think I'm falling in love with you."

"What?"

He was more confident as he repeated it. "I'm in love with you, Lacie."

As I stood there in complete shock, I suddenly heard an insistent banging on the door downstairs. Damn, those three! They were always doing this. I frantically grabbed my robe and Joe helped me put it on.

"Look, I've got to answer that. Get dressed and we'll talk some more about this, okay?" I gave him a quick peck on the cheek and rushed downstairs as the knocking became even more insistent.

"Okay, okay, I'm coming!" I yelled as I ran to the door and fiddled with the locks. I was sure it was Reneé and Dawn. "What are you doing here? I thought you were going to…" I was saying as I opened the door and saw Mama standing there.

"It's about time you answered the door. I've been knocking on it forever. What took you so long?"

I was about to answer her when I heard Joe coming down the stairs.

"Lacie, who's at the…" He stopped when he reached me and saw my mother standing there. "Oh," he said, looking embarrassed.

I saw why. He was bare-chested and had on only his boxers.

"Is this is why you didn't answer my phone calls last night?" Mama asked, eyeing my robe, my disheveled hair, and Joe's bare chest and boxers.

It was beginning.

CHAPTER 9

I was so embarrassed. I thought quickly and turned around. "Joe, would you mind going upstairs while I talk to my mother?" I mouthed, "And get dressed," to him.

"Oh, yeah, sure," he said and ran upstairs with us watching him.

I turned back around. "Mama, what are you doing here? I thought you said you'd call me?"

She looked at me incredulously. "Didn't you hear what I just said? I did call you, but no one answered the phone."

"Did you leave a message?"

"No. I'm your mother. I shouldn't have to leave a message and you know how much I hate answering machines. They're too impersonal."

I merely stood there with the door open and her on the other side.

"Are you going to let me in or not?" she asked.

"Oh, I'm sorry. Come in." I grabbed one of her bags and moved aside.

"Thank you." She walked in and put her bags down and I shut the door. "This place looks so cluttered, Lacie. I know you know better than this," she said, walking around and observing the apartment.

"Forgive me, Mama, but I haven't had time to clean up. It's been kind of hectic around here lately," I said, wondering why I was explaining myself to her. This was my place.

"I see," she remarked sarcastically, indicating upstairs with a nod. "Have you started on dinner yet?"

I shook my head, not bothering to answer. I knew what was coming next.

"Lacie, Thanksgiving is tomorrow and you haven't prepared anything?"

"Mama, I told you it's been hectic around here," I repeated. "I haven't had the time."

"So, you're going to ruin Thanksgiving over a good screw?" she asked.

I walked swiftly toward the kitchen. "Mama, why must you always start an argument?" I looked back at her as she followed me. "Do you want something to drink?"

"No, thank you," she replied. "And I'm not trying to start an argument. I'm only saying that you should have started preparing something by now."

"I'll have plenty of time to do that. I'm going to buy groceries today," I explained as I took out the orange juice from the refrigerator.

"Uh, huh, if you say so," she muttered. "Where's Reneé?"

"She's across the hall at Robert's. She and Dawn spent the night over there," I replied, reaching for a glass and pouring the orange juice in it.

"You mean with that gay guy?"

I looked at her in surprise. "How did you know that he was gay?"

"Oh please, Lacie. It's all over him. It's so obvious," she asserted, rolling her eyes. "So, Reneé and Dawn spent the night over there so you could have some quality time with him, huh?" she asked, pointing upstairs with a finger.

"Yes," I answered defiantly. "And his name is Joe, Mama. Joe Mitchell. He'll be spending Thanksgiving with us. Dawn and Robert will be here as well. And Mama, listen. I don't want any negative comments about Joe or Robert."

She tried to look innocent. "I'm not going to say a word. I have no problem with gay people. I just hope Robert knows he's going to hell, though."

"Mama!"

"It's true," she proclaimed indignantly.

"Mama, how do you know you're not going to hell?" I asked her. She was silent. I groaned. "Listen, this is Thanksgiving Eve. You wanted to come here and practically pushed this dinner on me. Now I would appreciate it if we could have a nice holiday without arguing. Dawn and Robert will be here and I've got someone upstairs who really cares about me and I don't want any of them to feel uncomfortable."

She looked offended. "What are you saying?"

I held up my hand. "I'm merely saying that I want this to go well, that's all."

"I want that too," she mumbled.

I just looked at her, got out a pad, and started writing a grocery list. Joe walked into the kitchen and gave me a peck on my cheek.

"Joe Mitchell, this is my mother, Josephine Taylor," I said.

"Nice to meet you, Ms. Taylor," he said and shook her hand.

She greeted him with a smile. "Nice to meet you as well, completely dressed, of course," she teased.

"Mama!" I exclaimed.

Joe chuckled. "It's fine. I'm sure Ms. Taylor wasn't expecting to see a half-naked man running down the stairs."

"You got that right," she murmured with a smile. "And call me Josephine."

Remarkably, Joe was right. His charm appeared to be working and Robert and Mama seemed to click as well. I came back from grocery shopping and found Dawn, Robert, Reneé and Mama playing spades, while Joe watched. He helped me with the groceries while everyone took a break from the card game.

"So how's it going?" I whispered to him while everyone was in the living room.

"Actually, it's been going quite well." He smiled. "I haven't had the least bit of trouble from her, but she is very inquisitive. She was kind of guarded at first, but she's warmed up some. I think she likes me."

"I see. Okay, I stand corrected. You were right," I admitted reluctantly.

"It's not about being right, Lacie. Your mother's a good woman. She's funny," he added, as he helped me unpack the groceries.

I stopped and looked at him. "Funny? Are we talking about the same woman here? Joe, I know my mother's a good woman. She raised me alone for a long time before she remarried. But I have never considered her to be funny—sarcastic, maybe, but not funny."

"Maybe you should try to get to know that side of her and not be so hard on her." After a moment, he said, "Lacie, I was thinking. Are you sure you want me to stay here? I mean, I would be more than willing to go back to my apartment if it's any trouble."

I frowned. "Of course I'm sure. Why would you ask me that?"

"Because your mother's here and everything..."

I scoffed. "Joe, I'm a grown woman, and this is my house," I asserted. "It's okay if you stay here."

"All right, if you say so." He lifted the turkey out of one of the bags and put it on the counter. "Lacie, how many pounds is this turkey? Are you trying to feed an army?"

"It's twenty-three pounds. Do you think it's too big?"

"Let's just say you're going to have to be very creative with the leftovers." He saw the look on my face. "What's wrong? Hey, I was just teasing," he said and hugged me.

"I want this to go well, Joe," I replied. "Yeah, I didn't want to cook dinner at first, but I've kind of gotten in the mood, you know?"

"Everything is going to be fine," he reassured.

"You keep saying that."

"Yes, but wasn't I right about your mother?"

I nodded. "You've made your point." We continued unpacking the groceries. "So Mama asked you a lot of questions, huh? What about?"

"Never mind what questions I asked him." Mama strolled into the kitchen. "That's just between us." She looked at all the food on the counter. "Did you get everything you needed?"

"Yes, and surprisingly, the store was fully stocked. I had to make only one stop," I answered.

"All right, let's get started then. What do you need help with?" she asked.

"Mama, that's okay. You finish playing the game. I'll take care of the cooking."

"I can fill in for your mother, if she doesn't mind," Joe offered, giving me an encouraging look.

"No, I don't mind at all," Mama agreed.

"All right, then. Mama, you can start on the white potatoes and I'll work on the collards." I gave Joe a mean squint as he slipped out with a devilish smile.

While Mama and I cooked, Dawn, Joe, Robert and Reneé continued to play spades. Occasionally, they'd take turns to check on us. They appeared to be enjoying themselves and amazingly, Mama and I were coping well with each other in the kitchen. But then, we always got along when it came to cooking. That seemed to be the only thing we had in common.

By the time it got to be late afternoon, everything was just about ready to be cooked for the next day. After the turkey soaked for a good while, I seasoned it and decided I wouldn't put it in the oven until later that night.

When the phone rang, I yelled for someone else to pick it up, but no one heard me. Mama was in the bathroom and I had stuffing all over my fingers. I quickly wiped my hands on a dish towel and picked up the phone.

"Hello?"

"Is the turkey in the oven yet?" Tony's voice greeted on the other line.

Hearing his voice was a surprise. "Oh, hi, Tony," I said uneasily. I peeked around the corner to make sure no one could hear me. "I just got through seasoning it. She's a big one."

He chuckled softly. "Good, good. Listen, I called because I was a little concerned about you."

"Why?" I asked as I started stuffing the turkey.

"You've been so distant lately and last night you left the party before I could say good-bye and wish you a happy Thanksgiving. The last time I saw you, William was cutting the cake and then you were gone."

Why did he have to mention last night?

"It was getting kind of late, so I decided to go ahead and leave," I lied. I couldn't tell him the real reason why I'd left. "Are you spending Thanksgiving with your family?" I asked, changing the subject.

"But of course," he said easily. "Simone and her father invited me to spend Thanksgiving with them, but I didn't want to break tradition, so I invited them to come with me."

Why did I suddenly feel a tinge of jealousy? The thought of him and Simone spending the holiday together irked me.

"Umm, sounds nice," I mumbled as I violently jabbed another spoonful of stuffing into the turkey. I had to get off the phone. "Tony, I'm sorry to be so abrupt, but I'm in the middle of getting everything ready and I'm really busy."

"Ahh...Joe must be there," he assumed. "That's no problem. I just wanted to check on you and see that you were okay and to let you know that William wants to meet with us Monday. I left some information about his company under your office door. You really impressed him."

"I did?"

"Yes, you did. I'll tell you about everything later. You have a wonderful weekend and enjoy your holiday. And Lacie?"

"Yes, Tony?"

"Happy Thanksgiving."

"Happy Thanksgiving to you, too," I said softly, and hung up the phone. Why was I so disconsolate all of a sudden?

"Tony?" Robert asked, coming from behind me.

"How did you know?" I asked.

"I didn't, but you just confirmed it." He hopped on to a free space on the counter. I slapped his butt lightly and motioned for him to sit at the table.

"Yeah, he called to wish me a happy Thanksgiving and told me that William Carr wants a meeting with us." I was silent for a second. Then I looked at him. "Do you know that Simone and her father are at his parents' house, spending the holiday with him?"

Robert shook his head. "You've got it bad."

"What?"

"Nothing." He sighed. "So, did you get to taste some of Joe's goodies last night?"

"Hey, there was no tasting on my part, only his," I replied with a mischievous grin. "Robert, let me tell you. That man knows his words and he backs them up one hundred percent. Everything is finally going the way I've always wanted it to." I took a deep breath. "This morning he told me that he's in love with me. Can you believe it? That man out there loves me!" I exclaimed, pointing to the living room.

"But how do you feel about him?"

"I care about him deeply, too."

"Uh, huh," he said.

"What was that for?"

"Lacie, you're going to have to be honest with him about your feelings. You can't keep him in the dark. He's fallen for you very hard."

"Who's fallen very hard?" Mama came in.

"No one, Mama," I answered. Robert just shook his head.

All that cooking Mama and I did reminded everyone that we had to eat something for the night. We ordered pizza and rented some movies. Around midnight, we were tired and ready for bed. Robert said he would come over early to help set up. Dawn had already gone to her room thirty minutes earlier.

Joe got off the sofa and stretched. "Lacie, are you ready for bed?"

I caught Mama's look. "Uh, I'll be up in a little bit, Joe. Reneé and I need to talk to Mama for a minute." I looked at Reneé and she nodded. Reneé had told me earlier that once everyone left, she wanted to tell Mama about her pregnancy.

"Okay, don't be too long." He gave me a kiss on the cheek and went upstairs.

"He's a nice guy. You did well," Mama said.

"Yeah, you're really lucky to have him," Reneé offered.

"Thanks, but I didn't pick him. He picked me," I said.

"Is he going to sleep upstairs with you?" Mama asked.

I nodded. "Yes, he is, Mama," I admitted calmly to her disapproving frown.

"Where will I sleep?"

"You can bunk in with Reneé. I don't think Dawn wants any company. She needs some time to herself."

"You have got to tell me about that child. I know that something's stressing her out," Mama said, shaking her head. She glanced at Reneé. "What's wrong, baby?"

Reneé looked almost green. Instinctively, I knew it wasn't the right time to tell Mama. It would have to be after the holiday.

Reneé caught the tone in Mama's voice and knew also. She tried to straighten up. "I think that pepperoni pizza didn't agree with me," she lied.

"Yes, I don't think that pepperoni was too fresh," I agreed. I didn't lie. It was a bit stale.

"Let me give you some Maalox, that usually calms upset stomachs." Mama reached into her purse.

"No!" Reneé and I exclaimed simultaneously.

Mama looked at both of us in surprise.

"Mama, I'll be fine. I just need to sleep it off." Reneé stood up, took a huge breath and walked upstairs.

"She'll be okay, Mama," I said.

"I certainly hope so. We're having a lot of food tomorrow."

I climbed into bed with Joe.

"Did you tell her?" he mumbled, hugging me instantly.

"No, we chickened out," I replied with a yawn and went to sleep.

Bang! Bang! Bang!

It was three o'clock in the morning. Joe was still asleep. I didn't see how. I put on my robe and opened the door and waited for the figure in front of me to come into focus.

"Lacie, we've got to take Reneé to the hospital immediately! She's been throwing up constantly for the past hour. I gave her some ginger ale, but she threw that up too. Does Joe have a car? Maybe he could drive us," Mama suggested frantically.

I awoke instantly. I couldn't tell her just yet. *Think, Lacie, think!* "Where is she?" I asked.

"She's in the bathroom. I'd swear I saw blood, Lacie!" she shrieked.

"Okay, calm down, Mama," I soothed, thinking that she was probably in shock and only imagined seeing blood. I walked into the bathroom with her on my heels.

"I'll hurry up and get dressed and get her coat," Mama panted at the bathroom door.

I walked in. Reneé was sitting on the toilet cover with a wet towel on her forehead. "You okay, kid?" I asked her. She gave me a weak smile. "I guess it was inevitable, huh?" She nodded weakly as she understood. I took a deep breath. "Well, get ready." I helped her up. We walked out of the bathroom door and almost collided with Mama.

"Okay, I got her coat and some clean panties because you never want to go into a hospital without clean underwear on…"

"Mama, " I said softly.

"…and heavy socks because it's too cold outside for this child…"

"Mama," I repeated louder.

"…to be ass out in a nightgown. Where's…"

"Mama!" I yelled.

"What!" she shrieked.

I took a deep breath. "Reneé is not sick. She's pregnant," I said gently.

There was dead silence as Mama looked at us. She didn't say one word as she turned around, walked slowly toward their room and slammed the door.

Reneé and I looked at each other sadly. She had to know. It was that simple. I helped her downstairs and knocked on Dawn's door. Mama and Reneé sharing a room for the night was definitely out of the question.

I explained to Dawn what had happened and she offered to sleep on the couch so Reneé would be comfortable. After tucking Reneé in, I went into the kitchen, put the turkey in the oven and set the oven on low.

I walked up the stairs tiredly. I knocked on the door several times, begging Mama to come out and talk, but she never answered.

This was great, just great.

CHAPTER 10

I woke up to the sound of pots and pans banging. It woke Joe also.

"You told her, huh?" he asked.

"Yeah. You missed a big scene last night. It happened while you were asleep," I explained. "I'd better go and talk to her." I put on my robe and went downstairs.

She was stirring something on the stove. I stood there uncomfortably for a while, not knowing what to say.

"Mama, do you want to talk?" I asked gently.

Her face was pure granite when she turned around. "No," she replied coldly.

I threw my hands up wearily. "Suit yourself. I'm going back upstairs. I only ask that you try to be a little considerate because some of us are still asleep."

Mama was silent the whole day. We worked together in the kitchen without saying a word to each other. Everyone noticed the tension in the air. Robert came over early, as expected, and helped set the table. Joe, Reneé and Dawn stayed in the living room and watched television.

The food looked appetizing as everyone sat down at the table. Joe sat at the head and I at the other end. Mama sat next to him. Joe said a blessing and after that we started eating.

"Lacie, this food is delicious. The turkey is so moist and tender," Joe said, breaking the silence.

Dawn, Reneé and Robert agreed in unison.

"Thank you." I smiled.

We ate heartily. Dawn, Reneé and Joe helped themselves to seconds. Robert had thirds. I was pleased that everyone was enjoying the meal, but was disturbed about Mama's attitude. She ate silently and it was obvious that she was angry. We had no choice but to ignore her and continue with dinner. I guess I shouldn't have told her in such a way. As if she read my mind, Mama finally spoke.

"I can't believe you let her get pregnant!" she exploded angrily.

We all jumped at her outburst.

"Okay, Mama, let's not talk about this now. We're eating," I said calmly.

"Lacie, I wake up in the middle of the night and find my youngest daughter crouched over a toilet, upchucking last night's pizza and then you just happen to tell me she's pregnant. I was about to give the child Maalox, for goodness sake! How can you expect me not to be upset about this? When were you going to tell me?"

"Mama, you slammed your door last night and wouldn't come out. You had plenty of time to talk to us, but you chose to stay in your room and sulk. Not to mention you had every opportunity to talk to me earlier this morning. I don't want to get into it now. We can discuss this later."

"No! We're going to talk about this right now. Everyone stop eating!" Mama commanded sharply. She didn't have to—they had already stopped.

"Mama, this is my house and I will not tolerate you being disruptive. It's Thanksgiving and we all want to eat peacefully."

"To hell with Thanksgiving!" she exclaimed and threw down her fork.

That did it!

"Okay, Mama, you want to talk. Let's talk!" I blared.

Joe, seeing my fury, cleared his throat and spoke. "Uh, Lacie, maybe you two should have this conversation in your room," he suggested.

I was adamant. "No. Apparently she's not concerned about anyone but herself, so let's all hear what she has to say."

Joe, Reneé, Dawn and Robert, clearly uncomfortable, put their forks down and waited. Mama and I glared at each other angrily. After a minute of strained silence, she finally spoke in a low, menacing tone, through clenched teeth.

"I can't believe you allowed this to happen, Lacie. I left Reneé in your care and this is what I get? How could you let her get pregnant?" Mama asked.

All eyes were on me as they waited for my response. "Mama, I didn't *let* Reneé get pregnant. Nobody *lets* teenage girls get pregnant. They have sex and that's how they get pregnant," I retorted. "She's seventeen years old, Mama, what did you expect?"

"I expected you to watch her so that this wouldn't happen. I should have never left her with you. You can't do anything right," she seethed. "You're so irresponsible."

I shook my head. "I'm irresponsible?"

"Yes," she emphasized, with an accusing glare.

"So who's been taking care of her for the past few months because her mother asked—no, excuse me— almost *begged* her to take care of her daughter because she felt she needed some time alone? Me, that's who. I didn't ask for it."

"You practically drop a seventeen-year-old girl with raging hormones in my lap, because you can't bear to talk to your child about sex, and now you want to criticize me and tell me I'm irresponsible? She's your child! You gave birth to her. She shouldn't have to come to me and ask me about sex, but she did. So I filled her ears up with as much information as I could because she needed to know. So don't come here and accuse me of doing anything but what I had to do. If you were so concerned about her, then maybe you should have been here to deal with it yourself."

"So you're going to blame me for this? Is that it?" Mama asked.

I didn't back down. "If you would take just a little time to communicate instead of keeping everything inside, then maybe you could have a good relationship with her. Maybe she wouldn't be in this predicament."

"This is pitiful," Mama scoffed. "I've got to come back home and clean up your mess!" she snapped. She rolled her eyes and turned her attention from me to Reneé. "It doesn't look like you're too far along. As soon as this holiday is over, we're going to the clinic and see about you having an abortion," she commanded sharply.

Reneé looked alarmed, but I was a step ahead. "She's not going to have an abortion, Mama. She's keeping it."

"What!"

"I think you heard me. We've already been to the clinic and Reneé couldn't do it. She wants the baby."

She looked from Reneé to me. "Then she's just going to have to go back, because she's not having it!"

I remained calm. "Yes, she is, Mama. It's already been decided."

She was definitely mad now. I could see the disgust in her eyes. "You did this, didn't you? You told her to keep the baby," she accused.

I shook my head. "I didn't tell her anything. She made this decision on her own. I had no part in it."

"Yes you did," she insisted. "This is payback from when you had yours. You want to get back at me because I made you abort yours."

Robert and Joe looked shocked at the statement. Dawn and Reneé knew, of course, but this was news to Robert and Joe. I wasn't embarrassed or shocked that Mama had called me out. It was typical of her to do something so vindictive and I wasn't going for her bait.

I shook my head. "This isn't about me. This isn't about you or anyone else except Reneé and her feelings and her right to choose."

"She doesn't have any rights!" Mama shrieked.

"She has every right! It's her child!" I shrieked in return.

No one said a word. Suddenly, Mama stood up, knocking her plate over in the process. She glared at me angrily, apparently not caring that she had messed up the table, which now had gravy dripping down the sides.

"You make me sick! I can't believe you actually agree with this child ruining her life by having another child. Well, go on, Lacie! Believe, feel, think, or whatever the hell you want. I don't care. But I'm going to tell you one thing. Reneé will have this baby over my dead body and I mean every word of it!" She marched to the coat tree, grabbed her coat and slammed the door on her way out.

With very little spirit, we managed to continue eating. It was very quiet and I knew that we were all thinking about the argument Mama and I had had. I took a few glances at Reneé every now and then and immediately felt sorry for going off the way I had. She was in an awkward position. I supported her choice to keep the baby, while Mama was against it.

After we ate, Dawn and I cleared the table and started putting the dishes in the dishwasher. I felt terrible.

"It's not your fault, you know." Dawn said suddenly.

I barely heard her. "Huh?"

"You and Miss Josephine," she prompted, delicately.

"Oh, Dawn!" I groaned as I leaned against the counter and put my head in my hands. "I feel so awful. I ruined Thanksgiving! I mean, this is a day when we should be thankful and enjoy having family and friends around, and I get into an argument with my mother."

She put a hand on my shoulder. "Lacie, you and Miss Josephine really need to talk. Whatever it is that's going on between you two has got to be settled. You can't keep putting Reneé in the middle of it. It was so obvious that the argument was not just over Reneé being pregnant."

I nodded my head slowly. "I know. I know," I whispered tearfully. "What am I going to do? What am I going to do?" I sighed. "She stormed out of here and didn't even tell me where she was going. Now I don't know what to think."

"I don't know what to tell you. You know my mother and I don't get along well either, so I'm the last one to give advice."

I looked at her and smiled faintly. "You just did."

"I did, didn't I?" She grinned and we both laughed.

"I am so glad to finally hear some laughter in here," Robert remarked as he, Reneé and Joe came to the doorway.

"Hey, listen you all. I apologize about dinner. I wasn't expecting to get into it with Mama. She just hit a nerve and I responded," I explained, wiping my eyes.

Joe walked over and put his arms around me. "No apologies necessary. We all know how family can be. We understand and we love you."

"Yes, we love you," Robert agreed. "Of course, we'd really love you if you agreed to play Monopoly with us."

"I'll only play if Dawn promises that she won't cheat," I said.

"For the last time, I do not cheat!" Dawn exclaimed.

We played Monopoly and had a wonderful time. It took my mind off the argument with Mama for a while.

Occasionally, I would check my watch for the time. I still hadn't heard from her and after a while I began to worry.

After the game, we watched television and shortly thereafter, Robert went to his apartment and everyone decided to turn in. I stayed up to clean a little more and wait for Mama. After cleaning, I began watching some television and had almost fallen asleep in the living room when I heard a knock at the door.

She stood in the doorway wearily. "Do you want to speak first or should I?" she asked.

I closed the door as she walked in and sat on the sofa. I sat on the love seat facing her. I waited until she got comfortable before I spoke.

"Mama, listen. I want you to know that I didn't like that argument we had during dinner at all," I said. "I didn't expect to get so upset."

"It didn't seem that way to me at all. I think you almost enjoyed it," she retorted.

I ignored her remark. It was getting late and I didn't want to argue anymore. "I know what I told you last night caught you off guard, but that was not an excuse for you to blow up like that—especially in front of company."

"Excuse me?"

I explained further. "Mama, everyone was uncomfortable with your little outburst. You made us put our forks down and stop eating just so you could vent your frustrations on me."

"Forgive me, Lacie, but I think I had every right to be upset."

"I agree, but did you really have to make such a scene?"

"Lacie, I don't care what people think. You should know that by now," she responded sharply. "Reneé is pregnant and you want to be Miss Bad Ass and act as if she's Cinderella and the prince has just put on her glass slipper." Mama had always had a way with words.

"That's not how it is, Mama," I defended. "I know Reneé can't go through an abortion. You should've seen her when we went to the clinic. She was scared out of her mind. She didn't want to do it."

"She should be scared. No one told her to open her legs and get knocked up!"

"Oh Mama, please!" I exclaimed. "How can you be so merciless about this? Reneé is going through a hard time right now and you want to point fingers."

"Lacie, if Reneé was scared then, what do you think raising a child is going to do to her? She's not ready for that. She hasn't even finished high school and you support her bringing a child into this world that she can't even take care of."

"Hey, I support her decision on this because this is her choice. It's her body, Mama, and she's..."

"Oh, will you please stop with this 'this is her body, her choice' crap, Lacie! That's such a politically correct thing to say," she vented. "She's seventeen years old, Lacie! She's not ready to be a mother."

"But she's pregnant, Mama! She wants to have this child and she's old enough to make that decision. You shouldn't force her into anything."

"Reneé will get over it. You did," she argued.

"What?" I gave her a stupefied look. "Mama, I never got over it and neither will she," I declared. "Do you realize the emotional strain Reneé will go through if you make her do this? I don't want her to go through what I went through. I wouldn't wish it on anybody and I'm warning you that if you make her do this, she'll wind up resenting you in the end."

"No she won't," Mama insisted.

"Yes she will, Mama, because I did and I still do!" I exclaimed.

It just came out. I surprised myself and apparently her, too.

She peered at me incredulously. "You resent me, Lacie?"

"Yes, Mama. I've been feeling that way for a very long time now." It was an incredible relief to finally admit it to her.

Mama stood and then I stood. She paced back and forth, letting what I'd said sink in. She looked hurt when she stopped in front of me.

"You're telling me…that you resent me? How can you say that?" she asked.

"Mama, listen…"

"No, you listen!" she interjected sharply. "Lacie, I was sixteen when I had you and I had to raise you by myself, with no help from your father or anyone else. I had to work and save every dime in order to keep food in your mouth, clothes on your back and a roof over our heads. There were times when I didn't know how we were going to make it. All this I did!" she proclaimed. "I know we may not have had the finer things in life, but I did the best I knew how.

And look at you. You've got this beautiful apartment, a good job and a man that loves you. You've done pretty well for yourself. So you give me a reason why my older daughter has just told me that she resents her mother," she breathed tearfully.

"Yes, you did take on all that financial responsibility by yourself. I'll give you that. But there is a lot more to being a parent than finances, Mama!" I returned, trying to hold back my tears.

She looked at me dubiously. "What are you talking about, Lacie?"

"You never talked to me," I replied simply. "We never had that mother and daughter relationship that people hear or read about. I couldn't even get you to talk to me about sex."

Mama looked at me as if I had lost my mind. "So you're telling me that you resent me because I never talked to you about sex? Is that it?" She threw up her hands. "Oh! Well, you seem to have learned pretty well by yourself!" She pointed to the stairs. "I watched you go upstairs and sleep with a man that's not even your husband. You did that right in front of my face, with no respect or consideration at all for me."

"This is my home, Mama. I can do whatever I want in my own house and if you want respect you have to earn it."

She glowered at me. "Lacie, I earned my respect when I brought you into this world!" She raised her hands. "So I didn't talk to you about sex." She shrugged. "Big deal. My mother didn't talk to me about it, either. When I grew up, that was a subject that we never talked about. So how was

I going to talk to you about sex when I was never educated on it myself?" she defended. "You may not have had the best education on sex, or anything else for that matter, but I supported you in each and every other way I knew how."

I threw my hands up in disgust. "Do you want a medal, Mama? Is that it?" I cried. "You supporting me was not a favor. It wasn't a miracle. It was your job. I didn't ask to be born. So don't act as if I'm obligated to you, because I'm not." I peered at her. "Do you know when I really started losing respect for you? When you married Martin, Mama, that's when!" I nodded my head to her widened eyes. "Yes, that's right. I hated the fact that you were more interested in him than in your own child. No real mother would ever forsake her child's feelings for her husband's."

"I didn't do that," she denied strongly.

"Yes, you did, Mama." I shook my head. "The sad thing about this is that you can't even admit it to yourself."

"What is it you want me to do? I can't change what happened," she cried. "You better wake up and stop dwelling on the past." She shook her head sadly and sat down. "I was on my own with you, Lacie. What was I supposed to do? I needed someone in my life and Martin was that person. I had needs just like any other woman."

My shoulders slumped sadly in defeat. She hadn't listened to one word that I had said. "I'm not saying you didn't, Mama. That's not what I'm saying at all." I sighed. "Listen, I'm tired. I know we have different opinions on this thing with Reneé but I am asking you to think this over thoroughly. I know you can't change the past, but you can do something about the future," I stated. "This isn't your life. It's hers. For once, think about your child."

I went up to my room and left Mama sitting in the living room alone. I had had enough. After all of that arguing, I felt we'd accomplished nothing.

The next few days were tense. Joe kindly decided to stay Friday and the weekend to divert my attention from the strained silence in the apartment. He took me to plays, to the movies and out to dinner. We had a great time and it was a comfort to have Joe around with so much hostility in the air.

He went to church with me Sunday, and I expected Mama and Reneé to go, but they were asleep when we left. He got a lot of stares at church and I was asked a lot of questions, which I avoided mostly. I didn't want any rumors of marriage to go around. After the service, Joe had a few errands, so he dropped me off at home and said he'd give me a call.

I walked into the apartment and saw Mama sitting on the couch, watching television. I nodded to her, put my coat in the closet and walked to the kitchen to start on dinner. I thought pot roast would be a good choice as it was a Sunday. I'd had enough of the leftovers from Thanksgiving.

Mama came in. She watched me for a moment, then proceeded to help me with the potatoes.

"Where's Joe?" she asked.

"He had some things to do, so he won't be back tonight."

"Oh," she said. "How was the service?"

"It was good. Reverend Jacobs preached a good sermon. Joe came with me and everyone asked about him." I glanced at her. "I'm sorry you missed church. You would have loved the sermon."

Mama sighed. "I wasn't feeling well this morning. I guess that's a good reason why I should have gone, huh?"

I smiled. She sounded just like me. "Probably so," I replied. "Reneé is still asleep, huh?"

"Yes. How did you know?"

"She's been like that for a long time. I guess it has something to do with her pregnancy."

Mama nodded. "Yeah. When I was pregnant with you that's all I did too." Suddenly, we both realized what she'd said and looked at each other uneasily. "Listen, Lacie…"

I stopped her. "Mama, look, I had a good time at church today, and…"

"No, listen, now," she insisted softly. "I don't want an argument either."

I sighed. "Okay. Go ahead."

"What I said about me not feeling too well wasn't exactly true. I heard you and Joe get up for church this morning but decided to stay behind and talk to Reneé."

"Oh," I said with surprise. "How did it go?"

"Very well, actually. Reneé did most of the talking and I listened."

"And?" I prompted.

She took a deep breath. "It's okay for Reneé to keep the baby," she said. "She really wants it."

I let out a small sigh of relief. "Yes, she does." I nodded. "What made you change your mind?"

Mama looked thoughtful. "What you said Thursday."

"I said a lot of things Thursday, Mama," I pointed out.

"That's true," she agreed. "But only a few things stuck in my head and made me think."

I didn't even want to know what I'd said that made her change her mind. I was just glad that she had.

Joe called just as he'd promised. We talked on the phone for at least three hours. When asked if I had any plans for Christmas, I told him I hadn't made any, but I knew that whatever I planned, Reneé and Mama had to be included.

I went back to work elated and full of energy, more than I'd had in a long time. The whole episode with Reneé and Mama had put a lot of stress on me. Now that Mama had accepted her condition and decision, albeit reluctantly, she wasn't going anywhere. Reneé still wanted to stay with me and Mama wasn't looking forward to returning to an empty house. Now my house was completely full. Mama, Reneé and Dawn were all living with me and I had no idea how I was going to cope with it.

Carrie was already at her desk when I arrived. She greeted me with a cup of coffee and followed me into the office with pen and pad.

I grinned. "You missed me that much, Carrie?" I teased as I sat in my chair.

"Yes," she admitted. "It got a little crazy while you were gone." She pointed to a small stack of pink slips on my desk. "Take a look at all the messages I left you. You've got a lot of things ahead of you, girl."

I picked up the slips. "I guess this is my welcome back, huh?" I asked dryly, looking through them. I recognized a few names from the dinner party the other night. "How was your Thanksgiving?"

"It was okay. Of course I did all the cooking while my in-laws complained the whole time. Lacie, before you get married, please make sure that you get along with his parents before you walk down the aisle. It could be a nightmare."

I laughed. Carrie had a good sense of humor and I was glad she was working with me. Besides Dawn, she was the only one that I really confided in on the job.

"So how was yours?" she asked.

I told her what had happened over the holiday and even about Joe. I knew that Carrie didn't approve, but since she was my friend, I felt she should know. I told her that we'd finally made that move and that I felt he was going to be a big part of my life.

"Lacie," she said, "if he makes you happy, then I guess that's all that matters."

"I guess so," I replied softly.

Tony and I spent the next week and a half meeting with prospective clients from Mr. Carr's birthday party. We also researched Mr. Carr's company's finances and history. I knew that in order to get big accounts, it was best to know everything about our clients and their business.

The day that we were due to have a lunch meeting with Mr. Carr, I spent the morning going over the prospectus.

It was almost time for lunch when Carrie buzzed me on the intercom.

"Yes, Carrie?"

"Uh, Lacie, your mother is here to see you."

Huh? Carrie sounded almost as shocked as I was. "Sure. Tell her to come on in." Mama walked in a second later. "This is a surprise." I greeted her with a kiss on the cheek. "You didn't tell me you were coming."

"I'm shocked you gave me a kiss on the cheek. Does this mean we're at peace, now?"

I smiled warmly. "I hope so."

"Only because you got your way, right?" she asked.

"Mama," I groaned.

"I was only teasing," she chuckled. "I haven't seen much of you lately because you've been so busy, so I decided to come by and ask you if you wanted to go to lunch with me. It's my treat," she said.

"Talk about surprises. You want to treat me to lunch?"

"Yes. Really I shouldn't, because it seems as if you're making some big bucks from the looks of this office," she remarked, looking around my office. "Lacie, this office is gorgeous and the view is incredible!" She strolled over to the huge glass window.

"It's only a start, Mama. You should see some of the executive offices. They make mine look like a cardboard box." I walked over and looked at the view too.

"You're doing well, Lacie. I'm very proud of you," she said suddenly.

I looked at her and cocked my head to the side. "Thank you. I believe that's the nicest thing you've said to me since you've been back."

Her expression was unrevealing. "Well, you know..." she said awkwardly. She took a deep breath and clapped her hands together. "So, are we on for lunch or not? It's still my treat."

The atmosphere was so peaceful between us at the moment that I was reluctant to turn her down. She sensed it.

"What's wrong?" she asked.

"I already have a lunch meeting with a client," I said. "The limo is probably waiting now. I wish I could change it..."

She held up her hands. "No, Lacie. You do your job, child, and make that money," she insisted. "It's my fault, really. I shouldn't have come here on such short notice. I just had some things I wanted to talk to you about, is all."

"What's up? Is something wrong with Reneé?"

"No, Lacie. She's fine. She had a little morning sickness, but went on to school nonetheless. What we have to talk about can wait. We can do this..." She was interrupted by a knock at the door.

Tony came in. "Hey, Lacie, are you ready? The limousine is waiting for us downstairs." Tony suddenly realized I wasn't alone. "I'm sorry. I didn't know you had someone in here. Carrie wasn't at her desk, so I figured it was all right for me to come in," he explained apologetically.

"That's okay, Tony. Carrie probably went to lunch." I smiled. "And this someone is my mother," I explained, putting an arm around Mama. "Tony, meet Josephine Taylor. Mama, this is my colleague, Anthony Douglas. He prefers to be called Tony."

He walked over, grabbed Mama's hand and kissed it like a perfect gentleman. "Nice to meet you, Ms. Taylor. I apologize again for the interruption. I should have known you were Lacie's mother. The resemblance is uncanny," he remarked, staring at us in awe.

Mama smiled politely. "We get that a lot and there are no apologies needed," she replied. "This is your place of work. I was hoping that Lacie would come to lunch with me, but she explained that she already had an important lunch meeting with a client."

Tony turned to me. "Lacie, would you like to go to lunch with your mother instead? It's no problem. I can meet with William and fill you in on everything later," he suggested.

"No, Tony. You know we do this together and I don't think it would look too good if I didn't go."

"I was only saying…" he began.

"No," I said firmly. "This is my job. It's what I do."

Mama had been watching the whole thing. She looked from me to him. "On that note, I'm going to go," she said with an amused smile.

"I'll walk you out," I said. I gave Tony a hard look. "I'll be right back."

Tony was sitting in a chair when I came back, but stood up as soon as I walked in. "What was that about?" he asked.

"I don't want you to do me any special favors, okay?"

"What are you talking about?"

"Would you have said that to anyone else, knowing they had an important meeting to go to?"

"Of course not."

"Exactly. So treat me with the same respect." I sighed. "Listen, I know there were a few concerns expressed when I got this promotion, and I don't want people to think that I've got it made, just because I'm a director now."

"We both know that you got this out of hard work, Lacie."

"Yes, but it's important that everyone else knows it as well."

He stared at me for a second and didn't utter a word. Then he smiled. "You've made your point." He held his hands up in surrender.

"Thank you."

"I see you're getting along with your mother," he observed.

"Yeah, I guess you could say that." I grinned. Then for some reason I said, "I told her, Tony."

For a minute he looked confused. "You told her?" he asked with a confused look. Then he got it. "Oh, you told her. About Reneé, you mean." I nodded. "How did she take it?"

"Not very well. She really didn't like it when I told her Reneé didn't want to have an abortion."

"An abortion? Wait a minute. You mean she was actually considering doing that?"

"Yep. That's why I was so stressed out the other week."

"Why didn't you tell me?" he asked.

I shrugged. "It was a family matter and anyway, Reneé didn't go through with it. Mama and I spent most of Thanksgiving arguing about it. She yelled and I yelled. She wanted Reneé to have an abortion, while I defended Reneé because she wanted to keep the baby. It was a big mess and it erupted right in front of everyone at the dinner table. It wasn't exactly a family affair."

"She seemed all right today, though," Tony remarked.

I nodded. "Yeah, I guess she is. It's been a while since that argument and she did finally accept Reneé's decision. I couldn't believe it. I was convinced that she would continue fighting with me about it."

"Maybe it was something you said," he suggested.

I nodded. "Yeah, that's what she said. I don't know. I did get a lot off my chest, though. You know, stuff that's been buried for a long time. We still have a long way to go, though, and I know it's going to be hard."

"Give it some time. All good things come when you least expect them," he said as his eyes locked with mine.

I abruptly averted my eyes and cleared my throat. "Now if it's okay with you, I'd like to go. We don't want to be too late for Mr. Carr." I grabbed my coat and brief-case.

"Whatever you say, partner," Tony said with a chuckle.

We arrived at the restaurant ten minutes late and saw that William Carr wasn't the only one at the table. Simone was there.

"It certainly took you two long enough. I hope there's a good reason why you're late," Simone huffed, looking directly at me. "Tony, come sit next to me," she commanded softly.

I really didn't like this woman. The more I saw of her, the more I disliked her. I had no idea why she was there because she knew nothing of the business.

"Take it easy, Simone. We weren't on time either," Mr. Carr said. He looked at us. "I hope you don't mind, but we took the liberty of ordering for you while we waited."

"No, not at all," Tony answered. "I'm sorry we're late. We got held up at the office."

"It's okay." Mr. Carr waved his hand. "I'm sure it couldn't be helped. Now, let's talk business, shall we?"

"Okay," I said. I reached into my briefcase and took out a folder. "Here are a few things we wanted you to look through, that we thought might be to your liking." When

I reached over to hand the folder to Mr. Carr, Simone grabbed it from my hand.

"I'll take a look at these." She flipped through it while the waiter filled our glasses. "This is outrageous!" She looked at me. "I hope you don't expect us to approve this?"

I nodded my head confidently. "In fact, I do. We've done extensive research on your father's company and this appears to be the best avenue to take. Those are rough figures, but I think they're just about right."

"I don't think so," Simone said sharply.

"Let me look at them." Mr. Carr gently took the folder from her. "Simone, I don't see anything wrong with this," he said after a moment. "Honestly, I think it's in the company's best interest. It looks good, Lacie," he commended.

I looked at Mr. Carr and gave him a grateful smile. "Thank you."

Mr. Carr appeared to be excited about the ideas Tony and I had and said he would get his lawyers and business partners to go over the deal with us. Simone, however, didn't appear to like anything. Everything that came out of my mouth, she challenged. There was no satisfying her. Her bitterness annoyed me, but I tried to conceal it from her. I just sat and tried to enjoy the meal.

"So what do you think? Are you excited about working with Mr. Carr's people?" Tony asked, once we entered my office.

"Yeah. Just as long as I don't have to deal with Simone," I replied.

"Why do you say that?" he asked. "You don't like her?"

My first impulse was to tell Tony what had happened the night of Mr. Carr's birthday party, but I decided against it and chose my words carefully. "Tony, she has a problem with me. Every idea I put out there today, she kept slapping away as if they weren't solid." I sat down. "She knows absolutely nothing about his company. You and I both know what's going on here. His company is in a financial crisis. They need us. So her attitude didn't help."

"This is a big account, Lacie. It would look good for us."

"So what are you saying? Do you want me to kiss up to her? Is that it?" I asked.

"No. I'm not saying that and you know it. I just want you to hold back your personal feelings. We won't be working with her, so I doubt your paths will cross."

"Good, because I don't like anyone criticizing my job, especially when they know nothing about it," I said.

The phone rang. It was Joe.

"Hey, baby. How are you?" he asked.

"I'm fine and you?" I smiled.

Tony caught the hint and motioned that he was going to his office.

"I'm great, couldn't be better," he chuckled. "Listen, do you have any plans for tonight? There's something I want to talk to you about."

Everyone had something to talk to me about. "No, I don't have any plans. Do you want to go out?" I suggested.

"No. I want to see you at your house. Maybe I'll order some takeout for everyone. How does that sound?"

"Fine," I said. "Call me when you're ready to come over."

My conversation with Joe made me wonder. What did he want to talk about? Did he want out? I shook it off. I was thinking too much.

I got out of a meeting later than anticipated and was about to ring my house to let Mama know that I was going to be late, when I noticed that Carrie had left me a message before she left. Mama had called. She and Reneé were going shopping for maternity clothes and they would be home a little late.

I hadn't heard from Dawn all day. When I left for work, she was still in bed and I hadn't seen her at the office today. I paged her and rang her cell phone, but didn't get an answer. I knew that that episode with Ronnie had really shaken her up and I was worried about her. I decided to go on home.

When I opened the door, I saw no signs of her in the house. If Dawn were home she would've been in front of the tube by now. So, I did have the house to myself after all. I went to the kitchen and saw a note Mama had left with the same message. I thought about her visit to the office. Her concern appeared to be genuine and maybe we'd learn to get along better.

I looked through my briefcase and realized that I had left some work at the office that I needed to go over. I'd just leave early the next morning and go over it then. Right now, I had to go to the bathroom. I walked to the downstairs bathroom because it was closer than running up the stairs.

I opened the door and was unprepared for what I saw. "What the...?"

CHAPTER 11

I sat in the hospital waiting room, silently praying that Dawn was going to be all right. I had found her lying on the bathroom floor with blood on her wrist and a razor blade on the floor next to her. The ambulance had arrived quickly and after working on her, the paramedics had said they thought she'd pull through. That helped calm my nerves somewhat, but I was still concerned about her emotional stability.

How could she have done this? An emotional wreck, I got up and paced the waiting room. I looked up and saw Mama and Dawn's mother, Rose, rush in.

"What happened, Lacie? Did they say she was going to be all right?" they asked frantically.

"She's being looked at now. On the way over here, the paramedics said they thought she was going to be okay. I think they're going to get some psychiatrists to look at her, though," I replied wearily.

Rose's face was torn. "I'm going to check with the nurses. I'm sure they'll let me see her and maybe they can tell me something more," she said and left us.

Mama and I exchanged somber looks.

"Do you want to go to the cafeteria and get some coffee?" she asked.

"No," I said. "I don't want to go anywhere until I know for certain she's okay."

"C'mon. Let's sit down then." She put her arm around my shoulder and we walked to two seats in the corner. "How are you holding up?" she asked.

I shrugged and ran a hand through my hair. "I don't know, Mama. I don't know. I didn't expect this. I'm really worried about her."

She nodded sadly. "I know. When you called, we were all surprised. We knew something was wrong though because we'd expected you to be home before us. Reneé was a little shaken up about this, so I asked Robert if he could stay with her. I didn't think it would be a good idea if I brought her here. I called Rose and then we came on over."

"You know, this is so unbelievable." I stood up abruptly. "I have never known anyone to attempt suicide before and I certainly would never have expected Dawn to do something like this." I started pacing in front of Mama. "I mean, have I missed something here? Have I been so concerned about my own problems that I didn't notice that she was going through something this emotional, that would make her want to take her own life?"

Mama stood up. "Don't do this, Lacie. You can't blame yourself. Dawn has some problems and she's going to have to handle them."

"But Mama, I don't know why she did it!" I exclaimed as I started to cry. "I'm her best friend. I should have recognized some signs."

Mama grabbed my face with her hands. "Lacie, just be glad that you found her before it was too late. Be glad that she's still alive. It could have been much worse." She sighed. "Come here," she said and hugged me.

"Hey, is everything all right, here?" I heard a male voice say.

Mama and I looked up. Joe and Tony were standing there with worried expressions. I walked over to Joe swiftly and he embraced me.

"Are you okay? Tony and I came to your apartment and Robert told us you were here, so we hurried over. What happened?"

Joe and Tony shook their heads sadly when I told them.

"Is there anything we can do?" Tony asked.

I shook my head.

"Has there been any word on how she's doing?" Joe asked.

"No. We haven't heard anything yet. Her mother went to check on her a moment ago, so hopefully we'll be hearing something soon," Mama answered.

Rose came into the waiting room then and said Dawn was doing fine, but the doctors wanted to admit her into the psychiatric ward for a couple of days for observation. They wanted to make sure she wasn't going to attempt suicide again. I breathed a sigh of relief. God was certainly looking out for her.

"She asked to see you, Lacie," Rose said wearily.

"Me?" I asked.

She nodded. "Yeah. She really wants to see you."

"Okay, I'll go,"

"Do you want me to come with you?" Joe asked.

I shook my head. "I'll be fine."

I knocked on the door and heard her weak voice say, "Come in." I opened the door and walked in.

"Hey," Dawn murmured.

"Hey." I walked over to her and grabbed her hand. "How are you feeling?"

She shrugged. "Despite trying to slit my wrist, I'm doing okay." She smiled weakly. "Some attempt at suicide. I got only a few stitches."

I closed my eyes and shook my head. "Dawn, please. Don't joke about this. You really scared me."

She nodded slowly. "I know. I just wanted to make light of the situation, so you wouldn't feel uncomfortable," she said.

"It's too late for that," I replied grimly. I had to ask. "Dawn, why did you do it?"

Her expression was somber. "It's not important, Lacie."

"What do you mean, it's not important?" I raised my voice a little. "I found you unconscious on the bathroom floor, with blood on your wrist and a razor blade next to you. I wasn't expecting to see that." I leaned closer to her. "Dawn, black people don't do that," I whispered earnestly.

She chuckled softly. "You always have a knack for making me laugh in serious situations."

"I really wasn't trying to," I said honestly. "I think that's the only way I can express my feelings right now, because I'm so shocked about this whole thing. You know what I mean?"

"Yes, I do." Suddenly tears rolled down her cheeks and when I saw them, my rainfall started also. "I really did it this time, didn't I?"

"Dawn, please don't."

"I can't help it," she said, choking with tears. She squeezed my hand tightly. "I'm sorry, Lacie. I don't know what's wrong with me."

"Hey, hey, hey," I soothed. "There's nothing wrong with you."

"Yes, there is, Lacie. My life is all screwed up. I can't get an acting or modeling job, my agent's about to let me go, I'm about to lose the one job that I have now, my boyfriend is sleeping with another woman, and I almost killed myself!"

She cried continuously as I hugged her. I cried also. I felt completely helpless. I sat with her for a good while until, finally, she went to sleep. Rose had mentioned that the doctors had given her some sedatives and evidently they had taken effect.

I closed the door behind me slowly, so I wouldn't disturb her. I was about to walk down the hall when I saw Tony out of the corner of my eye.

"Oh, hey, Tony. What are you doing up here?" I asked.

He looked sympathetic. "I came up here with Joe, but he got a page and went downstairs to make a phone call. He said he wouldn't be long and asked me to stay up here in case you came out." He put a hand on my arm briefly. "How is she?"

I wiped away some tears. "She's asleep now, thank God." I sighed and crossed my arms. "Tony, I've never seen her like this. That girl in there isn't the same girl I grew up with." I looked at him as if he had an answer. "I never would have thought she'd be capable of doing something like this." I shook my head. "I should have seen this coming, but I was so into my own affairs that I didn't think about what might be… "

"Wait, wait, wait a minute," Tony said easily. "This is not your fault, Lacie."

"That's what Mama told me," I said as more tears came down. "But somehow, I don't believe it." I pointed to Dawn's room. "My best friend is in that room because she attempted to take her own life, and what scares me is that if I had arrived just a few minutes later, she'd probably be dead right now."

"Yes, but she's not. That's all that matters, Lacie."

"Yeah, you're right," I agreed tearfully. "She's my best friend, Tony. I was so scared when I saw her on that bathroom floor, you know? I thought I'd lost her."

"I know," he said softly, holding me while I cried uncontrollably. "Shh…shh…" he soothed, stroking my hair and rubbing my back.

I held on to him and continued to cry. Once my crying had finally subsided, he handed me a handkerchief and looked into my eyes.

"Did that cry make you feel better?"

I nodded and blew my nose. "Yeah. I've been keeping it in."

He nodded. "I know. You're always trying to act stronger than you really are. It's okay to show your feelings, Lacie."

"I know, but… " I stopped and looked at him. "Are we talking about the same thing here?" I asked.

He shrugged and looked at me intently. "I don't know. Are we?"

I looked away and cleared my throat. "So, what were you and Joe doing before you two came over my house?" I asked.

He grinned, knowing that I had deliberately changed the subject. "Oh, we were hanging out together, catching up on a few things and talking about business. That kind of stuff."

"I thought you'd be out with Simone."

"Why would you think that?"

"Never mind," I said abruptly, regretting that I had even brought up her name.

He wasn't going to let it go that easily. "Why, Lacie?"

"No reason," I replied, shrugging my shoulders.

"Are you sure?" he asked.

Joe came around the corner before I could reply. "How's Dawn?" I shook my head vaguely. "She's going to be all right, Lacie. She's a fighter." He gave me a hug. "Now how are you feeling?"

"I'm doing a little better."

"That's my girl," he said softly.

Tony cleared his throat. "I think I'm going to go. I've got a few things to do before tomorrow."

Joe shook his hand. "Thanks, man. Thanks for coming. I really appreciate it."

"No problem. I wanted to make sure everyone was okay," Tony said and looked directly at me. "I'll see you tomorrow, man. You too, Lacie," he said and walked off.

Joe, Mama and I left the hospital, leaving Rose alone with her daughter. I couldn't help feeling sorry for Rose. I couldn't begin to fathom how she felt, knowing that her only daughter had attempted suicide. It was hard enough for *me* to deal with.

It was late when we got home and Mama went upstairs and left us alone. I sat down on the sofa heavily and Joe sat beside me.

We sat there silently while he held me and rubbed my arms. I finally decided to get up and fix something to eat, because I hadn't eaten anything since the lunch meeting with Mr. Carr. I asked Joe if he wanted anything and he said he wasn't hungry, but he followed me to the kitchen and watched me heat up some leftovers in the microwave. I didn't say anything. I couldn't. I had nothing to say.

Finally he came up behind me and put his arms around my waist. "Listen, I know this whole situation with Dawn is really eating at you, but I need to tell you something."

"What? What is it?" I asked, turning around to face him.

"Don't get alarmed, Lacie. It's okay," he assured.

"Then what is it?" I repeated.

"You know that my business here in New York is almost over, right?" I nodded. "I'm going to have to return to

Miami soon and work on some other projects for my company."

I nodded my head again. "Yeah, I figured you'd be getting ready to leave soon."

He took a deep breath and touched my face lightly with one finger. "Lacie, I want you to come with me," he said earnestly.

"What?"

"I want you to come with me," he repeated. "I really don't want to leave, but I do have a business in Miami to run and it calls for me to be there."

"I know that, but I can't leave. My family is here and my job is here. I can't leave just like that," I declared softly, with a snap of my fingers.

"You can work for my company," he offered. "I have a position that would be perfect for you and with more money."

I shook my head. "No, Joe. That's not the answer, baby. I've worked hard to get where I am with Ryan and Company. I like my job."

"Who's to say you won't like the job I'm offering you?"

"I may like it, but I'd be sleeping with you at the same time, Joe." That suddenly made me recall what had happened with Tony.

"So? I don't care about that."

"I know. But I care about it, Joe. You should know me better than that. I refuse to take a high paying job with your company just because you're my boyfriend," I insisted. "If things were different, I'd go with you, but there's my job and there's just too much going on right now. I can't leave and forget everything and everyone that's here."

"And I can't stay," he said.

There was a strained silence.

"So what do we do now?" I asked.

"I don't know. I don't like long distance relationships. I like to have the people that I love around me."

I shrugged helplessly. "I'm sorry, but I can't leave, Joe. This isn't the right time."

His expression was unrevealing. "Then I guess we already know what to do."

I helplessly watched him walk out the kitchen and leave. I don't know why I didn't stop him.

I was in a bad mood the next day at work. I hadn't heard a word from Joe after the previous night. I called him several times, but got the answering machine. This was our first argument and I didn't like it. We'd been getting along so well. Couldn't he see that I was unable to go? Didn't he understand that I had a life of my own? Oh, it was so frustrating!

Carrie sensed my mood and left me alone for the first part of the morning. I kept quiet during the meetings and noticed Tony giving me a quizzical glance every now and then. I didn't care. I was upset.

Mama called and suggested that we go out to lunch. It was her treat again. I agreed. I didn't have much of an appetite, but I knew that I needed some time away from the office.

"You're going to let your food get cold," Mama said.

"Huh?" I looked up.

"Lacie, that pasta's going to be up to your elbows if you don't stop twirling it around on that spoon," she remarked.

"I'm sorry." I breathed deeply. "I don't have much of an appetite."

Mama nodded her head. "You're upset about that argument you and Joe had last night, aren't you?" she asked, chewing her food.

"How did you know?"

She shrugged. "I heard some of it when I went to the bathroom," she replied. "So are you going to tell me what the argument was about?"

I ran a hand through my hair. "He wants me to move to Miami with him, Mama."

"So what's so bad about that?"

"Don't get me wrong. I would love to go with him, but I'd be giving up a lot if I did. Yes, a part of me does want to go, but I just got that promotion with Ryan and Company. I can't leave on a whim. That wouldn't be right."

"Didn't he offer you a job with his company?"

"Just how much of our conversation did you hear? Never mind," I said quickly. "He did offer me a job, but that's not the point. I can't accept his offer because it's a biased one. If I weren't involved with him, he wouldn't have offered me a job that easily."

"Maybe he wants more in your relationship than just you two dating each other."

"I don't know." I shook my head. "He didn't ask me to marry him. He just said he wanted me to move to Miami. That's a long way for me to go for a non-committed relationship, Mama. We haven't even been with each other for a year."

"Do you think he only wants you down there for a fling?" she asked.

"No, I don't think that. I'm only saying that he's expecting me to give up a lot for him and I don't know if I'm willing to do that just yet."

"Lacie, Reneé and I aren't going anywhere. We're family. We're always going to be there for you and if you move to Miami, then maybe we'll move also. I don't know. As for the job, you've got your degree and you've got experience. You shouldn't have any problem getting a job if you don't want to work for Joe's company. The only real question is whether your feelings are strong enough for him to make such a move."

I thought about what Mama had said on the way back to the office. I had a lot to decide. I felt Joe was right for me, but why was I so reluctant to leave with him? Why was this so hard for me?

When I walked into my office, I didn't notice that Carrie wasn't at her desk.

"What in the world!" I said, whirling around when I heard the door slam.

Tony stood there with an infuriated look on his face.

"Don't you know it's rude to slam doors?" I chided. "What's wrong with you?"

Tony came up to me and looked me straight in the eye. "I just came from seeing Richard. Joe's threatening to renege on our deal. He said that Joe wants you to work for his company and if you don't, he's going to back out."

I was taken aback. I couldn't believe what I was hearing. "Are you kidding?"

His expression was hard. "No, I'm not. Did you know about this?"

I sat down slowly in my chair, dumbfounded. "Are you sure he said this?"

"Yes. At least that's the way it was relayed to me. Now did you know anything about this?" he asked again, in an accusatory tone.

"No, Tony." He looked skeptical. "Okay, listen. Joe did offer me a job with his company and asked me to go to Miami with him, but he didn't mention anything about backing down on the deal."

"Oh. So you're actually thinking about taking him up on his offer?" he asked in that same accusing tone.

"I don't know, Tony." I hunched up my shoulders. "I mean, when he asked me, he caught me off guard. I told him I didn't think I could. Now I just don't know."

He glared at me for a while. "Okay," he said suddenly. "I'll explain everything to Richard. Maybe we can figure out what the hell is going on here."

I watched him march out the office. He was very upset. I quickly called Joe on his cell phone. This time, I got an answer.

"Are you trying to get me fired?" I asked loudly.

"No. What are you talking about?" he asked.

I reiterated everything that Tony had said. He said nothing. "Is this true?"

"Yes," he admitted. He sighed. "Lacie, listen…"

I didn't want to hear his explanation. "Joe, how could you do this? You know how much this job means to me. How could you give them an ultimatum like that? I thought you said I'd earned your account?"

"You did, but I told you that I like to get what I want, Lacie. If dropping my account from your firm is the only way that I can get you to move to Miami with me, then that's just how it's going to be."

"So in other words, just forget about what happens to me, is that it? Forget that this may jeopardize my career with this company, right?" I asked.

"It's not like that," he began.

I cut him off. "Joe, listen to me very carefully," I stressed. "If you think that I would move with you to Miami after you have ruined my job here, then you have really lost it. I don't appreciate it when a person claims to love me one day, then stabs me in the back the next day. I know you like to get what you want. You've already proven that. But let me tell you one thing. If you care for me and love me like you say you do, then you won't drop this account. If you do, then you can forget about me ever going anywhere with you!" I slammed the phone down.

Carrie walked in. "You have a fight with lover boy?"

I held up my hand. "Don't go there, Carrie. I'm not in the mood."

"So are you going to leave?" she asked directly.

"How did you hear about it so fast?"

"Are you kidding? Nothing stays secret around here for long. News travels fast. Plus, I heard you two through the door."

I just shook my head.

I was packing my briefcase and getting ready to leave when I heard a soft knock on the door. It was Tony.

"What? No slam this time?" I quipped.

"Uh, no. No slam. Just a friendly knock. I thought I should, since you almost bit my head off earlier," he replied.

I glared at him. "Excuse me, but I think you did the biting, not me."

"C'mon, Lacie. What did you expect me to do? I wasn't expecting to hear that Joe was going to renege on the deal and that you might leave and go to Miami with him. It caught me off guard." He sighed. "Anyway, Joe called. He's going to stay with us. He's not dropping the account."

I looked at him nonchalantly and grabbed my coat and briefcase. "I'm glad to hear that everything worked out. Maybe you won't be too quick to assume next time."

"I didn't assume..."

"Yes, you did, Tony. You did everything but accuse me of knowing about it and almost being behind it. Now, if you'll excuse me, I've got to be somewhere." I tried to get by, but he blocked me with his hand.

"Wait a minute." He paused. "Are you going to take him up on his offer?"

"I'm not even thinking about that right now. I just want to leave here and go straight to the hospital to see Dawn." I walked past him and headed toward the lobby.

He walked behind me. "Richard said he'd really hate to lose you."

I shrugged and pushed the down button on the elevator. "That's nice to hear, but like I said before, I'm not thinking about that right now."

"Let me give you a ride to the hospital," he offered as he began to walk back into the office.

The elevator came. "No," I responded sharply. "The elevator's here and I can't wait." I stepped in. "I'll see you tomorrow," I said as the door closed.

Dawn appeared to be in brighter spirits. She was animated and talkative.

"So what's the diagnosis? How long do you have to be in here?" I asked.

"Not long. They want me to stay another day, and then I can leave."

"Do you want to stay with me or with your mother?"

"I'm going to stay with my mom." She saw the surprise on my face. "I think this whole ordeal has really scared her and she wants to make sure that I'm going to be all right."

"That's understandable. I hope everything works out between you two."

She peered at me. "Your mother told me that Joe asked you to move to Miami with him. Are you going?"

"I don't know. Everything is happening so fast, you know?"

"I understand," she nodded. "You've got to realize, though, that men like him don't come easily."

"You keep telling me that, Dawn," I groaned.

"Yes, and I'm going to keep on telling you. Lacie, he is so in love with you. You should have heard how much he talked about you during Thanksgiving." She pointed to herself. "I don't have a man who loves me like he loves you. All I had was my own hopes and expectations of a man that I knew couldn't make me happy. And look at me now. You get what I'm saying?" She paused. "Lacie, I would give anything to have a man like him. Haven't you always said you wanted to get married and have children someday? Here's your chance. You've got him in the palm of your hand." She motioned with a slap of her hands. "What are you waiting for?"

"I'm not waiting for anything."

"So you say," she muttered.

I left Dawn shortly thereafter and went home. I walked into the apartment and saw Mama, Reneé, Robert and Joe sitting in the living room watching television. I raised my eyebrows at them.

Joe stood up. "Hi," he said tentatively.

"Hi," I replied. I took off my coat and hung it on the coat hanger. "What's going on?"

"We're all just hanging out. We were thinking of ordering something to eat," Mama answered.

Joe looked at me. "Can I talk to you in the kitchen for a minute?" he asked.

I shrugged. "Sure."

Once in the kitchen, he motioned for me to sit at the table.

"The first thing I want to do is apologize. I was wrong for the way I acted on the phone and definitely wrong for the way I handled everything with your job. That was selfish of me. I shouldn't have put you in that kind of predicament. I know how much you love your job. Are you still angry with me?" he asked.

"No, not really. I just don't understand what made you do something like that. It was like you didn't care about how I felt or what I thought," I replied.

He shook his head. "No, that's not how I wanted to come off."

"How did you think I was going to take it, Joe?" I exclaimed softly. "You threatened my boss with an ulti-matum and almost jeopardized my job."

"I know. I know." He nodded. "I'm sorry. I don't know what else to tell you." He opened his arms wide. "I got a little anxious, that's all. You know I like to get what I want."

"What about what I want?"

"I'm going to get to that in a minute," he said mischie-vously, grabbing my hand. "Listen, I was wrong. I can admit that. But I also admit that I am terribly in love with you."

"Joe, you've already told me how you felt…"

"No, hear me out first," he interjected softly. "Lacie, the first thing you need to know about me is that I'm not one for words at times."

I raised my hand.

He smiled and nodded. "Go ahead."

"What about all those nice things you said to me on our first date?" I asked.

"Oh, that was only so I could get you into bed," he joked. I slapped him on the arm playfully. "Just teasing," he said and laughed. "But it didn't work. I took you home and that was that. You get what I'm saying here? I have a problem expressing my true feelings. When I do try to express how I feel, it usually comes out the wrong way. What I'm trying to say is that, that whole issue with the account and everything was my way of trying to keep you with me."

I thought about what Mama said.

He continued. "I know what I did was bad and that made a mess of the whole situation. So after you hung up on me, I called Richard immediately and straightened out everything."

"Yeah, Tony told me."

He nodded. "Now, I'm going to make something else right."

He took my left hand and before I knew it, he'd slipped a huge diamond ring on my finger. I looked at him in awe.

He smiled tenderly and brushed my cheek with one finger. "I love you, Lacie. I have never met a woman like you before. You're smart, sexy, compassionate, sentimental, and you've got this unbelievably witty way about you that drives me crazy." We both chuckled softly as he leaned his forehead against mine. "Will you marry me?" he asked.

CHAPTER 12

I couldn't believe that he'd asked me that question. I took another look at my hand and realized it was true. I didn't know what to say at first. I glanced at his hopeful, expectant gaze and remembered what Mama and Dawn had said.

"Yes, I'll marry you," I answered decisively and smiled as he embraced me and then kissed me.

"Well, it's about time!" I heard Mama exclaim.

Joe and I looked up and saw Mama, Reneé and Robert standing in the doorway.

"How long have you three been standing there?" I asked.

"Just about the entire time," Robert said. "He told us that he was going to ask you."

I looked at all of their faces. "Oh really? So all of you knew?" They nodded in unison. "I should have known." I shook my head.

"Girl, hush and give me a hug," Mama said, chuckling as she walked over to me. "Congratulations, Lacie," she whispered, embracing me. "I'm very happy for you."

"Thanks, Mama," I murmured.

"So when's the date?" Reneé asked.

"We haven't decided that yet," Joe answered.

"Yeah, we've got a few things we need to iron out first," I said.

"Don't let it be before my baby's born. I can't be a bridesmaid with a big belly." Reneé indicated her stomach with a pat.

"Relax, Reneé. It won't be for a while," I said.

"Not unless I get her pregnant," Joe added.

"Joe!" I exclaimed.

He smiled. "I was only joking." He laughed and kissed me on the forehead.

"Well, don't do that!" I said.

"Aww, their first fight as an engaged couple," Robert cooed sarcastically. I caught the tone in his voice and gave him a look.

"Lacie, I promised to take your mother and Reneé to Macy's for a few things. Do you want to go with us?" Joe asked.

"No, I'll stay here. I've got some work to catch up on, so you all go ahead," I replied.

"Okay. You want to ride along, man?" he asked Robert.

"No, I think I'll stay back also. I need to talk to Lacie about something," Robert answered.

I closed the front door after Joe, Reneé and Mama left and leaned against it and looked at the ring on my finger. It was gorgeous. I smiled. Everything was going to work out just as I had always dreamed.

Robert stood outside the doorway of the kitchen. "Are you ready for a big brother talk now?" he asked.

I glanced at him suspiciously. "It depends on what you want to talk about. What was the reason for that look you gave me?"

"I wasn't trying to hide it. It was meant for you and you know what it was about," he said as we walked into the kitchen.

"No, actually, I don't, Robert." I took some cabbage out of the refrigerator and grabbed a knife from the counter to cut it up. I thought broiled lamb chops, cabbage and noodles would be nice to have for dinner.

"Lacie, what are you doing?" he said gently.

"What do you mean?"

"What in your right mind possessed you to accept Joe's proposal?"

I stopped cutting the cabbage and gave him a perplexed look. "Did you think I was going to say no?"

"I didn't think you were going to say 'yes'. An 'I'll think about it' or a 'maybe' would have been better than that," he retorted. "Why are you so determined to be with Joe?"

"Robert, have you noticed how good-looking Joe is? Have you noticed how he treats me? Have you noticed anything about our relationship? When a man like him proposes, you don't say, 'I'll think about' or 'maybe.' You jump on it."

"Joe is handsome. I agree with you. But you shouldn't marry him if you're not in love with him."

"Who says we're going to get married just yet?" I said defiantly. "I mean, we're not ready to go to the justice of the peace or anything. We're only engaged."

Robert shook his head. "Lacie, who are you trying to fool? Open your eyes, girl! That man is ready to take you to Vegas tomorrow and have you walk down the aisle with Elvis if he has to. He's not joking. This isn't a game with him, Lacie. He's in love with you and you're trying to play hackeysack with his heart!"

"Listen, I do love him," I defended. "I care about Joe a lot. He's exactly what I've been looking for in a man and I know that he loves me with all his heart and soul and that makes me believe that this is the right thing to do."

Suddenly Robert said, "What about your feelings for Tony, Lacie?"

"I…"

"See, you're not in love with Joe," Robert insisted.

"Dammit, Robert!" I slammed the knife down. "How do you know that? Huh? How do you know that I'm not in love with him?" I argued.

"If you were then we wouldn't be having this discussion, would we?" he asked softly.

I groaned and ran a hand through my hair. "Robert, listen to me. Just a few minutes ago, that man put a ring on my finger and that made me feel so good. Do you know how long I've waited for a moment like that? This is not an issue of how I feel about him, but how happy I am right now. Isn't that the most important thing? I mean, we can argue about this later or on another day, but for this minute can't you be happy that I'm happy?"

Robert looked at me fondly and grabbed my hands. "Are you really happy?" he asked, searching my face.

"Yes," I strained out.

"Liar," he said and we both laughed as he grabbed me in a big bear hug.

Joe, Reneé and Mama returned in a couple of hours, and almost immediately conversation turned toward plans for the wedding.

"Wait a minute. Hold up," I said. "It's too soon to be talking about wedding plans. We haven't even figured out a date."

"It has to be soon. I can't go through a long engagement. It's too stressful and you wind up spending more money than originally planned," Mama voiced.

"She's right, Lacie," Joe said as I sat on his lap. "Why don't we set a date?"

"For when?" I asked.

"How about in June? I've always wanted a summer wedding," he said.

"No, it's too hot during that month. How about September?" Mama suggested.

"A December wedding is nice and romantic," Reneé added.

This was going way too fast. I stood up from Joe's lap and grabbed his hand. "I need to talk to you for a minute."

As soon as we walked into the kitchen, he grabbed my waist. "What's up, beautiful?"

"Joe, I think we need to slow down a bit," I said carefully.

He frowned a little. "What do you mean?"

"It was only a couple of hours ago that you asked me to marry you. I haven't decided what I'm going to do about my job or when I'm going to move or anything. You just said that you have to leave for Miami soon and I'm not going to be able to make arrangements that easily."

He smiled. "Relax. I'm not expecting you to move that soon. Listen, I'm going home for Christmas and after I come back, we can discuss everything then. There's no rush," he said gently. He took a deep breath. "Tell you what. I'll let you decide on the date, so that way you'll be more at ease and then I won't have a nervous wreck on my hands."

I smiled. "Thank you for understanding."

"Hey, that's what I'm here for," he said, hugging me.

I decided to get an early start at work. I deliberated on whether I should wear the ring or not. I didn't want to make a spectacle of myself and I was sure once everyone saw it, they were bound to ask questions. I decided to wear it anyway. There was nothing to be ashamed of.

By the time I reached the office, I had forgotten that the ring was on my finger. The floor was empty except for a few janitors finishing their shift. I walked directly to my office and left the door open.

I was sitting at my desk reading some documents when Tony knocked on the door and peeped in.

"Hey, partner," he said. "Are you still angry with me? Is it okay if I come in?"

I smiled, shaking my head. "No, Tony. I'm not mad at you and yes, you can come in."

He grinned as he walked in. "What are you doing here? You usually don't come in this early."

"I should ask you the same question," I bantered with a smile. "Rarely do you ever come in at seven in the morning, Tony."

"Good point," he agreed with a nod. "I had some work to catch up on, and since we've got a few new clients coming in, I decided to get a good start," he explained.

"I know. I'm trying to do that also," I said with a groan, indicating the paper in my hand. "Can you come over here for a second? There's something I want to show you." He dropped his coat and briefcase on a chair and walked over to my side of the desk. "You see this? I've been going over this chart and the figures don't seem to be right. I can't figure out why. I know I put in all the information that I needed." I looked at him. "Do you think I forgot something?" I asked.

He pointed to a clear error that I had missed. "The percentage is off. That's why it didn't add up correctly."

"You're right. I guess I couldn't see the mistake because I've been staring at it for so long."

"You did forget something else, though."

"What?" I looked at the paper again to see what he was talking about.

"Are congratulations in order?" he asked, pointing to my finger.

I blushed and unconsciously tried to hide my hand. It had slipped my mind.

"It's no use trying to hide it now." He grabbed my hand to get a closer look. "Wow! That's a beautiful ring. I'm sure Joe paid a pretty penny for it," he remarked softly as he rubbed my hand and gazed at me. "I guess this is the reason you're in such a good mood. Joe mentioned that he had something important to ask you, but I didn't know he was going to ask you to marry him."

I felt uncomfortable and removed my hand from his grasp. "Uh, yeah, it surprised me also."

"I guess you've made up your mind, then, huh?" he asked. "You're leaving, then."

I shrugged. "There's nothing in stone or anything, but yes, I will leave eventually."

"Has a date been set?"

"No, not yet," I answered. "Joe did mention June, but it's not definite."

We heard someone cough. It was Carrie. "Sorry, Lacie. I didn't mean to interrupt you. I'm going to get some coffee and was wondering if you wanted any," she explained.

"It's okay, Carrie. You didn't interrupt anything," I replied. "Yes. You can bring me a cup and just put a little bit of cream and sugar in it."

"Okay," she said and left.

Tony watched her leave, then turned back to me. "Don't you think it's a little too soon for you and Joe to be considering marriage?"

"Not really," I replied calmly.

"Lacie, you two have only been dating for a couple of months," he reasoned. "You don't know each other well enough to be talking about marriage."

I took a deep breath before I spoke. "Tony, I just told you that we're thinking about June. That gives us plenty of time to get to know each other better."

He sneered and muttered, "You slept with him, didn't you?"

I was taken aback by his attitude, but recovered. I stood up abruptly. "That's none of your business, Tony! What is wrong with you?" I cried out angrily.

Apparently, he'd surprised himself also. "I...listen...I didn't mean..." he stammered. He stopped, composed himself, and then took a deep breath. He raised his hand. "I just think you're rushing into this, that's all."

I was unconcerned. "Well, I don't think I am."

"Lacie, why would you want to leave this company after all of the progress you've made? Things are going so well for you here."

I'd had enough interrogation. I was aggravated and he had ticked me off. "You know what? I'm not going to explain this to you. It's none of your concern. I'm doing what I want to do, Tony, and that's all you need to know."

"What about doing what's right for you?"

"I am doing what's right for me!" I blared indignantly.

He glared at me for a long time, then walked swiftly to the chair and grabbed his coat and briefcase. "Whatever. We've got a lot of meetings today, so be on your Ps and Qs. I don't want you to be too worked up to do business."

"Hey, I alway mind my Ps and Qs!" I retorted after his retreating figure.

Carrie came in. "What's going on? I could hear you two in the kitchen."

"Nothing," I murmured sharply, taking the coffee from her. "And what are you doing here so early anyway?" I demanded.

"You're just now realizing that?" she mocked, ignoring my question and pointing to my hand. "I take it Tony's not happy with that rock on your finger."

"That's not my problem." I glared at her. "Do you have something to say also?"

She held up her hands. "No, not at all."

"Okay, then."

"That is a beautiful ring, though, Lacie," she said.

"Thank you. Now let's drop it."

"Aren't we feisty?"

"Carrie," I warned.

"Okay, okay, I'll leave you alone." She closed the door.

I sat down and just held my head.

It didn't take long for news to spread that I was engaged. In the midst of all of the congratulations, I received a call from Mr. Ryan. He wanted to see me.

I knocked on his door.

"Come in, Lacie," I heard him say.

"You asked to see me, Mr. Ryan?" I asked, walking in.

"Yes, Lacie. Have a seat, will you?" He motioned for me to sit in front of his desk. "How's everything going downstairs? Is everyone treating you okay?" he inquired.

I shrugged. "Yes, of course."

"Good." He nodded with satisfaction, then leaned back in his chair. "Uh, Lacie, I'm going to get right to the point. When Joe threatened to renege on the deal, I was very upset."

"I know, Mr. Ryan. I'm sorry about that," I said.

He waved his hand. "Don't apologize. That's water under the bridge now. We had a long talk and we were able to work things out. He's going to stay with us." He paused. "I am concerned about something else, though. Tony informed me that you're still planning on leaving us to work for Joe's company. He was very upset. Aren't you happy with us?"

"Mr. Ryan..." I started to explain.

He held up his hand. "Lacie, please call me Richard. This is just a friendly chat and as far as I'm concerned, we're both colleagues here."

I cocked my head a little. "Fine...ah...Richard. Let me explain something," I began. "The past month or so has been incredible, what with the promotion and all. I don't exactly know what Tony said to you, but I doubt that he explained the whole story."

"So what's going on?"

I smiled. "Joe asked me to marry him and I accepted. As far as working for him is concerned, I doubt that will happen. I'm not going to marry Joe and work for him as well."

"Ah," Richard said. He leaned back in his chair and nodded. "Now I get the picture."

"I'm sorry that you didn't get the complete story from me first," I said. "A lot has happened and it was kind of personal..."

"I understand." He smiled kindly. "So when's the big day?"

"It's in the air right now. I'm still a little unsure of how I'm going to handle everything."

"That's understandable. Getting married is a big step." He nodded. "I've got to be straightforward with you, though. I love having you here. You're very proficient and zealous in your work and you've done a lot for this firm."

"Thank you. Tony said you'd hate to lose me."

"That's true. You'll be very hard to replace," he admitted. "I'd really like for you to stay on as long as possible. There's no need to rush, is there?"

"No, not at all," I replied.

"That's wonderful to hear. We'll continue to work as usual. Just let me know if there's anything I can do." He smiled. "Thank you for coming up here so that we could clear this whole matter up."

"You're welcome." I smiled and stood up to leave.

"Lacie." Richard's voice stopped me at the door.

"Yes?"

"I'm having a Christmas party at the Sheraton Saturday. It's a formal affair that I have every year and I'd like for you to be there. It starts at eight o'clock and you're welcome to bring Joe along."

"Thank you. We'll be there."

I had a considerable number of meetings to attend the rest of the day. It was hectic and Tony's attitude made it almost unbearable at times. He barely said a word to me and avoided sitting next to me. I was annoyed with his behavior and was so glad when five o'clock rolled around.

Joe came to get me.

"Hey, sweetie," I greeted him with a smile.

"Sweetie? You've never called me that before. What's up?"

"Nothing. I'm just glad to see you, that's all." I walked over and hugged him.

"That's good to hear," he said, returning my hug. "Are you ready?"

"Yes. Let me get my briefcase and coat." I walked to the closet.

"I just came from seeing Richard," Joe said.

"So everything is okay now, right?" I asked as he helped me with my coat.

He nodded. "Yeah. I don't think there are any hard feelings. Although we talked on the phone, I felt I should talk to him in person. I wanted to explain why I acted the way I did."

"I'm glad you did. I was in his office earlier today and we talked," I said. "He doesn't want me to leave, but he understood and congratulated me. He also invited us to his Christmas party Saturday."

"Yeah, he mentioned that to me also. I'm not going to be able to go," Joe said.

"Why not?"

"C'mon, I'll tell you in the car."

Joe told me that he was going to leave early for Miami for an emergency meeting and wouldn't be back until Saturday night.

"You have to go away again?" I asked. "I was hoping you'd be able to go with me."

"I'm sorry Lacie, there's no way around it."

"All right," I sulked. "I'll ask Robert. Maybe he'll go."

I continued to mope after Joe left for Miami. For some reason, his presence at the party meant a lot to me and I couldn't help feeling disappointed. Robert, however, agreed to stand in for him and that made me feel a little better.

Tony continued to avoid me as the week progressed, and I decided to just ignore him also. I was getting too old for foolishness.

Reneé at almost four months was starting to get a little stomach. She was glowing with happiness because Danny had reentered her life after she called him and told him she was keeping their child. He came by every other day. I was worried about how Mama would react to him, but they seemed to get along. Everything was going well for Reneé and I was really happy for her.

Mama and I were getting along also, though I had started to wonder how long it would last. We still hadn't had the talk she wanted and I was curious about it.

I heard from Dawn, who said that she was really getting along with her mother also. When I told her about my engagement to Joe, she was happy for me. She, in turn, told me that Ronnie had come by to ask her back, but that she'd slammed the door in his face. I was proud of her. My girl was growing up.

❧

At seven o'clock, the night of Mr. Ryan's party, Mama and I were upstairs and I was getting ready.

"Lacie, will you hold still? I'm having trouble zipping this up," Mama said.

"I'm sorry. I just had a little itch I had to scratch," I explained.

"You shouldn't have an itch after just taking a bath," she said. "Did you get all the important places?"

"Mama!"

"I had to ask," she defended.

"I know, but I think I'm old enough to know how to take a bath."

"Good. That means I taught you well," she said as she finished with the zipper. "Child, how much do you weigh? I sure had enough trouble with your zipper."

"Mama, I've worn this dress before. It's always been hard to zip. That's why I asked you to help me."

"Okay, I was just asking," she said. "Just so you know, it's hard to keep a man when you start gaining weight."

"Mama, where did you hear that?" I laughed.

"Don't worry about that. I've been around long enough to know these things."

I shook my head. My mother and her ideas. I changed the subject by asking, "Which of these do you think I should wear with this dress?" I held up a pair of pearl and a pair of gold earrings.

She took the earrings and held them up to my dress. "Wear the pearls. They look more glamorous. I don't want you going there looking like a hootchie-mama," she said, and we both started laughing. She put the earrings in my ear as we stood in front of the mirror. "Lacie, you look so pretty," she admired when she finished putting them in. "If Joe were here to see you, he wouldn't let you go out in that dress."

"Mama, I'm not going alone. Robert is coming with me," I reminded her.

"Yeah, but he doesn't count. He's not all man."

"Mama, that's not nice. You shouldn't have said that," I scolded.

"I know. I know. I do love that boy to death. I'm always teasing him," she said, brushing some lint off my dress.

I took another look in the mirror. "Mama, do you think this dress is all right?"

"Yes, Lacie. It's gorgeous and so are you." She smiled.

"Thank you. Now let's go downstairs, because Robert's waiting."

We walked toward the door.

"Lacie?" Mama asked.

"Yes, Mama."

"Do you ever wonder what makes them be that way?"

"Who, Mama?"

I should have known what she was talking about. "Gay people," she whispered anxiously.

"I have no idea. Why don't you ask Robert about that?" I suggested, shaking my head as I opened the door.

Robert and I arrived at the Sheraton just before eight. In the lobby I was suddenly worried about how I looked again.

"What?" Robert asked.

I turned toward him. "How do I look?"

"You look beautiful. This is your fifth time asking me that question. What's up with you?"

"I don't know. I feel weird all of a sudden and people are looking at us," I whispered.

"That's because we are both good looking people and you look stunning in that dress," he said confidently. "Why are you so nervous all of a sudden?"

I shook my head. "I don't know. I've got a strange feeling about this whole thing. Something is going to go wrong. I just know it." I peered at him. "Are you certain I look okay?"

"Lacie, if I were straight, I'd be attracted to you. Does that answer your question?" He huffed. "Can we go in now, please?"

"Yes, but one more thing."

"Yes?"

"Thanks for coming with me on such short notice. I really appreciate it."

He rolled his eyes upward. "That's okay. It's not like I have a man at home or anything," he remarked dryly. "I may find one, though. You never know." He put my arm in his. "C'mon, they're waiting on us," he said, indicating a doorman standing at the entrance of the ballroom.

The ballroom was magnificently decorated in the spirit of Christmas. A tall, green Christmas tree decorated with lights, tinsel, ornaments and fake presents under it, stood in the center. Angels surrounded the room on the walls and there were silver, gold and green streamers and balloons hanging everywhere.

Richard Ryan and his wife, April, greeted us immediately. I introduced Robert and explained that Joe couldn't make it because he had to go out of town. While they continued to welcome guests, Richard and April told us to enjoy the party and invited us to sit at their table.

"They seem like a nice couple," Robert remarked as we watched them walk away.

"Yes, they do," I agreed. "I don't know much about her, but Richard is very nice."

As Robert and I walked around the ballroom, I noticed a couple of people from the job, then saw Carrie and her husband. When we walked over to them, Carrie seemed surprised to see Robert, but I introduced him and explained why Joe wasn't there. We sat and talked with them for a while, until the band began to play a nice slow tune. Carrie and her husband got up to dance, and Robert stood up and held out his hand. I shook my head.

"C'mon, Lacie," he urged.

Reluctantly, I stood and we headed for the dance floor. Robert held me with ease as we danced.

"Umm, the way you're holding me, I'd swear you were trying to hit on me," I teased.

"Don't get any ideas. I don't go for women," he replied.

"I know. I know. Just wishful thinking, I guess," I bantered.

As we danced, the floor grew crowded. I noticed Carrie and her husband dancing near us, and when Robert turned me around suddenly, I saw Tony and Simone dancing cheek-to-cheek. Staring at them, I stiffened up immediately.

"Careful, your claws are showing," Robert murmured.

"No, they're not!" I snapped.

"Oh, please. If looks could kill," he suggested.

I looked at him abruptly. "Don't, Robert."

He shook his head. "I don't know why you do this to yourself," he said. "C'mon, I see Richard signaling us."

We walked off the floor leaving Tony, Simone and everyone else dancing. I was suddenly very irritated and didn't understand why.

Once we reached the table, Richard directed us to sit across from him. Just then, Tony and Simone came over hand-in-hand, and Richard also asked them to sit at the table. I avoided looking in their direction.

Simone, glowing with happiness, spoke first. "Well, hello, Lacie. It's nice to see you," she said, flashing that model smile. *What a liar!* I really wanted to kick those teeth in. "Aren't you going to introduce us to your new boyfriend?" she goaded.

Robert spoke up first. "My name is Robert and I'm not her new boyfriend. I'm a good friend of Joe and Lacie's. Joe couldn't be here, so I'm taking his place," he replied easily.

Simone looked at me with a cold smile. "Oh? Is there trouble in paradise already?"

"No," I replied evenly. "We're doing fine."

Robert chimed in. "As a matter of fact, they're engaged."

Simone, obviously pleased with the news, looked at Tony. "Really? Isn't that something? Tony, did you know that Joe and Lacie were engaged?"

Not answering Simone's question, Tony shot me a quick look.

Richard answered for him. "We all know, actually, and we're very happy for her. We'll miss her dearly," he said, giving me a smile.

I smiled my thanks in return.

"So Lacie, when is the big day? I assume you'll be leaving soon," Simone said eagerly.

"I'm not leaving the company just yet. Richard wants me to stay on as long as I can before I move to Miami," I replied.

"Oh." Dismay came over her face and her eyes immediately turned cold. When the waiter came over and filled our glasses with champagne, she took a gulp from her glass. "Are you sure that's the best thing? I mean, I'm sure Joe must want his fiancée with him in Miami."

I wanted to tell her to mind her own damn business, but I kept calm. "That's something Joe and I have to decide together. Besides, I'm sure there are more interesting things to discuss than my personal life."

Simone blinked her eyelashes quickly. "I was only curious," she said haughtily. "My father is planning on doing business with this company and it's imperative that his interest is protected."

Tony finally said something. "It is, Simone. Your father picked us because he felt confident that we would do just that," he remarked, sensing her hostility.

"I'm not so sure," she said obstinately. "I think someone else should have the account. Lacie may be too preoccupied with her personal business to handle it." She took another gulp of her champagne.

I got offended. "Are you questioning my ability to do my job?" I asked directly.

"Yes," she answered with a mean smile. "I don't want my father's account to be mishandled."

"Let me tell you…" I started.

Richard spoke up. "Uh, Simone…Lacie is very professional and capable of handling all the accounts that come into her hands. Your father was impressed with her work and requested that only she and Tony work on his account."

"Still I insist…" Simone began.

Tony interrupted her. "Simone, that's enough," he warned.

I didn't want to hear any more. "Excuse me. I have to go to the powder room." I got up from the table abruptly, leaving them all looking after me. I walked into the ladies' room and found it empty. I stared at my reflection in the mirror. "Lacie, don't let her get to you."

I took a handkerchief from my purse and patted my little beads of sweat off my forehead. After that, I checked my whole appearance. My makeup and hair still looked good and my dress was definitely saying something. I was presentable.

Suddenly the door opened and Simone stood there. *What now?* I continued to look in the mirror, determined to ignore her presence. She walked over to the next basin and started putting on lipstick.

"Well, well, well. It looks like someone insists on trying to make this difficult," she said.

"Excuse me?"

"I thought we reached an agreement the last time we spoke?"

I decided to play with her head. "Is that what you remember? I don't remember anything like that." I shook my head slowly. "No, can't say that I do." I sighed. "I don't know. I guess it's just something about ignorant and dim-witted statements that make them go in one ear and right through the other," I mocked.

With a look of contempt, she came closer to me and I could smell the alcohol on her breath. "You're really insisting on staying here and ruining what I've worked so hard to get back, aren't you? Why can't you just go to Miami and leave Tony and me alone?"

I looked directly at her. "Simone, what are you talking about? My decision to stay has nothing to do with you or

Tony. This is my life. Whether I decide to leave today or tomorrow is none of your concern."

"Oh, I disagree," she objected. "You see, ever since I came back into Tony's life, there's been this little barrier between us. At first, I thought it was my imagination that you and he got along so well, but now I know it's more that that."

I shook my head. This woman had some serious issues. "Simone, if you two are having problems, then maybe you should question whether you belong together."

She gave me a cunning smile. "Oh, I know we belong together," she declared.

"Then why didn't you stay with him the first—"

She cut me off sharply. "It's not important why we broke up last time. What is important is that we stay together now. There's no way in hell that I am going to let a black bitch like you get in my way!"

I blinked because I couldn't believe what she'd said. My first impulse was to punch her teeth in. I took a quick glance around the bathroom. We were alone and that meant I wouldn't lose face for what I was about to do. I swallowed my pride reluctantly and smiled.

"You know what? I'm not going to give you what you want, Simone, because I know you've been drinking a lot. So I'm going to leave and let you calm down," I said with composure. I started walking toward the door.

She grabbed my arm and blocked my way. Then she got in my face. "Don't walk away from me when I'm talking to you. You forget who I am. You mess with me and I'll have your ass off this account just like that!" she warned, snapping her fingers.

I knocked her hands off me angrily. "You know what? I don't care what you do, Simone, because I'm not going to be threatened by you. Go ahead and call me off the account. Go ahead and run to Daddy! I don't care. But I strongly suggest that you don't ever put your hands on me again!"

When she looked satisfied at my show of anger, I silently cursed myself for letting her get to me.

"Oh, my. Have I hit a nerve, Lacie?" She smirked. Our faces were inches apart. "Well, good, because I've got a little secret I want to tell you." She moved her face close to my ear. "I know you slept with Tony," she whispered.

Suddenly I felt as if I were on a soap opera. She saw my surprise.

"Don't tell me you're shocked that I know this," she taunted. "You should know by now that Tony tells me everything because we're so close. The ironic thing is that it doesn't bother me that you slept with him because he was only getting over me. It was nothing but a screw, that's all. Tony doesn't go for women like you—especially *black* women who sleep with their bosses just to get a promotion."

"I earned every bit of that promotion," I disputed.

"Is that what you think?" she scoffed. "You don't think you got that promotion because Tony was afraid you'd pull a sexual harassment suit on him? You don't think that was done just to shut you up?" She snorted. "You really are naïve, you know that? I hope you don't believe that he was actually falling for you." She laughed bitterly. "The worse part is that Joe is the innocent party in this whole turmoil that you created. How do you think he would feel if he found out just how much of a slut you are? Do you think he would appreciate the news that you slept with someone else, let alone his friend, while you two were seeing each other?"

I brushed past her and started toward the door again. She continued calling after me, still trying to get under my skin.

"What makes you think you're so special, Lacie? Huh? You're just like any other nigger trying to get ahead. You're nothing!" she yelled.

The use of the n-word stopped me in my tracks. I looked around to see if anyone else had heard it also. A few people had heard and stopped to look, but this time I didn't care. I had had it.

I turned around and glared at her. "What did you say?"

"I don't need to repeat myself. You heard me," she declared.

"Go ahead, Simone. Get it off your chest. You're on a roll now," I said calmly.

She didn't back down. I guess she had something to prove. "I said, you're just like any other nigg—"

I dropped my purse and headed for her. That was the last straw. Yeah, I'd made her say it again. I wanted to make sure I had a good reason for what I was about to do. She was due for an ass whipping and I was going to show her just how well a nigger like me could kick her ass. She hurriedly closed the bathroom door when she saw I was coming after her, but I had already made up my mind that I was going to get a piece of her by any means necessary. I had almost reached the door when I felt someone lift me up. I looked over my shoulder. It was Robert.

"Robert, put me down," I protested.

"Nope. I think it's time for us to leave," he said easily as he carried me, protesting, out of the hotel, with everyone staring, and into the next available cab. I was still complaining as he closed the door to the cab. "What did you do this time, Lacie?" he asked, turning to me.

I was shocked and insulted. "I didn't do anything," I protested. I began to tell him what had happened as the cab sped off into the New York traffic.

CHAPTER 13

"I mean, can you believe what she said!" I exclaimed to Robert as we entered my apartment. I flung my coat on the back of the sofa and Robert closed the door. "Man, I wish you'd let me clock her just once," I said vehemently, pacing back and forth across the living room floor. "It would've felt so good to get my hands around her throat and squeeze that skinny neck of hers."

Robert sat down on the sofa and shook his head. "Do you think that would have solved anything?"

I stopped pacing and looked at him. "No, but it sure would've made me feel better." I shook my head. "Robert, you didn't see how she was in that bathroom. She meant every word she said. It was as if she'd wanted to say those words to me for a long time and couldn't hold them back anymore. She delighted in my discomfort. She loved saying those words to me. I've done nothing to that woman but try to be cordial to her ever since I met her."

He nodded his head. "I noticed her heading toward the bathroom and sensed there might be some trouble, so I figured it was probably time for us to leave. I had just picked up our coats when I stopped you. I'm glad I did. You two would have been rolling on the floor if I hadn't."

"Excuse me—she would have been the one on the floor, not me." I sighed and flopped down on the sofa next to Robert. "I bet I've lost my job now, because of her. Tony's probably mad at me and I didn't say good-bye to Richard because you hauled me out of there so fast."

"You're being absurd. You're not going to lose your job over this," he said confidently.

I wasn't convinced. "Robert, I'm telling you, she has it in for me. She did everything she could to try to provoke me and now she's got something. I gave in to her taunts and you can bet she's going to use that to her advantage."

"I think you're being a little unreasonable. You're worrying about this entirely too much," he said, shaking his head. "Lacie, you didn't really do anything to her. She was intoxicated and even though you tried to leave the situation several times, she wouldn't leave you alone. You just exchanged a few words, the same as anybody would have if they had been provoked like you were. Richard loves you working for his company, Lacie, and I doubt very seriously that he'll let you go over something like this."

"Yes, but how many times has an employee attempted to beat a client's daughter's ass?" I said. "I would have succeeded too, if you hadn't stopped me."

Annoyed, Robert stood up and started walking toward the door. "This is useless. I'm leaving. You're still upset and unable to discuss this rationally."

I followed him. "You can say what you want, but I'll still waiting for the you know what to hit the fan," I insisted.

He turned around and kissed me on the forehead. "Goodnight. I'll see you later. Don't worry." He closed the door.

I walked to the kitchen, warmed up some leftovers in the microwave and got something to drink. I was still seething over the incident. Not caring that I still had on my dress, I flopped on the sofa to eat and watch a movie on cable. I didn't check on Mama and Reneé because I figured they were asleep upstairs. I wanted to be alone anyway.

I heard someone knocking and sat up, startled. I glanced at the TV. *Steel Magnolias* was almost at the end. Julia Roberts was in a coma and Sally Field was by her side, reading a book to her. I must have dozed off. As I stood up, I yelled that I was on my way. It had to be Joe. He'd said that he'd be back late tonight.

I was wrong. When I opened the door, it was Tony. He took in my appearance as I ran a hand through my hair.

"Waiting up for someone?" he asked, pointing to my dress.

I put my hands on my hips. "Yes," I answered. "I'm waiting up for Joe. He should've been here by now." I looked at my watch. "Anyway, what are you doing here at this time of night? Shouldn't you be with your darling Simone?" I asked more sharply, than I'd intended.

"That's one reason why I came over. Can you tell me what happened between you and Simone?"

I took a deep breath, opened the door wider so he could come in, then closed it. He walked to the middle of the living room and I followed.

"Tell me what she told you first," I instructed, standing in front of him with my arms crossed.

"Simone's very upset. She said you threatened her."

"That doesn't surprise me," I said sardonically. I sighed. "It's the other way around, Tony. She threatened me first. She called me all kinds of names and when I tried to leave the bathroom, she persisted in badgering me."

"Her version is the opposite. She said that when she came into the bathroom, you started calling her names and when she tried to leave, you threatened her and tried to fight her."

I scoffed. "She's lying," I said emphatically, shaking my head. "What reason would I have to do that, Tony? Why would I do that when we're about to land her father's account?"

"All I know is that she came to me crying hysterically, saying you tried to attack her."

This was getting on my nerves. "You know what, Tony? I want you to leave. It seems as if you've already formed your own opinion and damn whatever I say. I don't need this." I started walking to the door.

"Wait a minute, Lacie. I haven't formed an opinion. I'm just trying to get to the truth here."

"No, you're not. You're only worried about your precious Simone and losing the account."

"I want to know what happened, that's all."

"You want to know what happened? Do you really want to know?" I said angrily, walking closer to him. "Well, here goes!"

I reiterated everything that had happened in the bathroom, leaving nothing out. I told him everything she'd said, verbatim, and also took that opportunity to tell him what had happened at Mr. Carr's birthday party. As I spoke, his expression turned from surprise to anger. I was almost choking with tears as I remembered everything that had happened.

"Tony, you just don't know how much restraint I had to use when she called me a black bitch and a nigger. In all my twenty-seven years, I've never been called that. There I was, getting attacked from every possible angle and I couldn't do anything. All I could remember was how important this account was to you and the firm. It was the most demeaning and humiliating thing I ever had to go through."

Tony's face was solemn and contrite. "I'm sorry," he said. "I know Simone had a lot to drink but…" He stopped when he saw me wipe tears from my face. He came closer and reached for me. "Come here," he soothed.

I shook my head stubbornly and backed away a little. I was already upset that I had allowed the incident with Simone to affect me so much. "No, Tony. You told her what happened between us after you said you wouldn't tell anyone and she threw it up in my face." I searched his face for answers. "She said the only reason we slept together was because you were just getting over her and that I only got promoted because you were afraid I would threaten you with sexual harassment."

"Do you believe that?"

"I'm asking you," I pressed stubbornly.

"Why is that important to you?" He shrugged. "You're engaged to Joe," he reminded.

Ouch! I swallowed hard. "I want the truth, Tony, that's all. I want to know if the only reason I got that promotion was because of a good screw. Just tell me. I can take it. What I can't take is someone lying to me and making a fool of me."

"I've never lied to you and you should know that I take you seriously."

"Then answer my question!"

"No! The answer is no, no to both questions!" he exclaimed, backing away suddenly. "My God, Lacie!" He looked at me in disbelief. "Are you so blind that you can't see what's right in front of your eyes? How could you think that I would use you like that? How could you think you didn't earn your promotion?"

His response blew me away and I immediately felt a little foolish. "Well, because of what Simone said."

"I don't care what she said, Lacie. It's not true!" he exclaimed.

I took a deep breath. "Tony, why did you tell her? That was something that happened between us, not for anyone else to know," I said, scrutinizing him.

He shrugged and sighed. "I was upset about you and Joe being together. It was driving me crazy and I needed someone to talk to and she was there," he said simply.

We stared at each other in silence for a moment, and then I just shook my head.

"Listen, let's just drop it. What's done is done. It's pointless to talk about this anymore and I'm tired. I think you'd better go, Tony. Go home to Simone. I told you what happened and now it's time for you to leave."

"I don't want to leave you here like this," he said softly. "You look so sad." He reached out and brushed my face with his hand. A chill ran through my body as he did so.

I was tempted to back away, but didn't. I shook my head. "I'm going to be all right even though I'm going to have to deal with Simone until this business with her father is over."

He shook his head. "No. You're not dealing with her, Lacie. You shouldn't have to deal with any of that—not for any reason. I'm going to take care of Simone."

"You don't have to do that."

He nodded his head. "Yes, I do. She was absolutely wrong for what she said to you and how she treated you. I am so sorry you had to go through that." He looked at me longingly and reached out to touch my face again. "You know I hate to see you upset."

I backed away from him this time and shook my head. "You can't keep doing this, Tony."

"Why not? I just want to comfort you. Is that a crime?"

"Yes, it is. I already have someone else for that."

"He's not here, though, is he."

"That's not the point…"

Tony wasn't listening. He moved closer and stared into my eyes as he spoke. "Do you realize how beautiful you looked tonight?" He shook his head slowly. "Girl, it took every ounce of strength for me not to grab you and kiss you."

I didn't believe him. I was wondering why the conversation was heading the way it was and why I was participating in it. "Tony, I saw how you and Simone were dancing. It was like two dogs in heat," I said bitterly.

He cocked his head to the side. "You were watching us?"

"No," I answered quickly. "I just happened to catch a glance, that's all."

He moved even closer and his face was inches from mine. "That bothered you, didn't it?"

I tried to act annoyed, but it didn't work. "Of course not. Why would it?"

He put his hand in my hair and smiled. "It bothered you. Admit it."

"Tony, I'm telling you…"

He pulled my face to him and kissed me softly. I tried to resist and pull away, but he held me so firmly that I couldn't move. His kiss was gentle and insistent and I found myself opening my mouth, letting his tongue caress mine. My arms moved to his waist and I couldn't help getting lost in the kiss. His hands moved to my butt and he started rubbing it ever so delicately. Our tongues and lips joined together as if they'd found each other after being lost. But when I reached to cup his face, I came back to reality. I suddenly noticed the diamond ring that Joe had given me. Guilt tore into my soul at the sight of the ring. Here I was kissing one man while engaged to another. This was not good. Despite the insatiable desire in me, I broke away. Although I had only kissed Tony, I realized that at that moment, I had broken a trust. I had done it again. The tears started to flow and I turned my back before Tony could see them.

He came up behind me, laid his head on my shoulder and put his arms around my waist. "What's wrong?" he whispered.

I cried silently. "You need to leave, Tony," I managed.

He lifted his head from my shoulder. "Why?"

"Tony, just do me a favor and go, okay?" I pleaded.

He turned me around to face him and saw my tears. "Oh, Lacie," he said compassionately. He hugged me and stroked my hair. "Look, there's nothing going on between me and Simone. Regardless of how it looked, there never was," he explained, apparently misunderstanding the reason why I was crying.

"No, it's Joe," I clarified.

He gradually stopped stroking my hair, now realizing what we'd done, but still held me in his arms. "You're right. What are we going to do?" he murmured.

"I don't know," I uttered. "I don't know anything anymore." I moved away from him slowly. "You need to leave, though, Tony. This is too much for one night."

He looked tentative. I knew he didn't want to go. "Are you going to be okay?"

"I don't know." I smiled wearily. "I didn't expect this to happen."

He nodded. "Yeah, neither did I." He sighed. "I'd better go."

We walked to the door and stood there, unsure, digesting what had just happened. We gave each other empathetic smiles. Then his expression became serious again, and he took my face in both of his hands. His eyes were watery as they searched mine.

"I love you so much," he whispered, looking at me intently.

"I love you, too," I whispered in return, while a tear trickled down my face. I had finally admitted my true feelings to him and more importantly, to myself.

He smiled then, satisfied. "It made my day to hear you say that."

He bent down and kissed me passionately. I didn't resist because it felt so right. Another tear ran down my face, because I was sad and happy at the same time. We stood in the doorway for a while with both of our heads together and his hand on my neck. We didn't want to let go. Reluctantly, I finally broke it and he understood. I watched him walk to the elevator and push the button. It came immediately. He pulled the gate open, stepped in, turned around and waved a little good-bye. Tears were flowing down my face as I watched him disappear.

I went back inside and leaned against the front door and wiped my eyes. Man! What was I going to do?

"Well, that was certainly touching!"

I looked up and was startled to find Mama sitting on the sofa with her arms folded. Oh, here we go! Our silent peace treaty had ended.

I took a deep breath. "Mama, how long have you been down here?"

"Long enough to see you swapping spit with Mister Charlie!" she replied cynically.

"Oh, Mama, please." I headed for the kitchen.

"Don't, 'oh Mama, please' me," she voiced, following me. "I woke up and heard the television on and figured you were here. I came down to tell you that Joe's flight was delayed and that he won't be back until tomorrow. And what did I see? You sucking face with Mister Charlie!"

"Mama, don't call him that!" I snapped as I opened the refrigerator door and took out a Diet Pepsi.

"Oh, so now you're going to get defensive about him," she accused.

"Mama, you don't understand. It's…it's complicated."

She shook her head. "I knew you weren't telling me something. I could just smell it," she remarked emphatically, waving her hand around her nose.

"There was nothing to tell, Mama," I said, as she followed me back to the living room.

"Don't ruin your relationship with Joe over him," Mama warned.

Barely keeping my composure, I turned around to look at her and took a deep breath as I ran a hand through my hair. "Mama, you don't understand," I repeated.

"What, Lacie? You keep saying that I don't understand. You're supposed to be engaged to Joe and then I see you kissing Tony. What is there to understand?"

I just stared at Mama silently, aware of her aggravation and obvious disappointment. "Listen, I don't want to have this conversation right now. I'll talk to you later." I sighed heavily and began walking toward the stairs, too overwhelmed with everything to even attempt explaining what was going on. I couldn't even explain it to myself.

She called after me. "Lacie, talk to me. Don't go upstairs. Let's discuss this."

I walked up the stairs, tears streaming down as I did so. I stopped at the top and looked at her. She gave me a concerned and confused look. I said nothing, walked toward my room and closed the door behind me. I looked at myself in the dresser mirror, then at the huge diamond ring Joe had given me. I pulled it off my finger, tucked it away in my jewelry case, then lay down and cried myself to sleep.

I cried and tossed and turned the rest of the night. I was overburdened with guilt and frustration. At the same time, I was filled with happiness about Tony. Thinking about the complications involved made me weep even more. But I was no longer confused. There was no longer any doubt of who I wanted now. Because I had been careless, stubborn and denied true feelings, however, Joe was going to get hurt.

The next morning I went to church. Because I wanted to be alone, I didn't wait for Mama or Reneé. Ironically, the pastor's sermon seemed to cover exactly what I was going through and lifted my spirits a little. Afterwards, despite the cold weather, I decided to take a cab to Central Park and go for a walk.

Strolling through the park, I saw couples walking hand in hand, gazing into each other's eyes and kissing. This was exactly what I wanted with Tony. As painful as it would be, I knew what I had to do.

Not to my surprise, Mama was waiting in the living room when I came home. I said nothing as I closed the door, hung up my coat and walked straight into the kitchen. I hadn't eaten breakfast before I left for church and my stomach was growling. When Mama came into the kitchen, I still said nothing. There was no need. I knew she was going to start anyway.

"Are you ready to talk about it now?" Mama asked cautiously. She sat at the table and played with a napkin.

I avoided looking at her and got out some eggs, green peppers, tomatoes, cheese, bacon bits and onions. I was craving an omelet. I started silently preparing my meal. "I'm ready to talk," she said.

"Okay. Go ahead and talk, Mama. I'm listening," I instructed as I mixed the ingredients with the eggs. I remembered that the last time I was fixing an omelet, it was for Tony. I smiled secretly to myself, but Mama caught it.

"You're not smiling about him, are you?" she accused.

I turned around suddenly and slammed down the fork that I had been scrambling with. "What if I am, Mama?" I asked vehemently. "And his name is Tony."

Mama's eyes widened in surprise at my outburst. "Listen, I came in here to talk to you. You didn't want to talk last night, and when I woke up you had already left. I'm simply asking you to explain what's going on."

"What do you want to know, Mama?" I groaned.

"You already know that, Lacie. Let's not play twenty questions here. I have a right to know what's going on."

I turned around and put the mix in the skillet and turned the burner on low. I could feel her eyes on me as she waited for an explanation. I had to come right out and tell her. There was no other way.

"I'm breaking off the engagement with Joe," I said with a shrug.

"What!"

I turned back around and looked at her, so that she could see that I was serious. "I'm in love with Tony, Mama." I shrugged again.

"Lacie, you can't be serious." A bewildered expression on her face, she shook her head. "Where is this coming from?"

I turned around to the stove and folded the omelet over. "Mama, this has been going on a long time. I was just too foolish to recognize it."

"You're damn right it was foolish." she bellowed. "What about Joe? Are you forgetting about him? Don't you have any feelings for him?"

"Yes, I do. I care very deeply about Joe and I do love him, but I'm not *in love* with him. I'm in love with Tony."

"Lacie, you're already light-skinned. Don't you want your kids to have some color? Why on earth do you want to be with a white man?"

"I don't want to be with him because he's white, Mama. I want to be with him because I'm in love with him."

"No, you aren't. You only think you are."

"Don't tell me what I think. I know how I feel," I said indignantly. I put the omelet on a plate, grabbed a fork and sat down.

"Do you have any idea what you're doing?"

"Yes, I…" I stopped when Reneé came into the kitchen.

"What's going on?" she said sleepily.

Mama and I looked at each other hesitantly. Then she got up abruptly. "I'm going to get dressed and go out for a while. I'll talk to you later, Lacie," she said.

As Reneé and I looked at Mama's retreating figure, I shook my head. I knew Mama was upset, but she wasn't the only one I was worried about.

Mama came back downstairs, fully dressed, and left without another word to us. I decided not to worry about her, that she would eventually calm down. This was my problem and my life. I would have to live with my decisions.

When I explained everything to Reneé, she wasn't surprised.

"I knew it. I knew it!" Reneé exclaimed. "I knew there was something going on between you and Tony."

Later that morning Danny came by to see Reneé and they were up in her room when Robert stopped in. When I told him, he wasn't surprised either.

"I told you, I told you, I told you. Why don't you ever listen to me?"

"Okay, so you told me," I admitted grudgingly. "Are you happy now?"

"Not until I see a smile on your face," Robert said, pinching my chin.

I swatted his hand away. "Robert, this is serious!"

"So am I!" He grabbed my hand and pulled me out of the chair. "C'mon, get up. I'm tired of you being in a foul mood," he said. "Reneé! Danny! Come down here!" he yelled upstairs.

"Robert, what are you doing?"

"Hush. Don't say another word," he ordered.

Reneé and Danny came down and he told them to get their coats. He pulled me to the coat tree and helped me with my coat.

"Robert?"

"Hush, now. Just come with me."

Robert took us to a Christmas tree vendor nearby and we went down the aisles in search of the perfect tree. Once we found it, Robert insisted on paying for it.

We got home about two hours later and brought the big tree in. I was really glad my apartment had tall ceilings. Otherwise, it would have never fit. I dug out some ornaments and decorations from one of the closets, put on some Christmas music and we went to work. Robert's magic had worked and I was feeling a little better.

"Careful, I think I see a smile on your face," he teased.

I mouthed a thank you and we hugged each other. Unfortunately, my elation didn't last long. The front door opened and my mother and Dawn walked in.

"Isn't this festive? I didn't know we were going to decorate for Christmas today." Mama looked at all of us accusingly.

"It was a spur of the moment thing. Robert wanted to cheer me up, so we went out and he bought us this tree," I explained.

"I'm surprised you didn't get a white Christmas tree," Mama mumbled sarcastically, but loud enough for me to hear.

"Mama, stop it!" I belted out. She just couldn't leave well enough alone.

"Okay, okay, ladies," Robert placated. "Let's just have a good time and decorate the tree without any arguing." He looked at us.

"She started it," I said.

"Oh, no I didn't. You did, Lacie, when I caught you and…" Mama began. Dawn cut her off.

"Uh, Lacie…come with me for a minute." Dawn got between us and pushed me toward the kitchen.

"Oh! Do you believe her?" I voiced as soon as we entered the kitchen. "Here we are trying to get into the spirit of Christmas, and she starts an argument."

Dawn said nothing as I paced back and forth in the kitchen, just opened the refrigerator and got out a Pepsi. I stopped pacing when I noticed that she hadn't responded.

"What, Dawn?"

"Nothing," she uttered meekly and shrugged her shoulders.

"C'mon, spill it. I know Mama brought you here for a reason, so just say it." I commanded.

She looked uncertain at first, but shrugged and took a deep breath. "Lacie, your mother's very upset about this whole situation and about you changing your mind about Joe."

"Ah, now it comes out," I said, nodding my head. "I knew she'd told you as soon as you two came in." I leaned against the counter and folded my arms. "So what are your feelings about it? Oh, never mind. Don't answer that, because you made your feelings very clear a long time ago," I said bitterly.

"Lacie, I'm merely concerned about your mother's feelings," Dawn answered mildly.

"What about my feelings? Huh?" I argued. "Do you know how hard it was for me to come to this decision? Do you know how difficult this is for me?" I started pacing back and forth again. "Dawn, ever since that night with Tony in Washington and the night that we slept together, I've dealt with the whole world's feelings. I've thought about what people would say, how people would stare at us, what my family would say, what my mother would say and even what my children would look like if he and I got married. All of these things I had to take into account because the world is full of ignorant and close-minded people, who think love is beautiful only as long as people stick with their own kind. It's driving me crazy! I feel like I'm behind a line that I can't cross—a color line, if you will. *Oh, I can't possibly fall in love with him, because he's white and I'm black.* Think about it. Doesn't it sound insane and irrational to you when underneath we've got the same color of blood running through our veins?"

Dawn just stared at me in surprise. "You slept with him? When did this happen and why didn't you tell me?"

I looked at her in frustration. "Didn't you hear what I just said?"

She held up her hand. "Okay, I won't go there—yet," she said, as I started pacing again. Then she took a deep breath. "Listen, Lacie, this whole issue is much deeper than blood running through your veins. You know that. There's just so much bad history and distrust between black and white people. You can't just ignore that." Dawn shook her head. "I mean, do you honestly think you are capable of handling what you're about to get into?"

I stopped pacing and contemplated her question. "I haven't the slightest idea, Dawn." I shrugged. "What I do know is that I can't ignore how I feel about Tony anymore. I'm in love with him, Dawn. I've come to accept that now, and I will no longer pretend to love one man when I'm totally in love with another simply because of what society would say, what family would say or because he's the same color I am. I can't do it. I simply...cannot...do it," I breathed with emotion.

"Are you that certain?" she whispered, giving me a skeptical look.

"Yes," I said, wiping a stray tear from my eye.

Dawn and I eyed each other. She seemed to mull over everything I had said. I was hoping that I had effectively argued my case.

"Oh, girl, come here," she murmured with a smile, her eyes glistening with tears. She opened her arms wide and I stepped into them. We laughed and cried, grateful that the tension between us was now over. We stood there for a few minutes, both crying silently. We understood what our embrace meant. She was afraid for me and I was afraid for myself, but more importantly, she would stand by me. We finally let go and chuckled as we wiped away our tears.

"You know you've got to give me all the details about you and Tony, right?" she said. "You can't go over to the other side without giving up the info."

"Girl, what am I going to do with you?" I asked, wiping a final tear from her eye.

"Just love me." She smiled and we both erupted in laughter. "You know, I wish I were going to be here to see what the outcome is," she said, once we finally composed ourselves.

"What do you mean?"

She smiled mysteriously. "I'm moving to Miami. My agent finally came through for me and I got a small role in a low budget film." She noticed the questioning look on my face. "Relax. It's legitimate. The director is hot and upcoming and a major production company is handling it. I've checked into it already. My agent also booked me on some runway shows there after the movie, so that's why I'm moving."

"Well, what do you know? My girl is really getting her act together," I remarked proudly.

"Yeah, I'm really getting my act together," she repeated with a grin. "But I'm going to miss you."

I was touched. "Hey, I'm going to miss you too." I hugged her again and then let go quickly. "Okay, enough of this. Let's go back in there with everybody else," I instructed, already heading toward the living room. Dawn's voice stopped me.

"Lacie, I hope you know I really didn't mean to offend you a few minutes ago."

"Of course," I said. "And you also know that I would have cursed you out if you had."

She laughed and shook her head. "Girl, get on in there."

We left the kitchen and Mama came up to us and looked at Dawn expectantly, ignoring me.

"Well?" she asked Dawn.

Dawn looked from me to her and shrugged her shoulders. "She's set in her decision, Miss Josephine. I couldn't say anything to change her mind."

"You know, I really don't have any idea what I am going to do with you or Reneé." Mama shook her head in disappointment. "First, Reneé gets knocked up and now you tell me you're in love with The Man," she fumed, throwing down one of the lights for the Christmas tree. "I'm going upstairs. I'm not in the Christmas spirit and I've had enough of this." She started toward the stairs.

"Come on, Josephine. Don't go upstairs," Robert pleaded, looking at me helplessly.

I picked up an ornament and shrugged my shoulders nonchalantly in answer. "Let her go. It's just like her to do this. I knew our getting along wouldn't last."

Mama turned around in a huff when she heard what I had said. "I was trying to get along before I learned you decided to ruin a perfectly good relationship in order to act out a master and slave opera in your life."

"Well, Mama, if it's a master and slave opera, then so be it. You just remember that this is my life and I will damn well live it the way I want to," I returned angrily.

She looked at everyone and pointed at me. "You see? This is what I am talking about. Ever since I can remember, she has never listened to me, even when I was right."

"Mama, you were hardly ever right."

"But I'm damn sure right about this one! If you think for one second that I am ever going to approve of this, you are sorely mistaken."

"Actually, Mama, I never asked for your approval. If you were a real mother, then I wouldn't have to ask for it, now would I?" I retorted.

"Ooh, Lacie," I heard Robert, Dawn, Reneé and Danny murmur in unison. I didn't pay it any mind. Mama had pushed me there and there was no way I could have stopped it.

Mama's eyes widened. She looked around as if to get some help from somebody else, but Robert, Dawn, Reneé and Danny said nothing. I think they were unsure of what to say. Mama looked hurt.

"Fine," she uttered sharply, and walked rapidly up the stairs and slammed the door.

Everyone stood around and looked at each other uneasily. A knock at the door interrupted our silence.

"I'll get it," I said. I gave the ornament that I had in my hand to Reneé and walked to the door. Joe's smile greeted me as I opened it and he had an armful of gift-wrapped packages.

"Merry Christmas!" he said cheerfully.

Oh, Lord. This was definitely not going to be easy.

CHAPTER 14

"Merry Christmas," I murmured.

"Uh-oh." Joe frowned. "What happened? Why is everyone looking so glum?" He set the presents on the coffee table and looked at everybody.

"Mama and I got into another argument," I informed him.

"Why? I thought you two were getting along? What happened?"

"Nothing. I don't want to talk about it, right now." I took a deep breath. "So, you brought us presents, huh?" I looked down at the gifts.

"Yes. I thought I'd bring some gifts for my soon to be in-laws, since I won't be here for Christmas. Don't worry, yours is coming later," he said, kissing my forehead.

I shook my head. "Joe, you didn't have to do that."

"Of course I did. It's almost Christmas," he said simply. "Lacie, what's wrong?" he asked as my eyes started to water.

Robert came to my rescue. He put a comforting arm around my shoulder. "What's going on here? I know you two aren't going to let us do all the decorating by ourselves. We're trying to liven up the place, so your help will be appreciated," he announced, handing Joe a few ornaments. "Put these around the top left of the tree. It's a little naked around there and needs some color. Now hustle," he commanded.

Joe laughed as he walked to the tree and started helping. Robert waited for him to get out of earshot before he spoke.

"Whew, girl! Another minute and I was sure you were going to start boo-hooing," he remarked, wiping my tears with his fingers.

"Thanks for saving me."

"No problem," he replied, hugging me.

Danny and Reneé were teasing each other with tinsel and Dawn and Joe chatted away while trying to untangle some Christmas lights. We watched them for a moment.

"So when are you going to tell him?" Robert asked.

"I'm not sure. It's got to be soon, though. That I do know."

He nodded his head in agreement. "Listen, Lacie, don't let that argument with your mother get you down. I think this whole thing surprised her, you know? You shouldn't expect her to understand this soon. It's going to take a while."

"I know." I sighed and looked at Robert. "I sure did get myself into a mess, didn't I?"

"Yes, yes, yes, you did." He chuckled. "However, I'm sure you'll find a way to get out of it. Come on, let's help the others."

It was almost eleven when we finished decorating the tree and the apartment. It was gorgeous.

Since we hadn't heard a word from Mama, I asked Dawn to check on her before she left. She reported that Mama was asleep, so that cured my curiosity. Robert had complained of leg cramps and gone home thirty minutes earlier. Joe offered to drive Danny home and Reneé and I walked them to the door.

Joe turned around and looked at me. "Do you want me to come back tonight?"

"No, that's okay. A lot's gone on, what with the argument with my mother and all, and I really think I need some time to myself," I replied.

"I understand," Joe nodded. "You know, you never did tell me what happened between you two."

"I'll explain it to you later. Right now, I think you should take Danny home, or else he won't have a tongue left," I said, indicating Danny and Reneé tongue kissing in front of the freight elevator. "Goodness, you two! Do you think you can come up for air?" I shouted to them. They immediately stopped kissing and blushed. I smiled, shook my head and looked at Joe. "Teenagers, huh?"

Joe chuckled. "Ahh, come here, beautiful." He groaned softly as he held out his arms and I walked into them. "I missed you, girl," he said and kissed me. I wasn't that responsive and I think he noticed, because he gave me a strange look before he told Danny they had to go.

Reneé and I stood at the door and watched them get in the elevator and go down. I had to tell Joe soon. I just had to. I only wished it didn't have to be before

Christmas. What an incredibly tacky way to ruin a person's holiday.

Monday morning, I went to work early again, so I could finish up some research before the holiday. As I headed for my office, I noticed that a few people were already there. I was almost settled in when Carrie came in to greet me.

"Good morning, Lacie. How was your weekend?"

"Very interesting." I sighed, threw some folders on my desk and sat in my chair.

She caught the tone in my voice. "What happened?"

"I don't know if you've heard this, but Simone and I got into an argument at the Christmas party."

"What?" Carrie looked surprised and sat in the chair opposite my desk. "Is that why you left so soon?"

"Yep." I nodded my head. "She really showed her butt off. She confronted me in the bathroom and accused me of coming between her and Tony and started calling me all kinds of names. It was a big mess."

"What did you do?"

"I tried to ignore her at first. I really did. But she just pushed and pushed until I thought, forget this, I'm getting into that ass."

"Lacie, you didn't!" Carrie laughed.

"No, I didn't. Robert stopped me, pushed me into a cab and then we left."

"Oh, man!" Carrie said excitedly. "Did Tony find out what happened?"

"Yeah. He came by my apartment later that night, wanting to talk about it. Of course, Simone had changed the whole story around to make it seem like she was the victim. Fortunately, he believed me when I told him my side of the story."

I purposely left out what had happened with Tony because I didn't know what to tell her or if I was ready to tell anyone. Yeah, Tony and I had shared a special moment, but things between us were still up in the air. I didn't know where we stood. Until I knew what was going on, I planned on keeping my mouth shut. Furthermore, I still had to deal with Joe.

I must have slipped into deep thought, because I noticed Carrie studying me. "Why are you looking at me like that?" I asked.

"Lacie, you're not telling me something. What else happened this weekend?"

"Nothing," I answered, trying to sound nonchalant.

"Uh, huh," Carrie uttered, skeptically. "Whatever," she said as she stood up. "I'm going down to the cafeteria for a sausage and egg biscuit. Do you want me to get you one also?"

"Sure." I was elated to be off the hook.

Carrie shook her head as she walked out. Tony came in after her.

"Good morning." He smiled, closed the door and walked over to my side of the desk. "I saw Carrie leave and figured it would be best to talk to you while she was gone."

I nodded. "She just went to the cafeteria to get me something to eat."

"So how was the rest of your weekend?" he asked, leaning against my desk.

I smiled thinly. "You mean, have I talked to Joe yet?"

"Since you put it that way, yes."

I shook my head. "I haven't told him."

"Oh," he said, looking disappointed.

"Tony, I'm going to tell him. It's just that…" He put a finger to my lips.

"I know. You don't have to explain."

"Are you planning on talking to him also?"

"Yes." He sighed deeply. "Listen, how do you want to do this? Do you want us to talk to him together?"

"Tony, I don't know. I've never been in this kind of situation before. I don't want to hurt him," I said sadly.

"I don't want to either, but the fact is that whatever route we take, Joe's going to be hurt. But he's got to know."

"Oh man, I can't believe this is happening." I stood up and walked to the big glass window and looked at the street below.

"Hey, hey, hey," he soothed. He came over to me, put his arm around my waist and his head on my shoulder. "It's going to be all right."

I shook my head. "Mama and I had an argument this weekend. It was bad. Really bad."

"Oh, so that's the other reason you're upset."

"Yeah." I sighed. "She saw us kissing right before you left. Needless to say, she didn't like it—not at all. That started the argument."

"Is it because I'm not Joe?"

"Yeah, and because you're white," I said bluntly.

He chuckled. "Lacie, your mother's not the only one who'll have a problem with this. There's a whole world out there that's going to notice our difference and not like it. We're going to have to know how to handle it."

"Yeah, you're right." I took a deep breath. "Tony, listen, I think we should be discreet while we're at work," I said tentatively. "Joe and I haven't had closure yet and there are bound to be raised eyebrows about this."

"I thought you'd say that," he groaned softly. "But I'm not going to argue. I still need to talk to Simone also. I really don't like the way she treated you Saturday. Evidently, she's had the wrong idea about herself and me for a long time and I want to straighten her out about that."

"What about the account?"

"Don't worry about that. I'll take care of it. You've got enough on your hands already." He sighed. "Look at me," he said, turning me around to face him. He held my chin tenderly. "I'm going to make sure that everything works out, okay?" I nodded and he gave me a soft kiss. "Good. Now I'm going back into my office before I start getting ideas, because right now I...well, I'm not going to say it." We chuckled because we knew what he meant. "I'll see you at the meeting later," he whispered.

He walked toward the door, looked back and smiled encouragingly. He turned back around and almost bumped into Carrie.

"Good morning, Carrie," he greeted as he left.

Carrie, with a bewildered look on her face, looked back at his retreating figure and walked in, then looked at me. I tried to hide the smile on my face, but she caught it.

"Okay, Lacie, what's up? I definitely know that something's going on now, because Tony has never greeted me that cheerfully in the morning."

Reluctantly, I told Carrie the rest of what had happened over the weekend. She wasn't surprised. She said she knew it was bound to happen because the chemistry between Tony and me was just too strong and she'd decided not to say anything more to me—just wait until I realized it for myself.

"Thanks a lot, Carrie."

"Hey, I'm just telling it like it is," she defended. "You had to be with Joe because you thought that was what people would expect of you. You knew it also, but you were determined to prove it differently. It was very unsuccessful, I might add."

"Okay, that's enough. I've heard all of this from Robert already."

"Maybe next time, you'll listen," she shot back.

"You know, if I didn't like you and you weren't my friend, I'd fire you," I fumed.

"Yeah, and I love you too," she said, not at all affected by what I'd said. Then we laughed.

"Now listen," I said seriously. "I don't want you to tell anyone. And I mean no one, Carrie. Tony and I want to keep this a secret until we get everything straightened out. I still have to talk to Joe, you know."

Carrie hunched up her shoulders. "Who am I going to tell?"

"Oh please, Carrie!" I said emphatically. "You're the gossip columnist of this whole building."

She held up her right hand. "Okay, I won't tell a soul."

"Thank you," I said, satisfied. I knew her word was gold. I handed her a folder full of papers. "Here are some papers that need to be sorted, and if my mother calls, make sure that you put her through right away."

She saluted. "Fine, boss. I'll get on it right away." She grinned and I threw a pen at her playfully as she ducked and hurried out the door.

There was very little work to do as we came to the middle of the week and the holiday was just around the corner. Most of the people in the department seemed more relaxed. Tony and I managed to be discreet with each other at the office and I tried to keep busy by going over all the accounts and clients that we had acquired.

I hadn't seen Joe in a couple of days because he was so preoccupied with other business ventures and running around buying presents for his family. I was still dreading telling him, but decided that it had to be before he left for Miami. Tony offered again to talk to him, but I had made up my mind that I had to be the one to break the news to him first.

Since the argument over the weekend, I had hardly seen Mama. When I did encounter her, she barely spoke to me. I remembered the last words that I said to her over the weekend and felt bad. I decided to call her.

The phone rang four times before Reneé answered.

"Hello?"

"Hey, Reneé. Is Mama home?"

"No. She left just a few minutes ago. Do you want me to tell her you called?" she asked.

Darn! "No, that's okay. I'm taking a few extra days off along with the holiday, so I'll talk to her later," I said. "How are you feeling? Did you have any morning sickness today?"

"No. I've been feeling a little tired, but everything's fine," she assured me. "Listen…about Mama, Lacie," she began.

"Yes?"

"She's going to be fine. I think she knows that you didn't mean what you said."

"I hope so. It was out of anger, you know?"

"Yeah, I know all too well. Believe me." She chuckled. "Look, I haven't had a chance to talk to you about this, but I know you're going through a difficult time right now. I want you to know that I'm behind you."

"Really? What about Joe?"

"I like Joe. I'm not going to say that I don't, but the main thing is that you follow your own heart and don't listen to anyone who has anything negative to say."

"Isn't this something? My little sister is giving me advice," I acknowledged.

"Hey, I learned all of this from you."

I chuckled. "Listen, I've got to go. I'll see you later, sweetie."

As soon as I got off the phone, Carrie buzzed me and told me that Joe was on hold. I switched to the other line. "Hello?"

"Hey, beautiful. How are you?" he asked jovially.

"I'm hanging in there."

"You still worried about that argument with your mother?"

"Yeah, and some other things."

"I was really worried about you when I left the other day. You didn't seem like yourself. Do you want to talk about it?" he offered.

"Yes, but not on the phone."

"Okay. How about I come over to your house tonight and you tell me then? I'd like to spend some time alone with you before I leave and there are some things I want to talk to you about as well."

"Sure. I'll cook dinner and we can talk about everything. Do you think you can make it around seven o'clock?"

"No problem, beautiful. I'll see you tonight," he said and hung up the phone.

I called Robert and asked him if he could take Reneé and Mama shopping and to dinner on me.

"You're going to tell Joe today, aren't you?" Robert asked.

"Yes. It's not something I want to do, though," I said. "I don't know, Robert. Maybe this isn't the right time to tell him. I mean, isn't it kind of selfish to do this now, with the holiday and everything?"

"Lacie, it'll be selfish if you don't tell him. Honey, I know that it's the holiday season, but if you wait, then when would be the right time? After Christmas, there's New Year's, and then in February, there's Valentine's Day. So two months will have passed and you'll be unhappy because you're not with the man you love, and Joe will be unaware of everything that's going on. Baby, you've got to do it and do it now. It won't be fair to Joe if you don't tell him. The longer you wait, the harder it'll be."

"You really broke it down, didn't you?" I groaned.

"Hey, I had to," he said. "Lacie, be a good girl and do the right thing. Now that you've realized your true feelings, it's time for Joe to realize them also. I'll make sure Josephine and Reneé aren't home, but you just make sure you tell him tonight."

Robert was right. I had to tell him.

I was cooking when I heard the knock on the front door. Taking off my apron, I walked toward the door, hesitating before opening it. When I saw the huge bouquet of roses in his arms, I almost broke down right there.

"Hi, beautiful!" Joe greeted enthusiastically, kissing me lightly on the lips. "These are for you." He handed me the bouquet.

"Thank you." I managed a smile. "Come on in and shut the door. I'm going to put these in some water and I'll be right back. Dinner will be ready in about fifteen minutes or so," I said, walking toward the kitchen.

"Okay," he said, following me. "So, what are we having?" he whispered in my ear as he put his arms around my waist from behind.

"Shrimp scampi with steamed broccoli," I replied. I moved out of his arms easily to turn the burner on low.

"Sounds good," he murmured. He moved closer and put his arms around my waist again.

"Uhh, why don't you grab the plates and utensils and set the table," I suggested.

"No problem," he said, giving me a quick peck on the nape of my neck.

Out of the corner of my eye, I watched him whistle softly as he set the table and put two candles in the middle. I shook my head sadly, ready to cry any minute.

A few minutes later, dinner was ready and I carried the food to the table.

"Umm, this really looks good, beautiful. You did a great job," he commented.

"Thank you, sir," I joked lightly, with a salute. "Now, let's eat this food before it gets cold."

Joe did most of the talking as we ate. He was jovial and animated. While I listened to him, all I could think about was what Robert had said.

"You know, we've really got to talk, Lacie, because you look like you're going to cry any minute now. You've got to tell me what's been eating at you." He searched my face for answers.

"Uh, help me clear off the table, and then we'll talk," I suggested softly.

We cleared the table and I kept going over in my mind how I was going to tell him. Was I going to tell him about Tony first, or was I going to say that I didn't want to marry him first? *Oh, just tell him, Lacie. That's all you have to do. There's no easy way to do it.*

I took out a can of Pepsi and gave him one. Then we walked into the living room and sat on the sofa. He sat there patiently, waiting for me to begin. Although I had seen scenes like this on the soap operas, I'd never thought I'd be in a real one. I took a deep breath and hoped that I wouldn't start choking on my words as I talked.

"Joe, I don't think we should get married," I said quietly.

His expression was of shock, then amusing disbelief. "What? Why not?"

I gulped. "I've thought long and hard about it. I think it would be a big mistake. I'm not the right woman for you, Joe."

"Of course you are," he said tenderly.

I shook my head. "I'm not, Joe," I insisted softly. "Here, this is yours." I reached into my pocket, pulled out the engagement ring he had given me and gently placed it in his hand. Then I stood up.

"Wait a minute." He stood up also. "Where is all of this coming from? Why the sudden change? A week ago you accepted my proposal and now you're telling me that you don't want to marry me?"

"I really thought that was what I wanted."

"What do you want, Lacie? Is there something that I'm not doing? Is there something that you want me to do?"

"No, Joe. You've been wonderful to me. You've treated me like a queen the whole time we've been together."

He moved closer to me. "Then what is it? Whatever you do, don't tell me that you're not the right woman for me, because I know you are. I love you with every inch of my heart."

I didn't say anything as his eyes pleaded with mine. I couldn't say anything. I couldn't help him. He wanted me desperately and I couldn't give him what he wanted.

"Lacie?"

I was silent. He searched my face for an answer, then suddenly gave me a look that showed that he knew the reason.

"There's someone else, isn't there, Lacie?"

I was almost in tears. "Yes," I managed to utter.

He suddenly stepped away from me then, as if I had some horrible disease. There was so much hurt and anger on his face. "Okay. Let me get this straight. You're telling me that there's been someone else this whole time?"

"No," I replied meekly.

He looked at me and knew that that wasn't entirely true. "You're lying." He shook his head.

I moved toward him. "Joe, listen…"

"No!" he said sharply. "Don't come near me!" He started walking back and forth, then abruptly stopped. "Why? Why, Lacie? Why didn't you tell me all of this before?"

"I didn't know then!" I cried.

"You didn't know?" He looked at me incredulously. "You didn't know?" he repeated. "How could you not know, Lacie? I told you from the beginning how I felt about you and now you're telling me that all this time there was some other guy in the picture and you didn't know. What were you doing—sleeping with both of us at the same time?"

"No. It wasn't like that, Joe. Listen, it wasn't like that!" I touched his arm, but he jerked it away from me.

"Then tell me what it was like, Lacie. Tell me, because I really want to hear what your explanation is."

I stood there as if feeble-minded. I didn't know what to say at first, but then it started to roll off of my tongue. "Joe, when I started going out with you, I felt that I had finally gotten a man that was treating me with respect, romancing me and doing everything to please me. You were, in my eyes, the ideal man for me. However, there was this other guy that for some reason, knew how to push all my buttons, throw me into an emotional frenzy, and I had no idea why. I had you, the perfect man, the man of my dreams, right in front of me, but yet there was this other man that I had these strong feelings for. I tried so hard to ignore my feelings for him. Honestly Joe, I desperately wanted to get him out of my head, but… "

"You couldn't," he finished. "So, I'm the sucker in this little game you've been playing, huh?"

"Joe, don't say that," I pleaded.

He nodded his head insistently. "No, really. That's what I've been this whole time here, haven't I? You've been playing me all along, right under my nose and I've been the sucker in this whole game."

"Joe, I never meant to play you and it wasn't a game. I didn't mean for things to happen this way," I insisted.

"Bull!" He pointed at me. "That's bull! You should have told me about this a long time ago, Lacie. My God! I can't believe that you're doing this. You should've told me your feelings before I fell in love with you and before I asked you to marry me!"

"I know. I know." I nodded my head as tears started streaming down my face. "I thought that was what I wanted."

"You mean, you thought *I* was what you wanted," he said bluntly. "Evidently, I wasn't enough for you."

"That's not true, Joe. I care about you a lot."

"Apparently not enough," he retorted. "Did you sleep with him?" he asked abruptly.

I didn't say anything.

"Did you…sleep with him?"

I took a deep breath. "Yes."

"Before or after we started seeing each other."

"After," I replied reluctantly. I saw the look on his face. He was mad. "We hadn't been seeing each other that long, Joe. I didn't think we were getting serious."

He glared at me. "I did."

I watched him pace again in silence. He was hurt and angry and unfortunately, the worst part wasn't even over yet. As if hearing what I was thinking, he stopped pacing and stared me down.

"Who is he?" he asked directly.

Oh, boy. I was hesitant to answer him. He was already so pissed off. I didn't want to tell him it was Tony. I shook my head. "It's not important who he is, Joe." How could I have said that?

He repeated what I had thought. "How can you say that?"

"Because..." That's all I could say. I was trapped. Damned if I did and damned if I didn't.

He studied me then, with his head to the side. "You know, it's really funny that you didn't say the usual cliché. You said it's not important who he is, but you didn't say that I don't know him." I gulped and he noticed it. "I know him, don't I?" I said nothing. "Who is he?"

"Joe..." was all I could muster.

"No!" he said sharply. "If I'm going to be dumped, then I would like to know for whom. I'm owed at least that. Who is he?"

This was too painful. I didn't want to hurt him anymore, and I still didn't say anything.

"Tell me who he is, dammit!" he bellowed.

The tone of his voice shocked me and I knew I had no choice but to answer him. "Tony," I strained out and began to cry harder.

His face showed absolute stupefaction and incredulity. In complete shock, he just watched me cry. "Are you in love with him?"

I nodded my head slowly, continuing to weep. Seeing this, he abruptly headed toward the door without another word. I wiped my face and ran after him, but came to a closed door. I opened it and ran to the exit steps and called down after him.

"Joe!" I cried out, but he didn't stop.

Heavy-hearted, I headed back to my apartment door and came face to face with Mama, Reneé and Robert. Their arms were full of shopping bags and undoubtedly they had seen everything.

Mama gave me a chastising look. "You really know how to screw up a holiday, don't you?"

I didn't say a word.

"You had to do it, didn't you? You just had to do it!" Mama accused as we entered the apartment.

"Mama, I'm not in the mood!" I warned, furiously wiping tears from my eyes.

"I don't care what kind of mood you're in. You just wrecked that man's entire holiday. You should be ashamed of yourself!" She flung her bags down on the sofa.

Robert, aware that there was going to be another heated discussion, grabbed Reneé by the hand and started leading her upstairs. "Let's go watch some movies, Reneé. They're about to go at it again."

Mama waited for them to shut the door before she turned on me angrily. "How could you be so insensitive?"

I gathered myself together and tried to speak calmly. "He had to know, Mama."

"Why? You could have at least waited until after Christmas," she reasoned.

"He had to know," I repeated. "If I didn't tell him tonight, I was never going to tell him. I had to be honest with him." Mama sucked her teeth and rolled her eyes. I threw my hands up in the air. "What do you think I should have done, huh?"

Her eyes widened. "Oh, don't get mad at me! You're the one that sent that boy home crying to his mama for Christmas. You should've seen how he looked when he bolted down those stairs, Lacie. All of this you did because you want to be with Tony. How could you be so heartless?"

"Oh, Mama, don't go there!"

"Oh, I am going there!" she shouted. "How could you break that man's heart like that?

"Do you think I enjoyed doing that?"

"I don't know what to think about you nowadays, Lacie."

"Mama, you have no idea what I've been going through in the past few months and what I went through tonight. It took every ounce of willpower for me to tell him, to his face even, that I didn't want to marry him and that I was in love with his friend. Did you see the look on his face when I told him that? Did you see the anger and the hurt on his face? No, you didn't! *I* saw it with my *own* two eyes." I pointed to my eyes. "That man was in love with me and wanted to spend the rest of his life with me and I had to tell him that I wasn't in love with him!" I heard her footsteps behind me as I headed for the kitchen.

"You tell me what it is exactly that Tony can offer you that Joe can't. Joe's successful, he's handsome and he's intelligent. He has everything that Tony has. Why on earth would you want a white man when there's this beautiful black man right under your nose?"

"It has nothing to do with the color of their skin!" I looked at her in wonder. "Tell me, Mama. Is that all you see in Tony? Is his color the only thing that you see in him?"

"Girl, have you lost your mind? Have you completely lost your mind?" she asked in disbelief. She shook her head. "There is a big difference between white men and black men and I don't need to see anything else, Lacie. I've seen enough. I know all about white people. I've been through enough to know that blacks shouldn't mix with whites and I know enough to tell you that you're making a very bad decision," she asserted. "You had Joe, this handsome black man who treated you like a queen, and you blew it."

I rolled my eyes upward. "I'm not in love with Joe, Mama, and I'm not going to marry a man simply because he's black."

"Why not? You're black, aren't you?"

"I'm not going to answer that question." I shook my head.

"Lacie, listen, you have a whole world full of beautiful black men out there to choose from. They come in all shapes, sizes and colors."

"That's true. But I'm not in love with a world full of black men. There's only one man that I'm in love with and he just happens to be white."

She stared at me helplessly and shook her head. "Do you have any idea what you're getting yourself into? Do you know what people are going to say?"

"I don't care about that."

She shook her head. "If you insist on being with Mister Charlie, you'll see how people will treat you just because of your difference. And you won't like it, either."

"Look at how you're treating me now, Mama," I responded sharply. "Sunday, I told you I was in love with Tony and you had a fit. And for the last time, please give me respect and stop calling him Mr. Charlie!"

"Why not? He's white, isn't he?" she retorted.

I raised my hand to my head. "Yes, he's white, Mama. So what? So what?" I shouted angrily. "Am I supposed to disregard my feelings for Tony just because of that factor alone?" I shook my head. "Mama, all of those reasons that you gave me just a moment ago I was already aware of. And it's because of my *consideration* of those reasons that Joe is hurting right at this moment. I kept Joe conveniently near me, because I thought I was doing the right thing and in the end, I hurt him. I hurt him badly and unfairly, because I didn't want to admit that I was in love with Tony."

"Lacie, you only think you're in love with him," Mama persisted.

I looked at her wearily. "You see, this is exactly why we don't get along. You don't listen. I've repeatedly told you my feelings about Tony and yet you still refuse to hear me. So I'm not going to argue with you anymore. I spent all of those years with you and yet you don't know a thing about me or acknowledge my feelings. I tell you one thing and you tell me another. That's the way it's always been and still is. You don't know me, Mama." I shook my head sadly.

"I'm only trying to look out for you, Lacie."

"Well, don't. I needed a mother a long time ago and you weren't there. Don't try to make up for lost time now," I said as I left her in the kitchen and ran upstairs to my room.

CHAPTER 15

I woke up early the next morning and took off to do some last minute Christmas shopping. I was out of the house by eight-thirty.

Macy's was congested with people. Apparently a lot of people had the same idea that I had. Although the store was packed, I enjoyed being in the midst of the crowd and took my time looking for gifts. Christmas was my favorite time of the year.

When I came back home a few hours later, the house was empty. Reneé had left a note on the refrigerator saying that she and Mama had gone Christmas shopping. I was glad to have the house to myself.

I thought about the argument I'd had with Mama last night. She and I just never seemed to be able to get along and this thing with Tony had really done it. I should have known from the very beginning how she would react. She'd had always felt that way about interracial relationships.

What was I going to do? Yeah, I'd told her that I wasn't going to care what people might say or think about us, but that wasn't entirely true. I knew it would be a test of my willpower, but in retrospect, was I really willing to go through with it?

Then there was Joe. I'd broken his heart. That last look he'd given me just before he left the apartment was etched in my mind, and I knew that if he didn't already hate me, he was very close to it.

There was a knock at the door. When I opened it, Tony stood there, looking haggard.

"Hey," he murmured.

"Hey." We stood there silently for a second. "Come in, come in," I said.

He walked in and looked around. "Is anyone else here?" he asked as he walked to the stairs and looked up.

"No," I responded. "Mama and Reneé went Christmas shopping."

"Oh," he said. He looked at me. "About Joe…"

I sighed. "It didn't go well. I really hurt him, Tony. I don't know if he'll ever forgive me."

He nodded his head. "I know." He took a deep breath. "Joe came by my house after seeing you."

"How did that go?" I searched his face. He shook his head in answer. "Oh," I said. "I'm sorry, Tony."

"Yeah. He really blew up at my house." He smiled thinly and sighed. "You know, back in college we were always competing with each other for women. We both loved the challenge. Whoever got the girl first, won. But we never let that get in the way of our friendship. This time it's not so much fun."

"I'm sorry," I said again. "I didn't mean to come between you two like that."

"It's not your fault, Lacie." He shook his head and walked over to me. "It's mine. I knew what I was doing. I knew he had eyes for you, yet I kept pursuing you."

"To compete with Joe?"

"You should know that's not the reason." He looked at me tenderly. "When I saw you in that elevator for the first time I thought you were so beautiful. I knew I wanted to get to know you and when you told me where you worked and that you were getting a new boss, I was even more delighted because I knew I was him."

"Yet I told you that I wasn't interested."

He nodded and smiled. "Yes, you did. But your eyes and the chemistry between us told me differently."

"I knew it, too."

"I know."

"So..." I said.

"So..." he repeated.

"What do we do now?" I asked.

He shrugged. "You know...I'm not so sure. I expected to be in better spirits because I finally have you, but I'm not. I hurt my best friend."

"Yeah. I feel the same way. After all of the arguments with my mother and my breakup with Joe, I'm drained. There's just been so much conflict and pain. And for some odd reason, it's leading me to believe that maybe we're not supposed to be together yet. Does that sound strange?"

"No," he said.

"So, I guess we should..." I said quietly.

"Yeah, I guess we should hold off, " he mumbled in agreement.

We walked to the door slowly in silent agreement. As much as we wanted to be together, there were still some issues to overcome before we could be together. It wasn't our time.

He stopped at the door and opened it and smiled thinly. "Isn't it ironic that after all we've been through to get together, we're still not together?"

"Yes, it certainly does make you wonder."

We stared at each other. His eyes were sad and I was trying to hold my composure.

"Oh, here. I almost forgot to give this to you." He reached into his coat pocket and pulled out a small gift box.

"Tony?" I said with surprise.

"I saw it and thought of you," he explained. "Make sure you don't open this until Christmas. I know how nosy you are," he teased.

"Whatever." I rolled my eyes and smiled and we laughed.

"That's my girl," he whispered.

We looked at each other and knowing that it was what we both wanted, he cupped my face and kissed me. He held me for a while before he let go.

"Merry Christmas, Lacie," he said softly before closing the door behind him.

"Merry Christmas," I whispered.

Christmas day was surprisingly nice. I had made up my mind that despite everything that had happened, I was going to try my best to make it a good day. I'd make an effort at holding back my tongue when it came to responding to Mama.

Mama, I think, had that same idea. She, too, was trying to be on her best behavior, but because she was my mother, and I knew how she was, I didn't hold my breath.

Dawn and her mother, Rose; Danny, and his parents, Charlene and Danny Senior; and Robert and his friend,

Darren came over. Mama raised her eyebrows when she saw him. She came into the kitchen while I was fixing the sweet potato pudding.

"Did you see Robert's friend?"

"Yes, Mama," I replied. I knew where she was going.

"So…" she said as she chewed a carrot, "what do you think?"

"I don't think anything, Mama."

"Do you know if he's just a friend, or a 'friend' friend," she said, putting up her fingers and making quotation marks with them.

"I don't know, and I really don't care. Robert hasn't said anything to me about it and I'm not going to question him about it either." I put the potatoes in the oven.

"Look at him. You can tell he's gay."

I turned around swiftly and grumbled with aggravation, "Mama, stop. Just stop it. I don't want to hear another word about Robert's friend. His love life is none of your business."

She looked at me hard and put her hands on her hips. "Are we talking about Robert or you?"

I put my hand up to my head and closed my eyes. *Remember what you promised yourself, Lacie.* I opened my eyes and restrained myself from yelling.

"Do you remember what happened Thanksgiving? It was a disaster. Do you want that to happen again?" She shook her head like a child I was scolding. "Thank you. Now, can you do me a favor and set the table?"

I heard her mumble, "Don't get mad at me because you screwed it up with Joe," as she walked out the kitchen.

Dawn came in. "Girl, you've got this whole place smelling good!" She put a comforting arm around my shoulder. "How are you doing in here?"

"Fine," I said, trying to sound cheerful as I put some of my homemade rolls on a baking sheet. "I'm glad I bought a big turkey. Having Danny and his parents and Robert's friend was a surprise. I wasn't expecting this many people."

Dawn smiled. "I wasn't asking about the food. How are *you* doing?" I shrugged in answer. "Reneé and your mother told me what happened with Joe," she said gently. "Are you going to be okay?"

"Yeah, I'm sure I will. I'm more concerned about Joe. You should've seen him, Dawn. He was so upset and angry. I've never done anything like that before and I feel so horrible."

"I know," she nodded, rubbing my back. "Well, you've got what you wanted, right? You've got Tony. That's something to look forward to, right?"

"No." I shook my head. "I'm afraid not."

"Why not?"

"We kind of broke up, even though we were never really with each other. After all that happened, I think we felt that it wouldn't be right, simply because of how we got together. It was just too much. You know Joe and Tony were friends."

"So you're telling me that after all of that convincing and yelling you did at me the other day, you and Tony are still not together?" she asked with a dubious look.

"It looks that way." I shrugged.

She wiggled her finger at me. "You know what? You are not going to do this."

"What?"

"There's no way I am going to let you give up like that. You're going to call Tony and get back with him because I didn't get all of that yelling from you for nothing." She shook her head. "You're unhappy, Lacie. If I'm happy, then you have to be happy. That's the way it is and has always been, so you're just going to have to call him."

"Where is all of this coming from? I thought you were against me being with him?"

"At first I was. But I think I was using that as an excuse because I was envious of you."

"Why, Dawn?"

"Because you had two men in love with you, whereas I couldn't get the one guy I was with to be faithful to me. You also had this great career and I couldn't get my own career together."

"You shouldn't have felt that way, Dawn. You have a lot going for you, too," I suggested softly.

"Yeah, I know that now," she said confidently. "You've been with me through some hard times and I can't bear to see you this unhappy. Lacie, you had to tell Joe. Even though it hurt him, it was for the best. He'll get over it in time."

"Yes, but I don't think he'll ever forgive me."

"Don't worry about that, Lacie. You've got to think about yourself right now. You did you two a favor and if he's as intelligent as I think he is, then he'll probably wind up thanking you later on. Now, I won't feel good until my best friend is happy, so do me a favor and call Tony." She picked up the portable phone and handed it to me.

"I don't know," I said hesitantly.

"Just do it!" she commanded with a smile.

"All right, all right!"

Tony had given me all of his phone numbers a while ago when I started working for him. I looked up Tony's mother's home number in my organizer and dialed it. It was picked up on the third ring.

"Hello?" It was Simone's voice on the other end. "Hello?" she repeated.

I hung up.

Dawn looked flustered. "Why did you hang up?"

"Simone answered the phone."

"So? That doesn't mean anything."

"Maybe not, but I think I'll wait and talk to him when I see him at work. I checked the turkey and it was done. "C'mon, help me get the food on the table."

We all sat at the table, ate and talked amicably with each other. It was the first chance Mama and I had to talk to Danny's parents. They were a pleasant couple and seemed to really love their son Danny, who was their only child. As the dinner went on, somebody asked Robert's friend Darren what he did for a living.

"I'm a designer," he answered in a deep voice.

"What kind of a designer?" Mama asked. I gave her a look, but she ignored it.

"I work in fashion," he said with a smile.

Mama gave me an 'I told you so' look when he said that.

"So do you make a lot of money?" Mama questioned further.

"Mama," I groaned.

"I make out fine," he answered, chuckling.

I quickly thought of a way to change the subject. "Would anyone like dessert?" I asked. I noticed that most of the food was gone and that the turkey was now all bones.

"Sure. We'd love some," they all said in unison.

"Lacie makes a great apple pie," Reneé announced, and that started a new subject at the table.

After we ate, Robert and Dawn got up to help me clear the table while everyone else went into the living room and continued conversing.

"So, Robert, how long have you and Darren been seeing each other?" Dawn blurted out as soon as we entered the kitchen. I gave her a look. "What?" she exclaimed when she saw my expression. "No one else has asked him yet, so I thought I'd do it."

Robert grinned at her boldness. "Actually, we haven't been seeing each other—at least not the way you two and Miss Josephine are thinking. He's only a friend. He's from California and came here for a visit. He couldn't get a plane out in time, so I asked him to come along."

"Is he gay also?" Dawn asked curiously.

"Dawn!" I said.

Robert answered her question anyway. "No. He is definitely a heterosexual and always has been." There was a melancholy expression on his face that I had never seen before.

"Does he know that you're gay?" I asked gently.

He nodded. "Yes, he knows. He's known for a long time." He sighed. "Look, unless there's something else you need me to do, Lacie, I'm going back in there."

I shook my head. "No, you can go. Dawn can help me clean."

Shortly after Robert and Darren left, we decided to open the presents. Reneé opened hers first. She got a laptop computer from me, a gold necklace from Mama and an electric organizer from Dawn. Then Danny reached into his pocket and took out a suede ring case. Mama, Dawn and I looked at each other in surprise.

Danny got down on one knee and asked Reneé to marry him. She said yes and cried as he hugged her. Looking at them, I couldn't help remembering a similar scene with Joe. I shook my head and tried to blot out my thoughts. She and Danny were in love, so I knew it was going to work out. I smiled.

"Now let's just hope this one goes through," Mama said as she hugged Reneé.

I rolled my eyes.

Dawn, sensing a confrontation, said, "I'll hand out the other presents from under the tree." And she did.

All in all, everyone received some nice presents and I think we were happy with what we got.

"Oh, wait a minute," Dawn said. "I forgot this little one." She reached under the tree and got it. "This one is for Lacie," she announced.

I recognized the present immediately. It was the one that Tony had given me.

"I'll open it later. It's getting late and I want to go to bed," I said.

"No, Lacie. Open it now. We want to see what you got," Reneé urged.

I looked from her to Mama and from Mama to Dawn, who were looking at me expectantly. I took a deep breath. I really didn't want to open it in front of them.

"Okay," I said. Peeling away the wrapping, I found a long black suede box. I held my breath and opened it to find a gorgeous pearl necklace.

I felt Dawn and Reneé looking over my shoulders at the gift. "Wow! That's beautiful, Lacie!" I heard Dawn exclaim. "Is that from Joe?"

I didn't have time to answer. "No, of course not," Mama said. "It's from Tony, isn't it, Lacie? We should have known that if it was white it had to be from him."

"Mama!" Reneé exclaimed.

I just looked at Mama sadly. I didn't have the strength to argue. I stood up slowly.

"Mama, how many more digs are you going to get in until you've had enough?"

She ignored my question. "I bet you're going to get on the phone right now and thank him for that expensive gift, aren't you?"

"No, Mama."

"Why not? You've finally gotten what you wanted."

I sighed tiredly. "No, I haven't. We decided not to be together," I answered softly. I looked at everyone else. "Good night. I'm going to bed."

Bang! Bang! Bang! The persistent knocking on my bedroom door woke me up. Not again! I opened the door swiftly, prepared to get angry at whoever it was, but caught myself when I saw Mama's expression.

"Reneé's having cramps and she's spotting."

I didn't think twice. "I'll call a cab."

Reneé seemed to be in a great deal of pain and they took her into the examination room immediately as soon as we arrived at the hospital. Mama went in with her while I waited in the hall. I had called Danny before we left the house and was expecting him any minute. I was a nervous wreck and was praying that Reneé wouldn't lose her baby. It would devastate her.

When I saw Danny talking to a nurse at the nurse's station, I could tell that he'd been crying. I walked over to him and gave him a hug. He embraced me tightly.

"Mama's in there now with her," I said.

"Yeah, I know," he said, wiping his face. "The nurse just told me."

He needed to be in there with her. He was the father of her child, after all.

"Danny, why don't you go in there and tell Mama to come out here? Reneé is going to need you," I suggested.

He nodded and went into the examination room. A few minutes later Mama came down the hall, walking as if she were in a trance. She sat down next to me and merely stared ahead, without saying anything.

"Mama, how's Reneé?" I asked softly. "What did her doctor say?"

She sighed deeply and ran a hand through her hair. "They really haven't said much. They're giving her medicine to slow down the contractions right now and monitoring her and the baby's vital signs."

"Did they say why this happened?"

"No." She shook her head swiftly. All of a sudden, she broke down in tears.

I was stunned and didn't know what to do. I had never seen her like this. It was odd seeing her cry, and almost ironic that I was staying strong and she was weeping. If anything, it should have been the opposite, because I usually cried. I handed her a tissue awkwardly and she blew her nose.

"Lacie," she mumbled between blows, "would you mind getting me some coffee?" she asked. "A lot of cream and sugar, please."

"Sure, Mama," I replied quietly.

I came back a few minutes later and saw that she had collected herself and was now sitting up straight in the chair. I handed her the coffee and she thanked me.

"Ahh, that's some good coffee," she said after she took a sip. "Thank you, sweetie. I really needed that."

"You're welcome," I said, continuing to watch her.

She grinned and stared at the cup in her hand. "I guess I surprised you, didn't I? I know you didn't expect to see me cry like that."

"No, Mama, I didn't" I admitted, looking at my hands.

"There's always a first time for everything," she remarked and smiled when I looked up at her. "I do have feelings, you know," she said softly. She patted my leg lightly.

I shrugged in answer. "I've never seen you show them before. I didn't even know you could cry."

"Ahh, yes, Lacie." She chuckled lightly and put her head back. "I've shed my share of tears. Believe me when I tell you, I have wept many times. When it was just the two of us, I did it a lot. It was mostly because I was scared and a little lonely. I couldn't let you see that, though, because I had responsibilities and it wouldn't have solved anything." She looked down the hall and then checked her watch.

"She's going to be okay, Mama," I answered to her silent question.

"I know." She smiled weakly. "I'm concerned, that's all."

I nodded.

"I'm concerned about you too, you know," she said suddenly. She smiled when she saw me raise my eyebrows. "You're my first, Lacie. You should know that I'm always going to be worried about you."

When she gave me the key to the door that had been locked for so long, I opened it. This was my chance.

"Mama, why have you always been so hard on me? Why do we argue so much?"

She shrugged a little. "It's probably because you're just as stubborn as I am." She grinned. "Girl, you are exactly like me—in every way. You just don't know how many gray hairs I got because I was so worried about you." She paused. "I did it to myself, though, because I didn't know how to talk to you."

"Mama…" I started.

"No…" She silenced me with a finger to her lips. "This is long overdue. It's not going to be easy, so let me finish before I change my mind," she murmured tenderly. Her eyes started watering. "I am so sorry, Lacie. I'm sorry for not being the mother that I should have been and the mother you've always wanted. What I said about being young when I had you and not knowing how to be a mother, that was just an excuse. I was adult enough to have you and I should have been adult enough to be a mother." She shook her head slowly. "All of those arguments that we've had, especially since I've been back here, have made me realize all of the hurt you've been through. I am terribly sorry."

I shook my head when she finished. "I can't let you take responsibility for all of this. It's my fault as well. I apologize also, Mama, because there've been times when I didn't speak to you with respect. I was so focused on dwelling on the past and blaming you that I let my pride get in the way. I've been rude and disrespectful to you when you didn't deserve any of it. I think deep down, I knew that you did all that you could for me. I'm so sorry. Will you forgive me, Mama?"

By this time, we were both in tears and holding tissue to wipe our faces and blow our noses. She grabbed my hand.

"Sweetie, there's nothing to forgive. I think what we both should try to do is forget what's in the past and concentrate on building a better bond between us. Life is too short for this. We've wasted too much time already, so let's not waste any more, okay?" I nodded in answer. "I love you, Lacie. With my entire heart, child, you are dear to me. Don't you ever question my love for you," she scolded tenderly.

"Yes, ma'am," I nodded.

She grinned. "Now come here and give your mother a hug," she said and we both started laughing. We held each other for a long time.

"Mama?" I asked, after we finally let go of each other.

"Yes, baby?"

"Why did it take something like this to bring us together?"

"Oh child, please!" she exclaimed, dismissing my question with a wave of her hand. "I was planning on having this heart to heart with you early in the morning. This was just circumstance."

"Oh?" I smiled.

"Yeah, girl. When I saw how miserable you looked walking up the stairs tonight, I knew I had to talk to you. Uh, uh, I can't have my baby looking like that." She shook her head and I couldn't help laughing. "Now, about this Tony fellow…" she began.

I frowned. "Oh, Mama! Don't spoil this, please," I groaned.

She patted my hand lightly. "Now, now, wait a minute. Give me a chance. You haven't heard what I'm going to say," she defended.

"Okay, I'm listening," I murmured.

"Now, I've been thinking a lot about this whole situation with you and Tony. I talked to Reneé and Dawn about it also, and they made me realize something that I was too stubborn to want to see, even though you've been telling me this all along." She sighed. "Sweetie, you've got it bad for this Tony fellow. I mean, really bad. When you walked up those steps after opening his gift, you looked like someone had just taken your sweet potato pie away from you—and you know how much you love sweet potato pie." She chuckled when she saw my confused expression. "I know that was a bad comparison, but I think you get my point." She shook her head. "Baby, I've never seen you look that sad before and I certainly haven't seen you act that way about Joe or any of the other men you've dated. So you're just going to have to call him up or something, because I can't have my baby looking like this," she declared.

I grinned. "What about all of the Mister Charlie jokes and I'm black and he's white and everything?"

She tilted her head to the side. "Well, I still feel the same way, Lacie. I think there's always going to be a part of me that will be prejudiced, because I remember all too well what it was like when I was growing up. I come from a different generation than you do. However, you can't worry about how I feel about this. I can handle it and maybe, just maybe, I'll learn to accept it. I'll just refrain from calling him Mister Charlie in front of his face, that's all," she said.

"Mama!"

"I was only joking." She smiled. "Now go to the phone and call him," she commanded, lightly.

"Uhh…I can't."

"Why not?"

"Because we both agreed that it wasn't our time and…you know, I don't want to get into it. I just know that we're not together and anyway, I called his parents' house and Simone answered the phone."

"You mean that little wench you wanted to punch out the other day?" she asked, and I chuckled and nodded. She shrugged. "So what is that supposed to mean?"

"Well, it probably means he's gone back to her." I shrugged.

"Lacie, please don't act like those people in the soap operas. They just draw things out so." Mama groaned as she looked up toward the ceiling and rolled her eyes. "You can't assume these things, Lacie. That man loves you. I could tell that the first time I met him in your office that day. I really doubt that he's gone back to Simone, sweetheart."

"How do you know?"

She rolled her eyes. "Once again, don't think like those people on the soap operas. Now, I have reluctantly decided to come to some understanding about this whole issue with you and him, so you'd better do something soon, before I change my mind."

"You won't," I said confidently.

"That's true, but I thought I'd add that in there just to push you a little."

"Okay. I'll talk to him when I go back to work."

"Yes, you do that, dear." Mama nodded and patted my leg again. She stood up and sighed. "Now that I've patched up stuff here, I'm going to go check on my other daughter and see what's going on."

I watched her walk down the hall. "That's my mama," I said aloud.

CHAPTER 16

I was quite tired the next day. The doctor finally released Reneé around six o'clock that morning, under the conditions that she stay bedridden for a few days and that her temperature and blood pressure be checked around the clock. Her blood pressure was running a bit high, so he instructed her to come back to see him in a few days. Once we got her home, Mama and I took turns checking her blood pressure and temperature and making sure she was eating properly.

"How are you feeling?" I asked her during my round, while Mama slept on the sofa downstairs.

"I never thought being pregnant would be like this," she said as I wiped her forehead with a damp cloth. "But I'm feeling a little better."

"Don't worry. Once you see that baby in your arms, you won't even think about what you're going through right now."

"Whatever," she said, rolling her eyes upward. I laughed.

❧

"Good morning, everybody," I said as I walked through the department to my office.

"Good morning, Lacie," Carrie said, entering my office. "How was your Christmas?"

"You want to know if I told Joe, right?" I asked shrewdly.

"If you insist on telling me." She sat down in a chair.

"Let me put it this way." I flopped down in my chair and ran a hand through my hair. "If I were the last woman on earth and he the last man, I believe he'd kill himself just so the human race would be extinct."

"That bad, huh?" She looked sympathetic.

"Oh yeah. It was really bad." I shook my head. "Carrie, I never thought I could make someone so angry."

Carrie tried to look optimistic. "At least you told him. Now you and Tony can be together, right?" she said. "What?" she asked, when she saw me shake my head. "What's happened now, Lacie?"

After I told her everything that had happened, all she could do was just shake her head. "Are you really going to talk to Tony or did you just say that to appease your mother?"

"Why do you ask?"

"I know you, Lacie. You've got too much pride and I'm sure hearing Simone's voice on the other line probably shook you up."

"Yes, it did," I said. "However, I'm tired of not doing what everybody tells me to do. I get good advice from you and Robert and it goes in one ear and right out the other." I shook my finger. "Uh, uh. You all are not going to blame me for this one. I'm not going to mess this up."

"That's my girl. You fight for your man." Carrie smiled and stood up. "Do you want any coffee?" she asked, heading for the door.

"Not right now, thank you."

"Okay." She walked to the door and stopped abruptly. "Uh, Lacie, come here and look at this."

I frowned and walked to the door. Carrie pointed toward Tony's open door. In his office, we saw Tony and Simone in an embrace. Then letting go, Simone kissed him. *Damn!*

"Carrie, on second thought, I'll take you up on that offer. I'm going to need something strong after all," I said.

Carrie walked toward the kitchen and I closed the door and leaned against it. *Damn!*

"Sorry, Mama. You may think that I'm acting like those people on the soap operas, but I'm not going to make a fool of myself," I mumbled.

I tried to keep busy throughout the morning, but my mind kept wandering to that vision of Tony and Simone together. Every time I thought about it, my heart felt as if someone had sliced it with a knife.

I heard a soft knock. Carrie stood in the doorway with a strange look on her face. "Ah Lacie, there's someone here to see you."

Why did she have that look on her face? "Okay, send…" I stopped when Carrie stepped aside and Joe walked in. "Joe?"

His face was expressionless. "Do you mind if I talk to you for a minute?" he asked, once Carrie had closed the door.

"Sh...sh...sh...sure," I stuttered. I looked up at the ceiling. Lord, what was this man going to do? I gulped. "Do you want to sit down?"

"No, thank you. I think better when I'm standing."

"Okay," I managed to say as I tried to figure out what had brought about this unforeseen visit.

We stared at each other for a long time. I stared because I was expecting him to blow up at me again, but I had no idea why he was staring at me.

"You look good," he said suddenly.

"Thank you," I replied. I couldn't tolerate the suspense anymore. "Joe, I'm..."

"Shh..." he whispered, standing with his eyes closed for a moment. "Don't say anything. I'm trying to get my thoughts together to tell you why I came, so please, don't interrupt."

I nodded. "Alright."

"Thank you." He stuck his hands in his pockets and took a deep breath. "Uh...I thought a lot about the argument we had, on the way home and over the holidays. I was so angry and frustrated." He looked out the window. "I guess Tony told you that I went over to his house after I left yours." I nodded. "I wanted to punch his lights out, but Tony is a good fighter and I knew we would be scrapping for a while and I would miss my flight." He smiled thinly.

"We agreed many years ago that we'd never fight over a woman." He chuckled lightly. "Do you know that he blamed this all on himself?" He didn't wait for my answer. "He sure did. He defended you right down to the very end. I've never seen him do that for anyone." His expression was solemn as he looked at the floor. "That means he must love you very much. It's evident that you love him just as much." He took another deep breath. "I'm not a vindictive person, Lacie. I've never held grudges and I'm not going to start now. Life is too short for that, and Tony and I have been through too much together to end our friendship like this."

He sighed. "I guess in some way, I should be grateful to you, because you were right. It would have been a mistake to get married if you were not in love with me. It was hard for me to face it, but I'm glad that you told me now, instead of later—despite the bad timing. He's a lucky bastard, my friend Tony is. He always has been, and he's even luckier to have you. I think he knows that, though." He shuffled his feet. "Despite everything that's happened, I know you loved me in your own way, Lacie. So don't feel ashamed or sorry. You did the right thing by telling me and I'm going to do the right thing by wishing you two the best, because I love you both and I want you two to be happy." By this time he had reached my desk. I was sitting there with tears steadily streaming down my face. "Come here and give me a hug."

I stood up and he hugged me tightly. "I don't think I'll ever get over you, Lacie," he whispered in my ear.

"You will, in time," I murmured.

He let go, but held my face for a second. "Be good and stay out of trouble." He kissed my cheek and walked toward the door. He stopped before opening it and looked back. "Happy New Year, Lacie. Take care," he said and walked out.

I stood in my office in complete bewilderment. Then I sat down heavily in my chair and just stared at the walls.

When lunchtime rolled around, Carrie invited me to lunch with her. I accepted, because since my promotion, we rarely went out to lunch together. I made a mental note to make sure that we did that more often.

"So did everything go all right with Joe?" Carrie asked directly, as soon as the waiter left with our orders.

"Yes. Much better than I thought it would. When he walked in, I was so shocked. His face was like a mask."

"I know." Carrie nodded her head. "I didn't know what to think when I saw him either."

"Joe said that he'd had a long time to think about everything and he knew that it would have been a mistake if we'd gotten married. He's not going to hold a grudge against me or Tony and he wished us well," I said.

"Well, good! That means that you and Tony can get back together, right?" she asked excitedly.

"I don't think so Carrie. Not after seeing Tony and Simone cuddling up in his office. I'm not going to be the fool again."

She looked at me seriously. "You don't know that he's back with her, Lacie. You're only assuming."

"Maybe I am." I shrugged. "But I can't take that chance." She shook her head. "Carrie, you saw it yourself," I insisted.

"Yes, I did, but I think we should give Tony the benefit of the doubt. There could be a reason for what we saw."

"I doubt that very seriously."

She took a deep breath. "Did you at least tell him what Joe said to you today?" she asked. I shook my head. "Lacie!" she exclaimed.

"Look, evidently Tony's moving on, and I don't want to get in the way of whatever he has going for him," I said.

"You don't know that!"

I gave her a dubious look. "Carrie, please, I know enough when I see two people sucking face." I winced. I couldn't believe that I had used one of my mother's colloquialisms.

"Sucking face?" Carrie gave me a quizzical look.

"Oh, whatever," I dismissed. "Let's just drop the subject, okay?" I suggested as the waiter brought us our drinks.

℘

After lunch, I tried to avoid Tony as much as possible, but it seemed that wherever I turned, there he was.

It was five minutes to five o'clock when Tony tapped on my open door.

"Yes?" I asked, a little too rudely.

He looked startled at the tone of my voice as he cautiously walked in. "Uh…I just came in to check on you," he explained. "I saw Joe come in here earlier. Is everything all right?"

"Yes. Everything's fine," I answered brusquely, putting some documents into my briefcase.

I could feel his eyes on me. "What did you two talk about?"

I gave him a blank look. "Why do you want to know?"

He shrugged. "I was just wondering, that's all," he replied, looking at me curiously.

I smiled thinly. "Well, do me a favor and don't wonder, okay? From what we agreed on the other day, that's the last thing you should be doing, right?"

"Am I missing something here?" he asked, looking perplexed. "Are you angry with me?"

"Why would you think that?"

He shifted his feet. "Because of how cynical you've been with me ever since I walked in that door and how it seems as if you've been avoiding me. I've run into you several times, deliberately, I might add, and you've ignored me."

"Really?" I asked nonchalantly.

"Yes, really."

"Why are you so concerned?" I stopped what I was doing, glanced at him quickly, and then continued getting ready.

"Because you've been really cold toward me and I don't know why." He took a deep breath. "Listen, if there's something I did, just tell me!"

"I didn't say you did anything, Tony."

"Look, we're too old to be playing high school games," he said abruptly. "You may not have said anything, but your body language is telling me something else."

"Don't pay any attention to my body language, okay?" I voiced, putting my coat on. "It's not your job anymore."

I left Tony standing there as I yanked my briefcase off the desk and walked out. The elevator opened its doors as soon as I reached the lobby. I quickly pushed the button and watched as the door closed in his face.

When I arrived home, I heard Mama cooking in the kitchen. The aroma of the food was welcoming. I put my briefcase down and hung up my coat. She came out to greet me.

"Hey, sweetie," she greeted, wiping her hands on her apron.

"Hey, Mama," I mumbled.

She studied me for a second. "How was your day?"

I walked to the sofa and sat down tiredly. I looked at Mama and shook my head slowly.

Motherly concern came over her face. "What happened?" she asked calmly, sitting next to me.

She listened intently while I told her about my day. She didn't interrupt as I told her about Joe coming to see me and my seeing Tony with Simone.

"Mama, I was all set to give this thing with Tony another try and then I saw the two of them together." I shook my head.

She touched my knee lightly. "Why didn't you tell Tony what Joe said to you when he asked you?" she asked softly.

"I don't know Mama," I groaned. "All I could think about was Simone kissing him, and I got upset. So I forgot about it."

"Don't you think you should call him and tell him?"

"No." I shook my head and looked up at her. "It's not going to make a difference, Mama."

She gave me a loving smile. "How do you know that?"

I thought for a second, then said, "I don't."

We heard Reneé come down the stairs. She looked refreshed.

"What are you doing walking down the stairs?" I asked.

She sat down on the sofa. "Mama took me to the doctor today because I was complaining about being off my feet. After he checked my blood pressure and everything and saw that I was a little better, he said that I could start walking around again, but not to overdo it," she explained. "Are you okay?" she asked me.

I heard the phone ring and stood up. "Yeah, I'm fine. I'm going to get the phone in the kitchen."

Before I reached the kitchen, I heard Reneé ask Mama, "What's wrong with her?"

I answered the phone. It was Dawn.

"Hey, girl!" she said cheerfully.

"Hey," I replied.

"What's wrong?"

"Nothing," I dismissed.

"Uh, huh," she said. I could hear the doubt in her voice. "Listen, I called to ask you if you want to come see me off at the airport tonight."

"What? Why are you leaving so soon?"

"It's really not that soon. I start shooting the movie in a few weeks and I thought it would be a good idea to get used to my surroundings in Miami," she said happily.

"You don't have to sound that happy about it," I said in a crabby tone.

"Yeah, I'm going to miss you too, Lacie," she chuckled. "So are you going to come with me willingly or am I going to have to drag you?"

I was telling Dawn everything that had happened as the cab stopped at the passenger drop off at the airport.

Dawn shook her head as we got out of the cab. "You should have told him, Lacie."

"No, I shouldn't have," I said stubbornly.

"Do you actually believe he went back to her, Lacie?" She looked at me skeptically as I grabbed one of her bags.

We started walking toward the terminal. "I have no choice but to think that, Dawn."

Dawn stopped and gave me a stupefied look.

"What?" I asked. "Why did you stop?"

She shook her head. "Lacie, I love you with all my heart, but sometimes I really don't understand what goes on in that head of yours."

"What are you talking about?"

"You're being irrational."

"Dawn, I'm only looking out for myself. I don't want to get hurt," I asserted.

"Who says you're going to get hurt and who says that he and Simone are back together?" she said loudly.

I looked around nervously. "Dawn, you're making a scene."

We reached the line to get on the plane. "You know what? I don't care, Lacie," she scolded. "Don't you think you're being a little too presumptuous? You know he loves you. You know that. Why would he even think about getting back with her?"

"Because..." I started to say.

She held up her hand and stopped me. "Lacie, I don't even want to hear it." She shook her head as she handed the attendant her ticket. "How do you know what's really going on if you don't try to find out for yourself?" she asserted tenderly. "You don't." She grabbed me in a strong embrace as some people started going down the hall to get on the plane. "Lacie, life is too short for assumptions and pride." She kissed me on the cheek and walked backward down the hall. "Think about what I

said. I'll give you a call when I get to Miami. Love you."
She turned around and a few seconds later she disap-
peared onto the plane.

I stood at the window contemplating what she'd said
and waited until the huge jet took off into the dark sky.

When I got back home, I was surprised to find both
Carrie and Robert there with Mama and Reneé.
Evidently, they had been in some intense conversation,
but as soon as I entered the apartment, it immediately
stopped.

"Why did you stop?" I looked at all four of them
suspiciously. I turned toward Carrie. "I'm surprised to see
you. What brought you over here?"

All smiles, Carrie stood up instantly, walked over to
me and gave me a hug. "I came over to invite you to the
New Year's Eve party I'm having at my house," she
explained innocently.

"I didn't know you were having one."

She shrugged. "It was kind of a spur of the moment
decision. I haven't had a party in years, so I thought it
would be a good idea."

"Do you think you're going to have enough people
there? Most people make their plans for New Year's Eve a
month in advance."

"Oh, it's not going to be anything major, just be a few
friends that I know don't have any other plans for that
night."

"Oh, okay," I said thoughtfully.

"David and I were doing some shopping for the party
and since we were out, I thought I'd come over here and

invite you personally." She glanced around. "It's been a while since I've been here. You've done wonders with the place. This apartment looks really nice, Lacie," she complimented.

"Thank you."

"You're welcome." She smiled and glanced at her watch. "Got to go. I can't keep David waiting." She looked at me. "So, will you come to the party?"

"I'll see you at work tomorrow and let you know then."

She kissed me on the cheek. "Okay. Have a good night." She walked toward the door and turned around. "Goodbye, Miss Josephine, Reneé and Robert. Take care."

"Take care," they replied.

As soon as Carrie closed the door, I turned around and looked at the three of them. I put my hands on my hips.

"Okay, what's up?"

They looked at each other, feigning innocence.

"What?" Reneé asked first.

"You all are up to something because the minute I came in here, the chatter stopped. Now what is it?"

"Nothing is going on, Lacie. We were only talking about the New Year's Eve party that Carrie's giving. That's all," Robert defended.

I threw up my hands. "Fine. If you don't want to tell me what's going on, then I'm not going to worry about it. It's bound to come out sooner or later anyway." I walked toward the kitchen.

"So are you going?" I heard Mama call after me.

"I don't know. I haven't decided yet," I called back.

I heard them talking while I made a sandwich. I just knew they were talking about me. Robert came in as I was pouring water in a glass.

"Are you all finished talking about me yet?" I asked sarcastically.

"Of course. You know you're all we think about, Lacie. We don't even have time to think about ourselves," Robert quipped. I gave him a look. "Lighten up, will you? I was only teasing. I came in to see how you were doing. Your mother told me that you went to see Dawn off at the airport. How are you handling it?"

"I'm fine." I shrugged. "I'm happy for her and I'm confident that everything is going to work out for her. It looks like she's getting off to a good start and I'll just continue to pray that she does well."

"She'll be fine," Robert said. He took a deep breath. "So, are you going to the New Year's Eve party or what?"

I took a bite of my sandwich and looked at him pensively. "Robert, what's going on?"

He looked innocent. "Nothing," he replied.

I figured I couldn't get anything out of him even if I tried. I shrugged it off. "I don't know, yet. I haven't been so festive lately."

"Why don't you go to the party then? I'll come with you and I promise you'll have a good time. Carrie's planning a great party. It'll be fun. I don't have anything planned for that night and you know I'd be miserable staying here with you, watching Dick Clark bring in the New Year."

"What's so important about this party that everyone insists that I go?"

"Oh, come on, will you?" He sounded exasperated. "Let's start the New Year off fresh with new beginnings."

"Fine, I'll go," I relented. "What have I got to lose?"

The next few days went by fast.

Dawn called me as promised and said that she was doing fine. Her flight had gone well and she had met some interesting men on the plane. She was always such a free spirit. It was just like her to try to pick up some men.

The conversation Tony and I had had the other day seemed to have had an effect, as I saw very little of him. He rarely stayed in his office. Every now and then I would glance over at his office and see him in there, but as soon as I turned my head and looked back, he would be gone

Carrie was elated that I'd agreed to go to her party. "I can't wait! Watch! You're going to have a wonderful time."

"I hope so, considering I was coerced into doing this by you and Robert," I grumbled.

"We care about you, Lacie, and we want you to be happy. There's no need to be home when you can come over to my house and have a good time with the people who love you."

"Whatever," I uttered under my breath when she walked out the door.

"I heard that," she called back as she closed the door.

After work, I decided to go to one of the local coffee shops around the area. I needed some alone time before I headed home. I sat at a table in the back, ordered a cappuccino and took out some papers from work. A waiter came over shortly with my order.

I was enjoying my cappuccino and looking over some material when I felt someone standing over me.

"Lacie Adams," the male voice said.

I looked up and saw Steven Turner. "Steve?" I asked. "What are you doing here?"

"I saw you walk in and wondered what made you come in here. I've never seen you here before."

I ran a hand through my hair. "Yeah, well, it was just something I decided to do before I went home."

"Reneé is still there, huh?" He smirked.

"Yeah, and so is my mother. I've got a full house."

"Oh," he said, with a nod. After a moment of odd silence he asked, "Do you mind if I sit?"

"No, not at all," I said easily, indicating a chair opposite mine.

He sat and put his cup of coffee on the table. "So, how have you been?" he asked.

"Okay, I guess. How are you doing on your new job?"

"Fine," he replied. "I'm really happy there."

I smiled. "I'm happy for you."

"Thank you." He took a deep breath. "Lacie, I know it's been a while since we talked, but I want to apologize for the way I acted toward you that time in Washington. I was way out of line," he said suddenly.

"Hey, I was out of line, also." I shrugged. "I shouldn't have slapped you," I said sincerely.

He shook his head. "No. I deserved it. I was an ass and I'm sorry. Actually, I was an ass the whole duration of our relationship, if you could call it that."

I chuckled. "Listen, there are no hard feelings here, Steve. I just think we were too different, that's all. That's why I ended it. It was a waste of time for both of us."

"Yeah," he said, looking a little sheepish. "You're right. It was better that it ended."

"I am a little curious, though," I said. "What made you apologize? While we were seeing each other, you never apologized about anything."

He shrugged. "I realized that I messed things up between us. I didn't treat you right and I'm deeply sorry." He sighed. "I guess people never realize what they have until it's gone, huh?"

I didn't know whether he was asking me or making a statement. We took a sip from our cups, and then he stood up.

"Well, I've got to go. I just wanted to get that off my chest," he said. He was about to walk away, but then stopped. "Oh, Lacie, one more thing. If you have someone or ever have the chance to fall in love with someone, treasure that person while you can. Don't waste your time on nonsense, okay?" I nodded slowly. "Good."

He smiled. "It was nice seeing you again. Take care of yourself."

Speechless, I stared at his retreating figure as he left the coffee shop.

ℒ

It was New Year's Eve and I was searching my closet for something to wear. Mama walked in and sat on the bed.

"Are you in better spirits yet?" she asked.

I shook my head. "Not particularly. I'm starting to feel as if I should stay home, after all. I can't find anything to wear."

"What's wrong with what you've got in your hand?" she asked, indicating the black suede pantsuit that I had draped around my arm.

"Umm...I don't know..."

"Girl, that looks fine. You're only going to a party with friends. It's not anything formal."

I looked at the outfit. "You're right." I started to put it on. "Mama, do you believe that some people are meant to be together?"

"Yeah, I guess I do, honey," she replied, getting up to hand me my suede boots. "Shoot, that's the way I thought about your father, until his sorry behind decided to leave us."

"Mama, now you know that's not the way it happened. It was a mutual decision between the both of you," I reminded her.

"Yeah, well..." she muttered. "Why did you ask me that question?"

"I just feel as if everybody is saying the same thing to me over and over again, that's all."

Mama smiled warmly. "If you feel as if everybody's telling you the same thing, then don't you think you should start listening?" I was about to speak, but she cut me off. "Hush," she said, putting a finger up. "Just think about what I said, huh?" she murmured softly as she closed the door behind her.

CHAPTER 17

Robert and I arrived at Carrie's house on time. There were a few people there that I knew already, and I gave them acknowledging glances. Carrie greeted us and kissed me on the cheek.

"I'm glad you came," she exclaimed. "I wasn't sure if you were going to come after all."

"Yeah, right," I chided, looking at her skeptically.

"You're right," she said with a laugh. "Listen, make yourselves comfortable. The food is on the table in the dining room and there are plenty of beverages. Lacie, go on in and help yourself. Robert, may I talk to you for a minute?" she asked him, pulling him toward the kitchen.

Left alone, I peeked into the living room and saw a few people watching the big screen TV that stood near the wall. There wasn't much going on. My stomach started growling, so I took that as a hint and headed for the dining room.

The table was covered with food and it looked good. Carrie had definitely gone all out for this night. There appeared to be every dish that I liked on the table. No one was around, so I started piling my plate and wasn't embarrassed. I heard someone come in, but didn't pay attention as I continued going from dish to dish.

"Don't you think you should save some for everybody else?" I heard his voice say.

Oh no! I groaned inwardly. I wondered how long he'd been in the room. I turned around and looked at him. "There's enough here for everyone, Tony," I replied, indicating the huge buffet. "What are you doing here, anyway?"

"Carrie invited me."

"Oh?" I questioned. I couldn't wait to get my hands on her.

"Are you surprised?"

"I am, as a matter of fact. I would have thought you'd have other plans."

"No, I didn't have anything planned." He took a deep breath. "Actually, I'm glad she invited me. I was a little lonely."

"Really?" I asked indifferently.

"Yeah, really," he repeated.

Carrie and Robert came in with more food.

I walked to Carrie immediately and grabbed her arm. "Carrie, I need to talk to you."

"Sorry, I can't, Lacie. We've got to finish putting the food on the table," she replied. "Continue talking to Tony. Robert and I will be in the kitchen." She and Robert walked out.

I glanced at Tony. I had to get away from him. A few people came in and I nodded to them in greeting as I eased out and left him in the dining room.

I found a seat in the living room and ate while I watched the other guests mingle. They seemed to be in such good spirits about the New Year.

I noticed Tony in a corner of the room watching me and I turned my head. A minute later, I saw Carrie and Robert talking to him. What were they up to now? The three of them stood there talking for a moment, and then

Tony nodded and headed on over to a piano that was in a corner by the bar. Carrie and Robert must have asked him to play. Sure enough, they got everyone to quiet down and then announced that Tony was going to play.

Tony sat down at the piano. "Uh, this song that I'm about to sing is very dear to me. It's become my favorite actually, because I sang it to an amazing and beautiful woman on the same day I realized that I wanted her to be in my life forever." He cleared his throat. "Uh, I haven't sung in a while, so please bear with me." A few people laughed in good humor.

I stood up and was about to walk out when I heard the beginning notes of a familiar melody. I stopped and listened to be sure I was hearing correctly. I turned around when I knew the song. It was "You and I" by Stevie Wonder.

Standing there in complete shock, I watched him continue to play and sing with his eyes closed. Once again, he seemed to get lost in the music. I couldn't help staring. When he finished the song, everyone applauded and a few people whistled for an encore. He politely waved them off, but promised another one later. Then he stood up and walked toward me, his eyes fixed on mine.

I was at a loss for words, but somehow managed to say, "Who was that for?"

He smiled. "You already know the answer."

Suddenly, I noticed that all eyes were on us. "Excuse me," I said awkwardly and walked toward the kitchen.

I passed in through the swinging doors and heard them open and close again. I knew he was behind me, but I kept my back to him, afraid to turn around. My heart was racing and I felt an incredible wave of emotion come over me.

"Did you like the song?"

"Yes, it was beautiful."

"Do you remember the last time I played it?" he asked.

I took a deep breath. "Of course I do. It was the night we…"

"Made love," he finished. "I remember how complete I felt with you in my arms and how I didn't want to let you go."

"Tony, don't…" I pleaded weakly. "We agreed…"

"I know what we agreed to, Lacie, but I don't care," he interrupted. He turned me around gently so that I could face him. "I know what Joe said to you the other day. He came to my apartment before he left for Miami and told me everything. Why didn't you tell me what he said when I asked you?"

I hesitated.

"What?" he asked.

I took a deep breath. "Tony, I know about you and Simone."

He looked perplexed. "What are you talking about?"

"Tony, don't play games. I saw you and Simone in your office that day," I said. His bewildered look turned into a grin. "I don't see what's so funny, Tony."

He shook his head and cleared his throat. "Uh, what did you see, Lacie?"

Oh, so now he was going to rub it in? "You know damn well what I saw, Anthony Douglas!"

"No, I don't. What did you see?" he taunted.

"I saw her kiss you!" I exclaimed, frustrated that he'd made me say it. He appeared amused by my outrage and that angered me even more.

"So, by that you automatically assumed..."

I interrupted him. "There is no assuming, Tony. I saw you two with my own eyes," I said sharply. "You know what? Forget it. It doesn't matter anyway. This whole thing between us has been exasperating from the beginning and I've about had it." I sighed tiredly.

I tried to walk past him but his arm caught my waist. We were inches apart and I didn't want to look at him.

"Tell me. Did she kiss me like this?" he asked as he bent his head and gave me a peck on my lips. "Or was the kiss like this?" he asked again. He kissed me softly and lingeringly. I responded without hesitation. We continued kissing until he stopped briefly. "Which one was it?" he whispered and smiled as I tried to regain my composure.

"It was the first one," I murmured.

He put his forehead against mine and gently put his hands in my hair. "Exactly. There's a big difference between the two, isn't there?" he asked. I nodded weakly. He shook his head. "Simone gave me a friendly good-bye kiss, that's all. She left for Japan yesterday for another shoot," he explained. "Once again, there is nothing going on between us. There never was after I met you. I'm in love with you and only you. Can't you get that through your stubborn head?"

"But…" I began to protest, but he stopped me with an even more passionate kiss.

After a moment, he finally lifted his head and looked at me. "Did that convince you?"

"A little…yes," I said. "I'm sorry. I shouldn't have come to that conclusion so quickly."

"That's okay. I know about you and your assumptions by now," he teased, and we chuckled. "I'm just glad it wasn't too late."

"Yeah but…Carrie and Robert would not have let that happen."

He cupped my face and his eyes seemed to plead with mine. "Are you willing to give us a try, then?"

I thought for only a second, then said, "Yes."

He breathed a sigh of relief. "I didn't know if you were going to say yes or no."

"Actually, I think I knew the answer to that question a long time ago."

His expression was tender, as he said. "I love you so much."

"I love you, too. I really do," I returned as he bent his head and kissed me again, and I wrapped my arms around his neck without a second thought.

I was happy and deeply in love, and despite all of my reservations before, I no longer felt as if a line had been crossed. The difference in our color was not an issue to me and at that moment, I didn't think or care about the consequences that might come our way. I just wanted to be with him.

And that's all that mattered.

2007 Publication Schedule

January

Rooms of the Heart
Donna Hill
ISBN-13: 978-1-58571-219-9
ISBN-10: 1-58571-219-1
$6.99

A Dangerous Love
J. M. Jeffries
ISBN-13: 978-1-58571-217-5
ISBN-10: 1-58571-217-5
$6.99

February

Bound By Love
Beverly Clark
ISBN-13: 978-1-58571-232-8
ISBN-10: 1-58571-232-9
$6.99

A Love to Cherish
Beverly Clark
ISBN-13: 978-1-58571-233-5
ISBN-10: 1-58571-233-7
$6.99

March

Best of Friends
Natalie Dunbar
ISBN-13: 978-1-58571-220-5
ISBN-10: 1-58571-220-5
$6.99

Midnight Magic
Gwynne Forster
ISBN-13: 978-1-58571-225-0
ISBN-10: 1-58571-225-6
$6.99

April

Cherish the Flame
Beverly Clark
ISBN-13: 978-1-58571-221-2
ISBN-10: 1-58571-221-3
$6.99

Quiet Storm
Donna Hill
ISBN-13: 978-1-58571-226-7
ISBN-10: 1-58571-226-4
$6.99

May

Sweet Tomorrows
Kimberley White
ISBN-13: 978-1-58571-234-2
ISBN-10: 1-58571-234-5
$6.99

No Commitment Required
Seressia Glass
ISBN-13: 978-1-58571-222-9
ISBN-10: 1-58571-222-1
$6.99

June

A Dangerous Deception
J. M. Jeffries
ISBN-13: 978-1-58571-228-1
ISBN-10: 1-58571-228-0
$6.99

Illusions
Pamela Leigh Starr
ISBN-13: 978-1-58571-229-8
ISBN-10: 1-58571-229-9
$6.99

2007 Publication Schedule (continued)

July

Indiscretions
Donna Hill
ISBN-13: 978-1-58571-230-4
ISBN-10: 1-58571-230-2
$6.99

Whispers in the Night
Dorothy Elizabeth Love
ISBN-13: 978-1-58571-231-1
ISBN-10: 1-58571-231-1
$6.99

August

Bodyguard
Andrea Jackson
ISBN-13: 978-1-58571-235-9
ISBN-10: 1-58571-235-3
$6.99

Crossing Paths, Tempting Memories
Dorothy Elizabeth Love
ISBN-13: 978-1-58571-236-6
ISBN-10: 1-58571-236-1
$6.99

September

Fate
Pamela Leigh Starr
ISBN-13: 978-1-58571-258-8
ISBN-10: 1-58571-258-2
$6.99

Mae's Promise
Melody Walcott
ISBN-13: 978-1-58571-259-5
ISBN-10: 1-58571-259-0
$6.99

October

Magnolia Sunset
Giselle Carmichael
ISBN-13: 978-1-58571-260-1
ISBN-10: 1-58571-260-4
$6.99

Broken
Dar Tomlinson
ISBN-13: 978-1-58571-261-8
ISBN-10: 1-58571-261-2
$6.99

November

Truly Inseparable
Wanda Y. Thomas
ISBN-13: 978-1-58571-262-5
ISBN-10: 1-58571-262-0
$6.99

The Color Line
Lizzette G. Carter
ISBN-13: 978-1-58571-263-2
ISBN-10: 1-58571-263-9
$6.99

December

Love Always
Mildred Riley
ISBN-13: 978-1-58571-264-9
ISBN-10: 1-58571-264-7
$6.99

Pride and Joi
Gay Gunn
ISBN-13: 978-1-58571-265-6
ISBN-10: 1-58571-265-5
$6.99

Other Genesis Press, Inc. Titles

A Dangerous Deception	J.M. Jeffries	$8.95
A Dangerous Love	J.M. Jeffries	$8.95
A Dangerous Obsession	J.M. Jeffries	$8.95
A Drummer's Beat to Mend	Kei Swanson	$9.95
A Happy Life	Charlotte Harris	$9.95
A Heart's Awakening	Veronica Parker	$9.95
A Lark on the Wing	Phyliss Hamilton	$9.95
A Love of Her Own	Cheris F. Hodges	$9.95
A Love to Cherish	Beverly Clark	$8.95
A Risk of Rain	Dar Tomlinson	$8.95
A Twist of Fate	Beverly Clark	$8.95
A Will to Love	Angie Daniels	$9.95
Acquisitions	Kimberley White	$8.95
Across	Carol Payne	$12.95
After the Vows	Leslie Esdaile	$10.95
(Summer Anthology)	T.T. Henderson	
	Jacqueline Thomas	
Again My Love	Kayla Perrin	$10.95
Against the Wind	Gwynne Forster	$8.95
All I Ask	Barbara Keaton	$8.95
Ambrosia	T.T. Henderson	$8.95
An Unfinished Love Affair	Barbara Keaton	$8.95
And Then Came You	Dorothy Elizabeth Love	$8.95
Angel's Paradise	Janice Angelique	$9.95
At Last	Lisa G. Riley	$8.95
Best of Friends	Natalie Dunbar	$8.95
Beyond the Rapture	Beverly Clark	$9.95
Blaze	Barbara Keaton	$9.95
Blood Lust	J. M. Jeffries	$9.95

Other Genesis Press, Inc. Titles (continued)

Other Genesis Press, Inc. Titles (continued)

Eden's Garden	Elizabeth Rose	$8.95
Everlastin' Love	Gay G. Gunn	$8.95
Everlasting Moments	Dorothy Elizabeth Love	$8.95
Everything and More	Sinclair Lebeau	$8.95
Everything but Love	Natalie Dunbar	$8.95
Eve's Prescription	Edwina Martin Arnold	$8.95
Falling	Natalie Dunbar	$9.95
Fate	Pamela Leigh Starr	$8.95
Finding Isabella	A.J. Garrotto	$8.95
Forbidden Quest	Dar Tomlinson	$10.95
Forever Love	Wanda Y. Thomas	$8.95
From the Ashes	Kathleen Suzanne	$8.95
	Jeanne Sumerix	
Gentle Yearning	Rochelle Alers	$10.95
Glory of Love	Sinclair LeBeau	$10.95
Go Gentle into that Good Night	Malcom Boyd	$12.95
Goldengroove	Mary Beth Craft	$16.95
Groove, Bang, and Jive	Steve Cannon	$8.99
Hand in Glove	Andrea Jackson	$9.95
Hard to Love	Kimberley White	$9.95
Hart & Soul	Angie Daniels	$8.95
Heartbeat	Stephanie Bedwell-Grime	$8.95
Hearts Remember	M. Loui Quezada	$8.95
Hidden Memories	Robin Allen	$10.95
Higher Ground	Leah Latimer	$19.95
Hitler, the War, and the Pope	Ronald Rychlak	$26.95
How to Write a Romance	Kathryn Falk	$18.95
I Married a Reclining Chair	Lisa M. Fuhs	$8.95
Indigo After Dark Vol. I	Nia Dixon/Angelique	$10.95

Other Genesis Press, Inc. Titles (continued)

Indigo After Dark Vol. II	Dolores Bundy/ Cole Riley	$10.95
Indigo After Dark Vol. III	Montana Blue/ Coco Morena	$10.95
Indigo After Dark Vol. IV	Cassandra Colt/ Diana Richeaux	$14.95
Indigo After Dark Vol. V	Delilah Dawson	$14.95
Icie	Pamela Leigh Starr	$8.95
I'll Be Your Shelter	Giselle Carmichael	$8.95
I'll Paint a Sun	A.J. Garrotto	$9.95
Illusions	Pamela Leigh Starr	$8.95
Indiscretions	Donna Hill	$8.95
Intentional Mistakes	Michele Sudler	$9.95
Interlude	Donna Hill	$8.95
Intimate Intentions	Angie Daniels	$8.95
Jolie's Surrender	Edwina Martin-Arnold	$8.95
Kiss or Keep	Debra Phillips	$8.95
Lace	Giselle Carmichael	$9.95
Last Train to Memphis	Elsa Cook	$12.95
Lasting Valor	Ken Olsen	$24.95
Let Us Prey	Hunter Lundy	$25.95
Life Is Never As It Seems	J.J. Michael	$12.95
Lighter Shade of Brown	Vicki Andrews	$8.95
Love Always	Mildred E. Riley	$10.95
Love Doesn't Come Easy	Charlyne Dickerson	$8.95
Love Unveiled	Gloria Greene	$10.95
Love's Deception	Charlene Berry	$10.95
Love's Destiny	M. Loui Quezada	$8.95
Mae's Promise	Melody Walcott	$8.95

Other Genesis Press, Inc. Titles (continued)

Magnolia Sunset	Giselle Carmichael	$8.95
Matters of Life and Death	Lesego Malepe, Ph.D.	$15.95
Meant to Be	Jeanne Sumerix	$8.95
Midnight Clear (Anthology)	Leslie Esdaile	$10.95
	Gwynne Forster	
	Carmen Green	
	Monica Jackson	
Midnight Magic	Gwynne Forster	$8.95
Midnight Peril	Vicki Andrews	$10.95
Misconceptions	Pamela Leigh Starr	$9.95
Montgomery's Children	Richard Perry	$14.95
My Buffalo Soldier	Barbara B. K. Reeves	$8.95
Naked Soul	Gwynne Forster	$8.95
Next to Last Chance	Louisa Dixon	$24.95
No Apologies	Seressia Glass	$8.95
No Commitment Required	Seressia Glass	$8.95
No Regrets	Mildred E. Riley	$8.95
Nowhere to Run	Gay G. Gunn	$10.95
O Bed! O Breakfast!	Rob Kuehnle	$14.95
Object of His Desire	A. C. Arthur	$8.95
Office Policy	A. C. Arthur	$9.95
Once in a Blue Moon	Dorianne Cole	$9.95
One Day at a Time	Bella McFarland	$8.95
Outside Chance	Louisa Dixon	$24.95
Passion	T.T. Henderson	$10.95
Passion's Blood	Cherif Fortin	$22.95
Passion's Journey	Wanda Y. Thomas	$8.95
Past Promises	Jahmel West	$8.95
Path of Fire	T.T. Henderson	$8.95

Other Genesis Press, Inc. Titles (continued)

Path of Thorns	Annetta P. Lee	$9.95
Peace Be Still	Colette Haywood	$12.95
Picture Perfect	Reon Carter	$8.95
Playing for Keeps	Stephanie Salinas	$8.95
Pride & Joi	Gay G. Gunn	$15.95
Pride & Joi	Gay G. Gunn	$8.95
Promises to Keep	Alicia Wiggins	$8.95
Quiet Storm	Donna Hill	$10.95
Reckless Surrender	Rochelle Alers	$6.95
Red Polka Dot in a World of Plaid	Varian Johnson	$12.95
Reluctant Captive	Joyce Jackson	$8.95
Rendezvous with Fate	Jeanne Sumerix	$8.95
Revelations	Cheris F. Hodges	$8.95
Rivers of the Soul	Leslie Esdaile	$8.95
Rocky Mountain Romance	Kathleen Suzanne	$8.95
Rooms of the Heart	Donna Hill	$8.95
Rough on Rats and Tough on Cats	Chris Parker	$12.95
Secret Library Vol. 1	Nina Sheridan	$18.95
Secret Library Vol. 2	Cassandra Colt	$8.95
Shades of Brown	Denise Becker	$8.95
Shades of Desire	Monica White	$8.95
Shadows in the Moonlight	Jeanne Sumerix	$8.95
Sin	Crystal Rhodes	$8.95
So Amazing	Sinclair LeBeau	$8.95
Somebody's Someone	Sinclair LeBeau	$8.95
Someone to Love	Alicia Wiggins	$8.95
Song in the Park	Martin Brant	$15.95

Other Genesis Press, Inc. Titles (continued)

Order Form

Mail to: Genesis Press, Inc.
P.O. Box 101
Columbus, MS 39703

Name _____
Address _____
City/State _____ Zip _____
Telephone _____

Ship to (if different from above)
Name _____
Address _____
City/State _____ Zip _____
Telephone _____

Credit Card Information
Credit Card # _____ ☐ Visa   ☐ Mastercard
Expiration Date (mm/yy) _____ ☐ AmEx ☐ Discover

Qty.	Author	Title	Price	Total

Use this order form, or call **1-888-INDIGO-1**	Total for books _____
	Shipping and handling:
	  $5 first two books,
	  $1 each additional book _____
	Total S & H _____
	Total amount enclosed _____

Mississippi residents add 7% sales tax

Visit www.genesis-press.com for latest releases and excerpts.